I0591664

# ALEXANDRA

## LAUREN ROYAL
## DEVON ROYAL

June 2021 Edition
SWEET CHASE BRIDES: THE REGENCY

ALEXANDRA by Lauren Royal & Devon Royal

Published by Novelty Books, a division of Novelty Publishers, LLC, 205 Avenida Del Mar #275, San Clemente, CA 92674

June 2021 Edition

Cover by Kimberly Killion

Learn more about the authors and their books at www.LaurenandDevonRoyal.com.

ISBN: 978-1-63469-172-7

# MORE SWEET CHASE BRIDES BOOKS

~

## SWEET CHASE BRIDES

*The Earl's Unsuitable Bride*

*The Marquess's Scottish Bride*

*The Laird's Fairytale Bride*

*The Duke's Reluctant Bride*

*The Viscount's Wallflower Bride*

*The Baron's Inconvenient Bride*

*The Gentleman's Scandalous Bride*

*The Cavalier's Christmas Bride*

*A Chase Brides Christmas*

## SWEET CHASE BRIDES: THE REGENCY

*Alexandra*

*Juliana*

*Corinna*

## SWEET CHASE BRIDES: THE RENAISSANCE

*Alice Betrothed* (coming soon)

*For Alex Royal & Bella Royal,*
*because we were thinking of you*
*while we wrote this book.*

*With love and gratitude for your help!*

# PROLOGUE

*Cainewood Castle, the South of England*
*Summer 1812*

**I**T WAS ALMOST like touching him.

Lady Alexandra Chase usually sketched a profile in just a few minutes, but she took her time today, lingering over her work in the darkened room. Standing on one side of a large, framed pane of glass while Tristan sat sideways on the other, she traced his shadow cast by the glow of a candle. Her pencil followed his strong chin, his long, straight nose, the wide slope of his forehead, capturing his image on the sheet of paper she'd tacked to her side of the glass. Noticing a stray lock that tumbled down his brow, she hesitated, wanting to make certain she caught it just right.

Someone walked by the open door, causing Tris's shadow to flicker as the candle wavered. "Are you finished yet?" he asked from behind the glass panel.

"Hold still," she admonished. "Artistry requires patience."

"It's just a profile."

Alexandra flushed, though she knew better than to take offense. He was simply impatient. He'd always been an admirer of her work.

As well he should be. Alexandra made excellent profile portraits.

"You promised you'd sit still," she reminded him, injecting authority into her girlish voice. "Just this once before you leave." She'd been asking Tris to sit for her for months, but he never seemed to have the time. This would be her only chance.

"I'm sitting," he said, and although his profile remained immobile, she could hear amusement in his tone.

She loved his good-humored forbearance, just like she loved everything about Tris Nesbitt.

She'd been eight when they first met. Her favorite brother, Griffin, had brought him home between school terms. In the six years since, as he and Griffin completed Eton and then Oxford, Tris had visited often, claiming to prefer his friend's large family to the quiet home he shared with his father.

Alexandra couldn't remember when she'd fallen in love, but she felt like she'd loved Tris forever.

Of course, nothing would come of it. Now, at fourteen, she was mature enough to accept that her eminent father, the Marquess of Cainewood, would never allow her to marry plain Mr. Tristan Nesbitt.

But that didn't stop her from wishing. It didn't stop her stomach from tingling when she heard his voice, didn't stop her heart from skipping when he looked at her with his silver-gray eyes.

Not that he looked at her often. After all, as far as he was concerned she was little more than Griffin's pesky younger sister.

Knowing Tris couldn't see her now, she skimmed her fingertips over his silhouette, wishing she were touching *him* instead. She'd never touched him, not in real life. Such intimacy simply didn't occur between young ladies and gentlemen. Most especially between a marquess's daughter and a commoner.

The drawing room's draperies were shut, and the low light seemed to enclose them together—alone!—in the room. She desperately wanted to say something clever or diverting, something he would remember after they parted. But she could think of nothing. "Where are you going again?" she asked instead, although she knew.

Let him think she'd barely noticed he was leaving.

"Jamaica." He sounded excited. "My uncle wishes me to look after his interests there. I'm to learn how his plantation is run."

"Is that what you wish to do with your life?"

"He doesn't mean for me to stay there permanently. Only to acquaint myself with the operation so I can manage it from afar."

"But do you wish to become a man of business? To manage property? Or would you rather do something else?"

He shrugged, his profile tilting, then settling back into the lines she'd so carefully drawn. "He paid for my education. Have I any choice?"

"I suppose not." Her choices were limited, too. "How long will you be gone?"

"A year or two at the least. Perhaps more."

Everything was changing. Griffin would leave soon as well—their father had bought him a commission in the cavalry. Although Griffin and Tris had spent much of the past few years away at school and university, these new developments seemed different. They'd be oceans away. It wasn't that Alexandra would be alone—she'd still have her parents, her oldest brother, and her two younger sisters—but she was already feeling the loss.

"Two years," she echoed, knowing Griffin would likely be gone even longer. "That seems a lifetime."

Tris's image shook as he laughed aloud. "I expect it might, to one as young as you."

He seemed so much older, already twenty years of age. Alexandra could scarcely imagine being two decades old. And young boys experienced more of the world than girls, leaving home as adolescents to pursue their educations. They spent time hunting at country houses and carousing about London while girls stayed at home with their mothers.

She was counting the months until she'd finally turn sixteen and have her first London season. She used to spend hours dressing up in Mama's old gowns and playing with her younger sisters, imagining the balls, the finery, and the grand young lords who would sweep them off their feet. One of those charming gentlemen would be her entrée to a new life as a society wife. And she would love her husband, she was certain, although right now she could hardly imagine loving anyone but Tris.

"Will you bring me something from Jamaica?" she asked, startling herself with her boldness.

"Like what? A pineapple or some sugarcane?"

It was her turn to laugh. "Anything. Surprise me."

"All right, then. I will." He fell silent a moment, as though trying to commit the promise to memory. "Are you finished yet?"

"For now." She set down her pencil and walked to the windows, drew back the draperies, and blinked. The room's familiar blue-and-coral color scheme suddenly seemed too bright.

She turned toward him, reconciling his face with the profile she'd just sketched. She wouldn't describe him as pretty. His jaw was too strong, his mouth too wide, his brows too thick and straight. As she watched, he raked a hand through his hair—tousled, streaky dark blond hair that always seemed just a bit too long.

Her fingers itched to touch it, to sweep the stray lock from his forehead.

"It will take me a while to complete the portrait," she told him as she walked back to where he sat beside the glass, "but I'll have it ready for you before you leave."

"Keep it for me."

She blew out the candle, leaning close enough to catch a whiff of his scent, smelling soap and starch and something else she couldn't put her finger on. "Don't you want it?"

He rose from the chair, smiling down at her from his greater height. "I'll probably lose it if I take it with me."

"Very well, then." She'd been hoping he'd say she should keep it to remember him by. "I wish you a safe journey, Mr. Nesbitt."

She'd called him Tristan—or Tris—for years now, but suddenly that seemed too informal.

His gray gaze remained steady. "Thank you, Lady Alexandra. I wish you a happy life."

*A happy life.* She could be married by the time he returned, she realized with a shock. In fact, if he were gone two whole years, she very likely would be.

Her heart sank at the thought.

But at least she'd have his profile. When it was finished, she'd have a perfect likeness of his face, black-on-white in an elegant oval frame. And she'd been alone with him while making it.

As he walked from the room, she peeled the paper off the glass and hugged it to her chest.

# ONE

### RATAFIA PUFFS

Take halfe a pound of Ground Almonds and a little more than that of Sugar. Make it up in

a stiff paste with Whites of five Eggs and a little Essence of Almond whipt to a Froth.

Beat it all well in a Mortar, and make it up in little Loaves, then bake them in a very cool

oven on Paper and Tin-Plates.

*I call these my magical sweets... my husband proposed directly after eating only one!*
—Eleanor, Marchioness of Cainewood, 1728

*Cainewood Castle, three years later*
*June 1815*

"**NOT ALL OF IT!**" Alexandra Chase made a mad grab for her youngest sister's arm. "We're instructed to add a *little* more sugar than almonds."

Corinna stopped grating and frowned. "I *like* sugar."

"You won't like the ratafia puffs if they're *all* sugar," their middle sister, Juliana, said as she took the cone-shaped sugar loaf and set it on the scarred wooden table in the center of Cainewood Castle's cavernous kitchen.

"Here, my arm is tired." Alexandra handed Corinna the bowl of egg whites she'd been beating, then scooped a proper amount of the sugar and poured it into another bowl that held the ground almonds. Stirring them together, she shook her head at Corinna. "You really are quite hopeless with recipes. If you didn't look so much like Mama, I'd wonder if you're truly her child."

A sudden sheen of tears brightened Corinna's brilliant blue eyes. She quickly blinked them away. "She always made good sweets, didn't she?"

"Excellent sweets," Juliana said in a sympathetic tone, shooting a look at her older sister.

Alexandra felt abashed and maybe a little teary herself. She looked away, her gaze wandering the whitewashed stone walls of the kitchen. She'd meant only to tease her sister, not remind her of their mother. Mama had been gone less than two years, and memories could still be painful.

But the time for sadness was over...after years of loss and mourning, Alexandra and her sisters were finally wearing cheerful colors and ready to face the world again. In Alexandra's case, she was *more* than ready to put the sorrow behind her and get on with her life.

During her first London season, she'd received many excellent offers of marriage. But at her father's sudden death, all thoughts of a wedding had been abandoned, and she'd missed the rest of the season while mourning him. Shortly thereafter her dear mother had passed, followed by her oldest brother, and she'd missed this year's season in yet another anguished period of mourning.

All of the marriage-minded gentlemen who'd courted her had long since found other brides. But Alexandra wasn't sure she could endure another season, with all the attending frivolity, competition, and intrigue. She just wanted to be someone's wife. She wanted to forget past hardships and start over, to feel settled and secure in a new place and a new situation.

As for her younger sisters, they'd yet to be presented at court and were beside themselves at the thought of finally having a season. It seemed all Juliana and Corinna could talk of were parties, balls, breakfasts, dances, and soirees.

"I can hardly wait for next spring," Corinna said, echoing Alexandra's musings.

Juliana added a few drops of almond extract to the egg whites. "If Griffin has his way, we'll all be married long before spring. We'll *never* have a season."

"He cannot get you both matched up so quickly." Alexandra idly stirred the almonds and sugar. "You two will have your seasons. He'll have to be content with my marriage for now."

"If the 'magical' ratafia puffs do their job." Corinna handed the bowl of eggs back to Alexandra. "Here, now *my* arm is tired. This is hard work." Mopping her forehead with a towel, she looked pointedly through an archway to where a scullery maid stood drying a towering stack of dishes. "I cannot understand why you won't ask *her*—"

"If the magic is to work," Juliana interrupted patiently, "we must make the ratafia puffs ourselves, not relegate the task to a servant."

"Ladies aren't supposed to work in the kitchen." Corinna tossed her mane of long, wavy brown hair. "Holy Hannah, it's blazing hot in here with the coal burning all the day long!
"

"Chase ladies work in the kitchen," Alexandra said with a pointed glance at the ancient, stained journal that lay open on the long table. The heirloom volume was filled with recipes penned by Chase women going all the way back to the seventeenth century. Their foremothers had been renowned for their skill with sweets. "It's a tradition," she added, still beating the eggs. "Will you be the first to break it?"

"I might. Unlike you, I don't put much stock in tradition."

Alexandra beat the eggs harder. "Well, perhaps you should—"

"Girls." Always the peacemaker, Juliana took the bowl of stiffened eggs and dumped the almond and sugar mixture into it. "Why is there no ratafia in ratafia puffs?" she asked, adeptly changing the subject.

"Perhaps we're supposed to serve ratafia with them," Corinna suggested.

Alexandra laughed. "Griffin invited Lord Shelton to take tea, not spirits. I expect they're called ratafia puffs because they taste of almonds like ratafia does."

Corinna dipped a finger into the sweet mixture and licked it off. "Do you think Lord Shelton will propose today?"

Juliana rolled her lovely hazel eyes. "Alexandra could feed him dirt and he'd propose. Have you not seen the way he looks at her?"

"Like he'd rather eat her than the sweets?"

"Oh, do hold your tongues." Alexandra's cheeks felt warm. She *had* noticed the way Lord Shelton looked at her, and though she found it pleasing, she'd never confess as much to her sisters.

He really was quite perfect.

He was handsome and kind. He possessed a fortune of his own, so she knew he wasn't after her sizable dowry. And he lived nearby, so she would see her family often. What more could she possibly require?

As a fanciful child, she had basked in the illusion of romance. Now she knew better. Love wasn't a fairytale; it was two well-suited people choosing to make a life together.

And she was choosing to love Lord Shelton.

With any luck, the ratafia puffs would work their magic, she thought as she dropped shiny dollops of the batter onto a paper-lined tin baking sheet.

The Chase sisters were long overdue for some luck.

# TWO

*F*OR THE FIRST time in more than three years, Tristan rode over Cainewood Castle's drawbridge and into its quadrangle. As a groom hurried from the stables, he swung down from his black gelding, his gaze skimming the clipped lawn and the four stories of living quarters that formed a U around it.

Cainewood didn't look any different, although there was no reason it should. If he remembered right, the castle had been in Chase hands—save during the Commonwealth period—for close to six centuries. He shouldn't have expected it to change in the last three years.

But *he'd* changed, so it felt odd that this place hadn't.

Three years ago, with his new Oxford degree in hand and his comfortable future as a man of business assured, he'd been anticipating adventure. A far-flung paradise of—he'd imagined—fine weather, sandy beaches, and pretty girls awaited him.

Two years ago, he'd been unexpectedly called back from Jamaica to become the next Marquess of Hawkridge.

Things hadn't turned out quite like he'd imagined.

The young groom tipped his cap. "Take your horse, my lord?"

"Yes, thank you." Tristan handed over the reins. As his mount was led away, his gaze wandered Cainewood's ancient keep—still as tumbledown as ever—and past it to the old tilting yard that lay beyond. He smiled, recalling games played there with Griffin—and often, Griffin's little sisters—running through the untamed, ankle-high vegetation. Those summers spent here during his school years were memories he cherished. Griffin's family had been a jolly remedy for the lack of his own.

"Tristan. Or I suppose I should call you Hawkridge. Whichever, it's been entirely too long."

Lost in his thoughts, he hadn't heard Griffin approach, but now Tristan's pleasant nostalgia was replaced by apprehension. He'd no idea what sort of greeting to expect. Steeling himself, he turned and extended his right hand.

"Oh, hang it," Griffin said, and pulled him into a one-armed hug.

Filled with gratitude, Tristan clapped his old friend on the back. "Yes. Entirely too long," he echoed as he drew away. "Am I supposed to call you Cainewood?"

"Strikes the ear wrong after all these years, doesn't it?" Like the castle, Griffin's crooked smile was familiar. "Griffin will do. I didn't expect you until tomorrow at the earliest."

"Your note sounded urgent." Tristan walked with him toward the entrance. "I'd no idea you'd left the army."

"I haven't been here long. Just these few months past."

"I was sorry to hear about your parents. And Charles."

Griffin waved away the condolences. He'd never been one for solemnity.

Before they reached the front steps, the double oak doors opened. Cainewood's longtime butler stood between them. "Welcome back, my lord," he said with a little bow.

"Why, thank you, Boniface," Tristan returned, pleased to see him again. The man was aptly named, for he had a bonnie face—a youthful countenance that belied his forty-odd years. No matter how hard he tried to look stiff and serious, he never quite succeeded. And other than a touch of gray at his temples, the years hadn't changed him a bit.

Tristan couldn't say the same for Griffin. "You look older," he said as they climbed the steps. Faint lines were beginning to form around his friend's eyes and mouth.

Griffin nodded. "An old man at twenty-four."

Tristan chuckled. "Hardly."

"I'm aging quickly these days."

Tristan was surprised. "Surely managing the estate is less stressful than fighting a war."

"You would think so." They stepped inside. "But management is the least of my concerns. I've got three sisters to marry off—"

"They cannot already be old enough to wed!"

Griffin's rueful laugh echoed through the three-story-high entrance hall, all the way up to its stone-vaulted ceiling. "Mathematics never was your strongest subject." He led Tristan up the carved stone staircase. "Corinna—the baby—is nearly sixteen. Which means nearly old enough to find a husband."

Tristan frowned. "And Juliana and Alexandra?" he asked.

"Sixteen and seventeen." They turned on the landing and went up a second level to the family's private apartments. "Mourning has kept them from the marriage mart, but now it falls on me to see them all settled—and soon."

He ushered Tristan into a dark wood study. Waving him into a leather wing chair, he went to open a cabinet.

Tristan sat warily. Surely Griffin wasn't leading up to...? "Look, old man, I sympathize, but your letter implied a need for my assistance, not—"

"Ah, yes." Rather than sitting behind the massive mahogany desk, Griffin chose the chair beside Tristan's. "And I appreciate your response." He set two crystal glasses on the small table between them, unstoppered a matching decanter, and began to pour. "Despite your seclusion and, ah, recent troublesome circumstances—"

Tristan grimaced. He disliked any reference to his *circumstances*.

"—it seems you've become rather renowned as a talented manager, particularly of agricultural enterprises. Imagine my surprise!" He grinned to show he was fooling. "You must have learned a thing or two out on that island. I understand you've been able to make some remarkably clever—and profitable—improvements to the Hawkridge estate. With these qualifications in mind, I resolved to seek you out and implore you to consider—"

"I do not wish to marry!"

"—lending me your expertise." In the midst of handing Tristan a glass, Griffin blinked. "Marry? Do you presume I asked you here for the benefit of one of my sisters? Perish the thought!"

Tristan breathed deep of the brandy as he wavered between relief and annoyance. Never mind that he had no desire to wed any of Griffin's sisters—or anyone else, for that matter—he couldn't help feeling stung by the frank dismissal. "Why did you summon me, then?"

"I need your help. I've heard you've worked miracles with Hawkridge's vineyard."

"I had a hand in reviving it, I suppose. We've had two good harvests—last year's wine is particularly excellent. Or so I'm told." Tristan shrugged. He was more of a brandy man. "You're in need of wine?"

Griffin lifted his own brandy and took a sip that was

nearly a gulp. "Charles," he said, referring to his late older brother, "planted grapevines some three years ago—"

"Charles wanted to make wine?"

"It's the latest thing, apparently. With prices soaring during the war against France, I suspect he thought to make a killing." With affectionate satire, he added, "Charles always was a swell of the first stare."

"Yes, he was." Tristan sipped. He remembered the elder Chase son as a tall, dark man with an impressive air and impeccable taste. "Go on, then."

"I've been told not to expect a yield suited for production for another year at the least. But the vines should be bearing fruit by now, shouldn't they? They're not producing anything."

"Three years with nothing at all? Not even the odd bloom?"

"Nothing beyond leaves. I fear they may be dying. And I haven't the foggiest idea what to do. I was trained for war, not managing land and livestock," he said plaintively.

"Not to mention winemaking, which is another venture entirely."

"You do *sound* as if you know what you're talking about."

"Don't bother concealing your astonishment," Tristan said dryly. He finished his drink and placed the glass on the table. "But do enlighten me on one point. With an estate the size of yours, you cannot survive the loss of the vineyard? This is your emergency?"

Griffin colored. "I apologize if my letter made it sound dire. But...this was Charles's principal project. He invested quite a measure of our fortune in the vineyard, and I'd hate to see it fail." He hesitated. "I'd hate to think *I* failed where my brother would have succeeded." Finally, he met Tristan's eyes. "To be perfectly candid, I'm not at all confident that I'm ready for this role. I've never sought it, never wanted it. But I mean to make the best of it."

Griffin leaned back against the chair and downed the rest of his drink. Military men didn't make a habit of baring their souls, Tristan supposed. He appreciated his friend's honesty.

"I understand," he said aloud. "I wasn't raised to be a marquess, either." Quite the contrary, he'd been born the son of a second son, a mere mister who'd attended the right schools only on the largesse of his uncle. "You've only been doing the job a couple of months. You'll settle into it. I did, eventually."

Griffin nodded, looking uneasy.

"Shall I have a look at your vineyard?" Tristan began to rise.

"It will have to wait until tomorrow." Waving him back down, Griffin refilled their glasses. "It's a good hour each way by horseback, and I'm expecting another caller shortly. A very acceptable suitor for Alexandra's hand."

Alexandra. Tristan had always had a soft spot for the eldest Chase sister. He pictured long dark curls and round, thoughtful eyes. She would be seventeen now, no longer a schoolgirl. He wondered how she'd look all grown up.

"We'll ride over in the morning," Griffin added. "You'll stay, won't you? At least long enough to evaluate the situation?"

"I'll stay as long as I'm needed." Though Griffin's crisis wasn't as pressing as Tristan had imagined, he wouldn't turn his back on a friend.

Especially as he didn't have many to spare.

# THREE

"**Y**OU LOOK lovely, Alexandra." Standing in the high gallery, Juliana tweaked her sister's low, ruffle-edged neckline. "Lord Shelton won't be able to resist you."

"Especially after he tries your magical ratafia puffs." Corinna grabbed one of the small sweets from the tray on a marble side table and popped it into her mouth. She sighed as it dissolved on her tongue. "François said they turned out perfect."

"Lord Shelton won't be able to try one if you eat them all first." Alexandra lifted the silver tray, smiling at the little golden puffs, which had been beautifully arranged by François, their French cook. "Come along, now. Lord Shelton is surely waiting." She hurried through the gallery, lifting her blue sprigged muslin skirt with one hand while carrying the fancy tray with the other.

Her sisters flanked her going down the wide stone staircase. "Gentlemen expect to wait for ladies," Juliana said. "It's not the thing to appear too eager."

"I don't care to play those sorts of games," Alexandra said, gazing down at her sister.

Juliana was exceedingly short—so short she made Alexandra feel tall, although she and Corinna were rather average in height. Juliana, Alexandra had noticed in the brief time Griffin had been inviting his friends to pay calls, attracted young men like bees to honey—most especially the shorter ones.

Thankfully, Lord Shelton was tall.

On the first floor, Alexandra paused in the picture gallery outside the drawing room's door. Masculine voices drifted out. Griffin must have been entertaining her guest—or, more likely, pestering him into a proposal.

With any luck, his efforts would pay off.

She schooled her expression into a welcoming one and rounded the corner into the room. "Lord Shelton," she said graciously, "please excuse my tardiness. I hope these sweet confections will redeem me."

Lord Shelton turned and smiled, walking toward her. But her gaze shifted past him, to where another young man stood with her brother. As he turned slightly and she met his eyes— silver-gray eyes—her heart gave a little skip.

Tris.

He still had the same strong jaw, the same long nose, the same heavy, straight brows. His skin was unfashionably bronzed, as though he'd spent too much time outdoors, and his streaky brown-blond hair still looked tousled, as it used to —and still made her want to run her fingers through it.

The sight of him robbed her of breath.

"Good afternoon, darling," Lord Shelton said. "I was more than pleased to receive your invitation to take tea."

She tore her gaze from Tris. Lord Shelton looked wan by comparison, his skin pasty, his hair the lightest blond, his eyes an innocuous blue. Odd that his paleness had never made an impression on her before. It seemed as though he'd faded.

And he wasn't as tall as she'd thought.

And come to think of it, she didn't much like being called "darling."

"Thank you for accepting the invitation," she murmured, struggling to remember her manners.

"Girls, I'm certain you recall Tristan," Griffin called out.

Juliana and Corinna curtsied. "Mr. Nesbitt," they said in unison.

Dazed, Alexandra followed suit. "Mr. Nesbitt."

"The Marquess of Hawkridge now," her brother informed them.

Tris was titled? How had that happened? And where had he been all this time? She had a million more questions. She hadn't seen him in...good heavens, was it three years? While she hadn't precisely forgotten him in all that time, she *had* forgotten how looking at him made her insides melt like butter.

"Lord Hawkridge," she corrected herself.

"Lady Alexandra," he returned with a vague if polite nod. "And Ladies Juliana and Corinna. You've certainly all grown up since I saw you last." He turned back to Griffin. "Do you know what time of year Charles planted the vines?"

"I haven't the foggiest idea," Griffin replied.

Alexandra stood blinking. Next to the familiarity of their old relationship, Tris's dismissal felt rather frosty. Paradoxically, its effect was to heat her insides even further, past melting and on to simmering.

Lord Shelton stepped closer. "Lady Alexandra." His tone was syrupy sweet. Alexandra supposed he was trying to sound intimate and romantic. She probably would have reacted positively to that yesterday, but today she found it aggravating. She feared steam might begin pouring from her ears.

He lifted her gloved hand and pressed a kiss to the back. "Darling, you look exquisite."

She didn't feel exquisite. Right now she felt about as appealing as a puddle of steaming, boiling human-entrail soup.

Juliana elbowed her discreetly. "Perhaps Lord Shelton would like to taste one of your ratafia puffs."

Alexandra looked down to the silver tray, forgotten in her other hand. "Oh, not quite yet." Her laughter sounded forced to her own ears. "Don't you think we should pour the tea first?"

Ignoring her sisters' puzzled frowns, she walked clear across the room and put the tray on a gilt-legged table that sat against the wall.

Juliana began pouring. "The puffs can hardly work their magic from over there."

"Magic?" Lord Shelton inquired.

"Please do sit," Alexandra told him, leaving the tray safely distant while she made her way back across the room. She seated herself on one of the light blue velvet sofas instead of a chair; a tactical error, since Lord Shelton immediately took the place beside her.

That definitely wouldn't have bothered her yesterday. But his scent—a flowery Oriental mix—seemed suddenly cloying.

When Juliana handed her a teacup, she rose and went to Lord Hawkridge where he was talking with her brother. He smelled of clean soap and starch and that something else that was just him. "Tea, my lord?"

"Thank you." He took it while barely sparing her a glance. "Not every variety is suited to our climate," he said to Griffin.

"You're welcome," Alexandra murmured.

"Alexandra," Corinna called conspicuously, "since you're

up, why don't you get the ratafia puffs and bring them over here?"

"Not just yet." Alexandra marched to the sofa and plopped back down, giving her sister a pointed look. "I've decided I'm not certain I wish to serve the ratafia puffs at all."

Lord Shelton glanced between them, clearly confused. "And why not?"

"Yes, why not?" Corinna pressed. "They're supposed to be *magical*."

"Precisely." Alexandra accepted another teacup from Juliana and sipped. "I've no wish to employ magic."

"Magic?" Lord Shelton repeated.

Juliana stood. "May I speak with you in private?" Before Alexandra could disagree, she pulled her up by the arm and drew her out into the picture gallery, Corinna in their wake.

Juliana's hazel eyes radiated concern. "What's going on?"

"Nothing." Alexandra glanced away, her gaze landing on a solemn ancestor who glared from a canvas on the stone wall, looking exceedingly disapproving.

"Nothing?" Corinna, if possible, appeared even more disapproving. "Why won't you give Lord Shelton one of the magical ratafia puffs?"

"Magical?" Putting scorn into her voice, Alexandra focused on each of her sisters in turn. "Do you truly believe that eggs and sugar can be magical?"

"Of course not," Corinna said. "But don't you think it's worth a try?"

Juliana laid a gloved hand on Alexandra's arm. "If they *did* work," she said gently, "you could add a notation to Eleanor Cainewood's entry in the recipe book, verifying her allegation. It's a tradition."

"I don't care," Alexandra said blithely.

At least, she hoped she sounded blithe.

Her sisters stared at her with wide eyes.

"You don't *care*?" Juliana breathed. "About tradition?" She pulled off a glove and reached to touch Alexandra's forehead. "Are you ill?"

"No." Alexandra drew away. "I just don't care about this silly tradition."

"But, Alexandra…" Juliana hugged herself. "You're the most traditional girl I've ever met."

It was true. Juliana was known for her wild ideas—always meant to help, of course—and Corinna was a bit of a rebel. But Alexandra always did exactly as she ought. She ran her brother's enormous household like clockwork; she kept up with her correspondence; she visited the villagers and tenants, both healthy and ailing, always with some famous Chase sweets in hand. She could sing, play the pianoforte, make lovely profile portraits, and embroider—and if she wasn't exactly renowned for any of those talents, at least she was competent.

Alexandra was a perfect lady. The best single word to describe her was *traditional*. But right at the moment, tradition could hang for all she cared.

She set her jaw. "I don't want Lord Shelton to eat any ratafia puffs."

Her sisters exchanged matching looks of astonishment. "Why?" Juliana asked carefully.

Corinna cocked her head. "Are you *that* certain he'll propose without them?"

"I'm not certain I wish him to propose at all."

Juliana dropped her glove. *"What?"*

"You heard me." Alexandra drew a deep breath, relieved the truth was out. "I've changed my mind."

Juliana blinked. "But Griffin expects you to marry Lord Shelton."

When Alexandra only shrugged, Corinna frowned. "You always do what's expected."

"How very tedious. It's about time I broadened my horizons, don't you think?"

"Girls?" Alexandra's flabbergasted sisters were saved from answering when Griffin stepped into the gallery. "What are you all doing out here?"

"Talking." Juliana bent to retrieve her glove.

Griffin looked toward the stone-vaulted ceiling as though praying for heaven-sent strength. "Lord Shelton is inquiring after your presence." He lowered his gaze to Alexandra and smiled. "He likes your sweets very much."

"Oh!" she said, when she wanted to say "Drat!" Not that she believed in magic, but...what if the ratafia puffs worked? She didn't want to actually *turn down* Lord Shelton's proposal. Griffin would never forgive her.

"I'm not feeling well," she told him—and suddenly, it wasn't a fib. The thought of marrying Lord Shelton made nausea rise in her throat. "Please give Lord Shelton my apologies," she said. "I must go lie down."

# FOUR

*A*LEXANDRA SAT at her gold-and-white Chippendale dressing table, gazing at the oval cameo she'd dug out of the bottom of her jewelry box. "It's pretty, isn't it?"

"Beautiful, my lady." Mary, the Chase sisters' maid, deftly pinned one of Alexandra's curls. "I've never seen you wear it before."

"It's been put away."

Alexandra hadn't been able to find the note that had come with the cameo that exciting day it arrived, about six months after Tris left for the West Indies. But she'd read it so many times, she knew it by heart. *My dear Lady Alexandra,* it said in a bold scrawl so distinct she could picture it even now,

*Here is the gift I promised you from Jamaica. I expect it will arrive a year or two before myself, but I saw it in a shop and knew it for the perfect choice. The cameo reminded me of your profile portraits, and its subject reminded me of you. It is my wish that you'll wear it in the best of health and happiness.*

> *Yours,*
> *Tristan Nesbitt*

The cameo, set in a beautiful white gold bezel with three tiny diamonds, featured a girl carved of mother-of-pearl in profile on an oval of black jet. She'd cherished it and been thrilled to think the pretty, curly-haired young miss on it reminded Tris of her. She must have read the words *My dear* and *Yours* a million times. But after a year of wearing the cameo, she'd given up those childish dreams and put both it and the note away.

That same year, the year of her first and only season, she'd taken Tris's profile portrait from her wall and put that away, too.

And now, he wasn't even Tris anymore. He was Lord Hawkridge, a strange and distant figure—and a rude one! But after fuming in her bed all afternoon, vexation had subsided, letting hope rise to the surface. She couldn't help thinking that, now that he was a marquess, he was no longer unsuitable. Perhaps—

"Are you ready yet?" Corinna called from the doorway.

"Almost. Come in for a moment." As her sisters entered, she threaded a delicate chain through the cameo's bale and quickly fastened it around her neck. Then she lifted a little pot of clear gloss. Watching in the mirror, she slicked it on her mouth.

"A Lady of Distinction doesn't approve of lip salve," Corinna informed her. "In *The Mirror of the Graces*, she says—"

"A Lady of Distinction can go hang," Alexandra interrupted. "Do you expect Lord Hawkridge might have stayed for dinner?"

"Oh, yes." Juliana straightened Corinna's pink satin sash. "Griffin has asked him to stay the night, so he can assist him with some sort of problem at the vineyard tomorrow morning."

So that was what the gentlemen had been so busy discussing while Alexandra was trying to keep the ratafia puffs from Lord Shelton. If Lord Hawkridge would be here through tomorrow, she thought with a little frisson of excitement, perhaps she might have time to make him notice her.

"And has Lord Shelton departed?" she asked with not a little trepidation.

*His* presence could ruin everything.

"Of course. He was invited only to take tea, after all." Corinna sat carefully on Alexandra's blue damask bedcovering. "He said he hopes you'll feel better soon."

"I'm absolutely recovered," Alexandra assured her. Even more so now that she knew she'd escaped the dreaded proposal. She handed her maid a blue ribbon. "Lord Hawkridge didn't seem to mind staying?"

"Not at all." Juliana smiled at her in the mirror. "I don't mind him staying, either. He's quite handsome, isn't he? In a rugged way, I mean."

"He's *gorgeous*." Corinna flung herself back on the bed. "I want to paint him."

"He's mine," Alexandra said quietly.

The room fell silent. Alexandra's reflection had flaming cheeks, but she didn't take back her declaration.

"You cannot be serious," Juliana finally said. "You're marrying Lord Shelton."

"I am not. I thought I made that clear this afternoon." Alexandra nodded up at the maid. "Thank you, Mary. That will be all."

As the woman slipped from the room, Alexandra took a deep breath and squared her shoulders. "I mean to marry Lord Hawkridge if he will have me." Juliana gasped, but Alexandra rushed on. "I hope you two will support me in this. I'm aware it seems rash, but the truth is, I've loved him since practically the day I met him." Too mortified to hold her sisters' gazes, she trained her own on the floor.

Corinna recovered first this time. "Does he know?"

"Of course not," Alexandra said to her lap. "Last I saw him, he was a full-grown man of twenty and I was still in the schoolroom. He didn't even notice me."

"He noticed us," Corinna disagreed. The bed creaked, and Alexandra pictured her rising on her elbows indignantly. "He played with us quite often, and he used to tease us mercilessly."

Alexandra sighed. "That wasn't the sort of noticing I was hoping for."

"In any case, he was just a mister then," Juliana pointed out, "with no prospects."

"I never cared."

Juliana's skirts rustled. "Father would have cared."

Alexandra finally looked up. "I know. And I accepted that. But now everything's changed—"

"Father would have cared about what?" Griffin said as he appeared in the doorway.

Juliana gave her brother an innocent smile. "Father would have cared to see one of us wed to Lord Hawkridge."

Alexandra could have yanked her sister's hair out.

Griffin blinked. "Let us hear none of that. I didn't invite Tristan here as a potential suitor."

"Why not?" Corinna asked. "You've invited every other unmarried gentleman in all of Britain."

"Not quite yet, but I'm working on it." He flashed his crooked grin, then nodded toward a book on Alexandra's bedside table. "Have you been reading *The Mirror of the Graces*?"

"Oh, yes. Every night," she assured him, ignoring her sisters' muffled giggles.

Griffin had given them each a copy of the etiquette manual, authored by "A Lady of Distinction," in the hope that they'd learn to deport themselves in a manner conducive to winning fine husbands.

He was leaving no stone unturned in his quest to see the three of them married off.

"Excellent," he said. "I trust you're feeling better now?"

"Much better, thank you. Shall we go downstairs to dinner?"

Downstairs, she thought as she trailed her siblings out of the room, Lord Hawkridge was waiting. A jittery mix of anticipation and apprehension nearly made her knees buckle.

In this state, it'd be a wonder if she managed to negotiate the staircase, let alone a romantic intrigue.

## FIVE

*T*HE EVENING began pleasantly enough.

An efficient dresser, Tristan was first to the drawing room. He had a moment to appreciate the view from its large, south-facing windows before the four Chases entered together, Alexandra bringing up the rear in a fetching blue dinner dress.

*I always knew she'd turn out to be something special,* he thought.

The notion took him by surprise, though she certainly was spectacular. He'd scarcely been able to recognize her this afternoon. The rather gangly girl of his recollections was gone, replaced by a young woman with gentle curves softening her slender frame and long, sooty lashes accentuating her lovely brown eyes. Her chestnut hair was the only bit of her that remained exactly the same—so springy it seemed alive, refusing to stay pinned demurely atop her head. He couldn't help admiring her.

Truth be told, any man with eyes in his head would admire a girl like Alexandra.

But it wouldn't do to let her brother get the wrong idea.

Griffin had made his feelings very clear regarding Tristan courting any of his sisters: *Perish the thought,* he'd said. Keen as Tristan suddenly was to renew his acquaintance with Alexandra, he knew he'd better keep his distance.

Accordingly, when she caught his eye on entering the drawing room and gave him a furtive little smile, he merely inclined his head. She looked away.

He felt a little pang of regret.

Boniface arrived to announce dinner, and the party went through to the dining room. Tristan was dismayed to find himself stationed immediately across from Alexandra—who, as the lady of the house, had undoubtedly chosen the seating arrangement. Though her gaze seemed to linger on him through much of the first course, he resolutely kept their interaction to a minimum and his eyes directed elsewhere.

By the second course, he was beginning to suspect their proximity was no coincidence. Attending to Griffin's talk was growing steadily more challenging with Alexandra in his peripheral vision. From her coy looks to her peals of feminine laughter, every action seemed calculated to attract his attention. Even her habit of fiddling with the necklace that dangled enticingly near the swell of her—

He froze with a forkful halfway to his lips. She was wearing the cameo he'd sent her from Jamaica.

And he felt entirely too pleased to see it on her. Candlelight glinted off the three little diamonds and the planes of the pearly face.

He couldn't fathom what game Alexandra was playing with him. But he felt sure she was winning.

The meal stretched on for two more courses and an eternity. Tristan ate everything on his plate without a clue what he'd been served.

When their little party finally removed themselves to the

music room to be entertained by the ladies, he found himself sipping port at an impolite pace.

Corinna had a pretty voice, and the music Juliana coaxed from her harp was nothing less than exquisite. But Tristan had ears only for Alexandra. She'd removed her gloves, and her bare fingers, long and elegant, flew gracefully over the keys of the pianoforte. Though the resulting tune was proficient rather than masterful, her playing had him enthralled.

Watching her, he realized that he *had* always known she was special.

As an adolescent, he'd never paused to consider the source of his particular affinity for Alexandra. She always talked to him more than Griffin's other sisters, and although she'd been so much younger, he'd found something delightful about the mature, sensible-minded intellect living behind her china-doll face. But now that he was a bit older and wiser, he could see the connection between them plain as day. He saw it in the open, eager way she looked at him—the same way she'd always looked at him. The same way he himself used to look at girls he believed he was in love with, as if they were the answer to everything.

He couldn't bear the thought of dashing that look from her eyes.

"Would you care for more?"

Tristan looked up to find Griffin standing over him with the bottle of port. "My thanks," he murmured, raising his glass.

Griffin settled beside him on the small gold brocade sofa. "Civilized, aren't they?" He gestured toward his sisters, all seated primly on dainty chairs with brocade seats and gilt backs. His chuckle was low enough not to carry across the room. "Whoever would have thought they'd actually grow up?"

Tristan smiled to cover his misgivings.

Alexandra glanced over at him again, a shy smile of her own curving her lips. He looked away and sipped. He would have to have a talk with her. At the very least, he owed her an explanation.

"What is life like at Hawkridge?" Griffin asked quietly.

*Lonely*, Tristan thought. He hadn't realized how lonely before coming here. But he wasn't looking for pity. "I keep busy," he said. "Doing very ungentlemanly things."

"Are you implying you *work*?" Griffin asked in mock horror.

"Incessantly, I'm afraid."

Griffin's laughter brought Alexandra's head up once more.

"Hawkridge's restored vineyards are the least of my improvements," Tristan said, turning deliberately to his old friend. "I'm building a gasworks. And I've found that methodical land management produces significantly larger crops."

Griffin sipped slowly. "And I hear you've begun a new breeding program as well?"

"Yes, I'm importing stock from distant estates. Not just horses, but also common swine and sheep. I ascribe to the theory that interbreeding produces weak animals."

Griffin looked a bit overwhelmed. "I look forward to learning more of this."

"I look forward to explaining it," Tristan told him with a clap on the shoulder.

Miraculously, it seemed that he still had a steady friend in Griffin. Yet another reason to steer clear of Alexandra. It wasn't worth ruining such a long-standing friendship—the only one he had left—over something that could never be.

When the song came to an end, instead of launching into another, the sisters held a short, murmured conversation. Tristan saw Juliana nod before they all rose. As they started across the parquet floor, Alexandra's hand went up to touch the cameo.

"That was very nice, girls," Griffin said.

Alexandra sought Tristan's eyes, but he trained his gaze on the large gilt-framed mirror that hung above the white marble fireplace. The room seemed too hot. He tugged to loosen the cravat so carefully tied by the valet who'd dressed him for dinner.

"Are you overly warm?" Juliana smiled sweetly. "Perhaps a walk along the battlements in the night air would help."

That sounded like an excellent idea. "I believe I shall take your suggestion," he said, beginning to rise. He needed to get out of here. He needed to think. He needed to plan carefully what he would say to Alexandra. Out of sight of her, and her warm brandy-colored eyes, and the cameo he'd given her dangling just over her heart.

"I'm pleased you agree," Juliana said, still smiling. "Alexandra would be happy to accompany you."

# SIX

*A*LEXANDRA WAS shocked at her sister's bold suggestion, and even more shocked when Lord Hawkridge, after a slight hesitation, nodded rather grimly and said, "That would be delightful."

He sounded less than delighted.

"Tristan," Griffin said in a quiet tone laced with warning. But Lord Hawkridge ignored Alexandra's brother, rising and taking her elbow, and she was too excited to pay Griffin any heed. She'd never thought to disobey him before, but then, she'd also never wanted to do anything he'd prohibit. At seventeen, it seemed, she was suddenly developing a defiant streak.

Lord Hawkridge had agreed to walk with her. Out of doors. Alone. Whether he was delighted or not, it seemed too good to be true. This was the perfect opportunity to make him notice her in the short time he'd be here.

If only she knew where to start.

Her efforts so far had been disastrous. She'd hoped to engage Lord Hawkridge in conversation over dinner, but after deliberately seating him across the table from herself, her nerve had failed her. Each time she'd mustered up the courage to look his way, her powers of speech had fled. Her agitation had exposed itself in fits of nervous laughter and unladylike fidgeting.

But perhaps he'd failed to notice, for now he was touching her! Just her elbow, but still, it was something! His grip was strong—almost painful, in fact. In determined silence he steered her from the room. In silence they descended the staircase and walked outside into the quadrangle. In silence they crossed the groomed lawn.

After a while, the silence grew worrisome.

She couldn't help wishing he'd sounded happier when he'd agreed to this walk. Perhaps he'd only acquiesced to avoid embarrassing Juliana. Maybe he would rather have stayed inside with Griffin. Though there was a full moon tonight, his gray eyes were unreadable.

She averted her gaze before he could catch her looking. She had to say *something*. "My lord," she began.

"After all the years we've known each other," he interrupted, "you're not going to start addressing me formally now, are you?" Having spent enough time at Cainewood to know his way around, he guided her uphill toward the keep, which sat atop an ancient motte—a mound of earth built to give the castle's defenders the advantage of height. "You called me Tristan when we were younger. Or Tris. I always liked that."

Had he? Feeling her cheeks heat at the thought, she was happy when it grew darker as they stepped into the tower.

He let her lead the way up the winding stone staircase, following close behind—as a gentleman should—in case she should stumble in the darkness. She put a hand to the rough wall for balance. "You weren't a marquess when we were younger."

"I'm still the same person."

She wasn't so certain he hadn't changed in three years. Braver in the dark than she'd have been in the moonlight, she blurted the question she'd been dying to ask. "However *did* you become a marquess?"

Behind her, Lord Hawkridge sighed. "My father was a second son—a spectacularly unsuccessful one. It was my uncle—the marquess—who financed my schooling and university."

"So I gathered." She glanced at him as they stepped through the archway and back into the pale illumination. "But your uncle had heirs, didn't he?"

"The requisite heir and a spare, yes." By unspoken agreement, they began strolling along the top of the wide, crenelated wall. "My uncle had married well, an heiress who came with a large plantation in Jamaica. Her family lived on other property they owned on the island, and though she and Uncle Harold had a good marriage, she pined to see them from time to time. While I was in Jamaica learning the ropes, she brought her sons home for a visit. None of them returned. Weeks after they were due to arrive, my uncle learned their ship had gone down in the Caribbean. He sent for me earlier than I expected, only a year after I'd left England, because suddenly I was his heir."

"You've been back in England two whole years? And you never called on us?" To think, all this time she'd been picturing Tris in a jungle halfway across the world, and in truth he'd been half a day's ride from her front door!

"When I first returned, things were…difficult. My own father had died while I was en route, and I'd inherited his estate—which was little more than a mountain of debt. I was in dire straits."

He hesitated as though he wanted to say more, but she waited a while and he didn't. "I'm very sorry for the loss of your father."

"Thank you."

He reverted to silence.

"It must've been dreadful for you," Alexandra prompted. Still nothing. "An estate full of dependents suddenly counting on you to save them from destitution," she went on, "and you just a year out of school and quite on your own."

"Yes, but all that was solved when I inherited the marquessate," he said and hesitated again. Their footfalls echoed into the night. "But there's no need to call me Lord Hawkridge," he finally added, bringing the conversation back to where they'd started.

She was certain there was something else he hadn't told her, and besides which, the account didn't explain his two-year absence from the social scene. But she felt too shy to press. "You always called me Lady Alexandra," she said instead. "On the rare occasions you noticed me, that is." She glanced toward him and smiled—a blithe smile, she hoped. "Last time you saw me I was just Griffin's vexatious little sister."

If only he could see her as more than that now. Shadowed in the moonlight, his features gave her little insight to his thoughts. A lock of his tousled hair had fallen onto his forehead. His eyes looked hooded.

"I always noticed you, Alexandra."

No *Lady*. She should take offense, she supposed—they weren't close enough to warrant that sort of familiarity. Not anymore, in any case. But she *wanted* to be that close. And he'd said...

Sweet heaven, had he *actually* said he'd always noticed her?

"Did you?" she asked breathlessly, even knowing he couldn't have meant it the way she hoped. *I always noticed you.* "Probably because I bothered you," she said with a shaky laugh.

"Not at all. You used to talk about the most interesting things. Deep things."

She'd always been somewhat of a philosopher, even as a child. Her sisters were forever telling her she was too serious. She turned to the ledge and stopped, gazing out over the darkened landscape, the fields and the nearby woods. The River Caine glistened in the distance.

She felt rather than saw him come up to stand beside her.

"I hadn't expected you listened," she said quietly.

"Alexandra."

Something in his voice made her turn to him. "Hmm?"

"I listened to every word."

When he laid a hand over hers where it rested on the ledge, she realized she'd forgotten to replace her gloves after she stopped playing the pianoforte. And he wasn't wearing gloves, either. His hand felt warm and a little rougher than a true gentleman's hand should. Not that she'd ever touched another gentleman's bare hand.

The sensation was thrilling beyond words.

"Tris," she breathed, the only syllable she seemed capable of uttering.

He grinned, his teeth flashing white in the moonlight. "That's better."

"I...I don't think it's proper for you to be touching my hand."

"You're right. I most definitely shouldn't be touching your hand."

But instead of removing his fingers, he tightened them over hers, and his other hand came up to touch the cameo she wore.

"You kept it," he said.

"Of course I did." She wouldn't tell him she'd put it away after a year. "It was the best gift I'd ever received. I was so surprised when it arrived."

"I promised I'd send you something from Jamaica."

"No. You were supposed to *bring* me something."

"I couldn't," he said simply. And then, "Alexandra, there's something I must tell you."

Her breath caught in her throat. "Yes?" she all but croaked.

"I listened to you, and I've thought about you, all the time. More often than even I realized," he added with a fleeting smile. "I wanted you to know that."

Had he just said those words, the very ones she'd always daydreamed about hearing from his lips? *I've thought about you all the time.* Her heart seemed to swell in her chest. She was so excited, she barely heard what he said next.

"But I also need for you to know—"

"I always noticed you, too," she burst out.

He winced, as though her admission had hurt him. "I'm almost sorry to hear that, sweetheart. There are circumstances…"

Heavens above, he'd called her *sweetheart*!

He seemed to be gathering himself. She waited. And waited. She'd never realized she could hold her breath so long.

"We're not meant to be together," he said at last. "Your brother would never—"

"This isn't my brother's choice." Now that she knew he had noticed her, she wouldn't let Griffin or Lord Shelton keep her from Tris. The Prince himself couldn't stand in her way! "I shall have a talk with him."

He shook his head mournfully. "Even in the *extremely* unlikely event that Griffin might agree, I cannot allow—"

"Hush, Tris." She turned her hand over beneath his and gripped his fingers, hard. "You don't mean it." She moved even closer, so close she had to tilt her head back to search his eyes, looking for understanding and failing to find it. Then, without thinking, she reached up and swept that single rene-gade lock off his forehead.

All at once, something changed in that molten gray gaze, and he stepped closer, his scent overwhelming her—that clean-Tris scent. "Alexandra," he murmured, his fingertips grazing her cheek.

His warmth enveloped her, warding off the chill night air. He cupped her face in his hand and pressed closer, all but pinning her against the ancient stone wall. Closer, closer, until she could feel his breath teasing her lips.

She wondered fleetingly if she would faint from lack of air. Then his lips touched hers, and all thought fled for a long, glorious moment.

When he released her, she stood frozen in utter, giddy disbelief, relying on the wall for support.

Her first kiss, it had been, and it had felt wonderful. Soon, she thought dizzily, his surprising, thrilling words still swirling about in her head...*I've thought about you all the time*...soon, they would kiss again. Soon, he would be her husband.

She gave him a trembly smile. "That was nice."

"No." He shook his head and ran a hand through his hair raggedly. "That was wrong of me."

"Well, perhaps," she said, confused. She drew a shaky breath and let it out. "But such a small impropriety cannot really matter so long as we..."

"So long as we what?"

"So long as we..."

He hadn't proposed, and she couldn't bring herself to do it for him. But as she watched and waited, she saw under-standing dawn in his eyes. And then she saw his jaw set as he stepped farther back. "A kiss doesn't equal a marriage proposal, Alexandra."

His voice shouldn't sound so cold and resolute. Her giddiness seemed to pop like a soap bubble. "But I thought—"

"I'm sorry," he interrupted, and he did indeed look sorry. "I cannot marry you. There are circumstances...blast it, I knew I needed to think about how to explain this." She watched his Adam's apple bob as he swallowed hard. "Please accept my sincere apologies. What I just did was dishonorable, and I can only assure you it won't happen again. There's no chance I will ever take you for my wife."

# SEVEN

"*I* SEE," Alexandra said and immediately turned to leave.

Though he knew he should elaborate, Tristan held his tongue as he trailed her back to her family. Along the wall walk, down the winding steps of the tower, and across the quadrangle, he cursed himself a dozen times. Alternately, he considered the wording of his explanation. How could he make her understand that that no matter her feelings or his, an alliance between them would be the worst mistake of both their lives?

And in between all of that, his thoughts kept returning to that one extraordinary moment when, reaching out to touch his hair, her fingertips had skimmed his forehead.

It had been such an innocent gesture. Trivial, even. He couldn't fathom why it had affected him so. Perhaps he was no longer fit for genteel society, considering the smallest hint of kindness from a pretty girl could rob him of his wits.

He wouldn't—couldn't—allow anything similar to happen ever again.

On the steps in front of the double doorway to the castle's living quarters, he caught up to her. "Alexandra—"

The door opened to reveal Griffin. "My sister doesn't look happy," he said flatly.

He—or perhaps Juliana and Corinna—must have been watching them approach through one of the picture gallery's tall, narrow windows.

Alexandra stepped decisively into the stone entrance hall. "I'm fine."

Griffin didn't look like he believed her.

Following, Tristan shut the door behind them. "Alexandra, let me explain."

"There's no need." She raised her chin. "I understand completely."

As Griffin moved closer to his sister, Tristan looked between the two of them: Alexandra, calm and composed—she would never be flustered for long, nor, Tristan expected, was she the sort of girl to succumb to weeping—and her protective older brother. Theirs was a close-knit family; it seemed to make little difference that Griffin had been gone for years. Such closeness was so foreign to Tristan's own experience as to be nearly unimaginable.

He felt helpless in the face of their united front.

"I must explain," he repeated.

"You did," Alexandra said. "I shall have a word with Griffin and straighten this all out. Now."

Turning to Tristan, Griffin emitted a long-suffering sigh. "There's more port in the music room. Please help yourself."

Tristan heard the delicate notes of the harp wafting down the staircase. But he didn't need liquor or entertainment. What he needed was to go back to his secluded existence—the one he should never have left—and forget this mortifying episode.

"I believe I shall take my leave for Hawkridge," he said.

"No." Griffin stopped him with a hand on his arm. "You've promised to help me. Stay, please, at least until you've seen the vineyard in the morning."

It had been a long time since a friend—or anyone, truthfully—had wanted Tristan around. It was a nice feeling, and he gave into it with pitifully meager resistance. "I shall retire, then. Good night." Before he could change his mind again, he headed for the great carved stone staircase.

Boniface appeared from the shadows. "Allow me to accompany you, my lord."

"Thank you, but I know the way."

The butler handed him a lantern. "I shall send a valet to you posthaste."

Tristan didn't want a valet. He wanted to be alone. He'd been relieved to escape his own very fine and competent valet this morning and ride to Cainewood in blessed solitude, assuming this would be a day trip.

But he was a marquess now. Upon inheriting the title, the world believed he'd forgotten how to undress himself.

What he'd forgotten instead was his head. His manners. His principles, his integrity, his consideration for the fragile heart of a lovely, innocent young girl.

And then, as an encore, he'd made an awful situation worse with his blasted inability to explain the blasted *circumstances* that made any relationship between them impossible.

Holding the lantern high, he mounted the stairs, cursing himself. He cursed himself all the way through the picture gallery, across the arched dining room, and down the impossibly long length of the hammerbeam-ceilinged great hall. At its far end, he stomped down a corridor and slammed into the room he'd been assigned.

Seemingly endless rows of guest bedrooms lined this wing, and he'd never been given this one before. Of course, he hadn't been a marquess before. The Gold Chamber, this room was called, and it was saved, a chatty chambermaid had informed him, for the castle's most honored guests. Having been decorated for a royal visit in some previous century, it was filled with heavy gilt furniture and draped in golden fabric. It dazzled the eye. And had him tiptoeing his way around.

The makings of a fire had been thoughtfully laid on the marble hearth. Within Cainewood's thick stone walls, even summer evenings were chilly. No doubt the chambermaid hovered in the passageway, waiting for his summons to start it. In an act of defiance, he set the lantern on a gilded dressing table and bent to light the logs himself.

Straightening to retrieve the lantern, he managed to jostle an ornate painted vase and only just righted it in time. He groaned.

With any luck, he'd be leaving in the morning, right after inspecting the vineyard. But in the meantime, this gaudy room was no place to relax.

He sat gingerly on a carved, gold-leafed chair to await the blasted valet. Hawkridge Hall, the mansion he'd inherited, had its share of impressive rooms, including one very much like this. He rarely went in there. He hadn't been raised among such valuable trappings. He was almost afraid to touch anything.

He shouldn't have touched Griffin's sister, either.

~

"SIT DOWN, Alexandra."

Griffin waved her toward one of the study's leather wing chairs, then settled himself behind the big desk she still thought of as belonging to her father. Establishing his authority, she thought with an internal sigh. Well, it didn't matter. Everything had changed. She was finished being the obedient sister, and she wasn't going to let Griffin pressure her into marrying Lord Shelton—or anyone besides Tris.

He rested his elbows on the mahogany surface, steepling his fingers. "What happened out there?"

She had to say it. She squared her shoulders and opened her mouth before she could stop herself. "Tris kissed me."

"He did *what*?"

She struggled to maintain eye contact, but the shock on her brother's face was too much. Instead she looked down at her hands clenched together in her lap. "You heard me. We wish...we wish to marry." She'd have to do better than that if she meant to persuade him. She drew in a breath and all but shouted, "I don't want to marry Lord Shelton. I want to marry Tris!"

"I heard you!" Griffin snapped. He sat back in the chair, rubbing the nape of his neck. "He hasn't asked for your hand, has he?"

"Not exactly." Something in Griffin's eyes, in the tone of his voice, was making her uneasy. She managed to look up at him, though not with anything like conviction. "He seems to think you won't approve."

"He's right, and that's why he would never ask." He fixed her with a piercing green gaze. "The man's been accused of murder."

## EIGHT

"**M**URDER?**"** Alexandra's elbows gave out, and her energy seemed to drain on the spot. She couldn't have heard Griffin right. *"Murder?"*

"Murder. His uncle—the last Marquess of Hawkridge—died under suspicious circumstances."

She sagged in her chair, trying to wrap her mind around her brother's words. "What circumstances?"

"The old man went to bed with a mild fever and failed to awaken the next morning. Poison, it was rumored, and Tristan was with him at Hawkridge at the time. Since his father had recently drunk himself to death and left him heavily in debt, penniless and well nigh desperate, there are those who believe his timely inheritance of his uncle's title, property, and massive fortune proved rather too convenient."

"Poison?" With some effort, she righted her posture. "I don't believe it for a moment."

"Neither do I," Griffin said with a sigh. "He was never convicted—there was no solid evidence—but many still think him guilty of the deed. What we personally do or don't believe has no bearing on the fact that Tristan is not a suitable husband."

Alexandra smoothed her dress over her knees while she tried to remember to breathe. If what Griffin said was true, she had to agree that wedding Tris was out of the question. Although she could live without the social whirl, if her family aligned themselves with him by any bond so strong as marriage, their own good name would be ruined. Juliana and Corinna would find it impossible to make good matches for themselves...and despite Alexandra's new resolve to be less in thrall to societal convention, she wasn't selfish enough to doom her sisters' marriage prospects.

*If* what Griffin said was true.

"I don't believe it," she repeated. "I don't believe any of it. How did I never hear of this? It must have been an enormous scandal."

"It was. So major a scandal that Tristan has remained cut off from the respectable sphere. He hasn't claimed his seat in the House of Lords. He abandoned his friends rather than subject us to society's criticism. Did you never hear the murmurings, the nasty rumors? Well, of course you didn't," he answered himself. "You were hidden away here in the countryside wearing black."

Pushing himself up from the desk, he moved around it to lay a hand on her shoulder. He meant it to be comforting gesture, Alexandra knew, though his own discomfort with such familiar contact was obvious.

"I'm sorry," he said quietly. "But you cannot marry Tristan."

She stared past him at the empty desk chair for a long spell. She'd never been one for tears, but right now it took all her self-possession to hold them at bay.

It just wasn't fair.

Finally, she looked to her brother, nodding her acceptance.

He released her shoulder with evident relief and sank into the chair beside hers.

"I don't want to marry Lord Shelton."

"You wanted to this morning."

"Well, I've changed my mind. I realize now that I cannot be happy with him. Please don't make me—"

"I would never make you marry anyone. Anyone in particular, that is." The beginnings of panic flooded his eyes. "You *do* still want to marry? In general, I mean."

Under different circumstances, she might have laughed. "Yes, I still want to marry." She couldn't imagine what she would do with herself otherwise. From birth, her mother had trained her to care for a household and oversee its accounts, but she could only remain mistress of Cainewood until her brother took a wife. Besides, she'd always known that she wanted children of her own someday.

She didn't have a passion like Corinna's painting, or, like Juliana, a compulsion to meddle in other people's lives. She just wanted to live her own. "I only wish…"

Though her wish remained unspoken, her brother knew what she wanted to say. "Wishing won't get you anywhere," he said gently, and then added, "He shouldn't have kissed you," looking totally disgusted. "I'll send him away. Immediately. You won't have to face him at breakfast."

At hearing her brother say the word *kissed,* she flushed for what felt like the thousandth time today. "No, please don't! Juliana said you need his help."

"Yes, I do need his help." With an agitated motion, he unstoppered the crystal brandy decanter that sat on the small table between them. "But I don't need him seducing my sister."

The word *seducing* made her face grow even hotter. "He didn't. I swear it." She watched him pour two glasses, one much fuller than the other. "Honestly, Griffin, it was only a... a kiss. I'm sorry I even mentioned it."

"There's nothing *only* about a kiss. At the very least, I will have a serious talk with him." He handed her the glass with less brandy.

She stared at it stupidly. "I've never had brandy."

"Then it's about time you did. Drink up, little sister. You need it right now."

This was certainly a night for firsts. She swallowed a gulp and coughed.

Griffin laughed. "You're supposed to sip it." Cupping the glass, he took an appreciative sniff, then a small sip. "Like that."

Cradling her glass in imitation, she drew deep of the heady scent. She sipped carefully, feeling the spirits' heat trail down her throat and warm her inside.

"Nice?" he asked.

"Very nice." She took another taste. "Go easy on Tris. Please. I asked for that kiss."

His eyes widened. "Did you?"

Her face would never return to a normal temperature again.

She hadn't asked for it in the way he was assuming, of course, but she knew Tris wouldn't have kissed her of his own accord. Knew now, in hindsight, that he'd agreed to walk with her because he'd wanted to tell her of the scandal, to explain why there could never be anything between them.

But she hadn't let him. Instead, in her schoolgirlish desperation, she'd moved closer, linked her fingers with his, skimmed his hair from his forehead. What had happened afterward was just an impulsive reaction.

*She* had seduced *him*, she was startled to realize. She sipped more.

Griffin reached to pry the glass from her hands. The

empty glass. A corner of his mouth curved up in a sympathetic half smile. "I think you'd best get a good night's sleep."

She looked longingly toward the decanter, then sighed. The brandy was much stronger than the wine she was used to, and she couldn't even drink much of that. Her head was already buzzing, and more spirits wouldn't solve anything. "You're right. Just promise you won't send Tris away until he's done what you asked him here to do."

"Very well. But—"

"And promise you won't make him feel uncomfortable here, either."

"I suspect he'll feel uncomfortable around you no matter what I—"

"And promise you won't tell him I told you he kissed me."

"Would you let a man complete a sentence?"

She laughed. A heavyhearted laugh, but a laugh nonetheless. "Only if you're going to say what I want to hear."

"I pity the fellow who finally marries you." Griffin drained the rest of his brandy and set down his glass. "Of course, we have to find a fellow before I can pity him."

"We can wait for the season—"

"Good gracious, no." He looked horrified at the thought. "Securing two husbands next year is a daunting enough task." Steepling his hands again, he tapped his fingers against one another thoughtfully. "I know," he said, suddenly stilling. "We shall host a ball, and I will invite every unmarried gentleman of my acquaintance. At least twice as many men as ladies…that will ensure that no gentleman is monopolized by another girl, and you'll have ample chance to meet all of them."

Feeling bold with the brandy in her, Alexandra rolled her eyes. "You've no idea the preparation that goes into hosting a ball."

"Well, of course not. We didn't host balls on campaign." He poured himself another drink. "I do know how to play the proper host, though. And I have you to do the planning—"

"Me? I've never planned a ball!"

"You cannot tell me Mother never had you assist with the planning. We shall hold it in a month, I think. The season will be well over by then, and Charles will have been laid to rest a full six months by then, too, so our merrymaking won't dishonor his memory."

"A month? I cannot plan a ball in a month! Invitations should go out more than a month in advance. Mama spent all year planning Cainewood's annual ball." Realizing she'd as much as admitted she *did* know something of what it took to plan a ball, she rushed on before her brother could make a smug rejoinder. "We'll need two months, at the very least."

"Six weeks, then." Griffin raised his glass, admiring the way the candlelight illuminated the amber liquid. "You're nothing if not efficient, Alexandra. I'm certain you can plan a ball in six weeks."

# NINE

"SIX WEEKS." Pacing the music room and shaking her head in disbelief, Alexandra popped a ratafia puff into her mouth. They sure didn't seem to be working any magic. "He wants us to plan a ball in *six weeks*."

"We can do it." At her easel, Corinna sighed happily. "A ball! We'll all need new evening dresses."

"Alexandra isn't concerned about our wardrobes at the moment," Juliana chided. She rose from her harp and went to stop her sister's frantic pacing, placing a gentle hand on her arm. "I cannot believe Griffin is after another husband for you already. You haven't even recovered from the loss of Lord Hawkridge yet."

Alexandra wanted to protest that she couldn't have lost Tris when she'd never had him. But it *did* feel like an immense loss. "I don't believe he committed murder."

"Neither do we," her sisters chimed in unison.

"He doesn't have it in him," Juliana added. "Griffin had no right to forbid you to marry him." Juliana always wanted to see everyone happy. "You should elope; you could run off to Gretna Green—"

"Don't be a goose." Alexandra moved away from her sister and back to the ratafia puffs. "Have you thought about the effect such a marriage would have on your own prospects? Our good name would be ruined. You and Corinna would never find suitable husbands."

"Perhaps that wouldn't happen," Juliana said. "You cannot know for certain how society would react—"

"Oh, yes, I can. Look how they've treated Tris!"

"In any case, you shouldn't sacrifice your own happiness for us," she concluded loyally, looking to Corinna for agreement.

Corinna swallowed hard but nodded. "We shall survive, one way or another."

"Geese. I'm surrounded by geese." Alexandra resumed pacing, now wishing there were real ratafia in the ratafia puffs. Was she forever doomed to exercising enough common sense for all three of them? "I won't marry if the two of you will suffer as a consequence."

The look that passed between her sisters set her teeth on edge. If they were conspiring against her, it wouldn't be the first time. Juliana made a hobby of meddling in people's lives, and Corinna had played her willing accomplice more than once. But Alexandra was determined to undermine them, never mind that their hearts were in the right place.

"Tris hasn't asked me in any case," she informed them. "He doesn't wish to marry me."

Juliana and Corinna exchanged another glance. "He's hardly had time to propose," Juliana started.

"That doesn't signify." Alexandra feared her protests were falling on deaf ears. "He made his intentions—or non-intentions—perfectly clear. So don't go getting any ideas in your head. One little kiss doesn't mean—"

"A kiss?" Juliana interrupted. "He *kissed* you?"

"What was it like?" Corinna demanded.

Alexandra hesitated. Even if she could have found words to describe the marvelous sensation, she couldn't have brought herself to say them aloud.

Juliana came to her rescue. "I'm sure it was just a good-natured peck on the cheek. There's nothing so wrong with that."

"That's not what it says in *The Mirror of the Graces*," Corinna informed her. "A Lady of Distinction claims that 'good-natured kisses have often very bad effects and can never be permitted without injuring the fine gloss of that exquisite modesty which is the fairest garb of virgin beauty.'"

"Must you remember every word you read?" Alexandra asked with a huff.

"I cannot help being able to picture the pages in my head. And in any case, I didn't say I believed it. *The Mirror of the Graces* is dreadfully straitlaced."

Alexandra had had quite enough of this nonsense. She was tired and brokenhearted, and she wanted to go to bed. "Well, it wasn't a good-natured kiss, anyway," she said, leaving her sisters gaping as she quit the room.

## TEN

REAKFAST THE next morning was uncomfortable. Conversation was stilted, and Tristan couldn't help but notice Alexandra wasn't wearing his cameo. He wasn't sure whether he found that a relief or a disappointment.

After breakfast, Griffin and Tristan went out and called for their horses. Griffin waited in stiff silence while Tristan wondered what he should say. But it was a crisp, sunny morning, and once they were on their way to the vineyard, it felt good to be astride in the fresh air. Good and familiar.

"Race you," he challenged.

Griffin slanted a single look at him before digging in his heels.

They hadn't designated a stopping point, but it didn't matter. Tristan leaned over his mount, bunching his muscles along with the animal beneath him, enjoying the rush of cool wind, the pounding rhythm. Beside him, Griffin kept pace; they could both afford expensive horseflesh.

What Tristan *couldn't* afford was to feel this distant from the only friend he had left. They were neck and neck, yet farther apart than when they'd lived on separate continents.

When the horses were blowing, they slowed to a walk and rode silently for a while.

"You can still ride," Griffin conceded.

Looking toward him, Tristan raised a brow. "And I wasn't in the cavalry."

"Keep your hands off my sister."

"I will." He wondered how much Alexandra had revealed. "I'm sorry."

"I know," Griffin said.

Just like that, the tension eased. Such was the way of old friends. But Tristan felt very fortunate that their friendship had survived his indiscretion.

It had been a terrible mistake. They were all lucky the two of them hadn't been caught. In a sphere where a kiss was often as good as a declaration, an *observed* kiss was sometimes enough to compel a marriage.

And Tristan had not the slightest intention of marrying— not Alexandra or anyone else.

"Thank you," he said quietly.

"It's forgotten." Griffin raised his face to the sun. "I'm certain it won't happen again."

They rode in silence a few more minutes, but it was a comfortable silence this time. Tristan felt his muscles unclench and the stiffness ease from his neck.

"Why did your brother plant this vineyard so far from the house?" he finally asked.

"You think I understood Charles? Ever?"

"He was a dandy, if ever I met one. But he left this place in decent shape, didn't he?"

"Though it pains me to admit it, yes. He was good at what he did." They rode over a crest, but the grapevines still weren't in sight. "What made you decide to restore

Hawkridge's vineyard?" Griffin asked. "I understand the vines had long been unproductive. It must've been an arduous task."

Tristan shrugged. "It wasn't so much damaged as neglected. Grapevines are hardy, for the most part."

"Not mine, apparently."

"We shall see. In any case, I viewed the vineyard as a chapter of family history. It was planted more than a century ago, in the early 1680s."

"By whom? Do you know?"

"Oh, yes. Not only who, but why. The Hawkridge records are impeccable. An earlier marquess—one Randal Nesbitt— saw taxation rising under Charles II. With the extra duties imposed on French wine, he thought to try to produce his own. According to the accounting, his father-in-law was something of a gardening devotee and helped to establish the vines."

"And they survived all this time."

"Under the brambles, yes. I'll do my best to make sure yours survive, too."

At last, the vineyard loomed before them, tidy rows of staked vines lining a vast hillside. Tristan gave a low whistle. "It's large."

"Charles never did anything halfway."

"He did his research. They're spaced nicely and on a south-facing slope, both of which are ideal."

"But they're not thriving."

"Let's see why that may be."

As they rode closer, Tristan could see his friend was right: The vines' tendrils were drooping, the young leaves were wilted, and there was no fruit in sight. He swung off his mount and crouched by a particularly pathetic example, digging his fingers into the soil.

"You're getting dirty," Griffin said.

"You never got dirty fighting a war?"

"I wasn't a marquess then."

"For pity's sake, you're turning into your brother."

"That didn't come out right," Griffin protested. "I only meant that I didn't ask you here to do manual labor."

Tristan scraped away at the roots. "You want to grow crops, you have to expect to get a little dirty." He stood, pulling the whole vine up with him.

They both stared at the scrawny thing.

"The roots are stunted," Tristan finally said, stating the obvious.

"Do you expect Charles planted them the wrong time of year?"

"We'll never know. You say these are three years old?" Tristan thought back. "There may have been drought conditions the season they were planted."

"Drought? Here in England?" Griffin gestured to the blue sky, where seemingly ever-present rain clouds were gathering on the horizon.

"If you're unaware of the reality of drought, you clearly weren't trained to farming."

"You can say that again," Griffin muttered dryly.

"Those clouds?" Tristan flung a hand in their direction. "They may dump several inches on the next village yet leave the ground here bone-dry. English weather is nothing if not random and unpredictable. And drought or not, it seems Charles neglected to see his new vines received enough water."

Griffin looked skeptical. "I've never heard of irrigating vineyards."

"Established ones, no. It's commonly held that some water stress is optimal for producing fine wine. Irrigation affects both the size and the quantity of the fruit, but wine grapes shouldn't be allowed to grow as large as table grapes

—the sugar concentration is more important than overall yield."

"Well, then it seems to me—"

"That has nothing to do with cultivating young vines. The soil surrounding new roots should be kept damp until they're deep and established. I'd guess Charles neglected to do that here."

"Is it too late to save them?"

"Perhaps." Tristan considered. "But maybe not. Deep watering may cure the shallow roots even now. The vines are still young—it's worth an attempt." He scanned the landscape, focusing on a glistening ribbon in the distance. "We can pipe water from the River Caine."

Griffin shook his head. "The river is lower than this hill. Even I know that water runs down. Short of carting it by hand, there's no way to get it up here."

"Have faith, my friend." Tristan grinned. "You've summoned the right fellow."

"Come again?"

"I've just built a hydraulic pump to supply my new gasworks direct from the Thames. A water ram pump. You've heard of them, I presume?"

Griffin rolled his eyes. "Naturally. My sisters talk of little else."

Tristan ignored him, already deep in thought. "We'll need a drop," he mused, embracing the challenge. "If there's no waterfall nearby—a few feet is all that's required—we'll have to situate the pump in a pit and pipe the river water down to it."

"And the pump will force the water back up?"

"An amazing distance—thirty feet or more in height. It's a brilliant design; wish I'd thought of it myself."

"Will the force be sufficient to propel the water this far overland?"

He gauged the span to the river. Half a mile or so, no more. "That won't be a problem. You'll want to water very heavily, an entire day so the flow penetrates the soil to a goodly depth. Then repeat when the ground begins to dry. A week between sessions," he decided, his brain racing as he formulated the plan. "We'll run a pipeline along the top of the slope with caps every few feet. You—or your people," he amended, watching Griffin's face, "will cap and uncap different sections every day, so by the end of the week the entire vineyard has been deeply watered. Then begin again where you started."

"Where was this intellectual capacity when we were trying to figure a way out of our third floor rooms at Eton?" Griffin shook his head in undisguised awe. "For how long must the irrigation continue?"

"I'm not sure. A few months, if you're asking me to guess. You'll have to keep checking. When the taproots have reached three feet or so, you'll shut off the pump." Pleased with the plan, Tristan nodded to himself. "I'll stay until it's all in place."

"That won't be necessary," Griffin rushed to assure him. "If you explain how to build the pump—"

"I don't believe I can. It looks like a simple enough design, but the parts must be adjusted perfectly. The first pump I built was a colossal headache. I've thought of a better design since then, so I believe this one will be easier, but for someone unfamiliar with the basic concept—"

"How long will it take to set this up?" Griffin didn't sound happy. "Run the pipeline? Build the pump?"

Tristan hesitated, knowing Griffin's real question was the one left unstated: *How long will you be here tormenting my sister?*

Old friends or not, Griffin didn't really want him around.

But Tristan wanted to stay and help. He wanted to make

up for last night's folly. He wanted Griffin to have the satisfaction of making a success of his brother's failure. And he wanted to prove he was worthy of Griffin's extraordinary loyalty.

"It depends," he answered slowly. "Have you a foundry nearby to cast the pump's parts from my drawings?"

"Yes."

"A *cooperative* foundry, willing to drop everything at your request to take on this project?"

"I'm the marquess," Griffin said dryly.

"There is that." Tristan had learned he had power as a marquess as well, regardless of his state of disgrace. "Will you hire a goodly sized crew to construct the pipeline?"

"Of course."

"A week, then. We can have this in place in a week."

"I suspect it will take longer, but even a week isn't insubstantial." Griffin measured him a moment. "You'd take a week out of your life to build a pump and run pipeline that will be used a scant few months? Knowing it may not even achieve the desired results?"

"Do you want to save your brother's grapevines or not?"

Griffin hesitated only a beat. "I want to save them."

"Then we'll do what needs to be done." Tristan knelt to reseat the vine and pat the earth into place around the roots. "I'll draw up the pump design today, then return here tomorrow to take measurements." He climbed back up on his black horse, holding the reins with soiled fingers. "And choose a spot to site the pump."

"Thank you," Griffin said.

Tristan gave a deceptively casual shrug. "This is what friends are for."

# ELEVEN

"*L*ADY ST. Quentin," Alexandra said that afternoon in the drawing room, adding the name to their guest list in her careful, tutored script. "We cannot forget *her*."

"I'd like to forget her." Corinna stood and stretched and, leaving her easel, wandered over to where Alexandra sat at their mother's pretty rosewood writing desk. "She's a busybody."

Seated on one of the blue sofas, Juliana looked up from the menu she was creating. "Do you think we should serve beef or lamb?"

"Both." Corinna peered over Alexandra's shoulder. "Holy Hannah, how did this list get so long? I was unaware we even *knew* so many people."

"How many?" Juliana asked.

Alexandra pulled out a third sheet of vellum. "A hundred and thirty-eight, so far."

Juliana's eyes widened. "Griffin has hardly had time to become reacquainted with anyone these past months. Where did he come up with all these names?"

"He's always been friendly," Corinna said in a tone that

made the statement more like a complaint than a compliment. "Consider all the young men he's managed to bring around to meet us already. My hand is hurting just thinking about writing all these invitations."

"Think about the new evening dress you're going to make him pay for instead," Juliana suggested.

Corinna grinned. "It's going to be pink. With embroidery and seed pearls."

"I sent a note to the mantua-maker this morning," Alexandra said. "She should be here in a week."

"Excellent. I can scarcely wait!" Corinna plopped onto a coral velvet chair. "What shall we say on the invitations?"

"There's proper, accepted wording, I'm certain." Alexandra pointed her quill at her youngest sister. "You've finished reading *The Mirror of the Graces*. What does A Lady of Distinction have to say?"

"Nothing. She is distinctly opinionless concerning invitations. She discusses dress and deportment only. We're supposed to choose the colors of our new evening apparel by candlelight, you know. For otherwise, she says, 'If in the morning, forgetful of the influence of different lights on these things, you purchase a robe of pale yellow, lilac, or rose color, you will be greatly disappointed when at night it is observed to you that your dress is either dingy, foxy, or black.'"

"Black!" Juliana laughed heartily at that. "Perhaps A Lady of Distinction is colorblind."

"A Lady of Distinction is a twit," Corinna said.

"None of this is helping with the invitations." Alexandra frowned. "Mama always knew what to write."

"She had a book with examples of correspondence," Corinna reminded her. "Remember that slim volume with the dark green cover?"

"Oh, yes!" Juliana exclaimed. "I think I saw it in the library last week."

"Will you fetch it, then, please?" Alexandra asked. "We'd best get busy writing if we're to give everyone proper notice."

"Proper," Corinna muttered as Juliana rose and left the room. She went back to her easel and dabbed a brush in blue paint. "Everything must be proper."

Less than two minutes later, Juliana returned. "I think you'd best fetch it yourself, Alexandra. It's up too high for me to reach."

Alexandra was busy adding yet another name to the list. "Use the ladder."

"The ladder is at the far end of the room." Juliana sat on the sofa and picked up her menu. "And it's dreadfully heavy."

"It has wheels." Corinna set aside her paintbrush. "Was there ever anyone more lazy? I shall fetch the book. Where in the library is it located?"

"Lower level, at the top of the third bank of shelves on the right. The middle bookcase." Juliana scratched something out on the menu. "But I think Alexandra should go. She's taller."

"Only by an inch."

"I *think*," Juliana repeated meaningfully, "that Alexandra should go."

"Ohhh," Corinna said. "Is it up that high, then? Alexandra, perhaps you should go."

"We could have written a dozen invitations by now." Alexandra pushed back from the desk. "Third bank of shelves on the right? I shall return directly."

With a long stride that A Lady of Distinction would surely disapprove of, she hurried through the picture gallery, past the music room and the billiard room. Her sisters, she thought as she entered the two-level library, wasted entirely too much time on petty disagreements.

She strode down the red-and-gold striped carpet, then

stopped short. Precisely in front of the third bank of shelves on the right, at a round mosaic table, sat Tris.

She mentally revised her last thought: Her sisters wasted entirely too much time on conniving plots.

An inch taller, indeed!

Pencil in hand, Tris was engrossed and hadn't noticed her. While he erased a line and carefully sketched another, she watched. Even drawing a picture, he looked like a man of action. Lean, wide shouldered, his skin kissed by the sun. The same lock of hair flopped over his forehead.

She wished she could push it back.

It was pointless, she reminded herself—any wishing for him was pointless. But she so vividly remembered the intimacy of their kiss. The delicious warmth of his body. Herself melting against that delicious warmth.

He looked up, then bolted to his feet. "Lady Alexandra."

*Lady.* So they were back on formal terms. It was for the better, she decided, hoping he couldn't divine her earlier thoughts by the heat that had crept, once again, into her cheeks. "Sit, please. I didn't mean to disturb you. I just came in to get a book."

He didn't sit. "May I help you?"

"It's right behind you." Walking over, she slid between him and the shelves. The books were covered by doors of brass mesh in mahogany frames. In order to open them, she had to step back. "Pardon me," she murmured, wishing he would move.

Then, when he did, wishing he hadn't.

"It's right here," she said, rising to her toes to reach the top shelf.

"Let me help you." The words were soft by her ear. He reached around her and up, leaning outrageously close, his chest grazing her back. He was as warm as she remembered, and his scent seemed to surround her. Her breath caught in her throat.

"This green one?" he asked.

"Yes." The single syllable came out as a breathy sigh.

"Here you go," he said, sliding it free.

She whirled around, almost in his arms. Almost.

But if she expected to see her own feelings mirrored in his eyes, she was doomed to disappointment. With a polite smile, he handed her the book. Then he returned to his chair and lifted his pencil.

Apparently, while her knees had been threatening to give out, he'd only been getting her a book.

"Thank you," she said from behind him, feeling schoolgirlish and silly.

"You're quite welcome." He erased another line.

She clutched the book to her chest as though it could protect her from unwelcome emotions. "What are you drawing?"

"A water ram pump. I'll be giving these sketches to the foundry so they can cast the pieces. When I've built it, it will pump water from the river to Griffin's vineyard."

Peering over his shoulder, she saw two versions of the metal contraption: a view of the outside, and, below that, a cutaway view showing the inner workings. "That's very clever," she said.

He shrugged. "I've tampered with the design some, but I didn't conceive it. A gentleman in France came up with the idea."

"Well, it's still clever of you to be able to draw it—and build it." She waited for a response, watching him shade a portion of the sketch. "I must get back to my sisters," she said when it became clear he was going to remain quiet. "I'll see you at dinner."

"Of course."

Of course. It was as simple as that. She sidled out from behind him and began walking away.

"Alexandra," he called softly.

No *lady* this time. She stopped and turned to find he'd risen again. "Yes?"

"I want to apologize for last night. I should have explained."

"I understand. And I know you tried. It was as much my fault as yours—"

"Regardless, I had no right to...to make an advance. I beg you to accept my apology. It won't happen again."

A heaviness settled in her chest. That was the last thing she'd wanted to hear. Without a doubt it was the only prudent course, but that didn't stop her from wishing things were different. From wishing the rest of society had the faith in him that she did.

"I don't believe the rumors," she told him. "You don't have it in you to commit murder."

"I appreciate your confidence." His gaze remained steady, cool. He was very good at masking his feelings. Either that, or she'd only imagined those feelings last night.

She'd never considered herself an especially imaginative sort of girl.

He sat again, a silent dismissal. Suppressing a sigh, she turned to leave—and saw Griffin striding toward her.

He glanced at Tris, grabbed her by the arm, then marched her into the picture gallery, and, for good measure, through the door to the billiard room.

"I don't want to see you alone with him. Ever."

In her current state of emotional anguish, her brother's overprotectiveness was more than vexing. She wrenched her arm free. "I was only getting a book."

"Just keep clear of him, will you? With any luck, we'll complete this project in a week or so, and then he can leave."

"And in the meantime, am I supposed to avoid entire rooms in my own home?"

"If that's what it takes."

"You could trust me a little." In a huff, she leaned against the oak billiard table.

"Stand up straight," Griffin said. "You'll throw the table off balance."

She snapped upright, her composure threatening to snap, too. When her eldest brother Charles had become the marquess, he'd enjoyed lording it over his younger sisters. And now Griffin. "Stop telling me what to do."

"I'm only trying to protect you—one of my many responsibilities, in case you've forgotten. I'd appreciate your cooperation."

"We don't need you to watch over us. We had three months on our own before your arrival. We did just fine without you then, and we can do without you now."

Matching temper lit his eyes. "You want me gone? How convenient, since I'd just as soon not be here, either." With an angry twist of his wrist, he sent an ivory billiard ball across the table's green cloth surface. "My friends just defeated Napoleon without me." The ball bounced off a cushion and hit another ball with a *crack*. "Perhaps I should rejoin them."

"As you said, you have responsibilities now. Beyond me, beyond Juliana and Corinna."

"I had responsibilities then, too," he said, referring to his time as an officer. Time when, she supposed, he'd become used to everyone following his orders.

But if he was hoping for an apology, he was hoping in vain. She'd had enough of other people deciding what was right for her. "Sadly, you cannot leave."

"You want me to leave?" He raised his gaze from the table and watched her, waited for her to answer.

"No," she said at last on a sigh. Suddenly, she felt beyond

weary. All the fight drained out of her. The truth was, although Griffin might be a less than ideal guardian, she couldn't imagine her life without him. She'd missed him dreadfully the years he was gone. "I don't know what I want," she said.

He sighed, too. "I don't know what I want, either." Producing a handkerchief, he brushed the chalk dust off his fingertips. "Life hasn't been kind to us these past few years, has it?"

"Perhaps not, but I'm tired of feeling sorry for myself." She gave him a shaky smile. "As concerns Lord Hawkridge, you've nothing to fear, I promise you. Your friend has become a proper gentleman overnight."

If part of her regretted that fact, a larger part knew it was for the best.

"I'm glad to hear it." Griffin smiled back, a relieved smile, then took himself from the room.

Alexandra sent another ball across the table with a force that outdid her brother's. It bounced off two cushions and rolled neatly into a pocket.

If only her life would roll into place that perfectly.

# TWELVE

*T*WO DAYS later, Griffin woke on the wrong side of the bed. Or at least that was what Tristan surmised, given his friend hadn't strung more than three words together during their ride out to the vineyard.

Leading their horses by the reins, they walked along the riverbank, discussing their final plans prior to setting them in motion. "We'll site the pump here," Tristan said, "below-ground with a grating over the opening. Ten feet in depth. That will give us the drop we need to start the water flow through the mechanism." The day before, he'd staked off an area roughly six feet square. "Four straight walls. You'll want to line them with brick to prevent erosion, but that can wait."

Griffin nodded. "I'll instruct my men to start digging the pit immediately. Is that your drawing of the pipeline?"

Tristan handed him the sketch. "It's a fairly straight shot from here to the top of the rise."

"And these dotted lines are where you've divided the vineyard into seven areas for irrigation?"

"Each serviced by a section of the pipe that runs along the ridge."

"Capping and uncapping each section as needed." Griffin traced a finger along the path. "The water will run straight down the slope. It should work."

Tristan swung up onto his gelding. "Of course it will work. I planned it perfectly," he quipped, hoping to brighten the mood of the exchange.

Squinting up at him in the morning sun, Griffin didn't look convinced.

When he held out the drawing, Tristan leaned from the saddle to retrieve it. "We'll make it work," he added.

"We?" Griffin asked.

"Think of me as your schoolmaster. Your first assignment..." Grinning, Tristan folded the paper and slipped it into the pocket of his coat. "Race me back," he challenged, taking off before his pupil was mounted.

Long minutes later when their horses tired, they slowed to a walk. Their friendly competition had served to cut the time of their journey. Tristan had hoped the invigorating ride would also serve to end Griffin's brooding, but as they continued on in silence, it seemed instead that his low spirits might be contagious.

As the crenelated walls of the ancient castle came into view across the downs, Griffin's fists clenched on his reins. "Impressive, isn't it?" he said in a bitter tone that contradicted his words.

"Magnificent." Tristan slanted him a glance. "But you don't feel like it's yours, do you?"

"No," Griffin said flatly. "It was never meant to be."

"Hmm." Tristan debated whether to sympathize or knock some sense into his friend. The latter was tempting. "Is that why you hesitate to learn how to manage it?"

"I'm learning," Griffin protested in an ill-tempered manner. They rode a while longer in silence before he added, "Very well, hang it, I've been hesitating."

The first step was acknowledging the truth, which Tristan knew because he'd climbed all the steps. Dragged himself up them, one at a time. "You haven't been home long. I hesitated, too, when I first inherited Hawkridge."

"Two years, now. Tell me, do you feel like it's yours?"

"I do." He hadn't felt that way at first, but he'd *made* Hawkridge his, put his own brains and sweat into its improvement. "Cainewood will feel like yours, too, someday. You'll have a family here—"

"Whoa." Griffin held up a hand. "I need to find husbands for my sisters before I even think about myself."

"Why?"

"Why? A gentleman doesn't put himself first. Besides, I've no interest at present—"

"I meant, why are you set on marrying them off so quickly?"

Griffin shifted in his saddle, staring straight ahead. "The older two should be wed already, never mind their lack of offers being no fault of their own."

Tristan just looked at Griffin until he turned to meet his gaze.

"Very well," Griffin finally admitted. "I want my old life back. And while I continue to be responsible for the three of them—"

"You'll never have it," Tristan interrupted.

"Have what?"

"Your old life back. Your sisters have nothing to do with it, and the sooner you accept that fact, the happier you'll be. If you would find a lady—"

Griffin's laugh was so harsh it was nearly a bark. "I'm too occupied figuring out how to run this hulk of a place to entertain any thoughts of marrying." As their horses clip-clopped over the wooden drawbridge and into Cainewood's quadrangle, Griffin shot Tristan a speculative glance. "I shall look for a lady for you instead. One who isn't my sister."

"No ladies." Since scandal had tarnished his name, Tristan hadn't courted any girls at all. "I wouldn't ask my worst enemy to share my circumstances, let alone someone I cared for."

"Whatever happened to that girl you left behind in Oxford?"

"We were talking about your love life, not mine." When his friend remained closemouthed, Tristan shifted uncomfortably in the saddle. "Doubtless she's married with several brats. She made it clear she had no interest in waiting while I gallivanted around the globe."

How nonchalantly he could say that now. At the time, he'd thought he'd never get over her. He'd sailed for Jamaica with an empty cavity where his heart should have been.

"And the girl you wrote of from Jamaica?"

"What is this, an inquisition?" They dismounted, Griffin once more expectantly silent. "She decided against leaving the islands for England," Tristan explained in an offhand manner.

The truth was, she'd agreed to marry him, then left him at the altar the day before he sailed.

The women he loved *always* left him.

After a while, he mused as a groom took his horse and he and Griffin crossed the lawn toward the door, a fellow grew up and realized that love was nothing more than an illusion. It wasn't solid, binding, and secure, as Tristan had once believed. It was neither truth nor fact, but merely a fancy in one's own mind.

An image of Alexandra, her warm, round eyes aglow with that look of love, flashed across his vision. She was just as naive, just as vulnerable as he had been. She would blame her first broken heart on *circumstances,* he knew, but someday she, too, would see through the illusion.

He could only be thankful he wouldn't be there to witness it.

## THIRTEEN

"*W*HAT'S GOING on here?" Griffin asked a few days later, poking his head into the drawing room.

"We're choosing new evening dresses." Alexandra held up a swatch of fabric. "Would you care to help?"

"In the dark?" Entering, he blinked. "Why in blazes have you closed the draperies?" He strode toward one of the windows.

"No!" Juliana cried. "We must see the fabrics by candlelight."

"Whose bacon-brained idea was that?" Griffin turned to the mantua-maker.

Madame Rodale laid a plump hand on her ample bosom. "Not mine, my lord, I assure you," she said in her fake French accent.

"It was A Lady of Distinction's idea," Corinna informed him.

"A lady of what?"

"A Lady of Distinction. The author of *The Mirror of the Graces*."

"The book you bought for all of us," Juliana reminded him as she pawed through a box of lace. "To help us catch husbands. A Lady of Distinction says we must choose our dress fabrics by candlelight, because otherwise we might select a pale yellow in daylight that appears black by night."

"Yellow appearing black? What swill is this? It appears I've bought a manual authored by a complete—"

Griffin broke off, apparently unable to come up with a word to describe her that was acceptable in mixed company.

"Twit?" Corinna suggested.

"A twit, yes. Perhaps you girls shouldn't read that book, after all."

"Oh, thank heavens," Alexandra breathed.

Juliana nodded. "That twittish Lady of Distinction also says we should never paint our faces, and we should wear only modest clothing no matter the current fashions."

"Does she?" Griffin smiled. "Keep reading, then."

All three sisters groaned.

"What do you think of this yellow?" Corinna held a square of fabric to Juliana's cheek.

"Pretty, but bright," Alexandra said. "Didn't you tell us A Lady of Distinction favors pastels?"

"It's called *jonquille*," the mantua-maker put in. "And it's *très* fashionable."

Juliana gave a happy sigh. "I shall have it, then."

"How can you even *see* it?" Griffin complained loudly.

"Griffin?" Tris barged into the drawing room. "We must leave soon, if I'm to—" Locking gazes with Alexandra, he cut off. "Pardon me," he said quickly and turned to leave, much to her relief.

Grabbing him by the upper arm, Griffin pulled him back into the room. "Do sit down. You, too, can help my sisters choose their new evening dresses."

"Choose dresses?" Tris echoed dubiously. But he sat, arranging his rangy form on a sofa.

Alexandra would have sighed if she wasn't afraid it would draw too much attention. In the past week, for her own comfort and to mollify her brother, she'd done her best to avoid Tris. Happily, that had proved a simple matter, since he'd been feverishly working on his scheme to save the vineyard.

Tris had taken to rising at dawn and breakfasting before Alexandra, an early riser herself, even ventured forth from her room. He spent most of his daylight hours in the temporary workshop Griffin had set up for him off the quadrangle between the laundry and the dairy, effectively hidden from where her family lived on the two upper floors. And when he wasn't in the workshop building his contraption, he was at the foundry visiting workmen or out in the fields directing construction. Alexandra rarely saw him except at dinner.

Though all of that made things a little easier, she was impatient for him to finish and return to Hawkridge. For now, she decided, she would simply ignore him.

At least he was focused on Griffin at the moment, rather than her. "It's dark in here," he said.

A twinkle in Griffin's eye was apparent even in the dimness. "Did you not know," he drawled, "that dress material is best selected by candlelight, lest something pale yellow in the daytime appear black by night?"

"Black?" Tris crossed his arms. "What sort of addlepated—"

"We can open the curtains now," Juliana interrupted. "We've all chosen our fabrics."

"Look at mine." While Griffin went to pull back the draperies, Corinna held up a swatch of the palest pink. "It's called blush."

"It's lovely," Tris said. Although Alexandra was busy

ignoring him, she couldn't help but observe his amusement at the goings-on.

"And Alexandra," Juliana announced with a long pause for dramatic effect, "will be wearing amaranthus."

"Amaranthus?" Tris sounded even more entertained.

"A bright shade of purple with a pinkish tint." As a painter, Corinna was good at describing colors. "Show him, Alexandra."

Alexandra didn't want to show Tris anything. She wanted to smack her sister, but she supposed A Lady of Distinction wouldn't approve. Instead she reluctantly held forth a piece of the silk, which shimmered in the newly admitted sunlight.

"Hmm," Tris said.

Corinna grinned at her sister while addressing the room in general. "Can you believe it?"

"Believe what?" Griffin asked.

"That she would wear such a color. She always wears blue."

"Does she?"

"Her room is blue, the ribbons on her bonnets are blue, her shoes are blue—"

"Are they?" Griffin asked, looking perplexed. He stared at Alexandra's blue shoes where they peeked out from beneath her blue skirts. "I hadn't noticed."

"He's such a boy," Juliana said to no one in particular.

Corinna shrugged. "Madame Rodale showed Alexandra a stunning swatch of bishop's blue—"

"I'm tired of wearing blue," Alexandra interrupted. "I wish to wear a different color. *Many* different colors," she amended. "A new color every day."

The old Alexandra would have opted for blue, but then the old Alexandra would have spent weeks or months languishing after Tris as well. And she was quite over him.

She just wished he'd go home.

"You all made lovely choices," Tris said. "But, Griffin, we really must be off."

"Tristan has finished the pump," Griffin explained. "We spent the morning overseeing its installation. A perfect installation, I might add."

"We hope." Tris didn't look quite as confident as her brother. "Now that it's been running a few hours, I'd like to inspect it once again before I leave."

"You're leaving?" The words tumbled out of Alexandra's mouth before she had a chance to think.

"This afternoon, assuming everything continues well."

"Oh," she said. He was leaving. Her wish was coming true.

So why did she feel as though all the air had quite suddenly been sucked right out of her?

Juliana slanted her a glance. "The pump must be very impressive," she said to Tris. "May we all come along and see it?"

His gaze slid to Alexandra and back before he answered. "There's really not much to see."

"We could take a picnic!" Corinna gestured outside the bright windows. "It's a beautiful day."

"Yes, please." Juliana turned to Griffin. "We haven't picnicked in months. As a matter of fact"—she paused for effect—"we haven't done anything at all as a family in months."

Juliana sounded so sincere, Alexandra wondered if perhaps she truly did want to picnic, rather than just wanting to throw her together with Tris for an afternoon.

But on second thought, both her sisters looked entirely too expectant. It was definitely a ploy.

A ploy their brother was falling for.

"Perhaps we could picnic," he said, looking to Tris.

Tris raked a hand through his hair, messing it up as usual.

"I was planning a quick ride out, a quick look, and a quick ride back." A picnic would mean a carriage, considering they'd have to take baskets and blankets and other assorted paraphernalia. None of which brought to mind the word *quick*. "I was hoping to get home before dinner."

"You could have dinner back here before you leave." The look Griffin shot his friend was a mixture of pleading and apologetic. "The days are long this time of year, so you'll still have sunlight should you ride home later." When Tris shrugged, Griffin turned to Alexandra. "What do you think?"

Her poor, misguided brother was just trying to make his sisters happy. Which meant there was no way she could get out of this without looking like a cantankerous crab, even though agreeing would mean hours shut up in a carriage with Tris.

Well, at least they wouldn't be alone, she told herself, forcing a smile to curve her lips. "Why, I think it sounds delightful."

"Mesdemoiselles." Madame Rodale cleared her throat and held up a large scrapbook filled with fashion plates. "You have yet to select your designs."

Griffin strode over and took the book from her hands. "They can choose during the drive. You won't mind, will you, Madame?" He unleashed his charming, crooked grin. "If you'll but wait a few hours, I should be tremendously grateful."

Madame, who was old enough to be his mother, blushed to the roots of her graying hair. "Very well," she murmured, forgetting her fake French accent.

Griffin's charm could be lethal. No wonder he had so many friends.

"It's all settled, then." He turned his smile on the rest of them. "Girls, you have half an hour to wheedle a picnic lunch out of François and change your clothes should your feminine sensibilities require that. What does one wear to a picnic? A carriage dress? A walking dress?"

"A garden dress," Alexandra informed him, forgiving him his masculine ignorance.

When he was nice like this, she wanted to kick herself for telling him he should leave.

# FOURTEEN

"THAT WAS delicious." In the shade of a large elm atop a rise overlooking the grapevine-covered slope, Tristan leaned back on his elbows, stretching his legs out on the red blanket Griffin's sisters had packed along with the picnic lunch. He glanced into the empty basket and feigned good-natured surprise. "What, no famous Chase sweets to complete the meal?"

Sitting across from him, Corinna finished her last bite of cheese. "Griffin didn't give us enough time."

"Don't go blaming me," Griffin protested. "As though you, of all people, would volunteer to spend hours in the kitchen."

"My talents don't lie there." She put her dainty nose in the air. "A Lady of Distinction said that whatever is worthwhile to do, is worthwhile to do *well*."

"She was talking about dancing," Juliana said with a roll of her eyes. She looked to Tristan. "May we see the pump now, please?"

"Certainly, at least what little there is to see of it." He rose to his feet and stretched, gazing down to where Alexandra had her own nose buried in Madame Rodale's book of fashion plates.

She'd barely looked up to eat; in fact, she *hadn't* looked up at all during the long drive out here in the carriage. She'd positioned herself safely between her sisters and kept her eyes on the scrapbook, discussing each engraving in such detail it had made him want to scream.

While it was true he'd done his best to avoid finding himself alone with her, there was no reason for them to ignore each other in company. Once, years ago, he'd considered Alexandra a friend, one of only a handful of girls he'd ever really talked to. Perhaps she hadn't seen it that way—she seemed to think he hadn't noticed her when they were young. But he'd always watched her, and listened, and responded— in a proper, respectful way, of course. And he'd thought of her as a friend.

Though they could never give in to their troublesome attraction, he wanted that friend back.

He leaned down and shut the book. "Are you coming along?"

She looked up, startled.

"We're leaving to see the pump," he elaborated, his face still close to hers.

"Oh." Her pupils grew large, darkening in her brandy-brown eyes. Clearly flustered, she glanced around him as if noticing for the first time that everyone else was standing. Her sisters were donning their hats. "Oh, yes. Of course I'm coming along."

"Excellent," he said, straightening and offering a hand to help her up.

She hesitated before putting hers into it, and when she did, he thought he felt her give a tiny jolt. He knew for certain that a surge of something unsettling swept through him. As soon as she'd gained her feet he dropped her hand.

It was a good thing he was leaving tonight.

The walk from the vineyard to the river was pleasant in the sunshine. Alexandra hurried ahead to join her sisters. From Tristan's vantage point behind them, the three girls were a study in contrasts. By far the shortest, Juliana walked in the middle, flanked by her taller siblings. Juliana's straight, dark blond hair was swept up in a flawless style, Corinna's mahogany waves draped elegantly down her back, and Alexandra's springy dark curls seemed determined to escape their pins.

They gracefully made their way across the downs in high-waisted frocks, Juliana and Corinna in white and Alexandra in pale blue. From the fragments of chatter that drifted back, he surmised they were discussing their evening gown selections yet again. Though she always dressed well, he'd never known Alexandra to be so enamored of clothing.

"The men have nearly finished testing all the stations that will water the different areas," Griffin said, breaking into Tristan's reflections. "Everything seems to be working perfectly."

"You're not surprised, are you?"

"That it would work? No. You've proven your reputation is well-earned. But I *am* surprised it came together so quickly. I didn't believe you when you said you could do it in a week. I owe you my apologies—and my thanks."

"You had a cooperative foundry."

"Regardless, I appreciate your attention to the matter. And your…shall we say *lack* of attention to my sister."

Tristan's gaze went to Alexandra's slender form. Her laughter floated back to him. "I made a promise," he said.

A promise to keep his hands off. But he hadn't promised to abandon their friendship, and he was determined to salvage it.

By the banks of the River Caine, all five of them gathered around the square pit Griffin's men had dug, gazing down through the grille at the noisy gray metal pump. Rhythmic hissing sounds shimmied up through the air.

"I told you there's not much to see," Tristan said. "The workings are all hidden inside. I hope you're not too disappointed."

"It's very impressive," Juliana disagreed tactfully. "How does it work?"

"That pipe there runs from the river down to the pump." Everyone stepped back while he opened the hinged grating. "It provides the water, and the downwards motion of that water flowing into the pump creates the energy that the pump uses to send it back up." He descended a ladder into the pit and stood there looking up at the rest of them. "This slender valve took me longest to adjust," he said, indicating a shank that moved up and down with rapid precision. "It pulsates fifty to seventy times per minute—roughly once per second. Each of those pulsations provides half a pint of water."

With each pulsation, a bit of water squirted out. "It's losing water," Corinna said.

"Not much, and that's part of the design, not a leak. The vast majority of the water is sent into the main chamber here." He laid a possessive hand on the vibrating machine. "Inside, there's a flap to keep the water that goes up from coming back down, and air in the top forces it through the outlet and into the pipe that runs uphill to the vineyard."

Although Tris kept talking, Alexandra wasn't really listening anymore. She was thinking about how the pump looked exactly like the pictures he'd drawn in the library. He'd created this, and it worked to get a job done even when no one was here watching it.

She gazed down at him in the pit and thought about how he was so very intelligent. Intelligent and handsome and stunningly knowledgeable despite his few years. And honorable, too—never mind that momentary lapse when he'd kissed her.

She would have liked to kiss him again.

It was a good thing he was leaving tonight.

"Your lordship?" When a gravelly voice interrupted her thoughts, she looked up to see a man addressing her brother.

"Yes?" Griffin replied.

"The caps on one of the stations aren't working properly."

Griffin looked inquiringly at Tris.

"Go on," Tris said, climbing back up the ladder. "It's time for you to graduate. I won't be here to solve any problems tomorrow."

Griffin nodded. "I'll meet you all back at the blanket."

Alexandra watched her brother head for the vineyard with the man. "Griffin can handle it," she said when their voices had faded away.

"I have no doubt." Tris hopped out of the pit and turned to lower the grille. "Your brother is a very competent fellow. He led troops all over the Peninsula."

"Sometimes I forget that," Juliana said as they started back at a leisurely pace. "Sometimes he makes me furious."

"Sometimes you make him furious, too, I'd wager." Tris softened that with a smile. "Did you ladies finally choose your dress designs?"

"Oh, yes." Corinna gave a little skip. "Mine will be covered with embroidery and pearls."

Juliana hugged herself. "Mine will be off the shoulder, with puffed sleeves and silk flowers tacked along the hem."

"And yours?" he asked Alexandra.

"Oh, it will be very pretty."

She didn't feel like discussing her dress. A dress Tris would never see.

Other gentlemen would see it. Wearing it, she would smile and flirt and dance, and one of the other gentlemen would end up her husband. She knew she should be excited about that, but at the moment she could hardly gather her thoughts with Tris walking beside her.

It was a *really* good thing he was leaving tonight.

Juliana met her gaze, her eyes sympathetic. Alexandra looked away. To the north across the hedgerows, fields were planted, but the rolling land beneath their feet was covered only by untamed grass. The air smelled fresh. A kestrel hovered overhead in search of prey.

"Will there be a famous Chase sweet to finish my last dinner?" Tris asked.

"Perhaps." Corinna looked to be considering.

"Strawberry tarts." Suddenly enthusiastic, Juliana turned to him. "Do you fancy strawberry tarts?"

"Very much so—"

"François rarely keeps strawberries in the larder," Alexandra pointed out.

"No matter," Juliana said cheerfully. "There's a patch of them over there."

Corinna looked to where she indicated. "Wild strawberries!" Perhaps she had little talent for making sweets, but she was accomplished at eating them. "And this late in June, they ought to be perfectly ripe." She sighed, looking down at her white garden dress. "A pity we have nothing to put them in." Their skirts would surely stain should they use them to carry fruit.

"We have the empty picnic basket." Juliana grabbed Corinna's hand. "Let's hurry and fetch it."

Disconcerted, Alexandra watched her sisters run ahead. "That's not very ladylike," she muttered to Tris. "A Lady of Distinction wouldn't approve."

"Is that why you're not going with them?"

"No. I'm...I cannot pick strawberries. They make me itch."

"Even if you just touch them?"

She nodded. "If I eat them, my tongue swells and my throat starts feeling tight."

And Juliana had known that, of course. She'd taken advantage of the fact in order to leave her sister alone with Tris. Juliana, who always knew what was best for everyone—one had only to ask her to be informed of that—had been trying to maneuver the two of them together all week.

Tris reached to touch Alexandra's arm on the bare skin below where her blue puffed sleeve ended. When she jumped, he dropped his hand. "I'm glad you cannot pick strawberries."

Her arm tingling, she stopped walking and turned to him. "You're glad they make me itch?"

"I'm glad of the opportunity to talk with you."

The little hairs on her arm were standing on end. "Talk with me about what?"

"Although it's clear we've formed a romantic attachment —" He stopped when she opened her mouth to interrupt, and, raising two fingers, briefly touched her lips. "There's no sense in denying what we both know."

Now her lips tingled, too. "There's no sense in discussing it, either."

"But that doesn't mean we cannot talk at all, about anything. I always considered you a friend, Alexandra. I don't want to lose that, too."

Tristan watched her fight with herself, watched her swallow hard, watched her eyes go from glassy to clear as she came to a decision. "I'll be your friend," she said at last. "Always."

He took her hand and squeezed it. "I'm so glad to hear that."

He expected her to pull her hand away. Instead she squeezed his back, so hard he wondered how her slim fingers could take the force. Then she didn't let go as they continued on their way to the abandoned picnic site.

They strolled silently for a while. He was more aware of Alexandra's hand in his than he remembered being aware of any physical sensation, ever. And he knew it was the same for her.

"Tris?" she finally said.

"Hmm?"

"Do you believe there's only one perfect person for each of us in this world?"

He smiled to himself. This was the sort of philosophical question she used to bring up when they were younger. "Perhaps some of us have no perfect person."

"Be serious," she said.

He had been, but obviously she didn't want to hear that. "No. My father believed there was only one for him, though. I don't think I ever quite forgave him for that."

"What do you mean?"

"He wasn't always a drinker and a gambler," he said, wondering vaguely why he was telling her this, "although I barely remember him as anything else. But my uncle assured me he'd once been a kinder man, and respectable."

"What happened?"

"When I was seven, my mother left us."

Her eyes widened. "She didn't die? She just left?"

"Yes, she just left. Went to America—"

"With another man?"

He shrugged. "I don't know. I expect there's more to the story than anyone bothered telling a boy of seven." Over the years, he'd never asked. Perhaps he'd feared the truth. And when his father and uncle died, the facts had died along with them. "One day my mother was gone, and Father said she had gone to America. She took my sister with her. Susan."

"Tell me about her," she said softly.

She must have heard the wistfulness in his voice—an unintended wistfulness that had taken him by surprise. He'd thought he was past feeling pain from these particular wounds.

He took comfort from her fingers laced with his. "Susan was four years older, and my half sister, really—from my mother's previous marriage. The odd thing is, though I missed Mother something fierce, I missed Susan even worse."

"Dear heavens." She squeezed his hand. "You must have loved her very much."

"I worshipped her, to tell you the truth," he admitted sheepishly. "She was more a mother to me than my own mother, and I couldn't understand why she would leave me. Now I realize she probably wasn't given a choice."

"Have you ever tried to find her?"

"They both died. Of smallpox. We received a letter a year later. That was when my father became dispirited and never recovered. It reached the point where he eventually squandered all of his inheritance, endangering the viability of his estate and the people who depended upon it. Depended upon him."

"You were one of those people."

"I wasn't talking about myself, but yes, I suppose I was." He didn't like to think of himself as a victim. There was nothing to be gained by placing blame, he'd learned; it was better to get on with life. "You see—to get back to your original question—my father loved my mother, and I gather that until he saw that letter, he hadn't given up hoping she might return. But once he learned of her death, he was so convinced he'd never love again that he gave up."

"Did you want another mother?"

The sympathy in her tone all but killed him. "Desperately, when I was young—most of the other boys had one, after all. But perhaps it's just as well that my wish never came true."

He added to make her laugh, "With my luck, she would have turned out to be a mean stepmother like Cinderella's." When she did laugh, his spirits lifted. "Do *you* believe there's only one perfect person for each of us?"

"No," she said in a way that made it clear she'd thought on the subject before. "I've seen many of my family's acquaintances lose spouses and find someone new. Ofttimes they seem happier."

"Maybe the first person wasn't the right one and the second one was."

"Perhaps, in some cases. But I still don't think there's only one in the world for each of us. What would be the odds of finding him or her? God wouldn't make it that difficult for us to be happy."

He knew she was thinking about finding someone besides him. The sting he felt at that was unexpected—and entirely inappropriate. He hoped she'd find someone to make her happy, or two or three someones should she think that possible. With all the grief she'd suffered in the past few years, she was still optimistic about her future. Bless her for that.

Life had taught him to be more cynical.

As they came in view of the vineyard where her brother knelt by the pipeline in the distance, she slid her fingers from his with an abashed smile.

He was very glad they were friends again.

But it was a good thing he was leaving tonight.

◈

*G*RIFFIN MADE dinner that night into a celebration, toasting Tris and their success with champagne. Conversation flowed along with the bubbly wine. Her tongue loosened by spirits and Tris's offer of friendship, Alexandra was very much a part of it.

But while she watched everyone else eat Juliana's strawberry tarts, a melancholy mood began settling in. When Tris's horse was saddled and waiting, she defied her brother's wishes and walked Tris downstairs.

The stone entrance hall felt cold this evening; the carved beasts that topped the newel posts looked fierce and forbidding. Although it was still light out, the sun had shifted, throwing shadows through the open oak doors.

They both paused on the threshold. "I don't know when next I'll see you," she said.

"I wouldn't count on it being soon. I don't go about in society."

"You could visit again. You and Griffin are still friends."

Tris's gaze flicked to that friend, who stood on the staircase watching them like a hawk, his fingers gripping the marble handrail. "I won't be visiting for a while, I expect."

"Not until I'm married," she said to the floor.

In spite of Griffin's vigilance, Tris reached out and lifted her chin, forcing her eyes to his. "I wish you a happy life, Lady Alexandra."

Captured in his intense gray gaze, she remembered him saying the same words years before.

And as then, she had no reply.

## FIFTEEN

The **NEXT MONTH** passed in a whirl of preparations for the ball. Though she wasn't usually given to moping, Alexandra was grateful for the frenzy of activity that kept her from sinking into a fog of melancholy.

A mere four days from now, the great hall would be filled with the most eligible young men in all of England. Surely one of them would sweep her off her feet and make her forget Lord Hawkridge.

In fact, she'd dare say he was half forgotten already! She hardly thought of him at all these days. Bent over the household bills and attending with admirable diligence to her monthly preparations for Griffin's solicitor, she congratulated herself on successfully banishing the troublesome gentleman from her mind.

*Oh, drat!* Did thinking about not thinking about him count as thinking about him?

Shaking her head, she refocused on her neat columns of numbers. "Mrs. Webster is overpaying for meat again," she muttered, referring to their housekeeper.

Corinna mixed two colors of paint on her palette. "Griffin can afford it."

"That's not the point." Pushing back from her mother's rosewood desk, Alexandra wandered pensively to one of the drawing room's windows. Outside, the morning was gray and dreary. Her reflection in the glass looked rather dreary, too. "I shall have to have a talk with her and set her straight."

Juliana looked up from her copy of *La Belle Assemblée*. "You should be paying attention to other matters now, Alexandra."

"Everything for the ball is in place."

"I meant personal matters."

She turned from the window. "Like what?"

"You'll want to present yourself—"

"Your skin, yes," Corinna interrupted. "A Lady of Distinction says a flawless complexion is key." Adding a dab of white to the hue she was creating, she nodded toward Juliana's magazine. "I read in there that if you hang a sprig of tansy at the head of your bed, a few inches above the pillow, you won't be bitten by any bugs as you sleep."

"Not her skin. Her skin is beautiful." Juliana shook her head. "Her deportment. She needs to practice enticing gentlemen."

"Practice?" Alexandra scoffed. "I've never had trouble enticing gentlemen—I simply haven't been afforded the chance." She certainly hadn't had any trouble enticing Tris— that is, Lord Hawkridge—into that kiss. But since Juliana seemed to draw young men like moths to a flame, she couldn't help being curious. "What sort of practice?"

"For example, smiling in the mirror. You should have many smiles, you know, for many different occasions. And if you wish to make gentlemen fall at your feet, you need to practice *the look*."

"*The look?*" Alexandra and Corinna asked together.

*"The look."* Setting down her magazine, Juliana rose and faced them. "First you locate the young man you wish to entice. Then you command his gaze."

Her sensual, blatant stare had both her sisters swallowing hard. "And then?" Alexandra prompted.

"Look down, bowing your head slightly to display your lashes against your cheeks—lashes you will have darkened, no matter what that twit lady says—and then sweep your eyelids up, gaze at him full on again, and curve your lips in a slowly emerging smile."

When she demonstrated, both her sisters sighed.

"Where did you learn that?" Corinna asked.

"I was born knowing it." Juliana plopped back on the sofa and picked up the magazine, idly flipping pages. "But I have no doubt you can master it with enough practice."

Corinna stared hard at Alexandra, shut her lids, opened them again, and grinned.

"Not like that!" Alexandra rolled her eyes. "She's right— you need practice."

Likely they both needed practice. There were no mirrors in the drawing room, so while Corinna gave up and frowned critically at her unfinished painting, Alexandra turned back to the window to use her reflection.

Command his gaze, look down, then sweep your eyelids up—

She blinked at the scene beyond the glass. Astride a black horse, a figure was galloping toward the castle. A figure she'd have recognized at any distance.

Juliana heard her soft gasp. "What is it?"

As he rode around the side of the castle out of view, Alexandra turned from the window, apprehension twisting her insides. "He's come back."

## SIXTEEN

"DID YOU BRING the new pump?"

Tristan smiled. "Good morning to you, too."

"I'm sorry." Griffin had the good grace to look chagrined. "I'm a mite distracted these days." He ushered Tristan inside, letting Boniface shut the door behind them. "I appreciate your response," he said, then waited a beat before repeating, "So, did you bring the pump?"

"I haven't started building it yet," Tristan said, following his friend up the staircase.

Griffin glanced openmouthed over his shoulder. "I sent the note to you a full week ago."

"As I wasn't at Hawkridge, I received it only yesterday. I do have other properties." As they approached the first floor, something drew Tristan's gaze over the marble handrail.

Alexandra, watching from the picture gallery.

Suddenly he remembered why he shouldn't have come back here.

In the month since he'd last seen her, she had often visited his dreams. But these weren't the sort of dreams he'd occasionally struggled with in his adolescence; far from lustful, these dreams were oddly…sweet. He and Alexandra would dance together, pressed close. Or he'd release the pins from her mass of curls and comb his fingers through her hair. He had kissed her again, but only once, on her soft cheek. Mostly, they just talked and laughed together, but still it felt more intimate than anything. He'd no idea what to make of it.

And now, here in the flesh, she was even more lovely than the girl haunting his dreams.

And every bit as unattainable, he reminded himself.

Her sisters were with her. "Good morning, ladies," he called from the landing.

"Good morning," they replied in chorus, looking shocked to see him.

Griffin wasn't allowing time for pleasantries. "Come on up to the study."

Demonstrating a deplorable lack of resolve, Tristan's gaze lingered on Alexandra before he resumed his climb. "Didn't you tell them I was expected?"

"I hadn't the foggiest idea when you'd arrive," Griffin hedged. "Particularly when I failed to hear from you. I figured it would take you at least a week to build the pump—"

"Quite a bit longer to do it from home. The foundry here has the molds from my newest design." In the study, Tristan claimed his favorite chair. "Were your sisters unaware you contacted me?" he pressed.

"The ball is only four days from now," Griffin said in an apparent non sequitur.

But Tristan understood. "Ah," he murmured. Obviously Griffin was hoping that, in only four days, Alexandra would be betrothed and therefore safe.

Safe from him.

Well, she was safe from him already. He'd spent a month apart from her and had survived just fine. Perhaps he'd dreamed of her sometimes, but otherwise his life was tranquil and productive, and he had no intention of upsetting hers by fostering anything more than friendship.

He accepted the glass of brandy Griffin offered. "I'm not here to seduce your sister."

Griffin busied himself pouring another glass. "No. You're here, once again, to help me solve a problem." He sat and met Tristan's gaze. "Thank you."

"You're welcome." Tristan took a sip. "Why do you need a second pump? Your note was more than vague as to your requirements. Ram water pumps are known to be very reliable, but if the first one malfunctioned, most likely I can repair it. And instruct you—or one of your men—so you can fix it yourself next time. I should have demonstrated the workings before I assembled it. I won't make that error again."

"The first pump is working fine. Read this." Griffin rose momentarily to swipe a letter off his desktop. "It's from my cousin upriver."

Tristan set down his glass and took the paper. Judging from the careful, fancy script, Griffin's cousin was decidedly female. *Dear Lord Cainewood,* Tristan read silently,

*I write on behalf of my brother, Lord Greystone, who finds himself in London and unable to communicate. In his absence, his estate manager approached me concerning flooding in our southernmost fields. Upon investigating the matter, I have discovered this is a result of water runoff from your property, apparently due to an irrigation program you have initiated. I must insist that this irrigation cease, as the resulting marshland is detrimental to our crops.*

*My thanks for your immediate attention to this matter.*

*Yours Sincerely,*

*Lady Rachael Chase*

Tristan remembered Griffin's cousin Rachael; she was a quite distant cousin, if he recalled correctly, her family several generations removed from where their line intersected with Griffin's. But as they shared the same surname and lived close by, Rachael and her younger sisters had been great friends with Griffin's sisters and spent many a day here at Cainewood.

"So formal," he murmured. "Couldn't she come to you directly?"

"I haven't seen her in more than three years."

Tristan looked up in surprise. "Have you not paid calls since returning from the Peninsula?"

"The Greystone Chases were in London for the season; they've returned only recently." Griffin rubbed the back of his neck. "Upon receiving Rachael's letter last week, I rode out to assess the problem. Her conclusion was not in error. The way the land is contoured, all the runoff from my vineyard is creating a stream that drains onto Greystone's estate. Twenty-four hours a day, I'm essentially pumping water onto his land. The only solution I could see—short of ceasing the irrigation—is to direct all that water into another pipeline and pump it back to the River Caine."

"It's downhill. You should be able to dig a simple canal to direct it back to the river."

"Unfortunately, from where it's collecting, the only way to avoid running it through Greystone property is to direct it uphill before it can go down. Hence the need for the second pump."

"Sounds as though you've investigated this fairly thoroughly. But before I invest time in building another pump, I'd like to ride over and inspect it myself."

"Naturally. How quickly do you think you can build the pump and have it delivered?"

"Are you suggesting I build it at home? That could easily take a month." Perhaps that was a bit of an exaggeration, but though Tristan realized Griffin wanted him gone well before the ball, building the pump at Hawkridge wasn't the best solution. "The foundry there is infernally slow compared to yours, plus they would have to start from scratch to cast my newer design. As I said earlier, the foundry here has the latest molds. Assuming they haven't destroyed them, that is—we shall have to check on that."

"How long if they saved them?"

"Depends more on their schedule than mine. But given the correct parts, I can build and adjust the thing in a day, two at the outside. I know this design inside out now. How fast can your men construct another pipeline?"

"Depends on how much I pay them," Griffin said dryly. "If you think the pump can be ready and installed by Thursday, I will see that the pipeline is finished then as well."

"The ball is Friday?" At Griffin's nod, Tristan stood and began to leave. "Sounds like there's no time to waste. Let's go look at the site and have a word with the foundry," he said, opening the study's door.

Three startled faces were on the other side. The sight of one of them—Alexandra's, to be precise—all but knocked the wind out of him.

He couldn't quite call it a *friendly* reaction.

Griffin snorted. "You'd hear better, ladies, if you put an empty glass to the door."

"We weren't listening," Corinna protested in entirely too innocent a tone. "We were just...on our way to change our dresses."

"Yes," Juliana said. "We're wearing morning dresses, and we need our walking dresses now."

Tristan couldn't help but notice Alexandra wasn't saying anything. With her mouth, at least. Her eyes, focused on him, spoke volumes. Clearly she found his unexpected presence unsettling in the extreme. He prayed that his own similar feelings weren't written on his face.

What was wrong with him? Was he losing his wits? Never before had the mere sight of Alexandra—or anyone else, come to think of it—provoked in him this sort of response. He couldn't even say if it was a positive response or a negative one. But it certainly didn't *feel* pleasant.

"Where are you planning to walk?" Griffin asked.

"To the village," Corinna said.

"We baked lemon cakes earlier this morning," Juliana added, "planning to make some calls."

"Go on, then." Griffin waved a hand. "As I expect you heard, Tristan and I are likely to be gone for the next few hours."

Tristan watched Alexandra accompany her sisters through the high gallery, her skirts swaying gracefully to match her gait. When she disappeared into the corridor that led to their bedrooms, he released a silent sigh.

Or maybe it hadn't been silent. "What?" Griffin asked, looking at him sharply.

"Nothing." He shouldn't be here. "What's the difference between a morning dress and a walking dress?"

"How should I know?" Griffin started down the stairs. "You think I understand anything to do with girls?"

# SEVENTEEN

## SMALL LEMON CAKES

Take half a pint of milk and heat to boiling then pour over a like amount of bread crumbs
and leave until heat has abated. Melt 8 spoons of butter and to this add grated rind of
lemons, a fair measure of sugar and three eggs well beaten. Mix all together and pour into
buttered cake-cups and bake until browned.

*Medicine for the heart. These cakes will brighten the most melancholy of days.*
—Belinda, Marchioness of Cainewood, 1811

**T**RISTAN'S assessment of the drainage problem had proved in concert with Griffin's, and they were both relieved to find the foundry had saved the molds. If all went to plan, the pump would be installed by Thursday, and Tristan would be well gone before the first guests arrived for Friday evening's ball.

They rode home in high spirits, despite the gloomy gray skies. For once, everything seemed to be going right.

But no sooner had they passed beneath the barbican than Cainewood's big double doors opened to reveal an agitated

Boniface, hailing them as he hurried across the quadrangle. "You've a caller, my lord. Lady Rachael Chase."

Griffin swung down from his mount. "She must have come to see my sisters. Have they not returned yet?"

"No, my lord, they've not. But she asked to see you. Something about an unanswered letter?" The stern frown didn't sit quite right on the butler's pretty face. "She's been waiting for well over an hour."

As Boniface returned to his post, Griffin swore under his breath. Tristan dismounted and followed him toward the doors. "You must have received Lady Rachael's letter a week ago or more. Did you never reply?"

"I wanted to make certain my solution would work before I explained it."

Tristan had to take the steps two at a time in order to keep up. "So you simply ignored her?"

"Her brother, the true owner of the affected land, is currently away in Lon—" Griffin stopped short as they stepped inside. "Good afternoon, my lady."

"Lord Cainewood?" Perched on one of the entrance hall's carved walnut chairs, Lady Rachael peered at Griffin with her mouth open in a little "o" of surprise, as though he were quite different from what she'd expected.

Or much better.

Intrigued, Tristan turned to peer at Griffin, too—attempting to appraise him from the female perspective. His dark-haired, green-eyed friend had never wanted for admirers, he recalled. And the fellow *had* grown a few inches and honed some muscles during his time in the military. Still, Tristan couldn't see what the girl found so shocking.

At last Rachael closed her mouth, then rose abruptly to her feet. "I trust you received my letter?" She licked her lower lip.

"I did, indeed." Griffin blinked at her, staring rather indecently himself. *His* reaction was no mystery. Though Lady Rachael wasn't Tristan's type, she was stunningly…well…

He'd never say it aloud, but the only word he could think of for her was *sultry*.

"Did Boniface not fetch you refreshment?" Griffin asked. He gave an elaborate sigh, as though the butler's neglect of their visitor far outweighed his own. "It's so difficult to get good help these days. Don't you agree, Tristan?"

"Mr. Nesbitt." Lady Rachael nodded graciously, though her eyes remained on Griffin. "It's a pleasure to see you again."

Tristan executed a small bow, hiding his amusement. "The pleasure is mine, my lady."

"Mr. Nesbitt is Lord Hawkridge now," Griffin informed her. "The Marquess of Hawkridge."

"Of course." She finally turned to Tristan, her expression a mixture of apology with curiosity and a touch of alarm. "How could I have forgotten?"

Clearly she'd remembered the scandal. Tristan wished she'd go back to staring at Griffin.

"Let me escort you to my sisters, Lady Rachael," Griffin interjected. "You came to visit them, didn't you?"

"I came to see you, as your butler has informed you." She lifted her reticule off one of the ornate iron treasure chests. "Shall we discuss this somewhere private?"

"Very well," Griffin said and guided her up the staircase, his feet obviously dragging.

Tristan had a quiet laugh at his friend's expense. "I shall arrange for refreshment to be brought to you in the study!" he called after them lightly. And with that, he took himself off, leaving Griffin to the mercy of his sultry cousin.

There were no servants hovering about, so Tristan made his way toward the side door that led to the household offices and kitchen, hoping to find Boniface, or perhaps the housekeeper or cook. Then, hearing footsteps and feminine voices drifting from the quadrangle, he turned back.

Boniface reappeared from nowhere and opened the door to admit Alexandra, Juliana, and Corinna. "Welcome home, my ladies."

"Good afternoon, Boniface," they chimed in chorus, belying the gray day in cheerful straw bonnets and pale pastel dresses. Walking dresses, Tristan presumed, though for the life of him he couldn't figure out what made them such. They were high-waisted and slim-skirted, like all the other dresses he'd seen them wear this summer.

"Lord Hawkridge," Juliana said in surprise. "Have you and Griffin returned already?"

"No, he's a mirage," Corinna quipped.

Juliana laughed. Alexandra didn't.

"What have you there?" Tristan asked, indicating the baskets they all carried.

"Lemon cakes," Juliana said. "Or what's left of them."

"We've just come from the village," Corinna elaborated. "We were visiting with the infirm."

"All of the tenants and villagers look forward to our sweets," Juliana boasted. "Would you care for one?" Her gaze flicked from him to Alexandra and back as she reached into her basket and handed him a cake. "They're reputed to cure melancholy."

Did he look distressed? "How kind of you, then, to take some to the ill." He bit into the confection and smiled, wishing Alexandra would say something. "I was just on my way to procure some refreshment for your cousin, Lady Rachael. Perhaps she'd enjoy some of these."

"Rachael is here?" Corinna squealed. "Where is she? Did Claire and Elizabeth come along as well?"

"I don't believe she brought her sisters with her. She's with Griffin, in his—"

"Griffin?" She frowned. "Whatever does she want with him?"

"Oh, it has to do with some flooding on her land. I think." He laughed, remembering the way they'd interacted. "Has Lady Rachael previously shown an interest in your brother? Or he in her?"

"A romantic sort of interest?" Juliana looked intrigued. "She was little more than a child when he left for Spain."

"She's not a child now."

"Of course she isn't." Juliana handed Alexandra her basket. "Take this, will you? We'll see that refreshments are brought to the drawing room for when Rachael is finished with Griffin."

After a silent moment, she nudged Corinna with her elbow.

"Oh, yes," Corinna said. "Do take mine as well." After shoving her basket at Alexandra, she followed Juliana upstairs.

Alexandra shifted the three baskets awkwardly. "Well," she said as her sisters disappeared.

One word, Tristan thought. It was a start. "They do have a habit of leaving the two of us alone together, don't they?" Doing his best to appear nonchalant, he polished off the rest of the cake.

She crossed to one of the iron treasure chests, set down the baskets, and turned away to busy herself combining the remaining sweets into one of them. "They mean well."

Moving closer, he watched her in the large, rectangular looking glass that hung above the treasure chest. "What do you expect they're hoping will happen?" He kept his hands clasped behind his back.

Though her cheeks went pink, she met his eyes in the silvery surface and answered in her forthright way. "I expect they think you might kiss me again."

"I won't," he said quietly.

"I know," she said and lowered her gaze.

Since spotting him riding to their door earlier that morning, she'd endured a riot of emotions: surprise, happiness, annoyance, confusion. Confusion reigned supreme. She'd been looking forward to the ball, to meeting new—eligible— young men. In the past month, she'd thought she'd succeeded in relegating Lord Hawkridge to that role in her life labeled *friend*.

But seeing him this morning had cured her of *that* illusion.

Youthful stupidity could be her only excuse. And perhaps madness. Yes, that would cover it. She whirled round, knowing he stood close behind her. Their height difference meant his lips were at her eye level, and she remembered they had been softer than she'd expected. A lock of his hair had flopped over his forehead as usual, and she reached to sweep it away.

He caught her gloved hand. "That won't work this time."

"I know," she repeated.

Their hands dropped together. Slowly his fingers moved up her arm until he was touching bare skin. "You don't *want* me to kiss you, do you?"

"Of course not," she said quickly.

"Good," he said. "Because I cannot be with you, Alexandra. I cannot be with anyone."

She couldn't be with him, either—not and live with herself. But surely there were ladies who didn't have families to consider. "Do you mean to never have children? Not even an heir for Hawkridge?"

He wrapped his fingers lightly around her elbow. "I don't believe that to be my fate."

"Fate." She narrowed her eyes. "You believe God's plan for you involves spending the rest of your life alone?"

"That appears to be the trajectory I'm on. I've accepted it. One cannot be happy without accepting one's fate."

He certainly didn't *look* happy. "Perhaps He needs you to pull your own weight. Is it so wrong to hope for more? To work for more?"

"Of course not." He seemed to realize he'd been holding her arm, and let go. Stepped back. "But it's wrong to expect more as your due."

She remembered how, after completing university, he'd felt he had no choice but to work for his uncle. And now, it seemed, he felt he had no choice but to accept loneliness as his lot in life.

Thinking about that made a lump rise in her throat.

"I don't believe in accepting," she told him. "Or settling. I believe in striving for the things you want." He looked startled when she moved closer and grasped one of his hands in both of hers.

But he didn't pull away.

"Promise me," she said, "as your *friend*, that you won't stop trying to be happy."

"I am—"

"*Promise* me."

He didn't. Instead, following a tense silence, he leaned closer and kissed her on the forehead. Then he withdrew his hand and quit the room.

## EIGHTEEN

*R*ACHAEL WAS more businesslike than he remembered, Griffin thought, standing behind the safety of his heavy desk. She stood opposite with one hand planted on a cocked hip, her silly little reticule dangling from her wrist.

Why on earth didn't girls wear pockets?

He picked up her letter and stared at it, then looked back to her. "When I got this, I was picturing you as a schoolgirl with a plait hanging down your back."

She raised one arched brow. "I never wore plaits."

He certainly couldn't picture her wearing plaits now.

The lavender dress she wore was made of some light fabric that clung to her figure. Her eyes were large and the color of a cloudless sky—a hue Corinna would describe as cerulean—and beneath that startling blue gaze, she had full lips. Her chestnut hair was done up in a ladylike style, but the loose tendrils around her face weren't tightly curled as was fashionable, instead falling in soft waves that hinted at thick, luxuriant tresses.

He had never seen a girl in a day dress manage to look so…he couldn't think of the right word.

"Did you bother reading that letter?" she asked in a voice much huskier than Griffin remembered.

He swallowed. "Of course I read the letter. I invited Lord Hawkridge here as a result. He's assisting me in rectifying the problem."

"In what way?"

"We're diverting the water back to the river by means of pipes and a pump. The new system should be in place by Thursday."

Her eyes narrowed. "Why?"

"Why? Because I'm flooding your brother's land."

"I meant, why did you begin irrigating in the first place? Have we not enough rain on this all-fired island?"

"I'm attempting to save my brother's vines."

When her forehead crinkled, even that looked intimidating. "Vines?"

"Grapevines. I'm raising grapes to start a winery. Or perhaps I should say Charles was raising grapes, and as his successor, I'm doing my best not to kill them."

"Oh." She sobered. "I was sorry to learn of Charles's passing."

"So was I," he said dryly.

She licked her upper lip, watching him speculatively. "You don't fancy being the marquess?"

"Given the trouble I have sustaining the lives of mere grapes, you may pity the unfortunate tenants who rely on me for their keeping. Sit, please," he added, indicating one of the leather wing chairs.

She did, setting her reticule on the small table beside it. He sat, too, with some relief, as he'd begun wondering if his knees might give out.

He leaned his elbows on the desk and steepled his fingers,

watching her over them, his jaw tense. He found himself idly wondering if she'd lick her lips again.

"I'm sorry about your parents," he said.

"It's been two years."

"That doesn't mean it cannot hurt."

Rachael turned her face to the window. "I haven't cried in forever," she said, blinking rapidly. "Thank you for making me start now."

Even though she'd turned away, Rachael could tell that Griffin kept looking at her—no, she decided, *staring* at her. Whyever was he doing that? As far as she was concerned, he was an irresponsible scapegrace, and she very much would have liked to be offended by his staring.

But somehow, she didn't mind.

Three years in the military had changed her cousin. The rowdy, ungainly youth she remembered had grown taller and sturdier. His eyes were still a pure leaf green, but the face around them had gained a weathered, authoritative quality that fascinated her.

In a cousinly way, of course.

"I'm sorry," he finally said. "I didn't mean to bring up old feelings."

"It's time I dealt with them," she admitted, still gazing out the window. "None of us have, if you want to know the truth. We lost Mama and Papa so quickly—a road accident is such an unexpected shock. Even the staff seems loath to believe they're gone. A chambermaid cleans their rooms every day just the same as if they still lived there. Nothing of theirs has been touched."

"If keeping part of them with you makes you feel better—"

"It doesn't, not really. It just keeps us from moving on with our lives." She drew a deep breath. "I've decided to empty their suite before Noah comes home in September. He was still living at school at the time, and it never occurred to us to move him into their rooms. He was too young at sixteen to take on an earl's responsibilities."

"You were only seventeen," Griffin pointed out.

"But I felt much older than Noah, being the first child. And I knew the care of the estate better than he did, so it made sense for me to take over for him while he finished growing up." She finally turned back to her cousin. "Now, though, he's eighteen, and it's time for him to come into his own. The master suite should rightfully be his. It's time to let go. They're only things, anyway, right? Not so significant."

She couldn't believe she was asking for his opinion, his approval. Griffin, of all people.

But the tightness in her throat eased when he gave her a gentle, crooked smile. "Yes, they're only things. You won't forget your parents, Rachael. You can keep some of their more special items...and regardless, they'll always live in your heart."

She had to blink back the tears again. "When did you get so wise?"

"Oh..." He pulled out a very old sapphire and gold pocket watch that she remembered had belonged to his father. "About two minutes ago."

He'd always been able to make her laugh.

## NINETEEN

"**R**ACHAEL!" Alexandra and her sisters rushed across the drawing room to welcome their cousin.

"Whatever did you want with Griffin?" Juliana asked after they'd hugged.

"It's not important." Graceful as always, Rachael slid onto a sofa. "He's already solving the problem."

"We've been wondering when you'd return." Alexandra sat beside her. "How was the season?"

Rachael shrugged. "I'm still unmarried. Not for lack of offers, mind you," she added with an arch smile.

Sitting next to Juliana on the opposite sofa, Corinna frowned. "Were none of the gentlemen suitable?"

"Indeed, there were an earl and a baron among them. Worry not, dear, you'll find no shortage of adoring gentlemen when you head for London next year. It's only that none of them seemed right...for me."

All four of them released heartfelt sighs.

Juliana poured tea and handed Rachael a cup. "Is Noah getting frustrated?"

"Noah?" Rachael laughed. "If Noah had his way, I'd never

marry at all. Who would run his household while he's out chasing girls and ignoring his studies? Not Claire or Elizabeth, I can assure you!" She turned to Alexandra. "Who will run *your* brother's household when *you* marry?"

"Juliana and Corinna." Alexandra looked to her sisters. "Mama trained us all in the housewifely arts."

Corinna paled; evidently she hadn't considered the ramifications of Alexandra marrying. "But we haven't the aptitude that you—"

"We shall do whatever's necessary," Juliana interrupted. "Besides, we won't have to concern ourselves if we find a wife for Griffin."

"As usual, Juliana knows what's best." Rachael's eyes danced. "If she wasn't here telling everyone what to do, the entire world would go to blazes."

"Rachael." Juliana heaved an ever-suffering sigh. "It's not the thing for a lady to talk like that."

Rachael sipped, looking every inch the lady despite her language. "For all intents and purposes, I've been an earl for the past two years—with all the aggravations and frustrations thereof. I'm entitled to curse should I care to."

Juliana never allowed anyone the last word. "A potential husband may not think so."

"I'd have no respect for a gentleman who couldn't look beyond a spot of unconventional language."

Alexandra hid a smile behind her own teacup. "Griffin wouldn't care about that."

"Pardon me?" Rachael's lovely sky-blue eyes widened. "Whatever compelled you to say such a thing?"

"Tris. Lord Hawkridge. He told us you and Griffin seemed quite taken with each other."

"Well, Tris—Lord Hawkridge—is wrong!" A telltale flush stained Rachael's cheeks. "Why, Griffin might as well be my brother. We grew up together."

Corinna passed her a plate of sweets. "You haven't seen each other for years, though, have you? I'd say you finished growing up apart."

"He's my cousin."

"There's nothing in the marriage laws to prohibit the union of cousins," Juliana said quite reasonably. "Cousins wed quite often."

"I would *never* marry a cousin."

The words were stated with such vehemence, Alexandra's teacup rattled as she set it back on her saucer. "Whyever not?"

"Do you remember my cousin Edmund?"

"The monster?" Corinna asked.

"Don't call him that!" Rachael closed her eyes for a moment, then opened them and sighed. "You're too young to remember him. Edmund was a very sweet child. He just... didn't look normal."

Corinna looked shamefaced.

"He didn't think normal, either," Juliana told her sadly. "He couldn't even really talk."

Alexandra poured more tea. "Edmund died very young. It was terribly tragic."

"Yes, it was." Rachael licked her lower lip. "Perhaps you never knew that he was my aunt's child. My mother took Edmund when her sister died. Aunt Alice's husband didn't want his son."

"How dreadful," Juliana said.

"Yes. Everything concerning Edmund was sad. Aunt Alice lost many children before having him, and the doctors told her that the miscarriages, and poor Edmund's condition, were most likely because her husband was also her cousin."

The sisters were silent a moment. "Her first cousin, I'd wager," Juliana finally said. "Griffin isn't nearly so close a relation."

"That doesn't signify." Rachael bit into a lemon cake and changed the subject. "What does your family cookbook claim these are supposed to do?"

"Cure melancholy," Corinna said. "But to look at Alexandra, they aren't working."

Rachael turned to Alexandra. "Are you melancholy, dear?" She seemed relieved to have the attention focused elsewhere. "According to the last letter I received from you in London, you were expecting to soon be engaged. Has Lord Shelton failed to propose?"

Juliana took a cake for herself. "He'd propose in an instant if she'd let him within speaking range. But one look at Tristan, and she banished Lord Shelton forever."

"Tristan?" Rachael echoed, looking shocked. "You cannot be seriously interested in *him*."

"Why not?" Alexandra asked cautiously, afraid she knew the answer.

"He's tainted with scandal! Everyone knows he's been accused of murdering his uncle."

"*I* didn't," Alexandra pointed out. "How is it we never discussed this?"

"I don't know." Rachael reached for another cake. "It happened a couple of years ago, didn't it? It must have been one of those seasons when I was in town and you were stuck here. In any case, it *did* happen—and in light of that, you cannot consider Lord Hawkridge's suit."

"There's no suit." Alexandra clenched her hands in her lap. "Lord Hawkridge refuses to even entertain the thought of marriage."

"Good for him. He's retained *some* honor, at least."

Alexandra's eyes widened at her cousin's tone. "You cannot think he committed murder? He wasn't convicted."

"Not in the House of Lords. But in the hearts and minds of the people who matter—"

"Rachael! You know Tris. He cannot have done something so heinous."

"I don't know him. Not anymore. It's been years—"

"He hasn't changed," Alexandra insisted. "Not that much."

Rachael's lips curved in a faint smile. "You always have been the most loyal person I know."

"My loyalty isn't misplaced. Not in this case, anyway."

Rachael considered, then nodded. "Very well. But that still doesn't make him marriageable."

"My sisters don't seem to agree." Alexandra turned to Juliana. "You left us alone again. You're trying to push us together, and don't try to deny it."

Juliana didn't. "Is it working?" she asked instead.

"Yes," Alexandra admitted miserably. "But he hasn't kissed me again."

"He *kissed* you?" Rachael breathed. "And you allowed it with no intention of marriage?"

Alexandra measured her cousin for a long moment. "You've had four seasons. Have you never been kissed?"

"Well…" Rachael's cheeks flushed a delicate pink, then deepened when Alexandra looked pointedly at the fourth finger of her left hand. "No, I didn't marry any of them."

"*Any?*" Corinna burst out. "How many gentlemen have you kissed?"

Rachael's hand with the ringless finger curled into a fist. "They were only kisses!"

"Exactly," Alexandra said with not a little satisfaction.

Corinna snatched another lemon cake. "I must be the only unkissed girl in all of England."

"Not the only," Juliana disagreed with a sigh.

Alexandra sighed in sympathy. "You'll both have your seasons. But only if I *don't* marry Tris. So it's in your best interests to let him finish what he came here to do and leave…without us being caught in a compromising position, thanks to you."

"But what about *your* best interests?" Juliana insisted. "You don't care so much for society—you'll be happier married—"

"I won't be happy if you're not. And how many times do I have to tell you that Tris has no intention of marrying me regardless of your plans?" She took a lemon cake, too. "At the ball I shall dance with someone who will sweep me off my feet."

Rachael smiled. "Waltzing always makes me fall halfway in love."

"Waltzing?" Alexandra repeated, alarmed. "There will be no waltzing. We don't know how to waltz."

"Of course there will be waltzing! There hasn't been a society ball without waltzing since 1812."

"We've had no dance lessons since 1812—people in mourning don't dance." Juliana looked panicked. "There's no time to send for a dancing master—the ball is just four days away. Good gracious, how will Alexandra find a husband if she doesn't know how to waltz?"

"This isn't just about me," Alexandra snapped.

Rachael bit into another lemon cake and shrugged. "One way or another, you will all have to learn how to waltz."

## TWENTY

$\mathcal{T}$HE **GRAY DAY** had finally delivered on its promise, and rain pattered on the drawing room's windows. "Lord and Lady Charlford will be delighted to attend," Alexandra read off a sheet of heavy cream-colored paper. Seated on one of the blue sofas, she set the acceptance note facedown on the empty space beside her.

At the desk, Juliana flipped through the guest list. "Charl-ford," she murmured. "Ah, here they are." She made a mark. "Next?"

Griffin peeked into the room. "Is she gone?"

"Who?" Alexandra asked innocently.

Her sisters snickered.

"Rachael," Tris clarified, walking in. He moved the stack of responses aside so he could sit next to Alexandra. "Griffin would just as soon avoid her."

Griffin grunted as he plopped down on a chair.

"Rachael? You're afraid of little cousin Rachael?" Juliana walked over from the desk to hand her brother the last of the lemon cakes. "Here, this will cure your melancholy."

"I'm not melancholy," Griffin growled before biting into it anyway.

Tris's leg was scarcely a finger's width from Alexandra's, and she'd swear she could feel the heat radiating off of him. Not only that, she could still feel the imprint of his lips on her forehead from earlier. Right in the center above her eyes.

This would never do. What could Tris mean by coming so close? How was she to complete her task and—more importantly—hold herself together, with the cause of her broken heart all but sitting in her lap? She should be focusing on last-minute party details and looking forward to the ball, not battling this wretched attraction.

Rubbing her forehead hard, she rose and wandered over to see Corinna's latest painting. On the unfinished canvas, a young couple lounged, sharing a cozy picnic. Corinna often painted landscapes, but Alexandra couldn't remember her ever including people.

She watched her sister create the dappled shade beneath a tree. "That's not one of your usual subjects."

Corinna looked up from her easel. "Do you like it?"

"Very much," Tris said, suddenly standing beside Alexandra. "The two of them look like they're in love."

Corinna glanced at him and Alexandra before focusing on her scowling brother. "Griffin's in love," she teased.

"I am not," he mumbled around a mouthful of lemon cake.

She swirled her brush in gray paint. "Rachael took a fancy to you, too."

He swallowed, half choking. "She did?" They all burst out laughing while Griffin slowly turned red. "I'm sure she said nothing of the sort."

Alexandra started inching her way back to the sofa. "Of course she didn't, but we could tell."

"We're girls," Juliana added.

"As though I hadn't noticed with all your dressmaker's bills." Griffin swallowed the last of the sweet. "It doesn't signify, in any case. I cannot have an affair with Rachael."

Leaning against the painted stone chimneypiece, Juliana crossed her arms. "Of course you cannot. It would ruin her. You'll have to marry her instead."

"I don't intend to marry anyone at present." He gestured to the pile of letters Alexandra had left on the sofa. "Are those the responses?"

"Yes," she said, grateful to have an excuse to move farther away from Tris.

"How many have accepted our invitation?"

She reclaimed her seat and picked up the acceptance notes, straightening the stack on her lap. "More than a hundred."

"Including Rachael," Corinna added with a mischievous smile.

Alexandra thought her sisters had meddled quite enough. "Oh, do leave Griffin alone. Rachael made it clear she'll never marry him, anyway."

Though Griffin looked curious, he remained stubbornly mute. The rain sounded louder as they all waited.

"What did she say?" Tris finally asked for him.

"She will never marry a cousin."

"Just that?" Griffin burst out, apparently unable to help himself. "Just she will never marry a cousin?"

Juliana took the chair beside him. "Do you remember her cousin Edmund?"

Griffin shook his head.

"The monster," Corinna reminded him sheepishly.

"Don't call him that!" Alexandra burst out at the same time Griffin said, "Oh, yes," wincing at the memory.

He looked to her. "We all called him that."

"Well, he wasn't one. He was a sad little boy. And Rachael will get very upset if you call him that in front of her."

"Tell me about him," Tris said, sitting again by Alexandra.

Tantalizing warmth and clean-Tris scent. "Edmund looked very odd," she said, scooting away a little bit.

"Malformed," Juliana elaborated.

"I was trying to be diplomatic, but yes. And he couldn't talk. He only grunted." Alexandra rubbed her forehead again. "He died very young."

"His mother and father were cousins," Juliana said. "The doctors suggested perhaps that was to blame for Edmund's condition. And Rachael said that's why she'll never marry a cousin."

Griffin nodded thoughtfully. "When we were young, Edmund scared me out of my seven senses. I can understand why Rachael would be frightened of giving birth to such a mon...such a child." He released a tense breath, looking relieved. "Obviously, marriage between us is out of the question. I don't know that her fears are founded, but given her feelings, that hardly makes a difference."

"There are others who believe close marriages aren't wise," Tris added in support. "I concur with the theory that interbreeding produces weak animals."

Corinna snickered. "Griffin and Rachael aren't animals!"

"But they are...in the strictest definition."

"Look at our own Mad King George," Griffin pointed out. "A product, you must admit, of copious interbreeding."

"What a picture," Corinna said. "You and Rachael interbreeding *copiously*—"

"Kindly shut up." Griffin had gone scarlet from the roots of his dark hair all the way down to his collar and perhaps beyond. "Tell me what you've planned for the ball," he said tightly.

Alexandra rubbed her forehead some more. "The invitations went out last month, requesting guests arrive at eight. We've procured a band of music from Chichester, and we'll place them in a corner of the great hall—"

"Not the minstrel's gallery?" Griffin broke in.

"No," Juliana said. "That's too far removed from the dancers. We want the musicians to take requests and interact with the guests. We'll have dancing until one o'clock, when a handsome supper shall be served. After supper, the dancing shall resume until dawn, and, for those who stay the night, we shall serve breakfast between eleven and twelve."

"And how many of our hundred-plus acceptances are from young men?"

"Most of them!" Corinna grinned. "We'll have a much greater number of unmarried gentlemen than unmarried ladies."

"Excellent." Griffin looked pleased.

Tris reached for some bread and cheese, leaning against Alexandra in the process. "Your ball sounds like quite an ambitious undertaking."

Juliana turned to him with a smile. "We've yet to receive *your* response, Lord Hawkridge."

"I don't attend balls," he said quietly, brushing Alexandra again as he settled back in his seat.

"Tristan will be leaving before the ball." Griffin stretched his long legs and crossed them at the ankles. "Everything's all set for Friday night, then?"

"No." Alexandra rose abruptly and went to the desk, taking the response notes with her as a pretense. She sat and tucked them away in a drawer. "Rachael alerted us to a problem. We don't know how to waltz."

"Then we won't waltz," Griffin said easily.

"We can*not* not waltz," Juliana said. "Everyone who is anyone waltzes. It's the thing."

"*The thing* is, we don't know how. One of you shall simply have to explain to the musicians—"

"I know how to waltz," Tris interrupted. He stood and walked over to the desk. "I can teach you all."

"Wonderful!" Juliana clapped her hands. "Tonight?"

An exasperated Alexandra glared up at him looming over her. He began absently rearranging items on the desk. "Griffin and I must finish planning the pipeline tonight—we have men arriving first thing in the morning for instructions. We can dance tomorrow, while I'm waiting for the parts to arrive from the foundry."

"What will we do for music?" Corinna asked. "If we're all dancing at once—"

"We can hum," Juliana said.

"We cannot all be dancing at once," Alexandra pointed out, moving the inkwell back to where she liked it. "Tris is the only gentleman."

"I take offense to that," Griffin said with mock outrage.

"You don't know the dance."

Tris lifted a quill. "He can dance while he learns. But we'll need a third man." Looking contemplative, he stroked his chin with the end of the feather. "I know. Boniface."

"Boniface?" Juliana scoffed. "Butlers don't dance."

Tris raised a brow. "Butlers do as they're told." He reached with the quill to tap Griffin on the nose. "Go inform him. You're the lord around here."

Griffin batted the feather away and stood. "I'm doing this only because I want to see Boniface's expression when I tell him," he claimed in a transparent attempt to retain his dignity.

"I want to see his face, too," Juliana said and quickly followed him. "Corinna?"

"Wouldn't want to miss this." Corinna dropped her palette and ran after them both.

A Lady of Distinction would find her sisters quite vulgar, Alexandra thought. Releasing a long sigh, she rubbed her forehead.

"Have you the headache?" Tris asked, looking solicitous.

"No."

"But you keep—"

"No." She wasn't going to tell him she felt phantom lips on her brow.

He shrugged and smiled. "They left us alone again."

"I was just leaving." She rose and started toward the door, then, sensing him on her heels, whirled to face him. "Would you please stop following me around?"

"I haven't been—"

"Yes, you have. You're shadowing my every step."

"Am I?" He looked puzzled, as though he'd been totally unaware of his actions.

"Yes. And you keep touching my things." *Not to mention touching me,* she thought, plucking the feather from his fingers.

Rain pattered while he stared at his empty hand as though he hadn't noticed he'd been holding the quill, either. Taking it with her, Alexandra left him there and hurried off to the solitude of her room.

Men truly were the most oblivious creatures.

# TWENTY-ONE

## CHOCOLATED SPONGE CAKES

Take a measure of sugar and a like amount of butter and mix together well. To this add
two beaten eggs and then flour in the same amount as the butter and sugar. Put together
with a little milk to make soft and pour into your pan. Put in your oven for half an hour
until well risen, then cut into little squares, cover with chocolate icing, and decorate with
white icing strands to make them look like little presents on a plate.

*Mere acquaintances have been known to call on me hoping to find these offered. They*
*look like tiny gifts and are reputed to be irresistible!*
—Katherine, Countess of Greystone, 1769

*B*ONIFACE'S PRETTY face was even prettier with
red cheeks.

"Take her hand, Boniface," Tris said patiently, demonstrating with Corinna. "You can do it."

Even with their hands gloved, the butler held Alexandra's
fingers so hesitantly she had to cling to his to hold on.

"Put your other hand around her back."

Though Boniface complied, Alexandra could barely feel
his fingers grazing her spine.

"Music, please."

All three sisters began humming.

"The basic figure is a full turn in two measures using three steps per measure. Like this." Tris swept Corinna into the dance, the two of them turning so fast she was forced to rise to her toes. She stopped humming. Her laughter echoed through the cavernous great hall.

Alexandra hummed through gritted teeth.

Griffin and Juliana took a few tentative steps, then seemed to grasp the idea. "Oh, this is fun!" Juliana cried, leaving Alexandra humming alone.

She changed to la-la-la's. Boniface still stood there, limply attached to her, his blue eyes wide with apprehension. Unlike most families, the Chases didn't ban their servants from marrying, and Alexandra had sometimes wondered why he chose to remain a bachelor. Now she knew.

By all appearances, he was terrified of women.

"Shall we dance?" she prompted, abandoning the music. It was still raining—it had rained all night—and the drops sounded louder in the sudden silence. "Hum!" she commanded her sisters, turning back to Boniface when they took over. "Well?" she asked.

He nodded mutely, remaining riveted in place.

Tris frowned as he twirled past. "Go on, man. Give it a try."

"It's delightful!" Corinna called encouragingly.

Seeing her sister in Tris's arms, a stab of jealousy caught Alexandra by surprise.

At last, Boniface took a few jerky steps, and she lurched with him, trying her best to stay attached. She hardly noticed the three times he trod on her feet, busy as she was watching Tris guide her sister in whirling circles around the planked wood floor. He danced with admirable grace, looking handsome and debonair and dreadfully delicious.

"Enough," he finally said, saving Alexandra's toes. They all stopped humming. "Change partners. No, wait—allow me to fetch another sweet first." He walked over to where Alexandra had set up refreshments on a side table, taking his sixth bite-sized chocolate-covered cake. "These are truly excellent."

"So you've assured me," she said with a little smile.

He snatched another one and ate it quickly before returning. "Now we switch partners." To Alexandra's disappointment, he went to Juliana. "Griffin, you take Alexandra. Boniface, I think you'll find Corinna an accomplished waltzer already."

Corinna beamed. Boniface's face turned even redder, if that were possible. Alexandra and her sisters resumed providing the music, and everyone began dancing.

Griffin held Alexandra a bit awkwardly, but at least his hands were firmer than the butler's. Tris shouted occasional words of encouragement and correction. He and Juliana glided by, making the dance look effortless—and sparking envy that seemed to fill Alexandra from the top of her head clear down to her toes.

She wondered if she'd actually turned green.

"Stop watching him," Griffin muttered.

She focused up at the hammerbeam ceiling. "La-la-la."

His fingers gripped hers tighter. "You think I don't notice the way you look at each other?"

"La-la-la."

"Three days from now, this room will be full of eligible gentlemen, all vying for your hand."

"La-la-la."

"I hope you'll fall in love with one of them."

The great hall looked plain and empty today, but on Friday evening it would be crammed full of people, blazing with torchlight, and sparkling with the jewels adorning their guests. Guests who had been invited expressly to provide her with the chance to meet someone special.

And her brother wanted her to find love. He wasn't bent on marrying her off to the first young man who offered.

She stopped singing. "I hope so, too."

"I'm glad to hear it." Griffin smiled...until her gaze wandered again to Tris. "Pay attention to your dancing, will you?"

"I think I'm improving." She looked back at her brother. "You're a great deal better than Boniface."

"That's not saying much," he muttered as the butler stumbled by with Corinna.

"Switch!" Tris called, heading toward the cakes. While everyone else shuffled partners, he ate two more.

Then finally, just when Alexandra felt like she'd been waiting forever, he slipped an arm around her waist and took her hand. As he locked her body into the proper position opposite his, he locked his eyes on hers, too.

A bolt of energy rippled through her. And through him as well—she'd swear it. He couldn't look at her like that and not feel as she did, not sense the current that ran between them.

And then he began to dance. He moved so smoothly, she didn't have to think about what her feet did. All by themselves, they seemed to know the steps. She forgot to hum.

His smile seemed as intimate as a kiss—that second kiss she'd been thinking about but knew she would never get. "Now you can follow me around," he said playfully, "instead of me following you."

"I'm sorry about yesterday. I was in a mood."

"I understand."

The fact that she believed he *did* understand didn't make her feel any better.

His gray eyes watched her so intently, she feared she might lose herself in their depths. She fit perfectly in his arms, the two of them moving together as though they'd been born to share a dance floor. Where his hand rested on her back, heat seemed to spread out from his palm to warm every bit of her skin.

She feared all the hard work of forgetting, of piecing her heart back together, was unraveling in the space of a single dance.

The song came to an end. Corinna and Juliana stopped humming. The incessant rain pounded on the hammerbeam roof. Tris kept dancing, kept his gaze fastened on Alexandra.

She felt rather than saw Griffin's glare. "Switch!" he called, shoving himself between them. He handed Tris a sweet. "Time for another chocolate cake, isn't it?"

"Thank you," Tris said and stepped back, allowing Boniface to take his place.

For the next minute or two, Alexandra danced in a daze. Boniface had improved slightly. He actually held her hand, and he trod on her toes only once.

"Switch!" Tris called.

Alexandra noticed Juliana sweetly hand him a cake as she joined him. Sometimes her sister grated on her nerves.

"Why are you frowning?" Griffin asked, holding Alexandra a little too tightly. "You're supposed to pay attention to your partner."

"Thank you for the advice. You could write a book and call yourself A Gentleman of Distinction."

"Stop watching him," he growled low.

"I'm studying his technique. He's good, isn't he?"

"How would you know?" He swung her farther away. "You've never seen anyone waltz before in your life."

"Switch!" Tris called.

Not to be outdone by Juliana, Alexandra rushed to grab one of the little cakes before meeting him. Her sisters laughed, but the smile Tris gave her made her knees turn to jelly.

Yet when his arm came around her, his sure guidance kept her twirling in perfect rhythm. She felt giddy, lightheaded. As their gazes held, she wondered whether to attribute that to the motion or to him.

Him. Definitely him.

She wracked her brains for a neutral topic of conversation. "If you never go out in society, when did you learn how to waltz?"

"Directly after my uncle died, when I first inherited the marquessate."

Before the scandal broke out, then. "Did a dancing master teach you?"

"No." When she just looked at him, he added, "A girl taught me."

If she hadn't turned green before, she surely did now. "A girl? Who?"

It was possibly the rudest question she'd ever asked. Her stomach twisted with shame, but she had to know the answer.

"It doesn't signify," he said, somehow managing to sound both evasive and blithe. "Just someone who hoped to dance with me at many balls."

He spoke in past tense, Alexandra consoled herself. Quite obviously, that girl's hopes had ultimately been dashed. But she hated her, regardless.

Even though she couldn't remember hating anyone before.

"Switch!" Griffin yelled, sounding so furious she was glad her next partner was Boniface instead of him.

She gave the butler a big smile. "You're surely improving, Boniface."

"Thank you, my lady." He stumbled. "Pardon me."

"No, no, you're doing fine." Since he didn't seem to be leading her, she led him instead. "Just think, you'll be able to waltz at the next servants' ball."

"I think not, my lady. I don't believe waltzing is my forte."

"Oh, bosh," she said, although she agreed. "You're doing just fine."

"Switch!" Tris called.

Griffin started twirling her with a little more gusto than necessary. "What were you two talking about so intently?"

"Boniface fears that waltzing is not his forte."

"Not Boniface. You and Tristan."

"Goodness, Griffin. That was a good two minutes ago. I cannot remember the conversation, but I'm certain it wasn't anything significant."

"He was holding you too close."

"No, he wasn't. You're not holding me close enough. There's a reason old matrons think the waltz is a scandalous dance, I'll have you know."

"Switch!" Tris called. While Alexandra headed to fetch him a chocolate cake, he added, "You're all doing splendidly."

"Good," Griffin said. "Because we're all finished."

Alexandra turned to protest, her gaze swinging past her brother and over to Tris. As she met his gray eyes, their intensity evoked the memory of his warm hand on her back as they danced, his thigh grazing hers as he reached for the bread, his chest pressing up against her in the library, his fingers encircling her elbow, his lips touching her forehead, his breath tickling her cheek…

Alexandra's knees began to buckle.

Sweet heaven, Tris *had* been holding her too close.

And she'd been encouraging him, flirting with him, not to mention letting jealousy turn her head. It was all wrong, so wrong. Tris was wrong for her, wrong for her sisters, wrong for the future of her family.

She took the plate of remaining cakes and held it before her like a shield. "I'll go put these in the dining room," she said, keeping her tone as casual as possible. When Tris gave the sweets a longing glance, she released a tense laugh. "Don't worry; we'll save them for you. They'll go well with your port after dinner."

She didn't breathe until she'd escaped, leaving the sweets on one of the dining room's side tables and her heart in the great hall.

# TWENTY-TWO

ITH ONLY A day and a half left before the ball —and less than that before Tris departed— Alexandra was finding it hard to sleep. Still lying awake in her bed well after midnight, she sighed and lit a candle, leaned back against her pillows, and slid a copy of *Mansfield Park* off her night table.

Then sat with it unopened on her lap.

Unless one could count fleeting glances, she hadn't seen Tris in the two days since the dance lesson. He'd ordered his meals brought to the workshop, where he was building the second pump. But his rush to finish didn't really explain his avoidance.

Nor did it explain why, the few times she'd caught sight of him, she'd found herself walking the other way.

It seemed silly and childish—and *wrong* somehow—and each time it happened, she swore to herself it would be the last. But after all, it took two to play the game. She wondered if he, like she, had been unprepared for the heady experience of waltzing together. Unprepared and dismayed. For both their sakes, nothing like that must ever happen again.

If only…

According to Griffin, although the incessant rain had delayed completion of the new pipeline, the pump was ready, and Tris would be leaving after they installed it tomorrow. A full day before the ball, just as planned. Griffin was jubilant, but her feelings on the matter ran to dejection mixed with relief.

Well, she told herself sternly, staring into space wasn't going to change anything. With another sigh, she opened her book. But she hadn't read two paragraphs when her attention was claimed by the prolonged creak of a slowly opening door.

Apparently she wasn't the only one finding sleep hard to come by this night.

She heard furtive footsteps, followed by a soft knock and murmured conversation. Her sisters, she was sure of it. Puzzled, she waited for them to fetch her too, but instead their voices receded down the corridor, leaving her feeling very much alone.

In the next quarter hour, she read the same page of *Mansfield Park* at least a dozen times while wondering what Juliana and Corinna were up to and why they hadn't invited her to their middle-of-the-night rendezvous. Now hurt warred with all her other emotions. Only pride kept her from seeking them out.

Until she heard movement in the dining room, which was directly below her chamber. A thud, as though perhaps someone had stumbled. And other muffled noises.

Curiosity overcame pride.

She set the book aside and climbed from her blue-draped bed. Tying a wrapper over her nightgown and taking the candle, she tiptoed from her room past her sisters' open doors and downstairs.

Walking through the picture gallery toward the dining

room, she considered what she should say when she found Juliana and Corinna. Should she act wounded or surprised? Disapproving or conspiratorial? Would she join them or suggest they return to their beds?

She'd play it by ear, she decided, depending upon their attitudes. Hopefully, they'd all have a good laugh. That could go a long way toward releasing some of her tension.

Anticipating a little sisterly mischief, she rounded the corner into the dining room.

And stopped short, bobbling the candle in her hand.

Her sisters weren't there. Instead, Tris stood with his back to her, barefoot, wearing a long dressing gown of rich burgundy brocade belted loosely around his waist.

Though the only skin bared was that of his wrists and ankles, the sight of him in such intimate clothing made her mouth go unnaturally dry.

Standing by a gothic mahogany side table, he was devouring what remained of the little chocolate cakes she'd left there yesterday morning. The embroidered cloth she'd laid over them sat crumpled on the floor.

He had yet to notice her. Recovering her composure, she laughed softly and walked closer, determined this time not to flee in the opposite direction. "Sneaking sweets, are you?"

The last cake in his hand, he turned to her. "Alexandra."

Placing the candle on the side table, she knelt to retrieve the cloth. "We missed you at the last few meals. But you could have asked if you wanted more." She straightened, setting the cloth on the table, too. "I'd have sent them to you in the workshop."

He tilted his head, giving her a look so calculatedly innocent—his smile vague, his eyes deliberately blank—that she laughed again. "I'm going to tell everyone you're a sweet thief."

The cake fell from his fingers and landed with a little *plop* on the carpet. "Alexandra," he repeated and reached for her, dragging her into his arms.

Though stunned, she went willingly. With their faces just a hair's breadth apart, he hesitated, making her shiver with anticipation. Then their lips met—she couldn't tell who closed the gap—and her heart rolled over in her chest.

The way they were pressed together from shoulder down to navel seemed incredibly intimate and thrilling—and *very* different from the friendly or sisterly sort of embrace she was used to. She could feel the searing heat of his skin through the fine fabric of his dressing gown. He wrapped his arms around her back. She buried her hands in his soft hair. He tasted of sugar and chocolate and Tris, a deliciously sweet combination.

No, make that *dangerously* sweet.

It took a herculean effort to retreat the barest inch. "We cannot," she whispered.

The look he gave her was so odd and intense, it seemed to go right through her.

"I—I need to go back to my room," she stammered, removing herself from his arms. When he didn't reply, she added, "I'm sorry," even though she wasn't sure what she was apologizing for.

He nodded, his lips curving in a sad almost-smile.

"We should both go back to our rooms," she said more firmly. "Good night."

"'Night," he echoed and turned to exit the far end of the room.

Almost against her will, she followed him to the doorway and watched him slowly traverse the long length of the torchlit great hall, standing there until he disappeared into the dark corridor that led to the guest chambers.

He didn't look back.

She released a long, shuddering breath before retrieving

her candle and starting upstairs. All the way down the picture gallery, the little flickering light reflected off the canvases on the walls—all her solemn, disapproving ancestors.

She wasn't supposed to even *dance* with Tris again, let alone kiss him.

But now that it had happened, all she could think was that she wanted more.

She didn't remember actually going upstairs, didn't remember walking through the high gallery or down the corridor past her sisters' rooms. She was settled beneath her covers before she realized their doors had been closed and they must be safely back behind them.

So much for some sisterly mirth to release her tension and help her relax. She blew out the candle and listened to the rain, wondering how she'd ever get herself to sleep now.

## TWENTY-THREE

"*T*HERE'S OUR thief!" Alexandra proclaimed loudly when Tristan arrived late for breakfast the next morning.

Spreading marmalade on toast, Juliana tittered. "What can you mean?"

"Do you see the plate of chocolate cakes that *isn't* on that sideboard? Tris sneaked in here and finished them in the middle of the night."

Though Tristan was weary and distracted—thinking about how to fix the problem with the pump he'd discovered this morning—he vaguely wondered why Alexandra was suddenly so friendly and cheerful when they hadn't so much as talked in a day and a half. He dropped onto the chair a footman pulled out. "I did what?"

"Don't try to act the innocent," she accused gaily. "I caught you red-handed. Or perhaps I should say chocolate-crumbed."

"You did?" He raised a hand to his mouth and absently wiped away nonexistent crumbs. "Very well, I confess. I cannot resist your sweets."

Her sisters both laughed. Griffin frowned. And Tristan wracked his brain.

Despite his "confession," he had no memory of leaving his room in the middle of the night. While plastering a smile on his face, he groaned inwardly, more distressed by this news than he'd been by the broken pump.

Apparently, he was sleepwalking again.

All of his life, Tristan had been an occasional sleepwalker. For years, he'd suffered through mornings where people informed him of his own doings the night before—often comical doings, none of which he ever remembered. After some of these episodes, his schoolmates—Griffin included—had teased him mercilessly.

As he'd grown, the episodes had become fewer and farther between—eventually far enough between that he was able to discern a pattern. He was most likely to sleepwalk when under pressure of some sort. As an adolescent and even more so as an adult, the infrequent occurrences seemed to be brought on by emotional stress.

After a long spell of peaceful nights, he'd decided he must have outgrown the odd habit. But now it was back. Since he wasn't personally affected by Griffin's irrigation problems and had no great concerns of his own, that could mean only one thing...

He was more attached to Alexandra—and frustrated by his inability to do anything about it—than he'd allowed himself to believe.

He needed to install this pump and go home. For good. Isolation had its drawbacks, but it had afforded him a peace he could only hope to reclaim.

"You rose late," Griffin commented.

"To the contrary, I've been awake for hours." Tristan held out his cup for coffee. "I've been in the workshop. We won't be installing the pump today."

"Why not? It operated perfectly during the test last night—"

"Well, something—or someone—bent the shank. The valve no longer works. I don't expect you have any wild animals about the premises?"

"Nothing capable of—"

"Juliana and I are finished," Corinna interrupted. "May we be excused? Madame Rodale has arrived for our final fittings."

Looking distracted, Griffin waved a hand. "Go." When Alexandra didn't follow, he turned to her. "Aren't you going with them?"

"I'll join them in a moment," she said quietly and looked to Tristan. "Are you feeling quite well this morning?"

He noticed she was wearing his cameo again and wondered about that. "As well as I expect one can when one's work has been sabotaged." Not feeling hungry, he put down his fork. "The piece will have to be recast, and the entire pump taken apart to reinstall it. This will set us back a day, if not more. I've thought of going home and returning, but..." He trailed off, not wanting to sound selfish.

"That would cost you another two days of your life," Griffin finished for him. "Besides, I promised Rachael the job would be finished."

"Then you'll be here for the ball," Alexandra said, her expression unreadable.

Tristan hadn't attended a ball in two years, and he didn't intend to start now. "I may still be here at Cainewood, but I won't be attending." He rose and turned to Griffin. "You might think about placing a guard at the workshop when I'm not there—as it was never meant to be living quarters, it has no proper door. However this came about, we'll want to make certain it doesn't happen again."

In a dark mood, he headed off to the foundry.

## TWENTY-FOUR

*I*N CONTRAST to Tristan's mood, the atmosphere in the drawing room was jubilant. The rain had finally stopped, and summer sunshine streamed through the windows; if the weather held but a day, they'd have a beautiful evening for the ball.

Madame Rodale and her two assistants swarmed about, making last-minute tucks here and tiny adjustments there. While Alexandra slipped into her new dress, Juliana and Corinna chattered excitedly, admiring each other's choices.

"You look beautiful." Corinna tweaked one of Juliana's short, puffed sleeves, which were decorated with knots of pale yellow ribbon. "The *jonquille* is so becoming on you."

"A Lady of Distinction would approve." Juliana grinned. "Now, as for your pale blush pink…"

"I adore it." As Corinna twirled, her skirts belled out, pearls shimmering all over the sheer top layer. Entwined with strings of yet more pearls, a drapery of lace went all around the bottom. "Doesn't Alexandra look lovely, too?"

Trying to smile, Alexandra settled her skirts into place. The dress certainly wasn't blue; shimmering in the morning light, the pinkish-purple amaranthus hue looked almost shocking. The hem was embellished with white velvet roses and a wide rouleau of amaranthus. Below that, a row of delicate white tassels alternated with sparkling white beads, nearly skimming the floor.

She'd never felt so pretty. But she could no longer hold her tongue.

"You two did it, didn't you? I heard you leave your rooms last night, so don't try to deny it."

"Deny what?" All innocence, Corinna adjusted her bodice.

"That you ruined Tris's new pump." Alexandra didn't wait for confirmation. "And all for naught, as it turns out. He's determined to avoid the ball, and nothing you do will convince him otherwise. You ought to be ashamed of yourselves."

Though Juliana didn't try to play coy, she didn't look ashamed, either. "We did it for you. We thought if Tristan attended—"

"Our other guests won't welcome him. Stop dreaming, will you? I'm not going to marry him, and nothing you do will change that." Nothing Tris could do would change that, either. Not even middle-of-the night kisses that made her melt. "Now, Griffin is paying for this ball for the express purpose of finding me a husband. I'm planning to do my best to have a proper attitude and make the most of it."

The sound of applause came from the doorway. "I missed the majority of that speech," a voice came from behind them, "but I heartily approve of the last part."

They all turned to look at Griffin.

At the sight of them, his eyes all but popped out of his head.

"Aren't our dresses exquisite?" Performing a few happy waltz steps, Corinna turned in a circle.

"Um, yes. Pull your sleeves up, Juliana, will you?"

She tugged at them, but the dress was designed to be off the shoulder. "They won't go."

He eyed their dresses' high waistlines and scooped necklines, designed to accentuate the bust. "You're all going to cover"—at an apparent loss for words, he patted his own chest—"with one of those scarf things, right?"

"A fichu?" Madame sniffed. "I think not. These are evening gowns, my lord."

"They don't look like the pictures my sisters showed me."

"The pictures were but a starting point, my lord. By the time the fashion plates make it here from France, they're already beginning to pass out of style."

"We shall not be caught in last month's fashions," Juliana added. "These gowns are the thing."

"Not in this house, they aren't!"

"Griffin. Good news. The foundry will have the new part cast by the end of the day." Tris walked in, scanned the room with a low whistle, and settled on Alexandra. "By George, you ladies will put every other girl to shame."

"My sisters won't be wearing these dresses," Griffin said.

"Of course they will." Tris tore his gaze from Alexandra and turned to his friend. "While I take apart the pump, you'll want to head out to the vineyard and see that work on the new pipeline is resumed."

"Very well." Griffin turned to leave, then swiveled back. "I'm not paying for those dresses," he warned. "Not until they're made decent."

Madame Rodale gave a little French-sounding "hmmph."

Tris laughed. "Listen to yourself, old man. You've been on campaign far too long. Don't you want men to find your sisters appealing? Irresistible? *Marriageable?*"

"Not if they're men like…"

"Like us?" Tris suggested helpfully.

Griffin's "hmmph" put the mantua-maker's to shame. "I need to get to the vineyard," he muttered and left.

"Madame has finished with my dress and Corinna's," Juliana announced. "We'll just go to our rooms and take them off." Grabbing Corinna's hand, she pulled her out the door.

Madame's two pasty-complexioned assistants fluttered around Alexandra, pinning her dress here and there. Tris stood watching. Wondering what she should say now that they'd kissed again—wondering if they'd kiss yet more—she shifted uncomfortably.

"Stand still," Madame said. "Else Mariette might poke you."

She stiffened and met Tris's gaze. "Don't you need to work on the pump?"

"You're beautiful."

"Thank you," she whispered.

"Of course, you're always beautiful—it has nothing to do with the dress." He spoke conversationally. "You'd be beautiful in a shapeless burlap bag. And you'll be beautiful when you're a hundred years old, because your beauty comes from inside."

She didn't say anything, because she didn't know what to say.

"I want to apologize," he went on, "for the way I treated you the last time we were together—"

"Are you finished?" she interrupted, addressing the assistants. The two girls were standing back, watching her and Tris as though they were performing a most fascinating play.

"*Oui*," Madame said briskly. "Remove the dress carefully, please, and take it down the corridor to the armory, if you will." Since the armory was just an empty room with rusty weapons all over the walls—Alexandra figured it hadn't been renovated since before the Civil War—Griffin was allowing them to use it as their sewing room. "Come along, Mariette, Martina. We have much to do before tomorrow."

Tris waited until their footsteps had receded down the corridor. "Do you expect their names are really Mariette and Martina?"

She laughed. "No, I think their names are Mary and Martha."

They shared a smile before he sobered. "As I was saying..."

"Yes?" She'd never seen him look quite so uneasy.

"The last time we were together, I didn't treat you much like a friend."

"No, you didn't," she agreed quietly. He'd treated her as much more.

And they'd kissed.

"I didn't look at you the way one looks at a friend."

"I didn't look at you like a friend, either." They'd looked at each other like two people in love; there was no other way to put it.

And they'd kissed.

"I held you too close."

He certainly had; she could still feel his body against hers.

And they'd kissed.

"I'm sorry for all of that," he concluded. "I still wish, more than anything, to remain friends."

She blinked. That was it? He still wanted to be friends? Nothing had changed for him last night?

Of course, nothing had changed for her last night, either—on the surface, that was. Marriage still wasn't an option. But clearly they'd crossed some sort of line. Surely, regardless of the fact that they couldn't act on their mutual feelings, they could acknowledge them and admit that they were more than simple friends.

"I can scarcely even imagine going back to a distant, polite friendship," she said carefully.

"I'm so pleased you agree," he said, looking relieved. "The hours and days we've spent avoiding each other...I shouldn't like to go back to that ever again." He released a pent-up breath. "There are many definitions of friendship. We're both sensible people. Certainly we can control—"

"What about the kiss?" she burst out.

He blinked. "That was weeks ago. More than a month. I thought we'd agreed to forget it." Watching her, his gray gaze narrowed warily. "What about it?"

"What have you been talking about, then?"

"What do you mean, what have I been talking about? The dance lesson, of course. I held you too close, and that precipitated our latest—"

"What about last night?"

"What *about* last night?"

"We kissed again last night," she said, exasperated. "Am I expected to forget about that, too? Or shall I assume kissing is part of your definition of friendship?"

He visibly paled, his jaw going slack. "Are you sure?" he asked.

Evidently he *had* expected her to forget it.

"What do you mean, am I sure?" Every minuscule detail of that kiss was burned into her memory. Just thinking about it, she could feel his arms around her, his lips slanting over hers. She could taste the hint of chocolate. "How could I forget such a thing?"

"I meant..." He hesitated, apparently fumbling for words. "I meant, are you sure you wish that to be part of the definition? Because frankly, I don't think it should be." The color had returned to his face, and unlike a moment ago, he sounded quite certain. "I don't think I could handle that. I don't think I could stop with kissing."

Part of her was shocked at the implication, but she couldn't help being flattered, too. And although she'd never considered kissing to be part of friendship, she had to admit the idea was tempting. After all, despite his stated opinion, kisses didn't *have* to go further. Hadn't she told her sisters they were "only kisses," not meaningful in and of themselves? And Rachael had said the same thing.

"I'm sorry," he continued, interrupting her musings. "I seem to be apologizing quite often these days, but I assure you, I mean it. I've no idea what came over me, but I hope to remain friends. I won't be kissing you again."

"I wish you would," she said under her breath as he walked out.

# TWENTY-FIVE

*F*OR PITY'S SAKE, he'd kissed her in his sleep!

Descending the stairs two at a time as he headed for the workshop, Tristan couldn't decide which was worse: the fact that he'd done such a thing, or the fact that he'd missed out on really experiencing it.

The only thing he was certain of, he thought as a footman threw the front doors open wide, was that he needed to go home. He'd take the pump apart today and put it back together with the new piece tomorrow. Adjusting the blasted thing again would eat up the better part of the day, but that would keep him busy while everyone else was occupied with the ball. Saturday morning he'd install the pump and leave with a sigh of relief. He was counting the hours.

And hoping he'd find the strength to keep away from her.

*I wish you would.*

Had she meant him to hear that? No matter—he had. And —friendship aside—the thought that she might want him regardless of his reputation was enough to make him run the opposite direction.

Anything beyond friendship would prove a disaster for them both—there was no disputing that fact.

"My lord? Are you in need of something?"

Tristan blinked, realizing he was standing stock-still in the middle of the quadrangle. Servants crisscrossed the lawn, carrying baskets of laundry and buckets of water, slanting him curious glances as they went about their business.

"No," he told the footman. "Thank you for your concern."

He headed for his temporary workshop, a dim, doorless room meant for storing timber, but empty this time of year. After lighting a few candles around the pump, he stood waiting for his eyes to adjust.

No wonder she'd put on his cameo this morning—she thought their relationship had changed. To her, that kiss had meant something.

He wished he could remember it.

And he wished, more fervently still, that their circumstances were different. Because a tiny part of him was beginning to wonder, despite past experience, whether marital happiness—if not true love—might be possible with a girl like Alexandra. A girl who seemed to complement him in so many ways.

But all the sorrow she'd endured didn't change the fact that she'd grown up in the bosom of a large, loving family—a family that was unquestionably part of society's elite. She'd never known isolation, never faced disapproval, never walked into a room and felt the chill of icy gazes that stared right through her. Never had whispers behind her back sound louder than the thoughts in her own head.

And now that they'd kissed again, he feared the thoughts in her head might be telling her an alliance between them could somehow take place.

Well, he'd have to nip that in the bud.

Cursing under his breath, he set to removing the first bolt.

Blast this peculiar affliction. Not only had it suddenly reappeared, it seemed to be getting worse. He'd never before kissed anyone while sleepwalking—at least as far as he knew. Usually he just ambled around for a bit, although he'd been known to dress himself and go outdoors on occasion. Once in a while he'd heard reports of other activities, but he'd never done anything in his sleep that wasn't a trivial, everyday action.

At least…as far as he knew.

Sometimes he wondered.

# TWENTY-SIX

## MARCHPANE FRUITS

Take a Pounde of almonds, Blanched and Beaten in a stone mortar, till they begin to
come to a fine paste, and then add a Pounde of sifted Sugar and make it into a perfect
paste, putting to it now and then the white of an egg and a spoonful or two of rose-water.
When you have Beaten it sufficiently, separate into balls and colour as for fruit, red for
apples and cherries, yellow for lemons, orange for oranges, purple for grapes, and the
like. Shape small pieces of your coloured Paste into fruits and leave out to dry.

*These festive fruits are lovely for parties and elegant enough for a ball. Or anytime at all,*
*for like all sweets, they are truly delicious.*

—Kendra, Duchess of Amberley, 1690

THERE WERE NO wallflowers at Cainewood
Castle's ball.

Griffin's strategy had proved an unqualified success. So
many more gentlemen than ladies were in attendance that
even the plainest girl had barely a moment to sit and rest.
And in their fashionable new dresses, the Chase sisters were
anything but plain.

The three of them had been claimed for every dance, and

though it was barely two hours into the long evening—only ten o'clock—Alexandra's feet were already beginning to ache. Since she was now engaged in a rather staid country dance, she tried her best to ignore the pain—and the dull gentleman who was her partner—and take a moment to savor the results of her hard work.

The great hall hadn't looked so beautiful since before her parents' passing. The enormous Gobelin tapestries on either end of the hall had been cleaned and rehung, their colors more vibrant than Alexandra remembered ever seeing them. The ancient planked floor gleamed with polish, and the huge chamber was ablaze with light from torches mounted between each of the arched stained-glass windows. But what really made the room glitter was the people—all the guests in their gorgeous dresses and handsome evening suits. The ladies' necks, wrists, and hands sparkled with jewels, and diamonds winked from many a man's cravat.

The music came to an end. "Thank you for the dance," the gentleman said with a bow. Lord Haversham, or Haverstock, or Haversomething…she really couldn't remember.

She smiled and curtsied. "It was my pleasure."

A row of red velvet chairs beckoned along the oak-paneled wall. She was heading toward one of them when Lord Shelton intercepted her.

"May I have this dance?"

"I'd be delighted," she told him, ordering her feet to stop complaining. After all, she'd been dreadfully rude the last time she saw Lord Shelton, refusing to serve him ratafia puffs. She could hardly dismiss his invitation to dance. But when he offered his arm to lead her back to the dance floor, she took it and felt nothing. *Nothing.*

She could scarcely believe she'd once contemplated marrying him.

Thankfully, the musicians didn't strike up a waltz, but

another country dance. As she took her place across from Lord Shelton, she had to admit he looked handsome in his formalwear. Pale and blond and very, very English. But she still thought his scent was too flowery.

"I'm pleased to see you've recovered," he said. "You suffered from quite a lengthy illness."

Was that the excuse Griffin had used to keep her former suitor away? Bless him, he was a fine brother indeed. "Thank you. I'm feeling quite myself now," she assured Lord Shelton.

"May I call on you Monday morning, then?"

Oh, drat. "I'm afraid I have prior plans." Surely she'd need to wash her hair.

"I should like to resume our courtship."

So she'd surmised. "I expect you should speak with my brother," she said, mentally composing her apology to Griffin.

"I shall," Lord Shelton replied.

The steps then separated them for a spell, and when they came back together, Alexandra launched into a lively discussion of the weather. After she'd exhausted that novel topic, she steered the conversation to talk of the latest fashion in gloves and the best way to keep household account books. When the dance—which seemed to last at least half an hour—mercifully ended, she headed toward the chairs again, only to be stopped by Griffin this time.

"Alexandra, I have an old acquaintance for you to meet."

"My feet wish for me to sit. They're protesting my treatment."

"You can sit tomorrow."

Groaning inwardly, she put a smile on her face. The purpose of tonight, after all, was for her to meet young men. Just because she hadn't fallen head over heels for the last dozen didn't mean the next one might not catch her fancy.

Besides, she owed Griffin, though he had yet to learn it.

"Lord Shelton will be approaching you. He wishes to resume his suit."

"What am I to tell him? You're obviously in the bloom of health."

"Oh, you'll come up with something." She smiled as a young man approached. "Is this the gentleman you wish me to meet?"

Griffin scowled at her, then switched on the famous charm as he turned to greet his friend. "Lord Ribblesdon, I'd like you to meet my sister, Lady Alexandra."

"A pleasure," the young man said, bowing over her gloved hand. "Would you honor me with this dance?"

"I'd be delighted," she assured him.

Though Lord Ribblesdon wasn't as handsome as Tris, he was attractive, his hair dark and his eyes a pleasant blue. The musicians were starting a quadrille, so they formed a square with three other couples.

From another square nearby, Juliana grinned. *"The look,"* she mouthed silently.

Alexandra had completely forgotten. Now she dropped her gaze and then raised it, curving her lips in a slight smile as she met Lord Ribblesdon's eyes.

Looking a bit dazzled, he smiled in return. "Your home is beautiful."

"I like it. I've always felt Cainewood is a special blend of old and new."

"You would like my estate, too," he said, and proceeded to describe it in exquisite detail as they danced.

After a few minutes, she glanced at the tall-case clock that sat against a wall. Ten twenty.

Lord Ribblesdon droned on, describing his octagonal breakfast room, which apparently boasted an unusual chandelier. Next he waxed enthusiastic about a pond on his property that was filled with notable fish.

Why did these dances have to go on so very long? An hour passed, and she glanced at the clock again.

Ten twenty-five.

Catching Griffin's gaze across the hall, she gave him a tight smile. He shrugged and nodded, looking around for another candidate. She figured he'd been successful when he positioned himself at the edge of the dance floor to wait for her.

"I need to sit," she told him when the dance that would never end finally did. This time she headed for the small room where they'd set up refreshments and took a chair there. "Ahh," she breathed as she dropped onto it.

He snatched a few marzipan fruits and brought them to the table with two cups of punch. "What was wrong with him?" he asked, sitting beside her.

"The same thing that's wrong with every other gentleman here. They have nothing to say of significance." She munched on a miniature apple, hoping the sweet almond paste confection would revive her. "They talk only of themselves. Or their property."

He devoured a piece of marzipan in two bites. "Their goal is to impress you. What else should they talk about?"

"Why should they think I'll be impressed by the number of acres they own or the new horse they just bought at Tattersall's?" She drained the cup of tepid punch, telling herself it was refreshing. "I trust you wouldn't introduce me to anyone of insufficient means or a gentleman after nothing but my dowry. I don't particularly care what these men own; I'd much rather know what they think."

"About what?"

"Life. The state of the kingdom. Walter Scott's latest book. Anything."

"Have you asked them?"

"No," she admitted to both her brother and herself. She

hadn't. She'd let the gentlemen lead both the dances and the conversations, but perhaps it would be best to take the latter into her own hands. "I'll try that. Thank you."

"You're welcome. Ah," he added, rising. "Here comes Lord Sandborough now."

The next dance was a waltz, and Lord Sandborough was a superb waltzer. If it felt a bit odd to be held by a stranger, at least he was a dashing one. He had golden hair and merry green eyes, and his evening clothes hung nicely on his well-proportioned frame.

As they glided over the floor, she decided that, yes, she could imagine marrying this gentleman. She considered giving him *the look*, but instead she cast about for a good question, finally remembering one she'd asked Tris. "Do you believe there is only one perfect person for each of us in this world?"

"Indeed." He smiled, displaying nice teeth. "And I'm certain my person is you."

They'd only just met! Suddenly he wasn't so dashing. Stupidity—not to mention insincerity—had a way of tarnishing a person's appearance.

Griffin introduced her to five more young men, one after the other, and she danced on her aching feet with all of them. Three of them claimed she was their perfect person. Lord Jamestone said yes, he believed there was only one perfect person for each of them in this world, but alas, his lady had died. Though he assured her he was willing to settle for second best, for some reason she couldn't see herself in that role.

The fifth gentleman—whom she privately christened Lord Sapskull—apparently couldn't wrap his mind around the question. He simply declared that his mother had often assured him nobody was perfect. Alexandra assumed that was because he was very imperfect indeed.

Though the long great hall could be accessed from the dining room on one end and a corridor leading to the guest chambers on the other, it also had its own impressive entrance in the middle, complete with a grand staircase from the quadrangle. As the dance with Lord Sapskull came to its blessed end, three late guests appeared at the top of the stairs.

"Rachael!" Alexandra cried, hurrying to meet them. "And Claire and Elizabeth!" One by one, she wrapped Rachael and her sisters in welcoming hugs.

Her own sisters appeared, too, and the hugs were repeated.

"We're sorry," Rachael apologized. "I was certain we'd be your very first arrivals, but a carriage wheel broke on the way."

Though their estates adjoined, Cainewood Castle was at one end of Griffin's property, and Rachael's home was at the far end of Greystone. It took a good two hours to ride between them in a carriage, even one with all its wheels intact. "I understand," Alexandra assured her. "You'll stay the night, won't you?"

"Absolutely." Rachael's smile was impish. "We wouldn't want to miss the breakfast. Seeing how everyone looks in the morning is much more amusing than the actual ball."

They all shared a laugh. "All of you look lovely," Juliana said.

Claire, the middle sister, grinned. "Since Noah wasn't home to consult, we decided he would want us to have new dresses." She twirled in hers, white lace over pale violet satin with a neckline every bit as low as Alexandra's. Her unusual amethyst eyes danced, and she'd teased some of her curly raven hair into little ringlets that framed her face. At fifteen, Claire was already an accomplished flirt. "Do you like it?"

"How about mine?" Elizabeth, a year younger, wore blue and green stripes. They went well with her green eyes and the blue ribbons in her sleek dark hair. She dipped into a deep curtsy worthy of royalty. "My lady."

Alexandra laughed as she took her hand to help her rise. "You're more than ready for presentation at court," she told them, though that wouldn't be happening just yet. They'd been invited to the ball only because they were family and it was a country affair. "And you're both stunning."

But neither of them could match their eldest sister. A dress of poppy-red muslin sprigged with gold clung to Rachael's slim curves. Double rows of gold lace embellished the bodice and hem, and a broad band of gold lace circled the high waistline. Her hair was tucked into a headdress of gold and poppy satin, and the loose strands that framed her face weren't curled like her sisters', but left to fall in soft waves.

"May I paint you in that dress?" Corinna asked reverently.

"When Noah gets home, perhaps I'll be able to find time to sit."

"By the lake, I think," Corinna said, staring into the distance in that way she did when she was envisioning a piece.

Glancing around, Alexandra smiled to herself when she spotted Griffin staring at Rachael. He swiftly turned away, making her laugh again.

"What?" Rachael asked.

"Nothing." Alexandra knew she wouldn't appreciate his interest. "I expect dozens of young men are waiting to dance with you all, so let me take your reticules and put them in the ladies' retiring room."

She took their three pretty little purses and started across the hall toward the small side room they'd designated for the ladies' use. A succession of feminine gasps followed by the low hiss of whispered murmurings made her stop and look over her shoulder. Her gaze swept the great hall, searching for the cause of the commotion.

At the far end of the room, Tris stood, his chin held high.

Her first thought was that he'd look better in gray, to match his eyes. Her second thought was that he couldn't possibly look any better.

His tall, lean form was breathtaking decked out in evening wear. His formal suit was admittedly rather dated—the dark blue tailcoat would always be classic, but the white knee breeches were five years out of fashion, as were the ruffled white cuffs that peeked from beneath the coat's sleeves. Tris wouldn't have brought evening apparel along with him, so he must have asked a valet to scare up the outfit. It had likely belonged to her father or her brother Charles. But since several other country gentlemen hadn't bothered to update their wardrobes to the latest London offered, he didn't really look out of place.

Yet if the reaction of their other guests was any indication, he didn't belong here—and his clothing had nothing to do with it.

It wasn't that anyone confronted him. To the contrary, they all backed away, clearly snubbing him by keeping their distance. By the time she reached him—at the same moment as Griffin—he stood very much alone.

"You'd best turn up your noses," he drawled in a dry tone, "else your guests may conclude you think me worthy of more than the cut direct."

"You *are* worthy," Alexandra returned hotly.

Griffin was much more composed. "I thought you were determined not to attend."

Tris shrugged his elegantly clad shoulders. "I changed my mind. Quite obviously a foolish decision." His steely gaze skimmed the disapproving crowd. "It seems they have long memories."

Alexandra seethed at the sight of so many women whispering behind their fans. "How can they 'remember' something that never happened?"

"Regardless of the events leading up to it—or the lack thereof—the scandal happened, I can assure you." Tris managed a cool smile, which Alexandra sensed was for the benefit of their other guests. "It was very real."

"It was very wrong." She wasn't sure which made her more angry: her rude guests or Tris's blithe acceptance of their attitude. "Come dance with me. I wish to show them we're not swayed by their misplaced disapproval."

The slight shake of Griffin's head clashed with his plastered-on smile. "I don't expect that would be wise."

Tris nodded in agreement. "I shall take my leave before the two of you—and your dear sisters, by association—are irredeemably tarnished." He swept them a proper bow. "Good evening."

The guests turned, almost as one, to watch him leave. Instead of escaping down the corridor to his room, he walked, head held high, across the great hall and out the grand entrance. Alexandra supposed he wanted everyone to conclude he'd left Cainewood. But what would he do? Hide in the workshop all night?

The noise level rose as the other guests gossiped in earnest now—behind Tris's back. Alexandra looked to Griffin, clutching the three reticules so tightly her knuckles turned white. "They're all going to think we sent him away."

"All things considered, that's not such a bad thing."

"He's the best man here tonight."

"You wound me," Griffin said, grasping his chest as though she'd put a knife through his heart.

Normally that would make her smile, but she was too upset. "He's your oldest friend. Where is your sense of loyalty?"

"Right here," he said, pointing down at the planked floor.

"In this very room, with you and your sisters and your futures. Sometimes," he added between gritted teeth as he smiled at two guests approaching them, "we are forced to rank our loyalties, whether we like it or not."

"Lord Cainewood!" Lady St. Quentin, a rail-thin older woman who was a fixture in this part of the country, hurried closer. She had a pinched face, and her brows were far too arched, giving her a look of perpetual astonishment. Her beady gaze swept curiously over both of them. "Could you believe the nerve of that boy? You did the right thing sending him packing."

When Alexandra might have opened her mouth, Griffin shot her a look of warning. "Let us forget this unpleasantness, Lady St. Quentin. I see you've brought your son."

"I was hoping for the honor of a dance," her son said in a quiet voice, almost as though he were making up for his mother's loud one. Pale and long-faced, with a knife-edged nose and small eyes, he didn't compare to Tris.

But then, no one in the great hall compared to Tris. The more young men Alexandra danced with, the more she realized that although they were all perfectly acceptable, none of them were ever going to measure up to the only one she wanted.

Yet she had to keep an open mind, because anything more than friendship with Tris was impossible. If she wanted to be a wife and mother, she was going to have to settle, like Lord Jamestone, for second best. And if the thought of that made the marzipan congeal in her stomach, she was determined to ignore it. This was, after all, her family's celebration, their long-awaited reentry into society. It should be a happy occasion.

She put a smile on her face and looked up at Lady St. Quentin's son. She wouldn't marry him—the St. Quentin estate was notoriously ailing, and in any case, the thought of

Lady St. Quentin as a mother-in-law was enough to make her quail. But she didn't want the old prattlebox questioning her manners, either. The son seemed nice enough, if a bit of a milksop; certainly Alexandra could be polite.

"I should be delighted to dance with you," she told him with a wider, more determined smile. "Let me just dispose of these reticules, and I shall return posthaste."

## TWENTY-SEVEN

*W*HEN THE ELEGANT supper was all but finished and the majority of the guests had forsaken the dining room to resume dancing, Rachael moved to an empty chair beside Alexandra's. "Are your feet thanking you for sitting?"

Alexandra drained the final sip of the half glass of wine she'd allowed herself. "I've danced with so many gentlemen, my feet are numb now."

"How fortunate."

"How about yours?"

"You had a three-hour head start. Mine still hurt." Rachael reached to touch Alexandra's cameo. "This is very pretty."

It wasn't nearly as pretty as the diamond necklace that graced Rachael's neck, Alexandra thought, or the glittering jewels that adorned the other ladies. But she'd wanted to wear it tonight. "Tris sent it to me from Jamaica."

"You used to wear it all the time, didn't you? I remember it now." Rachael's smile was a little too understanding for Alexandra's comfort. "Have your numb feet led you to a future husband?"

"Not yet. Have your aching feet led you to anyone special?"

"Alas, they haven't."

"Alexandra!" Juliana hurried into the room, followed by Corinna. "Griffin is looking for you. Several more gentlemen have requested introductions." She turned to Rachael. "Have you danced with Griffin yet?"

"I'm not a whit interested in dancing with Griffin. But I will say he's managed to bring together an impressive array of eligible gentlemen for your sister's consideration." Rachael's eyes twinkled as they shifted to Alexandra. "You don't mind sharing with the few other ladies here, I'm hoping?"

Alexandra laughed. "No, I don't mind. I need but *one* for myself."

And that one, she feared, was outside tinkering in a timber room.

"Griffin hasn't found time to dance at all," Corinna said.

"That's a pity." Rachael leaned forward and pulled off her poppy red shoes. "My feet are killing me."

Juliana frowned. "You should go into the ladies' retiring room to do that."

"A Lady of Distinction would not approve," Corinna added with exaggerated primness.

"A lady of what?" Rachael asked, rubbing one of her stockinged feet.

Juliana rolled her eyes. "The author of *The Mirror of the Graces*, the manual that's supposed to transform us all into marriageable ladies."

"I've never heard of it." Rachael switched to massaging her other foot. "But if a gentleman won't take me the way I am, I expect I wouldn't want him anyway."

"Rachael would spit on A Lady of Distinction," Corinna declared with relish.

Figuring she'd better go find Griffin, Alexandra groaned as she got to her feet.

"Not numb anymore?" Holding her shoes in one hand, Rachael rose with an overstated wince. "I'd best see what Claire and Elizabeth are up to," she said as they all moved toward the door. "This is their first ball, and I don't think they ate three bites between them; they couldn't wait to get back to the dancing."

Griffin spotted the four of them the minute they entered the great hall. "There you are," he said, leading a handsome, dark young man toward his oldest sister. "Alexandra, this is Lord Shipworth."

As Alexandra made the appropriate responses and went off with the prospective suitor, Rachael tried to sidle away. Juliana caught her by the arm. "Rachael thinks it's a pity you haven't found any time to dance," she told Griffin. "She wishes to rectify that situation."

"I don't—" Rachael began before catching herself. Although the last thing she wanted was to dance with her cousin, refusing to his face would be dreadfully rude. "I don't...want to put on my shoes."

"Then don't," Juliana said gaily, taking the red slippers from her limp fingers. "Just dance in your stockinged feet. You've never feared scandal before. Ah, a waltz." Grinning, she grabbed Rachael's hand and put it right into Griffin's. "Enjoy yourselves, will you?"

"I'm not very good at this," Griffin muttered as he guided Rachael onto the dance floor and took a few tentative steps. "I learned to waltz only this week."

He was certainly holding her awkwardly. And at arm's length, as though he could hardly bear to touch her. But at least he wasn't trodding on her stockinged toes. "You're doing very well for a beginner," she assured him. "Especially considering you didn't wish to dance with me."

The pink flush that crept up his neck clashed with his green eyes. "I never said that."

"Liar." She laughed. "I'd wager you told Juliana you're not a whit interested in dancing with me."

A crooked half smile curved his lips. "I said nothing about a whit."

"Well, I did. I told her I wasn't a whit interested in dancing with you, but it seems she ignored us both."

"I'm all astonishment." The smile turned full-blown now, revealing creases in his cheeks that matched the slight dent in his chin. "That was a brave confession. I promise not to hold it against you."

"Do you expect I would care if you did?"

"Not at all. That's what I love best about you. In a strictly platonic way, of course," he rushed to add.

"Of course," she echoed pleasantly. Now that he'd relaxed, he was proving a much better dancer than he'd given himself credit for. He held her a little closer. He smelled of spicy soap.

It really *was* too bad they were cousins.

"Juliana deserves to be beaten," he said.

"You won't do it," she returned confidently.

"You're right. I'm an excessively ineffective father. And I never *dreamed* I'd be a matchmaking mama."

"A mama?" she echoed with a laugh. She'd never met a more masculine fellow than he. "That sounds more like a nightmare than a dream." As they twirled around the room, she noted all the ladies were on the dance floor while many extra gentlemen waited around the edges. "Given that you're a novice at matchmaking, I'd say you're doing an excellent job."

"But I have only"—he glanced at the tall-case clock—"four more hours to match Alexandra."

"Four hours? I hesitate to dash your expectations, but it's

likely to take longer than that. I've been searching for a husband for *four seasons*."

Four seasons, Griffin thought. Good gracious. If it took each of his sisters that long, he'd be practically middle-aged before he could concentrate on his own life. "Have you had no offers in all that time?"

"Oh, only about a hundred." She laughed with him a moment, but then sighed and licked her lips. Griffin suddenly felt too warm. "My parents shared a special love," she said softly. "I wish for no less. I'll wait until I find it."

"I see." Griffin danced silently for a few measures, wondering if his sisters were that idealistic. He wanted them to be happy, but four seasons was a long time. Of course, Rachael had been busy overseeing the earldom during that time, too. Perhaps she hadn't paid enough attention to her suitors. "Have you made progress preparing the master chamber for your brother's arrival?"

"Yes, much." Her good cheer returned. "It hasn't been as difficult as I expected. I haven't gone through anything very personal yet, but packing Mama's and Papa's clothes away has actually recalled many pleasant memories."

"I'm glad," he told her with a smile. She smiled back—a smile that lit up the entire great hall as they whirled across the crowded dance floor. No one else smiled like Rachael— she put her whole soul into it. He couldn't imagine why, in four seasons, no gentleman had managed to snatch her up. She was so open and refreshing.

The music stopped, but he held her a little longer, a little closer, thinking that when he did come on the market for a wife, he hoped he could find a woman like her.

Had he really thought that? he wondered, pulling back. He must be getting soft in the head. This matchmaking business was entirely too much pressure.

She looked bemused, her cerulean eyes wide and opaque. "Um, thank you for the dance."

"Thank you," he said, "for being such a sport. I shall have a talk with Juliana. It won't happen again."

## TWENTY-EIGHT

"**W**HAT DO YOU think of my son?"

"Oh, he seems a fine young man." Casting about for a way to redirect the conversation, Alexandra lifted a silver tray off a nearby table and held it out to Lady St. Quentin. "Would you care for another marzipan fruit?"

"Why yes, dear, I would." She chose a miniature bunch of grapes. "These remind me of your sweet mother."

"There you are!" Corinna barged into the refreshment room. "You must see something, Alexandra."

"One moment, Corinna." Alexandra smiled apologetically at Lady St. Quentin. "Indeed, Mama made these most every time she held an entertainment. We could but do the same. It's one of our traditions."

"I admire a traditional lady. Do you expect you and my son might suit?"

"Alexandra—"

"I'm pleased the marzipan brought back good memories, Lady St. Quentin. If you'll excuse me." Still carrying the tray, Alexandra hurried off with Corinna. "What could be so important?"

"Did you really want to answer her question about her son? Just come with me."

Huffing out a breath, Alexandra lifted her skirts and followed her sister to the far end of the great hall, into the corridor, and up a dark, narrow flight of stairs. "You know what a gossip Lady St. Quentin is. I danced with her milksop son, hoping she'd think well of us. Now she'll be telling everyone we're rude."

"Oh, do quit being such a fusspot," Corinna said as they stepped onto the landing.

Juliana was waiting there by a door. "What are you worried about now?"

"Nothing," Alexandra said.

"Not nothing," Corinna disagreed. "She fears Lady St. Quentin might think her less than a perfect hostess."

"If you'd quit worrying about what everyone thinks, maybe you could find happiness." With that cheeky proclamation, Juliana slowly opened the door. Music floated up and through it from the great hall. "Look," she whispered.

There, in the minstrel's gallery, stood Tris. His back to the door, he leaned on the balcony's rail, gazing down on the festivities below.

Alexandra didn't know whether she was cross with her sisters or grateful to them. She wasn't sure whether she should go to Tris or leave. Juliana solved her dilemma with a little push. By the time Alexandra turned around, the door had been quietly shut behind her.

The torches in the great hall threw light and shadow into the minstrel's gallery. For a moment, she just drank Tris in. His shoulders looked tense beneath the fine, dark blue tailcoat; his hair grazed the collar in the back. He'd be leaving before nightfall tomorrow. This might be the last time she'd ever be alone with him.

Taking a deep breath, she walked closer. "Would you care for a sweet?" she asked over the music.

Tris started, then turned to face her. "No. Thank you."

He looked different tonight. Perhaps it was the formal clothing, or perhaps it was because his hair was combed neatly for once. Or perhaps it was because the more time she'd spent with other young men, the more she'd become convinced he was the only one for her.

As he met her eyes, an odd tingle arose in the pit of her stomach. She held his gaze for a moment, finding nothing encouraging there, nothing to lead her to believe anything had changed for him. But over the course of the evening, everything had changed for her.

She was just now realizing how much.

Although he was stone-faced, she gave him a little smile. "How did you get back inside?"

"One of the servants' entrances, a few passageways, a set of back stairs. I learned my way around long ago, playing hide-and-seek with Griffin."

Of course. Tris had history here. It just wasn't with her.

"I thought you were determined to avoid this ball at all costs." The wooden structure held no furniture, so she balanced the tray carefully on the rail. "Why did you turn up?"

"To make a point." His gray gaze remained steady, resolute. "To prove to you, once and for all, that life with me would be unbearable."

The music swelled as she gestured over the edge of the balcony. "What I saw wasn't real life. I don't need those people." She swallowed hard, gathering her nerve. "I need *you*, Tris."

"You don't."

"I do. But I cannot ruin my family's good name." Her throat was tightening. Here she was, in the most beautiful dress she'd ever owned, and she'd never felt more wretched. "I don't know what I can do."

"You can go back down there and find another gentleman."

"I've tried—and I've failed!"

He looked startled at her vehemence. A long silence stretched between them, and the music from below was not enough to fill it. He just looked at her, and she just let him. Squashing every bashful instinct she possessed, she stood tall and brazen and watched him watch her. His gaze lingered on her face, then glided ever so slowly down the length of her body, and ever so slowly back up again. Finally it settled on the cameo, and his eyes softened.

It was time to go in for the kill.

Moving closer, she laid a gloved hand against his waist-coat. "I think I'm in love with you," she confessed quietly.

His eyes hardened again as he stepped back. "*Think* is the operative word. You cannot be in love with me."

"I know my feelings, Tris."

"You don't."

Her hands curled into fists. "Stop telling me what I do and don't feel."

"Stop pretending you can change our circumstances by wishing."

"I know I cannot." She heard tears in her voice and cursed herself for them. "But I cannot change my feelings, either."

He sighed, a sigh burdened with old memories. "I've thought I was in love before, too—more than once—but it was never more than a fantasy. I won't make such an error again. Neither will you, once I leave and you come to your senses. Day after tomorrow, Alexandra, you'll wake up free of me forever."

She'd never be free of him, not truly. "Will you tell me about the ladies you loved?" she asked carefully.

He turned to stare out over the dancers. "There was a girl in Oxford who wouldn't wait for me when I had to leave. And a girl in Jamaica who wouldn't come back with me to England." His fingers gripped the rail. "More recently, there was a girl named Leticia. Miss Leticia Armstrong."

When he stopped there, she laid a hand over his on the rail. "What happened?"

"She's the daughter of a local baron. I met her around the time I inherited, when everything in my life seemed charmed. She seemed charming, too, and I was certain she returned my feelings. In fact, she swore her undying love. I proposed, and she accepted happily enough. But then the scandal broke, and when I suggested her reputation might suffer should she stand by my side, she fled without a second thought."

Leticia. She must have been the girl who had taught him to waltz. Although Alexandra supposed she should be grateful that Leticia hadn't kept Tris for herself, instead she hated her—and the others—for hurting him. For filling his heart with cynicism.

She studied his shadowed profile—so like the portrait she'd done of him years ago. Except his jaw looked harder. "Leticia never loved you, or she'd have stayed with you. Perhaps she loved who you were—a marquess. She loved the life she imagined you'd give her. But when that life was threatened, her love disappeared. It wasn't true love."

"And neither was my love for her. Or the others. It always dissipates before long. As will yours. You'll make a nice life for yourself—with someone else." He finally turned to look at her, but it wasn't to offer hope. "I won't change my mind, Alexandra. Not for you or anyone else."

She'd heard that from him before—too many times before —but he couldn't fool her any longer. While she understood that he didn't want to be responsible for exposing his wife to society's derision, she also knew he didn't want to open himself up for more hurt. She knew he cared for her—he'd acknowledged as much more than once. But those three girls had damaged him more than he'd admit. He'd built a wall around himself.

She wished she could figure out how to scale it, even as she knew that, for her sisters' sakes, she couldn't.

Unless…

"What if you're proven innocent?" she asked, stunned that she hadn't considered this angle before. Should he be exonerated, society would welcome him—and his wife—with open arms. "Did you ever search for the real killer?"

He looked defeated before he even opened his mouth. "I'm not convinced there was a killer—my uncle hadn't been himself since his family was lost. Men often die in their beds naturally, from hidden illnesses or the weakness of old age. He *was* ill—a mild chill, we all thought, though it might have been something more serious. But yes, I tried to find a culprit. And no, I'm not going to reopen the investigation now."

"Why not? Perhaps we can find new evidence."

"We?" Something like panic filled his eyes. "Stay out of this, Alexandra."

"But I could help—"

"No. No, you cannot." Below, the musicians struck up a waltz. "The matter is closed. No one murdered my uncle. Forget it. Dance with me instead."

He pulled her into his arms, and they began twirling together across the wide, empty balcony. She found herself buffeted with warring emotions: frustration that he flatly refused her solution, sadness that this might be the last time they'd ever dance together, elation at finding herself this close to him if only for a short time.

He drew her even closer, much closer than he had during their lesson. His strong hand rested once again on her back, pressing her closer still. They whirled faster. A lock of his carefully combed hair came loose and flopped over his fore-head. Her heart seemed to beat directly against his, quick and unsteady.

She couldn't remember ever being so happy and so trou-bled all at the same time.

As for Tristan, *troubled* didn't begin to describe his state. Her declaration had set off an avalanche of jumbled feelings, churning and roaring within him so that he could barely hear himself think.

The most prominent of these feelings was abject horror.

*I think I'm in love with you.*

In the aftermath of Leticia leaving him, he'd made firm decisions, the main one being he would never again believe a girl's claims of undying love. He'd been burned thrice already, and he wasn't so dense as to put his hand in the fire a fourth time.

But mixed with the horror were guilt, anger, exasperation, and a dash of self-pity. And then there was the not-insignifi-cant corner of his mind that longed for her words to be true.

The idiotic corner.

Alexandra couldn't be in love with him—she just couldn't. She was too loyal, too sincere, too difficult to heartlessly deny. He couldn't cope with her love, with the guilt of leaving her, with the thought of her going to another. His only saving grace was his certainty that she was wrong. She didn't know love any more than he did.

The waltz was sweet torture, her softness pressed against him, her hand squeezing his so hard he wondered if their gloved fingers had gone blue. Beneath a fussy little bonnet, her hair was piled atop her head in a loose, sensuous arrange-ment, and he buried his nose in it, inhaling the fragrance and feeling the silky strands tickle his cheeks.

"I'm dizzy," she breathed as he spun her faster. "Dizzy and in lo—"

"Don't say it." Exasperation surpassed horror—though over both fell a flurry of what he could only call lust. "Just dance with me."

She leaned away from him, far enough to meet his eyes. "Why?" Even as she asked, her grip tightened on his hand, her other arm tugging him closer. "What made you ask me to dance?"

Abject horror, of course. He'd have done anything to stop her from continuing her line of questioning. The only thing more frightening than her talk of love was the murky uncertainty surrounding his uncle's mysterious death.

But he couldn't tell her that. "It was our last chance," he said instead, not wanting to encourage her but unable to come up with another explanation.

"And Griffin isn't watching."

"No," he agreed, "he's not."

When the music stopped, he twirled her once more before reluctantly releasing her.

"Will you kiss me?" she whispered in the hush that followed. "It's our last chance for that, too."

He shook his head. "I cannot." His reputation might be in shreds, but he still had his honor.

"You kissed me before."

He couldn't tell her he'd been sleepwalking. That would be humiliating for them both. "I cannot trust myself to only kiss you. I thought I explained—"

"Never mind." She began pulling off one of her gloves.

Below, the musicians struck up a jolly country dance. Tristan stared at her busy hands. "What are you doing?"

"I just want to touch you." She dropped the glove to the floor and started on the other one. "Do you remember when I made your profile portrait? Years ago, before you left for Jamaica?"

"Yes, but—"

"I wanted to touch you then. I pretended I was touching you while I traced your face. I've loved you for all that time, Tris. Maybe longer."

"You cannot have." As her second glove met the ground, he backed away toward the rail. "Young girls often have crushes on their older brothers' friends. You never let go of that. Now I understand."

"No. You don't understand." Following him, she raised a hand to his forehead and swept the hair from his brow. Her fingers were gentle, and she smelled sweet, and it took everything he had not to pull her back into his arms.

"That won't work," he said unsteadily.

She only shrugged and reached for one of his hands, tugging to loosen the glove, slowly and deliberately, fingertip by fingertip. As she slid the silk free and dropped it to join hers on the floor, a tremor ran through him, leaving a queasy ache in his belly.

Blast if she wasn't seducing him—and successfully, at that. His body was sending him all sorts of messages his brain couldn't accept. He should leave. Now.

The door was right there in front of him, but instead of leaving, he backed away some more. A smile curving her lips, she followed again, giving his second glove the same rapt attention as the first. When it dropped to the floor, she linked her fingers with his—both hands—and sighed prettily.

"I just wanted to touch you," she repeated.

He just wanted to kiss her. He couldn't. As she leaned into him, he took one more step toward the rail—

And knocked the silver tray clear off of it.

"Drat!" Alexandra cried, twisting sideways to lean over the rail. They both watched in horror as the tray hit the ground below with a resounding metallic crash, scattering miniature colored marzipan fruits all over the polished wood.

A few guests screamed, scattering along with them, while everyone else froze. The musicians stopped playing mid-note.

Alexandra wrenched her hands from his and pushed hard against his chest. "Run!"

She turned and fled, clattering down the stairs before he could even reach the door.

# TWENTY-NINE

*B*EFORE ANY servants could arrive to help, Alexandra skidded into the great hall and dropped to her knees on the floor, scrabbling for the miniature marzipan fruits. A Lady of Distinction would surely disapprove, but she couldn't bring herself to care at the moment.

"We'll have this set to rights in a minute," she announced to anyone who would listen, "and the dancing can resume. No need to panic."

Never mind that she was panicking herself. Her stomach was in a knot. Her breathing was quick and unsteady. Her pulse was racing even faster than it had when she'd been trying to get Tris to kiss her.

Tris! Good heavens, if anyone had glanced up and seen them there together…

Rachael knelt beside her, adding a tiny apple, orange, and strawberry to the dented tray. "What happened?" she whispered.

"Later," Alexandra muttered out of the side of her mouth. She stood, holding the tray with one hand while smoothing her skirts with the other. With a deliberate smile, she addressed the little crowd that had gathered around them. "Pray, continue." She waved a hand at the musicians. "If you will?"

The music resumed, and the guests began dispersing. A few ladies whispered behind their fans, but it seemed the worst was over. Alexandra's heart began to calm; her breathing began to slow; the knot in her stomach began to unravel.

Someone tapped her on the arm with a folded fan. "Lady Alexandra."

She turned to see Lady St. Quentin. "Yes?"

"Where are your gloves?"

She forced a light laugh. "Oh, silly me. I must have left them up in the minstrel's gallery."

"Well, then," Lady St. Quentin said, a keen glitter in her eyes, "shall we go recover them?"

"I'd be pleased to do that," Rachael offered quickly.

But Lady St. Quentin was already heading for the corridor, as unstoppable as a battleship under sail. A very narrow one. Alexandra shoved the tray at her cousin and ran to follow.

"I wonder what we'll find up there?" Lady St. Quentin asked.

"Nothing much," Alexandra said, knowing exactly what the woman would find: *two* pairs of gloves, one of them quite obviously a gentleman's. But she seemed helpless to deflect the meddlesome harridan. "I was overly warm," she babbled at the woman's bony behind as they climbed the stairs. "I was...yes, I was overly warm, so I went up to the minstrel's gallery and removed my gloves, and I was watching the ball from up there—so beautiful, it was—just resting a bit and cooling off, when I very unfortunately dropped—"

Alexandra broke off, fearing her heart might stop as the harridan marched through the gallery's door.

But there were no gloves. None at all. The floor was as bare as when she and Tris had danced on it.

Her knees weakened with relief.

"What happened to your gloves?" Lady St. Quentin turned on her, a predatory look in her eyes. "Do you suppose your lover took them as a souvenir?"

"Wh-what?" Alexandra stammered. Her knees weakened still more, but now it was with fear. "I have no lover."

"You were up here with a man," the woman accused in a low voice. "I saw you, so don't try to deny it." She smiled, the mean smile of an undeserving victor. "You're ruined, my girl."

"Ruined?" Alexandra breathed, raising a hand to cover her gasp. That was that. She'd undone her family. Disgraced herself, sullied their good name, tainted her poor sisters...and all for what? One dance with Tris?

The harridan was still talking. "Fortunately, my son is willing—"

"Your son is willing to do what?" Griffin interrupted from the doorway.

Rachael arrived behind him; perhaps she'd alerted him to the trouble. Alexandra didn't know whether to be comforted or petrified by their presence. How would they react? Would Rachael and her sisters share in their cousin's disgrace, too?

Lady St. Quentin lifted her pointy chin. "My son is willing to marry your sister."

"Would her sizable dowry have anything to do with that?"

"Does it matter? She should consider herself lucky. She was seen up here with a man."

"Was she?" He looked to Alexandra. "Were you up here with a man?"

"No, of course I wasn't." Alexandra said quickly. "That would be very improper."

"She wasn't up here with a man," Griffin calmly told Lady St. Quentin.

Two bright pink spots appeared on the woman's cheeks. "She was."

"She was not. Now, would you care to return to the ball? Or shall I have a footman escort you to your carriage?"

"I saw them," the woman insisted.

Griffin gave a long-suffering sigh and crossed his arms. "Let me put this another way, Lady St. Quentin. Should you spread the falsehood that my sister was seen with a man, neither you nor your son will ever receive another invitation to Cainewood...or anywhere else south of London. Do I make myself clear?"

All the color drained from her face, which looked even more pinched than usual as she sucked in her cheeks. The widow of a baronet was no match for the Marquess of Cainewood. "Indeed," she said stiffly.

"Excellent." His smile failed to reach his eyes. "I trust you know your way back to the great hall?"

Dumbfounded, Alexandra watched Lady St. Quentin make her muttering way down the stairs. What in heaven's name had just occurred? She felt like applauding. Or crying. Perhaps both at once. She could have kissed Griffin—in fact, she did just that, startling and embarrassing him in the process. He looked so awkward that she nearly dissolved in laughter, but for the sake of his pride she reined in her hysterics.

Rachael did applaud. "Bravo!" she said softly, her eyes shining as she turned to Griffin. "You were magnificent."

He gave a little bow.

"You *were* magnificent," Alexandra echoed fervently. "I thought we were ruined. I hope she'll keep her mouth shut."

"She will," Griffin said, sounding very sure. "Whom were you up here with, Alexandra?"

She swallowed hard. "Tris. Juliana noticed him watching the ball, and she and Corinna suggested I come up and keep him company for a short while." That was close enough to the truth. "He's leaving tomorrow."

He gazed at her for a long moment, his eyes unreadable. "There are six more gentlemen waiting to dance with you. We'd best go downstairs." He flipped open his pocket watch, looked at it, and closed it again with a *snap*. "You have two hours left to see if anyone catches your fancy."

"And if no one does?"

He shrugged. "We'll have to plan another ball."

A different brother might have said that in a threatening tone, Alexandra thought as she preceded him downstairs. But from Griffin, the statement had sounded matter-of-fact and good-natured. So good-natured, in fact, that she felt even more guilty for defying him. To think how narrowly they'd escaped, how close she'd come to damaging those she loved most in all the world...

Well, one thing was certain: the time for selfish, childish dreams had ended. She would never let herself see Lord Hawkridge alone again.

Though she still reeled from the night's highs and lows, the resolution gave her a sense of dull satisfaction. She squared her shoulders, determined to enter the great hall with aplomb.

She didn't want to disappoint her suitors.

# THIRTY

*A*LEXANDRA WAS having the most extraordinary, most incredible, most marvelous dream. Tris was kissing her. Long, slow kisses that made her senses spin.

Even in her dream, she was shocked, but as it was only a dream, she decided to let it continue. To just lie back and imagine this was real, that they could truly be this close to each other. Just lie back…

Indeed, she realized, she *was* lying back…on a bed. Her bed. Her eyes were closed, but she knew it was her bed regardless, perhaps because it was her dream. Tris was lying beside her. She'd never kissed Tris while lying down. It felt glorious, being sandwiched snugly between his body and the mattress.

Perhaps also because it was her dream, she didn't wonder if she was doing it right. The kissing, that is. This was nothing like any kiss they'd ever shared before. Their lips were parted, and their tongues were *touching*. It felt wonderfully bizarre. She didn't know if other people kissed in this fashion, but if they didn't, she felt sorry for them.

She sighed happily and wrapped her arms around his

shoulders, pulling him even closer. She could barely conceive of acting so forward in real life, but this was a dream, so she could do as she pleased. She slid her hands over his back, feeling his muscles through his dressing gown. He felt so warm and solid, and so very, very real—

Oh, no. Oh, no, no, no.

"Tris!" she cried.

"What?"

Her lids flew open. In the dim light from the dying fire, his eyes looked wide. "Where am I?" he asked, and she felt foggy, confused. He struggled to rise to an elbow, his gray gaze sweeping the room. "How on earth did I come to be here—"

He broke off as he focused on her beside him, then gasped.

"Oh, blast it," he ground out.

## THIRTY-ONE

*A*LEXANDRA snatched the counterpane up to her chin, but not before Tristan could observe that she wore nothing but a prim white nightgown. In the pale, flickering light, her eyes were pools of brandy mist. Her cheeks were flushed, her breathing sharp. Her hair was wild. She looked irresistibly beautiful.

His sluggish, sleep-addled mind refused to absorb the implications. He was in Alexandra's room…in the middle of the night…in her *bed*…wearing naught but a gaping dressing gown…

What on earth had he done?

"Blast it," he repeated hoarsely.

Abject horror had just returned in full force. He'd committed an unthinkable trespass—and having done the unthinkable, now he couldn't think. His faculties were overwhelmed.

Blast his traitorous body, or brain, or whatever it was that took charge in his sleep. His life might be in tatters, but—in his waking hours, at least—he still had his honor. Perhaps it was hanging by a thread, but he was determined to maintain it.

Somehow, he had to make amends.

"We shall have to marry," he said stiffly, forcing himself to look her in the eye.

She stared back at him, still clutching the counterpane like a barricade between them. Maneuvering under the cover, she propped herself up against the headboard. "I'd love nothing more," she finally said in a measured tone, looking infinitely more composed than Tristan felt. "But we cannot. Nothing has changed. My sisters—"

"Everything has changed," he snapped. "You could even now be carrying my child!"

"Carrying your child?" Her brow crinkled. "I might be a bit hazy on the details, but I've been given to understand it takes more than kissing to make a child."

"What?" He shook his head in an effort to clear it. "You mean to say we did naught but kiss?"

"Did you think we did something more?"

"I don't know," he said simply.

The words hung in the air. She waited, just looking at him, expecting an explanation.

Blast it.

There was nothing for it—he'd have to confess.

"I have no memory of our encounter," he said at last. "I don't even know how I got to this room."

"How can that be?"

"I was sleeping. Or rather, sleepwalking." He braced for her reaction. "The last thing I remember before waking here in your bed was going to sleep in my own. I realize that's difficult to believe—"

"Were you really sleepwalking?" she interrupted, confusion replaced by curiosity. She wasn't jeering him out of the room, at least. "I thought that only happened in books."

"It's happened to me all my life, on occasion. I'm sorry. I know it's a feeble excuse for ruining you—"

"You didn't," she said in her straightforward way. "I promise you I am not ruined."

"Are you certain?" he asked again.

She laughed. At a time like this, she laughed. "I'm positive. You only kissed me, Tris." She even lowered the counterpane, as if to demonstrate her faith in him.

He couldn't remember ever feeling more relieved, both by her assurances and her reaction to his explanation. She really was the loveliest, most understanding person he'd ever known—especially since he'd caused her nothing but trouble and heartache since the day he'd returned to Cainewood.

A tiny part of him wished he *had* ruined her, so they *would* be forced to marry.

He cleared his throat and swung his legs out of bed. "I thank you," he said formally, "for your forbearance. This won't happen again. As far as I know, I've never sleepwalked twice in a night." Gaining his feet, he busied himself securing his dressing gown.

She stopped him with a hand on his arm. "Please, stay for a while." Her eyes were wide, examining what she could see of his bare chest. "I know it's frightfully improper, but what's a few more minutes? I want to hear more about the sleepwalking. And you're leaving tomorrow."

He'd never spoken candidly to anyone about his affliction. The thought was appealing—but even more alarming. "I'm not sure it's a good idea," he dithered as he finished belting the dressing gown.

She jerked the covers back up to her chin. "I promise I won't attack you."

That earned a chuckle, though it didn't erase his qualms. But the plea in her eyes had him sitting down on the edge of the bed. Blast those warm brandy eyes.

Brandy...he could use a spot of brandy just now.

The fire was dying, and with it the light. He briefly considered rebuilding it, but then thought the darkness might make talking easier. And he wasn't cold. Being alone with Alexandra in her bedroom—and the both of them in night clothes—made him feel very warm indeed.

"What do you want to know?" he asked.

"Everything. When did you first sleepwalk?"

"As a small child. I used to do it quite often, but as I became older, I seemed to outgrow it. The episodes tapered off. Now it seems to happen only when I'm under stress of some sort. The occurrences have become quite infrequent. In fact, I was hoping they had stopped altogether. Until this week, I hadn't sleepwalked in more than a year."

"What is it like?"

"I don't know. I never remember." He'd guessed right that the darkness would help. Answering a disembodied voice was so much easier than responding to an expectant face. And yet more intimate in a way. "What did it look like to you?"

"My eyes were closed," she murmured. "I wasn't looking."

Her tone told him that if the room were lighter he'd see her blush. "How about the other night? When you caught me 'stealing' the chocolate cakes. What were your impressions then?"

"You were sleepwalking then?" Her voice was suffused with wonder. "Of course," she answered herself. "That's why you didn't remember our kiss. You seemed a bit...distant—well, other than during the kiss—and you didn't respond well to my questions. I thought you were being deliberately evasive."

"Others have said the same. A blank look in my eyes, responses that don't quite make sense." He sighed. "I never,

ever remember. It's rather frightening, if you want to know the truth."

"I wasn't frightened. I'd expect to be, but I wasn't."

Bless her for that. "I've never kissed anyone in my sleep before, let alone climbed into a girl's bed. It's frightening because I don't know what I might do next." For some reason he felt compelled to add, "And what else I might already have done."

*Blast.* What could have possessed him to broach that topic?

"Such as?" she breathed.

Whatever it was, it still had hold of him. He dropped his voice to an almost-whisper and continued, "Such as, possibly —though I don't remember it—poisoning my uncle."

There. He'd said it out loud. He prepared for her shock and immediate departure, but she didn't run screaming from the room.

Instead, she reached across the mattress, rooting around until she found one of his hands and took it in hers. "You don't really believe that."

His chest suddenly felt tight. Her unquestioning belief in him was...a gift. The most gorgeous surprise. A sort of acceptance he'd never experienced or expected. Though he couldn't see her in the dark, her hand squeezing his spoke volumes.

She had more faith in him than he had in himself.

"You don't believe that," she insisted. "Tell me you don't."

He found himself stretching out on the bed, moving closer to her voice. "I don't know. Sometimes I wonder what I did to deserve my life going so dreadfully wrong..."

He'd never told anyone this. Not even himself, he realized.

He wasn't the sort to brood over life's inequities, and until recently—very recently—he hadn't felt particularly deprived.

Even taking *circumstances* into consideration, he had so much more than so many others in this world. A beautiful and comfortable home, vast and diverse holdings to engage his talents and excite his ingenuity, and more wealth than he knew how to spend. Considering the hardship most people endured on a day-to-day basis, he would be absurd to complain.

It was only recently that he'd realized he was lonely. But that should be bearable. It *had* been bearable, until…until when?

The answer was obvious: until he'd seen Alexandra again.

"My uncle died in the middle of the night," he told her, scooting even closer, still holding her hand. "I had recently arrived from Jamaica to find my own father had passed. Uncle Harold hadn't been himself since the loss of his family —his wife and sons in the shipwreck—and I was staying with him at his request." He knew he'd told her some of this before, but he needed to put it in context. "As I was now his heir, he wished to instruct me, and I did my best to lift his spirits. Truly, I did. He was only in his early fifties; I expected him to live a long, long time. I had no wish for his death."

"I know you didn't," she said quietly.

"But, you see, I was there. I was residing in his house that morning when he failed to awaken. And I'd been sleep-walking—after peaceful nights in Jamaica, I'd come home to find my father dead and my financial life in a shambles, and I'd begun sleepwalking again. I don't remember murdering my uncle, and I felt nothing but love for him, I swear it. I didn't believe myself capable of killing anyone, let alone the man who'd fathered me more than my own father. But the fact remains that I was under great financial strain—strain that my uncle's demise would certainly have resolved—so a part of me has always wondered…"

"A very small part of you, I'm sure."

He wasn't sure it wasn't a large part. He tried to think about the affair as little as possible.

"That's what's kept you from digging too deeply to clear your name," she said. "You're afraid you might discover the opposite, that you were responsible for your uncle's death."

His first reaction was knee-jerk denial, but she sounded so reasonable he felt obligated to mull it over a moment. "Perhaps," he finally conceded. He'd always thought of it as putting the past behind him and getting on with his life. But he had to admit that what she said might be true.

And that she must understand him very well to have guessed it.

"That's ridiculous." She pulled her hand from his, leaving him alone in the dark. "Tris, you did not murder your uncle."

He recoiled from the temper she so rarely displayed. "It's a possibility," he disagreed. "Only a possibility, but—"

"It's *not*." He felt her fingers brush his face, and her voice gentled, but not much. "You're a good person. And I'm positively certain that, as such, you would never do anything while asleep that you didn't wish to do while awake."

It was an interesting theory, but he couldn't quite buy it. "How about *this*?" he retorted. "Coming to your bed in the middle of the night and nearly ruining you?"

She released a sigh, then probed until she found his hand again. He slid his other hand up her arm until he found her shoulder, then rested his fingers lightly on the skin just above her collar.

"Are you claiming you didn't want this?" she whispered.

He could hardly deny it. She felt more than good in his arms—she felt *right*. As though she belonged there.

But she didn't. No one belonged in his arms.

If he'd been resolved against marriage before, this evening's events had only served to reinforce his conviction.

Quite apart from the woes of public disgrace, how could he subject a lady to the menace of his unpredictable disorder?

And Alexandra's faith in him, though touching, was hardly convincing. How was she to know what he was capable of?

"I must go," he said, trying to pull away.

She gripped his hand tighter. "Stay. Please. A few minutes longer."

She didn't have to say why—they both knew that they would never be together like this again.

So he stayed. Her skin was so silky beneath his fingertips, her loose, long hair so fragrant. He closed the gap between their bodies and buried his face against her neck. He could feel her pulse, rapid and unsteady like his.

And when she fell asleep in his arms, he couldn't imagine a more tender moment.

He wouldn't succumb to sleep himself. He'd just lay with her a little longer. Soon, he would be gone.

He wouldn't sleep.

## THIRTY-TWO

*T*HERE WAS AN empty space at the breakfast table. True, it had taken a good half hour for the family and all their guests to make their bleary-eyed way to the dining room. But now it was nearly noon. And Alexandra —normally the earliest riser of them all—had yet to appear.

"Do you expect she's had a relapse?" Lord Shelton asked, his pale brow wrinkled in concern. "Could the evening have been too much for her in her current, fragile state?"

Griffin shrugged, secretly pleased. "Perhaps." With any luck, this would provide an excuse to put the poor gentleman off another month or so.

"Alexandra is the veriest picture of health," Juliana declared, to his annoyance. "I shall go fetch her." She began to rise.

"I expect Lady Alexandra is still sleeping," Lady St. Quentin said in her superior, all-knowing way. "I do believe she had a late night."

The low buzz of conversation ceased as all eyes in the room looked to her.

"We *all* had a late night," Griffin said into the sudden silence.

Lady St. Quentin blithely buttered a slice of toast. "Do you know," she continued conversationally, "I was rather restless during the night. All the excitement, I expect."

Juliana reseated herself. Griffin narrowed his gaze. "Go on," he said.

She would in any case, the old gossip.

"Well, I took a little stroll down the corridor, and what do you suppose I saw?" Enjoying her rapt audience, she paused to take a delicate bite, chew it leisurely, and swallow. "None other than the Marquess of Hawkridge, coming out of one of the bedrooms."

"Mother," her son interjected halfheartedly.

She waved him off, turning to Griffin. "I thought the marquess had departed after learning he wasn't welcome."

"You were mistaken," Griffin said with a forced smile.

"I'll go fetch Alexandra." Juliana rose again.

Lady St. Quentin raised her cup of chocolate to her lips, watching Griffin over the rim. "You'll want to go with your sister," she said pointedly.

He barely resisted huffing out a sigh. "And why is that?"

"Because when the marquess left his room, *he went upstairs*." She paused to let the significance of that sink in. "And he left his door open, and it still isn't closed, *and* he isn't inside. So I suspect he has yet to come back down."

"Why in blazes would you surmise that?" Rachael snapped.

Lady St. Quentin raised one of her overly arched brows. "My dear, you must learn to watch your language."

"Mother," her son repeated hopelessly.

She didn't even bother waving him off this time, ignoring him as she focused on Rachael. "I do believe Hawkridge is the man I saw in the minstrel's gallery with your cousin last night."

Several gasps were heard around the table.

"I'm going to fetch Alexandra," Juliana stated and headed from the room.

"I'm going with you." Corinna pushed back her chair and ran after her.

"So am I," Griffin added through clenched teeth.

Several more chairs rasped along the carpet as various guests rose to trail them. Griffin hurried after his sisters, refusing to look back. Gobble-grinders, all of them. Let the whole world follow, he thought as he took the stairs three at a time, passing Corinna and then Juliana handily. The St. Quentin woman would be red-faced before this was over. Alexandra was the most proper girl he knew, and after last night's close call, she wouldn't risk another blow to her reputation for anything.

Long-legged strides carried him rapidly through the upper gallery and down the corridor past Corinna's and Juliana's rooms. The two of them had to run—decorously, of course—to keep up. Reaching Alexandra's door before them, he twisted the knob and pushed it open.

Then slammed it closed.

He turned to his sisters. "Get rid of them," he gritted out, referring to the nosy guests making their leisurely way up the stairs and through the upper gallery. "Now."

"Why?" Corinna asked.

"Just do as I say for once, will you?"

Juliana's hazel eyes were as round as saucers. "They're both in there, aren't they?"

"Brilliant deduction. I'll give you your prize later. Now, go—"

He whirled to face the door as it opened again, from the inside this time, revealing a sleepy-eyed Tristan wearing a dressing gown. An improvement over a moment ago, when Griffin had seen the fellow in his sister's feminine Chippendale bed.

"Get back in there!" Griffin whispered, reaching to pull the door shut again, quietly this time.

"Aha." Lady St. Quentin's triumphant voice was unmistakable. "I knew it!" Elbowing past the other approaching guests, she made her way to the door and pushed on it.

It reopened with an ominous creak. Inside, Alexandra cowered in her bed.

"You're ruined, girl," Lady St. Quentin crowed. "Ruined!"

"She is not," Corinna protested, throwing Griffin a desperate, apologetic glance.

But it was too late. The crowd rushed to see, forming a loose semicircle in front of the door.

Alexandra *was* ruined.

"I sleepwalked in here," Tristan explained quietly, as though he and Griffin were the only ones there. A nerve jumped in his clenched jaw. "Unaware of my own actions."

"Balderdash!" Lady St. Quentin exclaimed. "I've never heard such a pathetic excuse. It won't save her reputation; that I can promise."

"Hang it," Griffin said dangerously. All the whispering behind him wasn't helping him think straight. He glared at Tristan. It was some consolation to learn Alexandra hadn't invited the son of a gun into her bed, but of all the accursed, unexpected… "You *still* sleepwalk?"

"Infrequently, but yes."

"You didn't have to stay once you got here," he bit out.

"You're right. My sincerest apologies. I'll leave now." Tristan started from the room.

"No, you won't." Griffin stopped him with an outstretched hand flat against his chest. "You stayed the night, you'll stay now. You'll marry my sister. By special license. Tomorrow."

Gasps rose from the onlookers. Tristan glanced down at Griffin's hand, then stepped back. "If that's what you wish."

Griffin's arm dropped to his side. "It's not what I wish, but it's what must be done."

"Nonsense," Lady St. Quentin cut in. "You cannot marry your sister to a murderer." Reaching back into the cluster of spectators, she pulled her son stumbling through to the front. "My Roger will be happy to marry her."

Her Roger looked mortified.

"For her dowry?" Griffin asked Roger's mother pointedly.

"Does it matter?" she returned.

Griffin's gaze flicked to where his white-faced sister sat motionless on the bed, her blue covers clutched beneath her chin. "Do you wish to marry Sir Rog—"

"You cannot let the chit decide this for herself," Lady St. Quentin scoffed.

Was there another woman in England as maddening? "As a matter of fact, I can should I choose to do so. And I can certainly solicit her opinion." Drawing a calming breath, Griffin turned back to Alexandra. "Do you wish to marry Sir Roger St. Quentin?"

She shook her head infinitesimally.

"No," Juliana said for her. "She most certainly does not."

Griffin and Lady St. Quentin sent her matching glares.

"I'll marry her," came another voice. Lord Shelton stepped out of the clutch of gawkers.

Despite his own distress, Griffin felt sympathy for the gentleman. If he knew Alexandra's mind, Shelton was about to be publicly refused. He looked back to her. "Do you wish to marry Lord Shelton?"

"No," Juliana started at the same time Alexandra said, "I'm sorry."

Thin and shaky, her voice barely carried from the room to the corridor. "My apologies, Lord Shelton. I'm honored by your offer, but I don't think we would be happy together." Suddenly, her eyes flashed—Griffin would swear he saw red in the medium brown. "And Lord Hawkridge is no murderer," she added loudly and perfectly clearly.

Griffin stood silent, cursing the fates that had put *him* in charge of his siblings. Two perfectly acceptable gentlemen had offered for his disgraced sister. If he forced one of them on her, this scandal would eventually blow over. She'd be miserable all her days, but their sisters would be able to marry well. If he allowed her to wed Tristan...

He felt everyone's eyes on him while his own vision swam. Never in his life had he found it so hard to make a decision. Not even on a battlefield with the enemy bearing down...although, given the antagonistic mood of some of those around him, that analogy wasn't so far off.

Rachael stepped close and laid a hand on his shoulder, drawing him away and down the corridor. The guests all turned to watch as she walked him to the end so they wouldn't be able to overhear.

"Your first instinct was good," she said quietly. "Let her marry the man she loves."

His gaze flicked to the curious onlookers. "But—"

"I, too, once thought this union inadvisable. But now that I've seen them together—"

"What they feel for each other has little bearing on the repercussions of this match."

"Have faith. She has faith in him."

Griffin had faith in Tristan, too—but that wasn't the point. "The *ton* doesn't mirror that faith."

"Will you allow that to influence your decision? That isn't the Griffin I remember. The one I imagined riding into battle with his principles held before him like a shield."

He stared at her. "You never thought of me that way. You thought I was a reckless rascal."

"Perhaps. I do recall you once telling me to ask for forgiveness, not for permission. But you were also stubborn as anything. You never let anyone else's opinions stand in the way of your goals."

His gaze swept the assembled guests, landing on the odious Lady St. Quentin. He could see her straining to hear.

Hang it. Rachael was right. He wasn't going to let that despicable, fortune-hunting woman decide his sister's fate. He couldn't consign Alexandra to a life of utter misery, even to save the rest of them from infamy. Not and live with himself, anyway.

With a sigh, he surrendered to the inevitable, marching back to face his old friend in his sister's doorway.

"Get dressed," he said tightly. "The Archbishop of Canterbury is half a day's ride, and you're in need of a special license."

## THIRTY-THREE

*A*LEXANDRA FELT queasy as she watched the last of their guests' carriages roll out of the quadrangle. "Why do I think they're all going to gather at the end of the road and have a good gossip?"

"Because they will," Juliana said.

"The repercussions have begun already." Alexandra turned to follow her siblings back inside. "They didn't even stay long enough to finish breakfast."

"That's only because it was stone-cold," Corinna said, sitting on an old, ornate treasure chest.

"No, it wasn't." Tired and shaky, Alexandra lowered herself to one of the walnut hall chairs. "No one wants to associate with us. Dear heavens. What am I going to do?"

"You're going to marry Tristan tomorrow." Griffin sat on the third step of the staircase, leaning forward with his elbows on his spread knees, his hands dangling between them. "And you're going to be happy. I demand it."

"How can I be happy when the rest of you will be miserable?" A single tear rolled down her cheek.

An expression of outrage stole over his face. He sat up straighter. "You're marrying the man you claim to love. There's no crying allowed. You hear me?"

"She's not crying for herself," Juliana said, moving to pat Alexandra on the shoulder. "She's crying for *us*."

"I'm *not* crying," Alexandra said, swiping at the rogue tear with a frustrated motion.

In truth, she wasn't sure why she was crying. She was a quivering bundle of emotions. One moment she was elated to be marrying Tris, the next racked with guilt that it meant making pariahs out of her siblings. She was more than disgusted with her failure to keep her resolution for even a single night. And she was humiliated beyond belief—absolutely mortified that half of society had seen a man come out of her bedroom.

"Why did I let him stay in my room?" Why had she *asked* him to stay in her room? "I'm mutton-headed."

"You're seventeen!" Juliana returned loyally. "And you're human."

"I'm sorry." Alexandra gave a long, wretched sniff. "I've ruined all your lives."

"Good gracious," Griffin said. "Cheer up, will you? You don't see any of us crying."

"We're *thrilled* for you," Juliana put in.

Alexandra looked around at all the grim faces. "Indeed."

"We are," Corinna insisted. "We're just a little…shocked. You've always been the *good* sister."

"Well, I've been changing, in case you haven't noticed. It seems my transformation is now complete. From a paragon of traditional femininity to an utter tart, and all inside of a single summer."

"No one thinks you're a tart," Juliana said.

Corinna nodded. "A little fast, perhaps, but—"

"She's about to be a married matron," Juliana interrupted, glaring at her younger sister. "There's nothing fast about that. Griffin, you did exactly the right thing."

"Thank you," he said dryly.

Alexandra sighed. "There *was* no right thing."

"Does Tristan really sleepwalk?" Corinna asked her brother.

He nodded. "All of his life." His jaw clenched. "I'm going to kill him."

Alexandra jumped up. "You wouldn't dare!"

"Sit down. I was fooling." Rubbing the back of his neck, he added, "I'd *like* to kill him, but I'll restrain myself. For your sake."

"Thank you." She plopped back down.

"Just be happy. That's all the thanks I require."

But she couldn't be happy—not when she'd ruined her family's reputation. She wouldn't be happy until she fixed that. Until her sisters could win any young men they wanted. Until Griffin didn't have to defend his fallen sister or his decision to allow her to marry Tris.

Until, she realized, the seeds of an idea taking root in her brain, she found the evidence that would clear her husband's name.

Her *husband*. It suddenly struck her as uncanny that by this time tomorrow, she would be a wife. She put that from her mind for the moment.

"Just give me a week or two," she told her siblings. "Then we'll all be happy."

Corinna's blue eyes narrowed. "What do you mean?"

"I'm going to find whoever murdered Tris's uncle." She could do it. She had to do it. "Then Tris won't be shunned anymore, and you'll be able to make a brilliant match. After all, your older sister will be married to a handsome, popular marquess who is well known for his expertise in machinery, animal husbandry, and land management." Alexandra tried for a brave grin.

"You're going to find his uncle's murderer," Griffin said flatly. Disbelievingly.

She raised her chin. "Yes. I am."

"How?" Juliana asked.

"I don't know. I'll need to investigate matters at Hawkridge Hall."

"Tristan doesn't think there *is* a murderer," Griffin reminded her. "He thinks his uncle died in his sleep."

"Well, we'd best all pray he's wrong, because a natural death will be much harder to prove. But if that's the case, I'll find a way, because it's the only hope for us all."

"Surely it's not as dire as all that," Juliana said.

But no one spoke up to agree with her, because it *was* as dire as all that.

Alexandra sighed into the silence.

"Holy Hannah!" Corinna exclaimed after a long moment.

Juliana turned to her. "What?"

"She's going to investigate matters at Hawkridge Hall. She's going to *move* to Hawkridge Hall."

"Tomorrow," Griffin said matter-of-factly. "I expect Tristan will want to leave directly after the wedding."

"She cannot leave tomorrow!" Juliana shook her head. "She's made no preparations, she has no trousseau, she—"

"She has no choice." Griffin stood, one hand on the staircase's marble rail. "I'm going to change my clothes and head out to the vineyard. Since Tristan has abandoned me, I'll need to install his pump." He started upstairs, looking over his shoulder at them as he went. "You'd better pack your things, Alexandra. And choose a wedding dress. With any luck, I'll be finished and back for dinner."

"A wedding dress," Alexandra breathed.

Corinna nodded. "A Lady of Distinction suggests white."

"I don't even *own* a white dress."

"You can borrow one of ours," Juliana said. "We'd best get busy."

# THIRTY-FOUR

$\mathcal{T}$HE SUN WAS sinking in the sky by the time Tristan returned, special license in hand, to learn that Griffin was at the vineyard. A change of horses and a brisk gallop got him there just before dark. Griffin's crew was completing the pipeline, lighting lanterns to provide illumination while they finished. As Tristan rode up, one of the men approached him, holding two of the lamps.

"I was just taking these to Lord Cainewood, my lord." He nodded in the direction of the newly dug pit.

"I'll take them for you," Tristan offered, sliding off his mount. He tethered the horse and headed toward the pit, both lanterns in one hand. Slipping his other hand into his pocket, he toyed with the ring he'd detoured to Hawkridge to pick up. A simple gold band, wide but worn thin from centuries of use. A family heirloom for traditional Alexandra. Though it was plain, he hoped she would like it.

Curses were coming from the square pit. Colorful ones. Still holding the lanterns in one hand, he started down the ladder, his eyes widening as he saw what was going on inside. "What on earth do you think you're doing?" he said as he reached the bottom.

"Installing your accursed pump." Griffin's wrench slipped, eliciting another burst of strong language.

Tristan set the lanterns in a corner on the dirt floor. "I would have done it if you'd waited."

"When? In the middle of my sister's wedding night?" Griffin mopped his brow with the back of a grimy hand. "I think she'd have my head. Besides, it's time I learned how to do this myself. Given the way my luck has been running, I'm likely to need another pump or a dozen soon."

"Let me give you a hand." Tristan took the wrench.

"One of the hands you couldn't keep off my sister?" Griffin snatched it back. "No thanks."

Heedless of the dirt, Tristan leaned against the wall, crossing his feet at the ankles and his arms across his chest. The pit exuded the pungent scent of recently turned earth. As fresh and sharp as his friend's mood. "You're cross with me."

"Give the man a prize."

"I didn't compromise your sister on purpose."

"No, you were sleeping. Just waltzed in there unaware. Or so you said—"

"Hey—"

"All right, I believe you." Griffin banged the wrench against a pipe, wincing at the sharp *clang*. "That doesn't mean I have to like it." He whacked the pipe again.

"You want to hit me?"

He looked all too intrigued by that idea. "No."

"Go on. Hit me. It'll make you feel better."

"It'll make *you* feel worse."

Tristan just shrugged. "You cannot but admit I deserve it."

Tapping the wrench against his palm, Griffin stared at Tristan for a few long, tense moments. Then he dropped the tool to the dirt, drew back a fist, and rammed it into his friend's shoulder.

Though pain exploded, Tristan didn't flinch. "You can do better than that."

"You're right." Griffin hauled off and punched him in the mouth.

Tristan saw stars. His friend looked wavery through his watering eyes. Tasting blood, he flexed his jaw. "Feel better?"

"Not yet." Gritting his teeth, Griffin took half a step forward and drove his fist full force into Tristan's gut.

The wind rushed out of him as he doubled over in pain and surprise. When he came up, gasping for air, he returned the favor with a blow to Griffin's face that sent him careening into the wall.

"Hey!" Griffin said.

"That's enough."

"I think not," he ground out, coming back swinging. "You compromised my sister. It will never be enough."

Tristan took two punches but ducked the third, straightening to throw a left-handed jab that landed solidly in his friend's midsection. Griffin retaliated with a right-handed hit that was even harder. From there, Tristan lost track. The blows flew fast and furious until finally they both stood there, panting and exhausted, neither of them possessing the energy to continue.

Griffin dropped to sit on the dirt floor, his legs sprawled out before him, his face cradled in both hands. "I think you broke my nose."

"No, I didn't. You're such a widgeon." Leaning against the wall above him, Tristan spit out blood. "I think you loosened my teeth."

"I hope so." Griffin grinned up at him, then winced. "You feel worse now, don't you? Just as I predicted."

Tristan slid down to sit beside him, groaning at new

assorted aches. "Nothing you do could make me feel worse. Believe it or not, I'm more upset at this turn of events than you are."

"I don't believe it. You didn't just ruin two of your sisters' lives."

"No, I ruined three of *your* sisters' lives instead."

"Three? Alexandra was dying to marry you."

But the way Tristan saw it, she could die *because* she married him. Who knew what he might do the next time he sleepwalked? He was scared stiff.

"Besides," Griffin added, "she's going to clear your name, and then no one's lives will be ruined."

"She's going to *what*?"

"She's determined to find your uncle's killer."

"My uncle didn't have a killer. He died in his sleep."

Griffin began to shake his head, then apparently thought better of it. "I told her you'd say that."

# THIRTY-FIVE

## CORIANDER BISCUITS

Take eight eggs, a little Rose water, some Madeira, and a pound of fine Sugar; beat them
together for an Hour; then put in a Pound of Flour and half an Ounce of Coriander seeds;
then beat them well together, butter your Pans and put in your batter, and set it into the
Oven for half an Hour; then turn them, brush them over the Top with a little of the Eggs
and Sugar that you must leave out at first for the Purpose, and set them in again for a
quarter of an Hour.

*These biscuits are perfect to take visiting. My mother always bakes some when we're to*
*meet someone new.*
—Lady Elspeth Caldwell, 1691

"**W**HAT ARE YOU doing up so late? It's three o'clock in the morning."

"Is it?" Startled, Alexandra turned to see her brother standing in the shadowed entrance to the kitchen. "I'm making coriander biscuits to take along to Hawkridge." She beat Madeira into a bowl of eggs, sugar, and rose water. "I cannot arrive there with nothing."

"You don't have to bribe Tristan's people to accept you. You'll be their marchioness."

She added flour to the mixture, dumping half of it onto her shaky hands in the process. "Chase ladies always bring sweets."

"Tomorrow will be a big day for you. Go to bed, for goodness sake. If you truly feel a need to bring something, you can ask François to make it in the morning."

Sound advice, except she was too excited—and nervous—to sleep. "We missed you at dinner," she said, changing the subject. "And afterwards." As he walked closer, she blinked and set down the bowl. "What on earth happened to your face?"

He touched it gingerly. "Your soon-to-be-husband happened to it," he informed her dryly.

"Tris? Whyever would he hit you?"

"Perhaps because I hit him first?" He looked around the cavernous kitchen. "Is there anything to eat in here besides raw biscuit dough? We just finished installing the pump. It works beautifully, but I'm about to expire from starvation."

"And Tris?"

"Said he's not hungry. Went straight to bed."

"I meant, does he look like you?"

"Not much." He crossed to where François had left out some bowls covered with cloths. "His hair is lighter, and his eyes—"

"Griffin!" Walking over, she playfully punched him on the shoulder with a flour-coated fist.

"Ouch!" He waved at the white powder flying in the air. "I hurt everywhere, so keep your hands off."

"How much did you hurt *him*? Will I have to keep my hands off my husband as well?"

Her brother's face flushed red beneath the bruises. "I'd prefer to avoid the topic of you touching...that man. Or any man." He rooted in a bowl of fruit and came out with an apple. "You know," he added, polishing it on his grimy shirt, "there is one advantage to your being ruined. Saves me from having to explain about the wedding night."

Now it was Alexandra's turn to blush. "I wasn't ruined, Griffin."

"I beg your pardon?" He bit into the apple with a juicy crunch. "Of course you were! Why else would I marry you to someone wholly unsuitable?"

"Don't talk with food in your mouth." She moved toward the pantry. "In society's eyes, yes, I was ruined. But not in truth."

He swallowed this time before responding. "What do you mean?"

She busied herself rifling through a drawer. "Nothing really happened last night. With Tris, I mean. We…we kissed is all. Then he woke up and we just talked. And then we fell asleep." She located the cloth she'd been seeking.

"You just talked," he said. "In your bed."

Mortification sparked her temper. "Yes, we just talked!" She flung the cloth in her brother's face. "Wipe your chin." Turning away, she started putting dollops of batter on one of the two pans she'd prepared.

After a long silence, she said in a small voice, "You believe me, don't you?"

"I suppose. Though it does boggle the mind." She heard the crunch of another bite. "I cannot imagine just *talking* to a girl in bed!"

"I'm so glad to hear you say that," she said to the biscuits.

"Hear me say what?"

"That you've done more than talk to a girl in bed."

He made a strangled sound. "Whyever would you—"

"Because, being unmarried as you are, I wasn't precisely sure you had knowledge of…of matters pertaining to the bedroom. But I'm glad that you do, because that means you'll be able to explain everything to me." Hearing a great deal of coughing, she turned to him. "Are you all right?"

He nodded wildly. Between the coughing, the bruising, and the embarrassment, he'd turned red as a beet. She waited patiently while he regained his breath.

"You *will* explain, won't you?" Part of her wished Tris had finished what he'd started last night. At least then she'd know.

He pounded on his chest with a fist. "Can I have some of that Madeira first?" He gestured toward the open bottle.

She handed it to him, looking around for a glass.

"Don't bother," he said and drank directly from the bottle.

She watched him take several gulps. "Madeira should be sipped."

"Oh?" He chugged another swallow and wiped his mouth with the cloth. Studying the floor, he took a deep breath and opened his mouth. Then closed it again. He took another deep breath. "You see, there are birds, and then there are bees, and—"

She giggled. "You don't have to start there. Mama told me all of that. Didn't she explain it to you?"

"Father did." He raised the bottle again, taking a more normal sip this time. "And if Mother told you all of that, what on earth do you need from me?"

"I want to know what will happen on my wedding night. *How* it will happen."

He hesitated. "Do I have to spell out everything?"

She nodded. "I shall bake all night if you don't. Please, Griffin."

Sighing, her brother held the bottle up to a candle. Only a swallow or two remained. He drained it. "We're going to need another bottle," he said dryly.

## THIRTY-SIX

*T*RISTAN COULD scarcely believe he was married.

The wedding had been a simple affair, held in the old family chapel, witnessed not only by Alexandra's siblings and three female cousins, but the effigies of her ancestors dating back to the fourteenth century. When the minister asked if anyone present could show just cause why he and Alexandra should not be lawfully joined together, Tristan had half expected a five-hundred-year-old marble statue to pop up, sword in hand, and take exception.

After all, it took a lot of nerve for a disgraced man to wed a lovely, proper Chase daughter.

He'd practically held his breath until the ceremony was over, until they'd shared a kiss that was decorous and chaste but sweet nonetheless. And then he *still* didn't quite believe she was his wife.

He couldn't have a *wife!*

The wedding breakfast—which was actually a luncheon— had been a haze of delicious food mixed with feminine chatter and laughter. Alexandra, he'd been unable to help noticing, had spent a lot of time looking at him and very little time eating her meal. The latter wasn't all that surprising. His own stomach felt a bit out of sorts from shock paired with exhaustion.

And anticipation.

That truth didn't quite hit him until they were in the barouche he'd borrowed from Griffin, making their way toward Hawkridge and hoping to arrive before dark.

It was a warm day with no threat of rain, so they'd left the top down to enjoy the setting sun. It was fortunate there were only two of them traveling, since Alexandra's luggage took up all the remaining room. In fact, Tristan couldn't even stretch his legs out. But with her seated beside him, snuggled against him, that seemed but a minor incon-venience.

She yawned, daintily covering her mouth with a gloved hand.

He took it to draw off the glove. "You're sleepy," he said, keeping his voice low so Griffin's coachman couldn't hear.

She swallowed nervously as he slipped the silk from her fingers. "I was up most of the night." With her free hand, she motioned toward a covered basket perched carefully on top of her other belongings. "I made coriander biscuits for your staff."

Removing her second glove, he stifled a smile. Such a gesture was all but unheard of, but so very Alexandra. "They're certain to be surprised."

"Pleasantly surprised, I hope."

"I have no doubt." He pressed a kiss to her bare palm. Carefully, because his bottom lip was still tender where Griffin had bashed him in the teeth. But he'd have endured any pain to hear the little gasp that escaped her.

Smiling into her palm, he kissed it again. "I wish I'd known you were baking. I would have kept you company."

"Griffin did, instead," she told him, obviously struggling

to appear unaffected. "He was rather cheerful despite the blood and bruises."

Tristan shrugged. "In an odd way, it felt good to fight."

She shook her head. "Heaven help me, I've married a lunatic."

Chuckling, he kissed her palm once more and felt her shiver.

After composing herself, she slanted him a curious glance. "He said he hit you first."

His smile spread into a grin. "But I got the better of him, didn't I?"

"You look rather the worse for wear yourself." She ran gentle fingers over his bruised jaw and across his sore lip, then blinked and snatched her hand away, apparently surprised to find herself touching him so boldly in public. "But the black eye Griffin woke up with this morning was more colorful."

"He was suffering from the headache this morning, too, I do believe."

"*That* was because he drank most of a bottle of Madeira." Her smile was the fond smile of a sister. "Why did he hit you?"

"Because I told him to."

She blinked up at him. "Whyever would you do that?"

"More evidence of my lunacy."

Shaking her head, she looked back toward the road. Her hair, which had been covered by a lace veil for the ceremony, was very simply dressed. Several strands had blown loose. Sweeping the baby hairs off her neck, he leaned closer to kiss her nape.

She shivered again, not hiding it this time. He laid a hand on her cheek to turn her face toward him and brushed his lips across hers.

"The coachman," she whispered.

"He's not watching."

"He has only to turn his head."

"We're allowed to kiss. We're married."

She blushed and looked down. "Yes, we are," she said, twisting the wide gold band on her finger. "I didn't expect you'd have a ring on such short notice."

"On the way back from London, I stopped at Hawkridge to pick it up."

"It fits me perfectly." She rubbed the plain surface, burnished from years of wear. "Is it old?"

"Very. A family heirloom," he said, reaching to gently pull it off. "There are names and dates inside." He handed it to her so she could see.

"So many!" She held it up to the setting sun, squinting at the tiny, engraved letters. "Henry and Elizabeth, 1579. James and Sarah, 1615. William and Anne, 1645. Randal and Lily, 1677." She looked up at him, her eyes shining. "And more. So many generations."

Such a long, noble line whose reputation he'd destroyed. And now, Alexandra's and her family's, too.

He wouldn't think about that, he decided as he watched her admire the ring. Maybe tomorrow he would think about those things, but not tonight.

Their wedding night.

He smiled. "I'll have our names and year added the next time we're in London. You don't mind that it's old?"

"Heavens above, no." She slipped it back on her finger possessively. "I cannot imagine a more perfect ring."

Knowing how she valued tradition, he'd hoped she'd feel that way. But he hadn't been sure. "I'm glad," he told her.

She leaned her head on his shoulder. "Do you suppose all the other wearers were happy?"

He shrugged. "I haven't the faintest idea."

"I think they were," she said decisively. "And we will be, too," she added through a yawn.

He wished he could be so confident.

He wasn't at all sure that she'd adjust well to his isolated life. That she wouldn't come to resent him. That she'd retain her calm assurance without society's stamp of approval.

That he wouldn't unknowingly do her harm.

That, in the long run, he wouldn't lose her.

Her family would always be there for her, and she could at any time decide to run back into their comforting arms. There she could make a different life for herself. Husbands and wives who lived apart were all too common among the aristocracy.

Her head felt heavy against his sore shoulder. He reached up to stroke her hair, welcoming the dull ache, because it reminded him that she was his, at least for now. Because, anxious as he was, he couldn't bring himself to be sorry they'd married. Not now—not with the sun sinking quickly and their wedding night just over the horizon.

"Tris?" she murmured sleepily.

"Hmm?"

"I love you."

His stomach clenched. His fingers tangled in her tresses and stilled. Not *I think I'm in love with you*, but *I love you*. Three simple words said with a quiet conviction he could never, ever return. Such was beyond him.

She fell asleep waiting for the response he couldn't give.

## THIRTY-SEVEN

"WE'RE ALMOST home," Alexandra heard softly in her ear.

She startled awake, lifting her head to look around. The road they were on followed the Thames, and as they turned off it and started up a wide drive, Hawkridge Hall came into view. Although it wasn't a castle like Cainewood, the symmetrical H-shaped building looked large and imposing, three stories of red brick.

The sight of it brought her crashing down to earth. She'd spent the past day in a haze of disbelief, but now her new home loomed before her. A new place. A new life...one that had cost her family dearly.

Tris squeezed her hand as they approached. "What do you think?"

Sweet heaven, she loved him. She swallowed hard, resolving to tuck the negative thoughts away—at least for today. It was her wedding day. How long had she dreamed of this day with Tris, never daring to hope it might actually happen?

Besides, she was going to prove he was innocent—so her family's reputation would be saved.

"Very impressive," she replied with a smile. She was *not* taking her happiness at the expense of her family. Not in the long run, anyway. She just needed a week or two to set everything to rights. "Is the house very old?"

"Seventeenth century, down to the furniture." He smiled at her bemused expression. "You'll see when we get inside."

As they skirted the old stone statue in the center of the circular drive, the arched front door opened. Servants poured out onto the two sets of stone steps, their expressions a mixture of curiosity and welcome.

Alexandra watched as they arranged themselves carefully, men along the left and women on the right. "They knew we were coming?"

"I told them yesterday, when I stopped by to get your ring and my wedding clothes. I suspect they've been in a frenzy since then, getting the house all ready for a new mistress."

She disengaged her hand to reach forward and grab her basket. "I hope they'll like me."

"They'll love you." He turned her face toward him and pressed a kiss to her lips, quick but heartfelt. "They won't be able to help themselves."

Seeing grins spread on several of the staff's faces, she blushed wildly. And wished he'd said *he* wouldn't be able to help loving her. She'd have to give him time. Though she was determined to knock down that wall around him, it was looking like she'd have to do it brick by brick.

Another project for the coming weeks.

Directly in front of the door and all those smiling faces, the carriage rolled to a halt. A footman rushed to help Alexandra down. "Welcome to Hawkridge Hall, my lady."

"Thank you,…?"

"John," Tris provided as he climbed out behind her. "Uncle Harold called all the footmen John."

"Well, that's just plain silly." Here, finally, she felt in her element. With two years' experience running Cainewood Castle, she knew how to handle a household staff. She reached into her basket. "Would you care for a coriander biscuit? And pray, what is your given name?"

"Ernest," the man said, looking at the biscuit in his gloved hand as though he'd never seen one before. "Thank you, my lady."

"Thank *you*, Ernest." She started up the wide stone steps, where the butler waited, looking very stiff and serious.

Tris came up beside her, taking her arm. "This is Hastings," he said by way of introduction. "I couldn't run this place without him."

Gray-haired Hastings was older than Boniface and not nearly as pretty. But hearing Tris's praise, his stern features relaxed, revealing a pleasant face with brown eyes. "Welcome, my lady."

"Why, thank you, Hastings." She smiled, handing him a biscuit before heading for the first of a half-dozen footmen lined up beside him, all dressed in blue livery. "And your name is?"

"Will. Welcome, my lady."

"I'm so pleased to be here, Will." She handed him a biscuit and moved on. "And you are…?"

"Ted. Welcome to Hawkridge Hall."

She reached for another biscuit. "Thank you, Ted."

"John," the next man said. When she gave him a dubious glance along with his biscuit, he added, "It truly is John, my lady. My father was John, and his father before him."

"A fine name," she assured him. "So long as it belongs to you."

It turned out there were *two* Johns among the footmen.

After Alexandra met the rest of the butler's staff and an array of outdoor servants, another man stepped out of the house. Dressed like a perfect gentleman, he was tall and big boned. He had a wide nose, full lips, and skin the color of a moonless night.

"My valet," Tris said quietly, obviously noting her surprise.

Though she'd never spoken with a black man before, she went up to him unhesitatingly. "Would you care for a coriander biscuit, Mr....?"

"Vincent. Just Vincent. I have no second name." His deep voice and musical accent made her think of palm trees swaying on a beach. "Welcome to Hawkridge Hall, my lady. My master is bound to be in better spirits with you here."

"I hope so," she told him, mentally filing the interesting tidbit that Tris's valet thought he'd been in poor spirits of late. "Thank you."

Vincent smiled, displaying a mouth full of large, white teeth. He was impeccably groomed and well mannered, and she liked him very much. But although it wasn't uncommon for servants to call their employers master and mistress, his use of the term, coupled with his lack of a surname, made her wonder if he was a slave.

She looked at Tris, unable to picture him as a person who would own another. With a cryptic smile, he took her arm to cross her over to the women's side.

Her questions would have to wait for later.

"My indispensable housekeeper," he said. "Mrs. Oliver."

A short, slight older woman with pink cheeks and sparkling chocolate eyes, Mrs. Oliver bobbed Alexandra a curtsy. "If you don't mind me saying so, my lady, we're so pleased that Lord Hawkridge has wed."

"He was lonely," Alexandra said softly.

Mrs. Oliver darted Tris a glance. "Yes."

"Thank you for taking such good care of him."

She beamed. "I expect you'll do that now."

"I'm going to try my best." Alexandra handed Mrs. Oliver a biscuit and moved on.

Although the housemaids had all been called Mary, only one bore that actual name. There were so many that Alexandra despaired of remembering them all as she worked her way down the line, smiling and exchanging pleasantries.

A middle-aged maid named Peggy bobbed a curtsy as she accepted a biscuit. "Will you be needing a lady's maid, my lady?"

She looked friendly, with pale green eyes and a mop of slightly graying brown curls beneath her starched cap. Alexandra returned her smile. "Why, yes, as a matter of fact. I shared my maid with my two sisters." She looked to Mrs. Oliver for approval, and when the older woman nodded, turned back to Peggy. "Would you like the position?"

"I should be honored, my lady. I served the last Lady Hawkridge. I'm very good with hair."

"I'm pleased to hear that," Alexandra assured her and moved on to meet everyone else.

When the introductions were finally complete, she handed her basket to the cook, a plump woman in her forties with a button of a nose and pale blond hair pulled back in a severe bun. "Will you all share the rest, Mrs. Pawley? And I hope you won't mind me invading your kitchen now and again. I do adore making sweets."

Mrs. Pawley's merry blue eyes looked surprised, but she quickly hid that with a smile. "I do adore eating sweets, my lady."

"Then we should get along famously," Alexandra said.

Tris took her by the hand. "Shall I show you the house?"

She'd forgotten to replace her gloves, and her fingers tingled in his, reminding her of what was to come tonight.

The servants hurried past them, returning to their tasks as she stepped into her new home for the first time.

The entry led straight into the great hall, a beautiful rectangular room with a floor of black and white marble squares. Above Alexandra's head, a large octagonal opening in the ceiling was railed all around, so those standing above could see down to where she stood. It lent an impressive height and grandeur to the room.

Before she could say as much, though, a huge dog came bounding down the stairs. It slid across the marble floor, jarring their hands apart as it rammed straight into Tris.

"Oof!" he said with a laugh. "This is Rex. Rex, your new mistress. Shake."

Fawn colored with a black mask and ears, Rex obediently raised the most enormous paw Alexandra had ever seen. She shook it, wondering if it were her imagination or if the canine looked mistrustful. "He must be twice my weight! You never said you had a dog."

"He's not my dog. He came with the house."

Rex was trotting happy circles around him. "He seems to have adopted you. Did your uncle name him, then?"

"Yes. But it's not as though he had a choice. According to family lore, there has always been a mastiff named Rex at Hawkridge Hall."

"And why is that?"

"I asked the same question, but Uncle Harold didn't know. That didn't stop him from naming this one Rex, though. The Nesbitts are big on tradition."

Looking around the room, she could see what he meant by that as well as his earlier comment that the house was seventeenth century *down to the furniture*. Indeed, although the various tables and chairs were lovingly cared for—beautifully carved, polished to a high sheen, and reupholstered in rich fabrics—they were heavy pieces compared to modern furniture. And the gorgeous paneling on the walls, though recently refinished, obviously dated from earlier times as well. "Goodness. Is everything just the same as when the house was built?"

"Tradition," he repeated with a smile. "But if you look carefully, you'll see some recent improvements."

Alexandra's gaze followed his gesture to a lamp attached to the wall, containing a yellowish open flame protected from drafts by a glass chimney. Her mouth dropped open in astonishment. "Gas lighting? Indoors?" Although gas was increasingly being used to illuminate London's streets, she'd never seen it in a house.

"Yes," Tris said proudly. "Installed it myself. With help from two of the Johns." He shook his head. "Make that one John and Ted."

She smiled, appreciating his willingness to adapt—not just his attitude toward the servants, but to the latest advancements. She supposed she shouldn't find it surprising that a young man who employed progressive farming techniques, who built things like pumps, would also implement gas lighting. "Did you design the lamps yourself, too?"

"No, but I believe I've improved on the original design some." He showed her the key mechanism by which she could turn the gas on and off or adjust the height of the flame, and he watched her practice until he was satisfied she understood. "You catch on quickly."

"It's not difficult. Where does the gas come from?"

"I'm burning coal in a closed iron vessel outdoors, a safe distance from the house. The resulting gas is piped inside."

"How very clever."

He shrugged. "This is a small system, conceived as an experiment. Now that it's proved successful, I'm currently building a large gasworks that will be used to supply the entire village. When it's finished, all the streets and businesses—and homes, should people like—will be lit by gas. And once that's complete, I hope to form a group to pursue an enterprise wherein we approach larger towns and cities to build gasworks and supply them via gas mains."

He was so different from the other young men she knew. "A gentleman doesn't aspire to enterprise," she teased. "Such an undertaking would limit his time for amusements."

Too late she realized he wouldn't be welcome in any gentlemen's clubs or the other places young men frequented to amuse themselves. But he seemed as determined as she was to avoid thinking of such unpleasantness, because he just shrugged again in a genial manner. "I'm afraid I'm tainted by my common roots."

Though she loved his dry humor, her smile was mostly one of relief. "You seem to like having the very best and newest, though."

"Tradition is fine, but progress can also be good. And progress will march on regardless, so we may as well make ourselves part of it." He took her hand again. "Let me show you the rest of the house."

While Rex followed at their heels, Tris led her through the ground-floor rooms, tickling her palm with his thumb all the while so she could hardly pay any attention. She gleaned little more than general impressions, and even those were muddled. The main parlor looked pretty and comfortable, the dining room had a beautiful two-toned parquet floor, and the study—which, oddly enough, was accessed through the dining room—had a heavy, ancient-looking desk. There were also some lovely guest rooms and Tris's uncle's rooms—which Tris seemed reluctant to go into.

"I can see them later," she told him. "Where am *I* going to sleep?"

For truly, beautiful as the house was, now that they were inside she could think of little else besides the room she would share with Tristan tonight. She hoped familiarizing herself with the setting ahead of time might help calm her nerves, as learning what to expect from Griffin had done.

Finally he led her up the massive oak staircase, a feature clearly built to make a statement. Rex bounded up ahead, his huge body taking the wooden steps with amazing ease. Alexandra skimmed her free hand along the polished wood handrail, the panels beneath composed of boldly carved cannons, muskets, lances, and other trophies of war, all high-lighted by sparkling gold leaf.

"Goodness," she asked Tris, "were your ancestors very savage?"

"Not that I'm aware," he said with a laugh as they reached the landing. He rubbed the dog's giant head. "Although I understand this house was used as a base of operations to plot against Cromwell in the Civil War."

The next room looked to be a gallery of sorts. "The round gallery," Tris clarified.

It wasn't really round, but a long oval. It was a room mainly used to access others, sort of a very wide corridor with a hole in the middle of the floor—the large, railed octag-onal opening where one could see down to the great hall below. But she didn't take time to look, as she was gaping at the paintings on the walls.

"Corinna is going to die when she sees these," she said.

He brushed a loose strand of hair off her cheek. "Hmm?"

"You know she paints. I cannot believe what you have here." She gestured to the many gilt-framed canvases. "Rem-brandt, Van Dyck, Rubens—"

"That one was painted by one of Rubens's students."

"Regardless. She'll sit here and study these for hours. She'll forget to eat."

"Like you at our wedding breakfast?" he asked with a tender smile. "What were you studying, sweetheart?"

*You.* But she wouldn't say that, even though he'd just made her melt by calling her sweetheart. "I simply have a ladylike appetite," she informed a staid Dutch woman in one of the paintings.

Laughing, he took her elbow to guide her into a corridor, Rex following close behind.

Peggy was in the next room, already unpacking Alexandra's things. "Enjoying your tour, my lady?"

"Very much." Alexandra blinked at the sumptuous furnishings. Behind a balustrade in the French style, an enormous state bed sat on a raised parquet dais. Hangings of rich turquoise were heavily embroidered with gold thread, and great poufs of matching ostrich feathers crowned the bed's four corner posts. The ceiling was elaborate painted plasterwork, the walls hung with heavy, old tapestries.

"It looks fit for a queen," she breathed.

"Queen Catharine of Braganza, Charles II's wife," Tris confirmed. "It was decorated for her visit."

That was easy to believe. The streaked marble fireplace was adorned with gold crowns. "Is this to be my room?"

"Not a chance," Tris said.

Peggy didn't even hesitate, let alone cease unpacking. "My lord, Mrs. Oliver wanted your new lady to have the best Hawkridge has to offer. The last Lady Hawkridge enjoyed this room very much."

Alexandra was taken aback by her audacity, although she supposed that if Peggy were a shy one, she wouldn't have so boldly asked for the position of lady's maid. But while the chamber was gorgeous, she couldn't imagine being comfortable among such opulence. Goodness, what if she spilled something on Queen Catharine's antique counterpane? "It's lovely," she said tactfully, "but—"

"Lady Hawkridge will be sharing my rooms," Tris interrupted. "While we dine, please move her things."

Peggy blinked. "But—"

"You may ask two footmen to assist you with the trunks. While you're downstairs, please inform Mrs. Pawley that we'd like a light supper in half an hour." He took Alexandra's hand to draw her from the room.

"That was a bit harsh," she said once they were out of earshot. "I know she defied you, but—"

"I've never liked that one."

"Why have you kept her on, then?"

"She's been here since she was a girl. What kind of person would I be if I turned her out?" He drew her down the corridor, Rex trotting by his other side. "Are you certain you want her for your maid?"

"Since I've already given her the position, I'll wait and see how we get along. As long as you don't mind."

"Whatever makes you happy," he said, squeezing her hand. "Stay, Rex." As they entered another chamber, he closed the door behind them. "My rooms," he announced. "And yours, too, as soon as Peggy moves you in here."

A huge bed dominated the space—an old-style four-poster hung with dark blue velvet bordered in yellow silk. The walls were hung with blue velvet panels on a yellow background, and, set before the fireplace, two cushioned armchairs were upholstered in blue-and-yellow striped fabric. "It's beautiful," she said. "And much cozier than the Queen's Bedchamber."

"I didn't want you in a separate room," he said low, making her eyes dart to the bed as butterflies fluttered in her middle. Then he grinned. "Although I was half tempted to leave you there as revenge for putting me in your Gold Chamber."

"Thank you for resisting." She heard the heavy thumps of Rex padding away down the corridor. "If you don't allow him in here, where does he sleep?"

"Given his size, I'd say anywhere he wants. But a man is entitled to a bit of privacy, don't you think?" He pulled her closer. "Besides, he snores something terrible."

She began to laugh, but he cut her off with a kiss.

And what a kiss it was.

Both times they'd kissed since becoming husband and wife—during the wedding and in the carriage afterward—had been perfunctory. Before that, they'd had only stolen kisses, ones tainted by feelings of shame and remorse.

This time there was no one watching. This time there was no guilt, no heartache. This time there was only the two of them, together, without a single obstacle keeping them apart. She sank into his arms, into his kiss, into the impossible truth that he was finally hers.

A brisk knock sounded, and the door swung open. She and Tris jerked apart.

"In here," Peggy directed.

Her head swimming, Alexandra endeavored to steady herself while four footmen marched in carrying two large trunks.

"Through the sitting room to the dressing room," Peggy added briskly.

Alexandra had been so focused on Tris, she hadn't even realized there *was* a sitting room or a dressing room. She watched him now, breathless.

Her new husband—*husband!*—looked just as dazed and frustrated by the interruption. He sighed and took her arm. "Shall we have supper while she puts away your things?"

## THIRTY-EIGHT

*L*IGHT SUPPER at Hawkridge turned out to be a three-course meal. But for the second time today, Alexandra found herself unable to eat much of anything. Though she'd been pleased by her lovely new bedroom, seeing their marital bed had done nothing to set her at ease—although, paradoxically, spending time alone with Tris *had* served to increase her anticipation. Tension jangled about in her stomach, leaving but little space for food.

Sipping sparingly from a glass of the estate's fine wine, she did manage a few spoonfuls of the delicious shellfish soup. But she surreptitiously fed Rex bites of her cornish hen and carrots, reaching under the dining room's long cedar-wood table and praying his huge jaws wouldn't snap off her fingers along with the food.

While she picked at her potato pudding—which, unfortunately, she had no way to feed to the dog—she and Tris discussed the staff. She learned Peggy wasn't the only servant long in residence at Hawkridge Hall. To the contrary, many of the staff had been born here. The butler, Hastings, had inherited the post from his father; Mrs. Oliver's mother had held the housekeeper's keys before her; and the groundskeeper's great-great-grandfather had first laid out the gardens. Likewise, many of the lower servants' families had served Hawkridge for years.

"Tradition," Alexandra said with a smile.

"Mrs. Pawley is Hawkridge's first female cook, however." Tris, of course, was eating like the proverbial horse. Nothing —not even the upheaval of a hasty marriage—affected a young man's appetite. "Her father was the cook, and his father before him. When Pawley failed to sire any sons, he taught his daughter the culinary skills instead. Uncle Harold was a mite uneasy about that."

So Mrs. Pawley wasn't married, Alexandra reflected as a footman removed her plate and replaced it with the sweet course. The cook still bore her father's name, the *Mrs.* only a courtesy often extended to upper servants. "Your uncle eventually accepted her, though?"

"During the Peace of Amiens in 1802, when it became clear her father's retirement was imminent, Uncle Harold sent her to Paris to study under a master." Tris dug into his strawberry trifle. "Male, of course. Apparently, being French-trained made up for being the wrong gender."

"Her food is delicious."

"I'm sure Rex thinks so," he teased with a grin.

The mastiff was snoring contentedly in a corner of the dining room. Alexandra pushed her trifle around on her plate, trying to make it look smaller so as not to offend the cook.

"I shall have to tell Mrs. Pawley you cannot eat strawberries," Tris said.

"It doesn't matter. I'm not hungry, in any case." He was nearly finished, and she still hadn't brought up the servant she found most curious. "Tell me about Vincent."

He sipped his wine, raising a brow at her over the glass's rim. "Do I strike you as someone who would own a slave?"

Her cheeks heated, but she lifted her chin. "You cannot blame me for wondering." Though trade in new slaves had been outlawed since 1808 in all British territories, there was nothing in the law to liberate those already in captivity. Many in England still owned slaves, particularly those who had plantations in the West Indies and brought their slaves with them when they came home.

With a sigh, Tris set down his glass. "Vincent served me well during the year I spent in Jamaica. I bought him and freed him before I left."

She released the breath she hadn't realized she'd been holding. "That was a generous thing to do."

"Merely decent. I cannot countenance one man owning another."

"But your uncle could."

He shrugged his ambivalence. "Uncle Harold inherited the plantation—and its slaves—as part of his wife's dowry. Under his ownership, the slaves were treated well, and during the time I spent there and after I returned, we talked many times of freeing them. He wasn't particularly comfortable owning men. But he feared the financial repercussions of setting them free, and he was of the opinion that it was only a matter of time—a short time, in the scheme of things—before legislation would emancipate them all and take the decision out of his hands. I agreed with him on that point."

"There has been no legislation."

"There will be. Soon." He polished off the last of his trifle and sat back, lifting his glass. "Uncle Harold wanted to wait. He felt sorry for the slaves' plight, but he feared they'd be in a worse situation as free men on a plantation that could no longer compete successfully in the marketplace."

"And you agreed."

"In theory, perhaps. In practice, no." He paused for a sip. "The first action I took upon inheriting the marquessate was freeing all our slaves in Jamaica."

She'd known he was kind. She reached across the corner of the table to take his hand. "And have there been consequences?"

"Making a profit has proven difficult," he admitted quietly. "But does it matter? There are more important things than property values and income." He squeezed her fingers. "A fellow has to live with himself if he's to sleep at night."

Sleep. She'd wager he hadn't noticed his own reference, but this, she knew, was not a man who could commit murder. Not even unknowingly in his sleep.

He drew a deep breath and released it, setting down his wineglass. "Are you finished?"

She nodded, suppressing her discomposure. There was no reason to fret, she told herself sternly. She had no doubt she'd be happy with Tris—being a wife was a big change, to be sure, but his home, his disposition, and his values were all more than she could ask for in a husband. Not to mention, he was more than attractive—why, she could happily do nothing but kiss him for the rest of her life! The marriage bed was a normal part of every marriage, and Alexandra was ready for it.

Wasn't she?

She found herself inordinately relieved when Tris stood and asked, "Would you like to see more of the house?"

"That would be lovely," she said with a grateful smile.

As they exited the room, Rex rose with a gigantic yawn. He trotted after them across the great hall, up the stairs, and through the gallery with the open floor. Alexandra resisted pausing to gawk again at the famous paintings. At the other end of the gallery, a door led to a large, square room with gilded paneling on the walls and various chairs and sofas set about.

"The north drawing room," Tris said.

"It's beautiful." She walked over to an exquisite harpsichord, its case inlaid with multicolored woods. Sitting on the petit-point stool, she hit a few keys experimentally. "Johannes Ruckers," she read out loud from where the maker's name was painted above the keyboard.

"Has he a good reputation?" Tris asked from behind her.

"I haven't the slightest idea. This looks very old. I don't expect his company is making instruments anymore."

"Can you play it?"

"Probably." Since the harpsichord was much narrower than a pianoforte, the keyboard was split in two, with one half over the other. She swiveled on the stool to face him. "I shall enjoy trying it. But is there no pianoforte?"

He shook his head. "I'll get one for you."

"You needn't go to so much trouble—"

"I want you to feel at home here." He raised her to stand and pressed a warm kiss to her lips.

Rex barked. His tail thumped the wooden floor, sounding much like a slap.

"I don't think he likes me kissing you," Tris observed.

"He's jealous. Until now you were all his."

"He's not mine. I told you—"

"That's not what *he* thinks."

Tris stared hard at the dog, opened his mouth, then shut it. "Well, he's going to have to get used to sharing me. Come see the long gallery."

Rex followed them through another door into a lengthy tunnel of a room. A room that called for quiet. Woven matting on the parquet floor muffled their footsteps. Large paintings in heavy gilt frames were spaced evenly along the dark paneled walls.

Even Rex kept quiet as they walked along slowly, gazing at the pictures. The painters here weren't important; this gallery was all about their subjects. Gentlemen in silks and velvets, ladies in stiff white neck ruffs.

"Some are older than the house," Alexandra observed softly. "Are they family?"

"Nesbitts, one and all."

A few of the names were familiar from inside her ring. Henry and Elizabeth. James and Sarah. She stopped to study a canvas whose brass plaque read WILLIAM AND ANNE. The painting showed that particular Lord Hawkridge standing behind his seated lady, who held a white kitten on her lap. Her blue eyes looked kind, and Alexandra could almost see her graceful fingers stroking the silky, purring cat.

"They look happy," she decided.

The next couple, Randal and Lily, looked happy as well. "1680," she read off the plaque. The man had gray eyes, like Tris's. His hair looked like Tris's, too, but longer, and a huge dog that looked just like Rex sat at his feet. A small child stood at his side, still in skirts so she couldn't tell its gender. The man's hand rested on the shoulder of his pretty, dark-haired lady, who beamed a smile at the baby in her arms.

Alexandra smiled in response. "Everyone here has been happy. I can feel it, can't you? This is a good house. A real home." History and tradition fairly oozed from the walls.

"My uncle wasn't happy," Tris disagreed quietly.

"Not after his family died, of course. But before?"

"He was happy," Tris conceded. Evidently unwilling to promise that they would be happy too, he gave her another kiss instead, short but heartfelt.

She would swear she heard Rex snort.

"The library is through here," Tris said.

It was a lofty, two-story chamber with dark shelving crammed with important-looking books. Alexandra walked over to pull one out and flip idly through it, the old pages crackling as she turned them.

"You don't want to read now, do you?" Stepping up behind her, Tris bent to kiss her neck.

"Not really." Tingling warmth spread from where his lips met her skin. He reached around her to take the book from her hands and set it on a small table, and she turned in his arms.

Rex's bark echoed up to the laurel wreath in the center of the high ceiling.

"See why I lock him out of my rooms?" Tris asked with a sigh.

"I hope it's not because you kiss a lot of girls in there."

"Only one," he said with a soft smile that made her skin tingle even more than the kiss. "Would you like to escape the beast and go there now?"

Her heart thumped harder than Rex's tail. "Aren't there more rooms I haven't seen?"

"None that cannot wait until tomorrow." He skimmed his fingertips over her cheek, ignoring Rex's protest. The pad of his thumb brushed her lips.

She pressed a hand to her chest. A faint smile curving his bruised mouth, he lifted that hand and skimmed his lips over the knuckles before lacing his fingers through hers.

Rex dogged their steps all the way back through the long gallery, the north drawing room, and the round gallery. Tris quickened their pace into the corridor and past the Queen's Bedchamber. By the time they reached his rooms, they were running. Alexandra laughed at the absurdity. When they finally dashed through his bedroom door and he whirled and all but slammed it in Rex's face, she laughed even harder.

Rex whined once, barked three times, then padded away, his big feet thudding with each step.

"He knows when to give up," she observed with more

giggles. Laughing had relieved her feelings, calming her nerves.

"You find this humorous?" Tris returned with mock severity. Without waiting for an answer, he dragged her into his arms and silenced her with a kiss.

It was a kiss of desperate tenderness, a kiss that quickly escalated. Though she wondered if the pressure hurt his swollen mouth, she wasn't about to pull away. Tris-scent filled her senses: fresh air and soap and that elusive something she thought of as him. He tasted of Tris and the wine from dinner, and she thought it was the most delicious flavor she could imagine.

When he finally released her, she was unsteady on her feet.

"You're not laughing anymore," he said with a smirk.

"Laughing? I think I forgot to even breathe."

The smirk widened as he walked away to turn down the gas lamps. There were four of them mounted on the walls, two on each side of the room. Even battered and bruised, he moved easily, gracefully, so tall and striking in the wedding outfit his valet had cobbled together.

Sweet heaven, what had she done to deserve him?

"There," he said when the room was bathed in a softer, hazier glow. "Isn't that nicer?"

"It is." Watching him watch her, she smoothed the white lace dress she'd borrowed from Corinna. "Thank you."

He shrugged out of his black tailcoat and draped it over the back of one of the striped chairs before he began untying his cravat. As his long fingers worked at the knot, she noticed his tanned hands, their backs lightly sprinkled with hairs that glowed golden in the gaslight. She wanted to walk closer and help him, but she didn't trust her knees. She was forgetting to breathe again.

After all those years of hopeless, girlish dreaming, to think he was really hers...

It was unbelievable. She swallowed hard—so hard she feared he'd heard it.

"Are you nervous?" he asked, sitting on the chair.

He *had* heard it. "Not really. Griffin told me what to expect."

He looked a bit startled. "Did he?"

She nodded.

In truth, this wasn't going at all the way Griffin had led her to believe. Despite her blithe words, her anxiety was returning. Her legs were trembling. She was grateful when Tris beckoned her over to take the other chair—until he pulled her sideways onto his lap.

Her brother hadn't said anything about lap-sitting. What else had he failed to mention?

She couldn't remember the last time she'd sat on anyone's lap. Sitting on Tris's lap, leaning into his warmth, made her feel both very childish and very adult at the same time. He began plucking the pins from her hair—which Griffin also had not predicted. "Do you know," Tris said conversationally, "how much I've wanted to do this?"

"How much?" she whispered.

"Too much." He lowered the heavy mass, finger-combing the curls down her back to her waist. "It's beautiful."

"It's terribly unruly."

"I like it."

"When are you going to leave so I can get ready for bed?" she asked, her voice coming out a bit shrill.

He gave her a puzzled smile. "I was planning to get you ready for bed myself."

"Pardon?" That wasn't the way it was supposed to happen. Griffin had said Tris would leave her, so she could change into her nightgown, and then he'd return wearing a dressing gown. "You're supposed to leave so I can prepare myself and wait for you in the bed."

His silvery eyes narrowed. "Says who?"

"Griffin. Griffin told me—"

"Griffin is a muttonhead." With a hand on her cheek, he turned her face toward him. "Forget whatever he told you, sweetheart. He is singularly unimaginative." Tris smiled so winningly she couldn't help but smile back. "Besides which, we needn't follow anyone's directions. We'll simply make it up together as we go."

Still holding her face, he kissed her again—and her anxiety melted away.

Later, as she drifted off to sleep wrapped in her husband's arms, she honestly couldn't recall what had worried her so in the first place.

# THIRTY-NINE

### GINGERBREAD CAKES

Take three pounds of flour, one pound of sugar, one pound of butter rubbed in very fine,

two ounces of ginger beat fine, a large nutmeg grated then take a pound of treacle, a

quarter of a pint of cream, make them warm together, and make up the bread stiff. Wait a

while and then make round balls like nuts and bake them on tin-plates in a slack oven.

*These are reminiscent of home, and excellent with a good gossip.*
—Helena, Countess of Greystone, 1783

*A*LEXANDRA WOKE first and watched Tris sleep in the dim early light. His lashes lay dark against his cheeks, making him look young and sweet and vulnerable. His chest rose and fell in a slow, even rhythm, his breath drifting in and out between slightly parted lips.

She breathed along with him. She wanted to do everything with him, but for now, breathing would have to do.

When he opened his eyes, she gave him a sleepy smile. He closed the inches between them and pulled her to him. Settling her head beneath his chin, she sighed happily. "I love you."

He pressed a slow, warm kiss to the top of her head, making her feel all melty inside. But he didn't say he loved her.

It didn't signify, she decided, ignoring the stab of hurt. He'd shown her how he felt last night. His wariness was an understandable reaction to his romantic history, and he certainly wasn't the first young man who found it hard to say those three words. She'd just keep telling him, assuring him, and he'd respond in time. Soon.

He raised his head to peek at the clock on the oak mantel. "Do you always wake before six? I thought ladies all slept until noon."

"I had a house to run for my brother. And now a house to run for you."

"For us," he corrected, making her heart turn over in her chest. Then he kissed her again, his body against hers still overwarm from sleep. She'd always risen immediately upon awakening—but she decided she could get used to lingering.

Sometime later, he rang for Vincent and Peggy, and by seven they were both dressed and in the dining room.

Alexandra smiled at him across the breakfast table. "I cannot believe how happy I am."

"I'm glad." His smile more tentative than hers, Tris sipped from a steaming cup of coffee.

"What shall we do today?" She lifted the pretty little jam pot that matched the crested breakfast service, hoping for marmalade but setting it down when she saw the contents were red.

"I believe those are cherry preserves. I asked Vincent to tell Mrs. Pawley you cannot eat strawberries."

"Oh!" She dipped her knife and happily coated her toast. "Would you care for some?"

"I cannot abide anything sweet in the morning." He spread butter on his own toast, then speared a bite of eggs.

"In answer to your earlier question, I'll need to make a circuit of the estate today, having been away for a while. There are matters that will require my attention. And I must spend some time at the new gasworks; I've left the builders long without my supervision. Would you care to accompany me?"

Alexandra hesitated, realizing that what happened in the bedroom might be the easy part of marriage. Finding the rhythm of their days was going to be more difficult. She had no right to expect a honeymoon following such a hasty wedding, and she suspected Tris would rather not be distracted as he went about his business. Although she wanted to see everything at Hawkridge, this house was her domain.

"If you wouldn't mind," she finally said, "I'd prefer to stay here. I have much to learn to run this household."

"You have Mrs. Oliver for that."

"It's still my responsibility to oversee everything properly." She set down her teacup.

She had another matter to broach, and there was no sense putting it off.

But as he bit into his toast, she found herself putting it off anyway and looking about the room instead. "How unusual to see wood gilded in a mosaic pattern like that," she said inanely, referring to the walls.

"It's not wood." He set down the toast and lifted his cup. "It's gold-stamped leather."

"Is it? I've never seen anything like it."

He sipped and gave her a wry smile. "It was all the rage a hundred and fifty years ago. I'm told it's supposed to absorb the smells of food, but it doesn't seem to me that it works."

"Well, thank goodness for that. A century and a half of accumulated food scents would be a bit much, don't you think?"

He chuckled, and she drew a deep breath. "How long will you be gone today?"

"I'm not certain. It depends upon what I encounter. Perhaps a few hours, perhaps until evening." He sipped again, watching her over the cup's rim. "My offer is still open for you to come along."

Although it sounded like a sincere invitation, he didn't look like he particularly wanted her to accept it. "I think I should stay here," she repeated and squared her shoulders. "But when you return later, perhaps we can discuss strategy."

"For removing scents from the walls?"

"For mounting a new search for your uncle's murderer."

His cup clattered back to its saucer. "No."

"We must clear your name, Tris," she said carefully. "For my sisters' sakes if not our own."

His gray gaze was resolute. "I told you before, I have no wish to reopen that coil of a case. There can be no good outcome. Either my uncle died in his sleep, in which case there's nothing to find, or..."

His voice trailed off.

The haunted look in his eyes broke her heart. "You cannot think the only other alternative is that you killed him."

But clearly he *did* think that. "Just leave this alone, Alexandra."

She swallowed hard. She had to make him understand. "Does my happiness mean so little to you?"

"Not ten minutes ago, you told me you were happy beyond belief. Have your feelings changed that quickly?"

"For myself, I'm happy. But there are others to think of."

"You had alternate offers," he reminded her. "Perhaps you should have accepted Lord Shelton or Roger St. Quentin."

A lump rose in her throat. Had he been hoping she would choose someone else, that morning they were discovered together at Cainewood?

"I apologize," he said stiffly, watching her. "That was unfair."

"No, you're right. I wanted you," she said, suddenly fearing she'd made a terrible mistake. "But I also want your name cleared. And, Tris...you're *not* responsible for your uncle's death. There's no reason not to investigate."

His jaw tense, he sat silent a long moment. "I must be off," he finally said in a neutral tone. "We shall continue this discussion tonight."

After giving her a perfunctory kiss, he left.

She sat stunned for a while, her wonderful mood shattered. She tried to finish her tea, but she couldn't swallow past her tight throat. Finally she rose, fed the rest of her toast to Rex, and went upstairs to grab her family's cookbook.

Then, as she often did when she was upset, she headed for the kitchen.

Unfortunately, she had no idea where it was—Tris's tour last night hadn't included anything as mundane as the servants' quarters. But this morning she'd noticed a back passageway off the great hall, so she decided to try there first.

No sooner had she wandered into the gray-painted corridor than she bumped into a housemaid hurrying the other direction. "Pardon, my lady!" The girl's cheeks turned bright pink.

"Goodness, it was my fault entirely." Alexandra wracked her brain for the girl's name. "I wonder, Anne, if you could direct me to the kitchen?"

Anne beamed. "Right this way, my lady." Carrying a mop, broom, and bucket, she led Alexandra down another chilly corridor to a staircase. "It's in the basement. Shall I show you?"

"I'm certain I can find it. Thank you, Anne."

"Thank *you*, my lady." Still smiling and juggling everything, Anne gave an awkward curtsy and walked off while Alexandra went down the stairs.

A row of leather buckets hung overhead, pointing the way to the kitchen—always the biggest fire hazard in any house. Busy plucking a chicken, Mrs. Pawley looked up when Alexandra entered her domain.

"Good morning, my lady! I wasn't expecting you to 'invade my kitchen' quite so soon." She wiped her hands on her wide, white apron. "Did you enjoy your breakfast?"

"Very much." The room was a hive of activity: kitchen maids chopping and slicing while scullery maids scurried here and there, hauling pans and implements off to be washed. A small boy stood turning a spit. Alexandra sighed. "I thought to perhaps make some gingerbread, but—"

"Come in, come in." Mrs. Pawley shooed two kitchen maids away from the large central table. "Show me your book."

Alexandra handed it over. "It's been in my family for well over a century."

The cook flipped several pages. "This sounds delicious. And this." She looked up. "Are all the recipes for sweets?"

"The Chases do all share a sweet tooth." Despite her blue mood, Alexandra smiled as she reclaimed the old book. "Each lady in the family adds a recipe every Christmas. I'll have to return it to Cainewood, where it belongs. I've only borrowed it to copy my favorites, as Lord Hawkridge and I were married, ah…"

"In a hurry?" Mrs. Pawley's blue eyes danced.

"You could put it that way, yes. Have you flour and sugar?"

Beneath her starched white cap, the blond bun at the nape of the cook's neck bounced as she nodded. "We have everything you need, my lady. You've only to give me your list."

Half an hour later, they stood companionably side by side,

their hands coated in flour, forming small balls out of the gingerbread dough. Mrs. Pawley, as it turned out, wasn't only an accomplished cook, but also an unrepentant gossip. "I did notice where your ancestor claimed these cakes are excellent with a good gossip," she said with a laugh.

"I expect she meant eating them, not making them." Alexandra sneaked a taste of the sweet-spicy dough. "Though I do confess some curiosity about the past happenings here at Hawkridge."

"I remember when your husband first arrived here from Jamaica. In a bad way, he was, his father dead and not a penny to his name. The last Lord Hawkridge took him under his wing, but he weren't in a good way, either."

"Yes, I've heard that. He was ill, wasn't he?" Alexandra scooped more dough. "Do you remember the morning the last Lord Hawkridge passed away?"

"Oh, most vividly." Having filled the first pan, the cook dusted flour on another. "We all loved the last Lord Hawkridge. Not that we don't feel the same toward your new husband. Do you know, it was he who suggested Lord Hawkridge send me to France for training. Saved my position here, he did. And he couldn't have been more than ten at the time; even as a boy, he knew the way of things. Your husband has a business head on those shoulders."

A vision of those shoulders—bare, smooth, and bathed in candlelight—made Alexandra's face heat. "When the last Lord Hawkridge was discovered in his bed, was poison suspected immediately?"

"Mercy, no! Who would poison a fine man like him?" Mrs. Pawley plopped another ball on the pan. "He died of a broken heart, I tell you. We all know that here. No matter what the outsiders say."

Alexandra was relieved to hear that Tris's staff didn't

suspect him. "Were there any outsiders here at the time? Anyone suspicious?"

"No one at all. Lord Hawkridge was in the dismals—he weren't taking visitors. Excepting your husband, of course. The house was still draped in black—"

"No one? A concerned neighbor? A salesman or tradesman?"

"Not that I remember." Rolling dough between her plump hands, the cook eyed Alexandra speculatively. "Why all the questions, my lady?"

Alexandra made another ball before she answered. She knew Tris wouldn't be happy she was asking questions. But did she have a choice? His fear that he'd killed his uncle was completely unfounded, and her sisters' happiness was at stake.

She set the ball on the pan. "I'm hoping to clear my husband's name, Mrs. Pawley. If I can prove someone else killed his uncle, he'll be welcomed back into society."

The cook nodded as if she'd thought as much. "I'd like to see Lord Hawkridge's name cleared as well. But there's no one here thinks the last Lord Hawkridge was poisoned. He died in his sleep, plain and simple."

"Do you find it upsetting to answer questions?"

"I suppose not. I didn't see anything that night to help you, though. 'Course, I'm stuck down here in the basement; I'm not aware of all that goes on upstairs." She reached over to pat Alexandra's hand, puffing flour into the air in the process. "If you're that determined, perhaps you should ask the others."

Exactly what Alexandra wanted to do. Perhaps she'd be risking her husband's anger, but she couldn't see where either of them would be happy with this cloud hanging over their heads. And it wasn't as though she'd be combing the countryside for clues—she'd only be talking to her own staff. People she should be getting to know anyway.

If a little voice told her that was a rationalization, she decided to ignore it. With any luck, she might uncover important information and solve the mystery before Tris even arrived home.

# FORTY

*A*N HOUR LATER, Alexandra and a large platter of gingerbread cakes sat in the main parlor, which had a lovely trio of windows looking out toward the Thames. The walls and upholstery were sage green damask, the ceiling painted with fat, cavorting cherubs to oversee the proceedings. Hastings—who'd had no new information to add to her investigation—showed the next servant in, bowing as he backed from the room.

"Please have a seat, Ted." She waved the footman onto the sofa opposite hers, reaching to the low table between them to pour tea, in hopes of making him comfortable. "Would you care for a gingerbread cake? They're still warm from the oven."

The footman seated himself carefully. "The others told me what you're asking, my lady. I regret that I have nothing to add. But we all know the marquess is innocent, and we do admire your efforts to clear his name."

"I'm determined." How ironic that everyone here thought Tris was blameless—except Tris himself. That only cemented her resolve to prove his innocence in spite of his protests.

Since Ted hadn't reached for a cake, she put one on a small plate and handed it to him. "Are you certain you saw no one suspicious around Hawkridge that night or the morning after?"

"None that I recollect."

"And was there anyone here—living here, I mean—whom you feel could possibly have had motive to harm the last Lord Hawkridge?"

"I'm afraid not. Lord Hawkridge was a fair man, much admired by all."

"So I keep hearing." She sighed. "If you think of anything that might help me, please let me know immediately. You may go. And feel free to take your refreshments with you," she added with a smile. "I suspect there may be a small party in the servants' parlor."

And so it went. She questioned all the footmen and other manservants, the housemaids, the chambermaids, the kitchen staff, and everyone in the stables and on the grounds. Over and over she heard the same answers, the same insistence on everyone's innocence. Four hours later, the pile of gingerbread cakes had dwindled, and there were only the upper servants left to interview.

"Good afternoon, my lady," Peggy said when Hastings ushered her in. She had put aside her maid's uniform and wore a clean but very outdated dress. "I've been wondering when I might be summoned."

"This is nothing for you to fret about," Alexandra assured her, thinking she'd fetch a few dresses for her the next time she went home to Cainewood. Lady's maids generally expected to wear their mistresses' cast-off clothing. She poured tea and set the cup and saucer on the low table between them, along with a gingerbread cake. "Please make yourself comfortable. I just have a few questions, that's all."

Peggy sat and fluffed her skirts. "You're looking for evidence to clear Lord Hawkridge's name."

"Yes. Word does get around." Peggy had done an excellent job unpacking and arranging Alexandra's things last night—even pressing her wrinkled clothing before putting it away—and this morning she'd worked wonders with her often unruly hair. So far, Tris's opinion notwithstanding, Alexandra was very pleased with her. "Do you recollect anyone visiting on the evening or morning of my husband's uncle's death?"

"No, my lady. No one." Peggy calmly sipped her tea. "And I know what you're going to ask next," she added, setting her cup back on the saucer. "I don't believe anyone here had any reason to harm Lord Hawkridge, either. He was well liked and respected, and we had all known him a long time—many of us all of our lives."

"I'm aware of that." Alexandra sipped a bit of her own tea to be polite, although she'd long ago had quite enough. "Is no one new ever hired here at Hawkridge?"

"There are rarely any openings and usually young people waiting to fill them." Peggy bit into a gingerbread cake, chewed, swallowed, and smiled. "Delicious, my lady."

"Thank you. It's an old family recipe." But the "good gossip" the cakes were purported to inspire wasn't netting her much in the way of results. "So you don't remember anyone who might have been new at the time? Anyone who could possibly have been less than loyal to the last Lord Hawkridge?"

"No, we're all here from way back." Peggy reached for her cup again, then stopped. "Wait." She frowned, narrowing her pale green eyes. "There was Vincent, of course. He'd recently arrived with your husband." She shook her head, her mop of brown curls bouncing. "But Vincent is a big sweetheart. He'd never kill a fly, let alone a man."

"I'm sure you're right," Alexandra said, hiding her surprise that she hadn't thought of Vincent herself. It was obvious that at the time he'd have been a new arrival. "Thank you, Peggy. I'll be calling on you to help me change before dinner. Would you inform Hastings that I'm ready for Mrs. Oliver?"

"Of course, my lady." Peggy smiled and left.

While Alexandra waited for Mrs. Oliver, she stared blankly out a window toward the peaceful river, her mind racing. Could Vincent have killed Tris's uncle? He didn't seem the type; she had liked him on sight. But Uncle Harold, after all, had owned Vincent when he was a slave. It was certainly possible for resentment to build under those circumstances. And Vincent had to bear Tris a strong loyalty, considering Tris had bought and freed him.

Might Vincent have been willing to kill his former owner in order to save Tris from destitution?

She didn't think so. But she owed it to Tris—and her sisters—to at least consider the possibility.

When Mrs. Oliver arrived, she brought news. "Lord Hawkridge has sent word, my lady. He's been detained at the gasworks and may not make it home until after dinner."

"Thank you, Mrs. Oliver." Alexandra forced a smile. The news was disappointing, but not altogether unexpected. And if this was to be her life, she might as well get used to it. "Please do take a seat. I hope you won't mind answering a few questions."

But although they had a nice conversation, Mrs. Oliver had nothing new to add to Alexandra's investigation.

And at long last, she had only one servant left to speak with: Vincent.

Vincent wore an immaculate black suit, a crisply tied cravat, and a wide, bright smile. He entered the room with such an easy manner that she couldn't imagine he was afraid of anything, much less worried he'd be arrested for murder.

"My lady," he greeted her in that musical voice that made her picture faraway islands. "I've never seen your husband as happy as he was this morning. I can only thank you for entering his life."

"Surely you exaggerate." How could she suspect such a charmer? "Have a seat, please, and tell me what you remember of the night my husband's uncle died."

"The man was feeling poorly, and one morning he failed to wake up." He seated himself, seeming to take up the whole sofa across from her. "I saw nothing to suggest there was foul play involved and nothing to rule it out, either. However," he added, his deep voice brooking no argument, "Lord Hawkridge had no part in his uncle's death. I'll hear nothing of that nonsense."

"I agree with you entirely." When she handed him a cup and saucer, they looked like toys in his big hands. "I hope to find the real culprit, to clear my husband's name and restore his place in society."

"He's aware of your investigation?"

Was it her imagination, or did he know Tris would disapprove? "I've told him of my intentions."

He sipped, regarding her over the cup's rim. "Most here think there was no culprit. They believe Lord Hawkridge's uncle died in his sleep. They're convinced no one here had any reason at all to consider murder."

"You don't agree?"

He shrugged his brawny shoulders. "I don't pretend to know. I had come to Hawkridge but recently, so I wasn't as well acquainted with the rest of the staff as they were with one another. Two years later, I still don't know many of them well."

He wouldn't. Upper servants rarely fraternized with those

lower, and she couldn't picture him becoming fast friends with Hastings, Mrs. Oliver, or Mrs. Pawley. He struck her as the sort that would keep to himself. Which doubtless suited Tris just fine.

She offered him a small smile. "If you think of anything that could help me, please let me know."

"I will," he said, draining his tea before rising to his feet. "Your husband is a good man, Lady Hawkridge. The best. If there's anything I can *ever* do to help him, you can wager I will."

He bowed to her from his lofty height, and she watched him quit the room.

After he left, she thought about him for a long time. She was usually a good judge of people, and she couldn't imagine him a murderer. He seemed friendly and open, and she liked him.

But he'd made it clear he'd do anything to help Tris.

Could *anything* extend to murder?

$\mathcal{I}$T HAD STARTED raining around sunset and hadn't let up since. Dripping wet and miserable, Tristan was surprised when Vincent met him at the door. Predictably, Rex met him at the door, too, bounding down the stairs and sliding across the great hall to greet him.

"Welcome home, my lord," Vincent said. Rex barked his agreement.

Tristan stepped inside, immediately creating a puddle on the black and white marble floor. He rubbed the dog's head before shrugging out of his sopping greatcoat and handing it to the valet. "Where's Hastings?"

"Sleeping." Vincent took Tristan's soaked hat, too, holding both away from his own pristine clothing. "Everyone's sleeping. It's half past one in the morning."

"Blast! I had no idea." Tristan dug out his pocket watch, but of course his valet was right. "Problem with the construction at the gasworks," he explained, snapping it shut. "I shall have to return first thing tomorrow. I expect Lady Hawkridge is abed, too?"

"I imagine so. Haven't seen her for hours. Should you like a late supper, sir?"

He suddenly realized he was famished. "Yes, and my thanks. Take it to my study, if you will. I have weeks of paperwork to catch up on."

Boots squishing all the way, Tristan headed across the great hall to the dining room and through to the study, Rex at his heels. He briefly considered changing out of his damp clothes, but decided he couldn't spare the time. He'd waded through less than half the mail when Vincent showed up with a platter of cold roasted chicken, sliced cheddar, and a small round loaf of bread.

From where he was snoozing in the corner, Rex perked up and sniffed.

"Just leave it here on the desk," Tristan said, reading a letter from his steward in Jamaica. "And take yourself off to bed. I can undress myself."

"Thank you, my lord."

Vincent hesitated.

Tristan looked up. "Yes?"

"Since your lady is asleep, I just thought you might like to know that she questioned everyone, but I don't believe she uncovered any new evidence."

He set down the letter. Slowly. "What do you mean, she questioned everyone?"

"About the circumstances surrounding your uncle's death." Vincent peered at him in the yellowish gaslight. "She assured me you were aware of her intentions."

"She did make her intentions clear, yes." And he'd thought he'd made his clear as well. "Thank you, Vincent. I'll see you in the morning."

"Good night, then, my lord."

Tristan waited for his valet's footsteps to fade from his hearing, then counted to ten. Then counted to a hundred.

Then told himself he'd be better off eating his supper and waiting for his anger to ebb, rather than stomping upstairs immediately to wake his new wife.

He ate two bites of chicken, tossed the cheese to the dog, and took a hunk of the bread with him.

Chewing savagely as he squished up the stairs, he considered the best way to wake Alexandra. A light tap on the shoulder? A whisper in her ear? Perhaps he should jerk the sheets up and dump her out of the bed.

He was sorely tempted as he squished through the round gallery and down the corridor. Having wolfed down the cheese, Rex caught up to him just in time to get the door slammed in his huge, hopeful face.

Seated in one of the armchairs, Alexandra looked up from her book. "You're home."

Tristan slumped back against the door. "You're not sleeping." He couldn't dump her out of bed after all. "You're not even undressed." All she'd removed were her shoes and stockings.

She set her book on the side table and smiled. "I thought *you* liked to do the undressing."

"I thought…"

Seeing her now, he could hardly remember why he'd been angry. She looked gorgeous with that beckoning smile, her eyes glazed from lack of sleep, her cheeks rosy in the gaslight, her soft curves evident in the slim dress she'd no doubt donned to eat dinner alone.

Gritting his teeth, he yanked his thoughts back to the matter at hand. "I thought I told you to stay out of my business."

Her rosy cheeks went white. "You've heard."

"Of course I've heard. Every servant here is loyal to a fault."

"So I learned today. They were all loyal to your uncle

while he lived, and now they're all loyal to you. No one thinks you poisoned him, and no one believes any of the others were responsible, either. They all stand together and behind you, Tris." She rose and crossed the distance between them. "It's extraordinary, when you think of it. Servant turnover is an enormous problem on most estates. Yet everyone here, it seems, has been here forever."

Rain pattered against the windows while he considered her speech and fought to control his temper. Perhaps all was over and done with; perhaps now the matter would be closed. "You didn't learn anything incriminating."

"Incriminating to whom? We both know you're not at fault. But no, I learned nothing to incriminate anyone here. Not even Vincent."

"Vincent?" he snapped. "Why should you mention him?"

He saw her swallow hard. "He was the only one new to the staff. The only one without a long-standing loyalty to your Uncle Harold. The only one, in fact, who had a reason to resent him."

The anger surged anew. "Whatever do you mean by that?"

"Your uncle *owned* him, Tris. Don't you think that could have made a difference? After you freed the man and then found yourself in dire straits, haven't you ever wondered if it's possible he considered murder a way to both revenge himself and solve your problem?"

He hadn't. Not for the barest moment. "I'd sooner believe I murdered my uncle myself. Just because the man has dark skin—"

"This has nothing to do with his skin!" Outrage brought color back to her cheeks. "I cannot believe you would think that of me. I happen to like Vincent very much. We had a nice chat. He cares about you—"

"Then why? Why would you accuse—"

"I'm not accusing him!" Her eyes were now flashing rather than glazed. "Shall you fault me for simply considering the possibility? For looking everywhere I can to find someone to blame so we can clear your name and get out of this mess?"

He realized they'd both raised their voices, but he didn't care whom they might wake. "I do not want this *mess*, as you put it, stirred up again. I thought I'd made that perfectly clear. Do you understand me this time? Or do I need to write it down on a blasted piece of paper?"

"What are you afraid of, Tris? That you'll find yourself a murderer? I *know* that won't happen." She looked beautiful in her righteous fury, her cheeks red as rubies now, her hair escaping its pins and curling about her face. "All I wanted was to ask around and see what I might turn up."

"And all *I* want is for you to stop!"

"Well, then, you have your wish," she said, suddenly sounding defeated. "I've talked to every single person on this estate, and no one had anything the least bit helpful to contribute. There's no one else to ask." She drew a deep breath, her chest heaving with the effort. "It's over," she added in a voice so dead and quiet it was startling following all the shouting.

The silence reigned for a space of time, stretching awkwardly between them.

"I am sorry for defying your wishes," she said at last. "But I confess I'd do it again. It's over, but if it wasn't, I'd do anything I could to find a way to clear your name."

He couldn't summon any more anger—what he felt edged closer to guilt. After all, it was his fault—his sleepwalking, his failure to leave her room—that had landed them in this impossible marriage.

Maybe a tiny part of him had hoped she'd be successful. Hoped she'd find a way to erase the stain on the Nesbitt name. Hoped she'd prove able to keep that stain from spreading to her own family.

Of course, a much larger part of him—the part that was scared stiff of what she might have found—overshadowed that tiny part.

But it was there. Maybe.

"I'm glad it's over, then," he said. "And I'm sorry, too." He wasn't quite sure what he was sorry for. Given the chance, he'd try to stop her all over again. But he did feel sorry. And guilty. And a little angry still, and he didn't know what else.

She sighed and moved the few inches between them to lay her head on his chest. "You're damp."

"I had to ride home through the rain."

She snuggled closer anyway. "I guess we've had our first fight."

"I didn't know you had it in you," he said, wrapping his arms around her. "You're always so calm."

"When something matters to me as much as this does—as much as you do, as much as my family—I will *not* be calm."

"I'll keep that in mind," he said dryly.

She felt warm and soft in his arms. Irresistible. Though his emotions were still running high, he'd never been able to resist her pull.

Never.

"It's very late," he said regretfully. She obviously needed sleep, which meant he'd just have to do his best to resist. "Do you want to put on a nightgown?"

"All my nightgowns are so plain," she murmured against his chest. "I borrowed a pretty one from Juliana, but it's really much too short. I didn't have time to acquire a proper trousseau. I shall have to hire a seamstress—"

"Another servant here for you to interview?" he said bitterly. "I think not."

She tilted her chin up to see him. "Was there a seamstress here at the time?"

She looked dead serious, which he found less than thrilling. Very much less than thrilling. "I thought you said you were finished."

"Only because there's no one left to question."

"It's over. You said it was over."

"If there was another person here at the time—"

He silenced her with a kiss. Exasperated, he could think of nothing else to do.

He half expected her to protest, but she reciprocated instead. He lifted her into his arms and laid her on the bed without breaking the kiss. She smelled heavenly and tasted divine, and he would never get enough of her.

And, in this moment, there was just enough anger left swirling inside him that he didn't care if she was too tired.

~

"**SWEET HEAVEN,**" Alexandra whispered later. "I cannot move."

Tristan chuckled, feeling more than a little done in himself. With effort, he raised himself on an elbow. He ran a finger alongside her face and kissed the wide expanse of her forehead. "I knew the hour was too late. I'm sorry."

"Don't be sorry." Her eyes drifted shut. "I'm not sorry."

Although she couldn't see him, he smiled.

She lifted her lids and met his gaze. "I love you, Tris. Even though we don't always agree, I love you."

The only answer he could give her was a kiss. He poured all the tenderness he possessed into it and still knew it wasn't enough. It wasn't what she wanted.

But much as he cared for her and desired her happiness— more than he wanted happiness for anyone else in the world

—he knew it wasn't really love. And he couldn't say words he didn't mean.

Finally he pulled away. "I'll get the lights."

He walked around the room, dousing the gaslights one by one, his gaze fastened on her as he went. He still couldn't believe she was his.

He still didn't believe he wouldn't lose her.

If he woke in the night, he wanted to be able to see her. He left the last light burning.

# FORTY-TWO

*T*RISTAN WOKE in his study.

At first he just blinked, disoriented. Slowly he noticed the light coming in through the shutters, the ticking of the clock on the desk. The dog snoring in the corner, rattling the windows.

He swung himself upright on the leather sofa and rubbed his face. The sofa was too short, and his legs ached. He stretched them out before him, wondering how many hours he'd slept cramped in that position.

Hours. Hours? For pity's sake, he must have sleepwalked here during the night.

Thankfully, his sleeping self had donned a dressing gown. He wrapped it tighter and retied the sash. Yawning, he stood and left the study, intending to head upstairs.

No sooner had he stepped foot in the dining room, however, than Hastings popped in. "Good morning, my lord. Will you be wanting breakfast?"

"What time is it?"

"Half past eight."

Blast it. He needed to get back to the gasworks. He'd

promised to arrive with the sun. "Yes, breakfast, please. Is Lady Hawkridge up and about?"

Hastings looked at him curiously. "No, my lord. She's yet to make an appearance."

"I'll let her sleep," he decided, amused. He must have worn her out. Rather than risk waking her, he'd have breakfast now and then quickly dress after she'd arisen.

When he'd downed his last bite of eggs and drained his second cup of coffee and she still hadn't appeared, he returned to his study to finish going through his mail. An hour later, he sent a footman to the gasworks with a note. An hour after that, he hurried upstairs, concerned.

No matter how late he'd kept her up, a girl who habitually rose at six didn't sleep until after eleven.

"Alexandra?" He knocked softly. "Alexandra?"

He opened the door. Curled up under the covers, she looked so peaceful he had to smile.

He walked closer and shook her shoulder. "Alexandra, it's time to wake up."

She slumbered on.

"Alexandra." He shook her harder. "Alexandra!" Still no response.

Fighting panic, he drew a deep breath. And suddenly felt lightheaded.

For a moment he just stood there, a vague prickling in his brain suggesting the woozy feeling should mean something significant. Shifting uneasily, he glanced around the room. And noticed the gas lamp he'd left lit.

Only it wasn't.

His pulse stuttering, he rushed over and twisted the key, hoping it wouldn't move.

It did move. The gas line had been open. It had been open with no flame, and Alexandra had been breathing gas for who knew how long.

He prayed to God as he scooped his wife and the covers from the bed, ran down the corridor, and turned into the Queen's Bedchamber.

"Alexandra!" He laid her on the turquoise and gold counterpane and crawled up beside her, his heart pounding so hard he had to yell over the roar in his ears. "Alexandra, wake up!" Kneeling on the mattress, he gathered her into his arms. "Oh, God, please, let her wake up." He rocked her back and forth. "Wake up!"

Her lids fluttered halfway open, then closed.

He held his breath. His heart seemed to stop. "Alexandra?"

"Just…"

Had he imagined that single, breathy word? He'd had to strain to hear it.

"Just…wait a moment."

A moment. Wait a moment.

He'd wait as long as it took. Hours. Days. Until the end of his days. If only she'd wake up.

He waited.

"You're holding me too tight," she finally said.

His heart started again.

He was shaking all over.

"I mean it," she murmured, her eyes opening at last. Warmed brandy. He'd never seen anything so beautiful.

She blinked up at him. "Let go of me, Tris."

"I can't." He did loosen his hold, though even that small compromise took effort. "I think I'm going to hold you for the rest of our lives."

Her little chuckle was the most glorious sound he'd ever heard. "What happened?"

"Good God, I almost lost you." He sent a thank-you up above.

"What *happened*, Tris?"

"The gas. The lamp I left burning last night. The flame went out, so gas leaked into the room, and you were breathing it."

"You're shaking."

"I know. You were breathing it, and you could have died."

She struggled to sit up on his lap. "Don't be so melodramatic. I'm fine."

"Thank God that room isn't airtight. It may have been leaking for hours."

"I've never heard you talk so much of God," she said with a little smile.

"Hours," he repeated, feeling the blood drain from his face.

"Tris?" She levered off his lap and knelt facing him on the bed, drawing the covers over her shoulders and around her. "Are you all right?"

"Yes. No." His heart was pounding again. "I must have extinguished the flame."

"What are you talking about?"

"I sleepwalked again last night. Woke up this morning in my study. Before I left the room in the night, I must have extinguished the flame in my sleep."

"That's ridiculous." The blanket slipped off a shoulder, and she pulled it back up. "It was stormy last night. A draft blew it out."

"The glass chimney is there to protect the flame. A draft cannot blow it out. It had to have been put out deliberately."

"Anything can happen, Tris."

He wanted to believe her. He didn't want to believe he was capable of harming his own wife in the middle of the night. What kind of person would that make him?

A dangerous one.

What would that do to their marriage?

"I know what you're thinking." She sighed, sounding so

much like hale-and-hearty Alexandra he wanted to hug her despite his dread. "Even if you did put out the flame—which I am not at all convinced is the case—surely it wasn't intentional. For heaven's sake, you did it in your sleep. You must have meant to turn it off and mistakenly extinguished it instead."

"Maybe," he said—because he knew that was what she wanted to hear.

"Absolutely." Having settled the matter—to her mind, in any case—she scooted to the edge of the high bed and slid off, swaying a bit on her feet.

He landed beside her and caught her by the elbow. "Careful."

"I'm *fine*." Hitching the blanket back onto her shoulders again, she peered up at his face. "Better than you are, I'd wager. What are your plans for today?"

He winced. "I need to ride out to the gasworks. I was supposed to be there hours ago. But I cannot leave you—"

"Don't be a goose. I told you I'm fine. I'm going to make some sweets and take them with me to meet the villagers." He'd barely opened his mouth when she added, "I know what you're thinking. I won't be asking anyone any questions about your uncle's death."

"That's the second time you've said you know what I'm thinking."

She shrugged prettily and smiled. A smug smile.

He kissed that smug smile off her face.

While they were still embracing, Rex plodded in, nudged Tristan with his huge head, and barked. They broke apart.

"He doesn't like me," Alexandra said.

"He just wants some attention. Which I cannot give him right now." He rubbed the dog's head. "I need to get dressed." He turned to leave, then turned back and pulled up the blanket that had slipped off her shoulder again. "Make certain to take Peggy with you."

"Of course I will."

"And a footman for good measure—and a carriage. I shouldn't like to see you walking or riding after what happened here this morning. You may not be as fine as you believe." He gave her one more short, hard kiss, ignoring Rex's bark, then headed off to find Vincent.

No matter what Alexandra claimed, he was certain she couldn't read his mind. Because there was no chance she'd let him walk away if she knew what he was thinking at this moment:

If he *had* poisoned her with gas while sleepwalking—intentionally or otherwise—then it was even more likely he had also poisoned his uncle.

# FORTY-THREE

## SUGAR-CAKES

Take Sugar and half again as much Butter, Beaten together, and add Eggs. as much Flour

as sugar, a little Cream, some Sherry, a generous amount of Currants and a spoon of

shaved nutmeg. Shape into thin round cakes and Prick all over, then bake in a warm oven.

Cover with icing Sugar mixed with white of egg and return to oven until Crisp.

*These travel well and are good for visiting.*
—Lady Diana Caldwell, 1692

*I*T TOOK A LOT of sugar cakes to feed a village.

At half-past noon, barely an hour after Tris left, Mrs. Pawley took the fourth pan out of the oven and brought it over to where Alexandra was spreading glaze on top. "Might I pour you more sherry?"

"No, thank you, Mrs. Pawley." The small glass Alexandra had finished was quite enough—just enough, in fact, to take the edge off her disappointment. Just enough so she could smile and laugh and pretend that everything was all right.

Although, of course, it wasn't.

Now that her investigation had failed, it would never be all right.

More than half a glass of anything alcoholic made her very giggly or put her to sleep. When the cook had suggested they have a wee taste of the sherry before adding it to the recipe, she hadn't expected to finish the bottle. But Mrs. Pawley was making a good dent in it.

"I'll just have another myself, if you don't mind." The cook filled her glass for the third time and sipped, watching Alexandra swirl the sugary mixture onto the cakes with a knife. "You do that very prettily, my dear."

"Thank you. My mother taught me how to do this. And my father's mother taught her, I expect, considering the age of the recipe."

Mrs. Pawley smiled and sipped again, one eye on all the activity in the kitchen. While Alexandra wouldn't normally approve of her cook drinking wine while working, Mrs. Pawley seemed unaffected, and she couldn't argue with the woman's results. Her meals were exquisite, and her kitchen was spotless.

The woman did, however, have a smudge of flour on her little button nose that Alexandra itched to wipe away. "I know your father was Hawkridge's last cook," she said to distract herself, "but did your mother work here as well?"

"Bless her, she did. Started as a scullery maid before she caught m'father's eye." The cook's blue eyes danced. "'Course she became his assistant in short order."

Alexandra smiled. "I imagine she did like that better than scrubbing dishes."

"No one aspires to stay a scullery maid long. If a girl cannot expect advancement—"

At the sudden silence, Alexandra looked up from the pan of cakes. "What is it, Mrs. Pawley?"

"I just remembered. We had a scullery maid—Beth, she

was called—who went to Armstrong House for a better position. She was here that night—the night his lordship's uncle died. Will you be wanting to ask questions of her as well?"

"Goodness, yes." The news lifted Alexandra's spirits more than an entire bottle of sherry could have done. "How far is Armstrong House?"

"An hour or less on horseback. You'll just need to follow the river."

"Lord Hawkridge would prefer I take a carriage." There was no reason to ignore his wishes completely. He'd doubtless be cross she'd gone at all, but she couldn't very well ignore an opportunity to solve their problems, could she?

"May I prevail on you to finish these?" She shoved the pan toward the cook. "I have to change my dress, and have a carriage brought round, and find a footman to accompany Peggy and myself." She was already headed toward the door. "They need only a few more minutes in the oven; when the icing has hardened, they're done."

Half an hour later, plans for her journey in place, she returned to fetch a few sugar cakes to take along with her to Armstrong House. She couldn't very well arrive empty-handed.

After yesterday's rain, the day was beautiful. She opened the carriage windows to let in the sunshine and fresh air. Ernest, the footman she'd recruited to accompany her, rode up on the box with the coachman, and Peggy sat with her inside. No sooner had they started rolling than Peggy pulled a basket out from under the seat and began filling plates for them both.

"What's this?" Alexandra asked.

"Luncheon. You missed breakfast. I won't have you wasting away from starvation."

Alexandra laughed, suddenly realizing she'd forgotten to

eat. She supposed she'd been too upset to really care. But now that her investigation was open again, she felt famished.

Peggy truly was a dear for taking care of her so well. She piled cold meats, cheese, pickles, and fruits on two plates. "No strawberries for me," Alexandra told her. "I cannot eat them."

Peggy handed her a plate before adding a few strawberries to her own. "Why is that?"

"They make my tongue swell and my throat feel tight. It's really quite dreadful. The last time it happened, I thought I might perish from a lack of air."

"That *is* dreadful," Peggy said, her eyes wide.

Throughout the drive, Peggy kept up a running conversation that required little more than nods and murmurs from Alexandra. Sooner than she expected, they arrived at Armstrong House. Although smaller than Hawkridge, it was obviously the home of a wealthy man. It looked to have been extended many times over the years and was now a sprawling mishmash of styles—medieval, Tudor, Stuart, and more modern.

"Wait here," she told Peggy. "I shouldn't think this will take long."

"Oh, but I haven't seen Beth in more than a year," Peggy said in a pleading tone.

"Very well, then. Come along."

Alexandra put a smile on her face as she approached the door with her sweets. "Lady Hawkridge," she told the green-liveried manservant who answered, her new name sounding strange on her tongue. "Here to visit with the lady of the house, if you please."

"Pardon me, but there is no lady. Lady Armstrong breathed her last in the spring."

Only then did she notice his black armband. "Oh, I'm so sorry. Is there no one to whom I may pay my respects?"

"Lord Armstrong has gone up to London. Only Miss Leticia is at home."

*Miss Leticia Armstrong.* Good heavens, wasn't that the girl who had once been engaged to Tris? Alexandra hadn't put two and two together when Mrs. Pawley mentioned Armstrong House, but now she was dying of curiosity.

She reached into her basket. "Would you care for a sugar cake?" The footman looked startled but took it, having little choice if he wasn't to be rude. "Could you please tell Miss Armstrong that I'd appreciate a few moments of her time?"

The man walked off, cake in hand, looking dazed. Behind her, Alexandra heard Peggy try—and fail—to suppress a snort of laughter. Glancing back, she gave her a small smile. She knew it was a bit odd to offer sweets to all and sundry, but the Chase ladies had always done so and been well loved for it, so she wasn't about to stop now.

"He should have invited us in," Peggy said disapprovingly.

"You're right, of course, but I believe he was a bit flustered."

Leticia appeared a minute later, wearing a fashionable black dress—as befitted a daughter in mourning—and approaching with small, graceful steps that A Lady of Distinction would surely approve. Tall and willowy, she had clear green eyes and beautiful flaxen hair swept up in a sophisticated style.

Try as she might, Alexandra couldn't bring herself to hate her. She knew what it felt like to lose a mother, and Leticia looked like a perfectly lovely young lady.

Until she opened her mouth.

"John told me you are Lady Hawkridge?"

"Yes." Alexandra wondered why Leticia's voice should sound so cold. "It's a pleasure to meet you, Miss Armstrong. Please accept my condolences on the loss of your mother."

Curious whether all the footmen here were called John, too, she reached into her basket. "May I offer you a—"

"You're not welcome here."

The sugar cake dropped from Alexandra's fingers. "I beg your pardon?"

"You heard me. The Hawkridge name has been disgraced. Please leave." Leticia began closing the door.

"Wait." Alexandra shoved a hand against the wood. She was reeling with shock, but she'd come here for a purpose. "Have you a maid here by the name of Beth?"

Leticia stared right through her.

"Beth is a dear friend of mine," Peggy said, stepping out from behind Alexandra. "My mistress brought me here to see her." She lowered her voice, sounding pained. "I...have news concerning her family."

Peggy, Alexandra thought, was a consummate actress. She almost had *her* convinced the invented news was dire.

Apparently Leticia did have something approximating a heart, since she nodded at Peggy. "Come inside. I'll fetch Beth."

She pulled Peggy in by the arm and closed the door in Alexandra's face.

Alexandra stood there for a stunned moment, then walked slowly back to the carriage. There was nothing else to do. She climbed inside and waited, fighting the nausea rising in her throat.

Although she'd known she would face difficulties as the wife of a pariah, she hadn't realized how it would feel to be an object of scorn. She'd expected to be whispered about or ignored, of course, but Leticia had really seemed to *despise* her. No one had ever despised her before, not in her entire life!

At least, no one who had said so to her face.

Her heart ached for her sisters. This was the treatment

they would receive, too. And, unlike her, they had no husbands to love, no one to hold at night to make facing the disgrace a little easier.

It seemed forever before Peggy finally came out. "Beth knows nothing," she reported even before she entered the carriage.

"You asked her all the questions?"

"Everything you asked everyone else, my lady." She sat across from Alexandra. "Beth believes Lord Hawkridge died in his sleep."

"Thank you for trying," Alexandra said, her heart sinking even more. It seemed Tris's uncle *had* died in his sleep. And that was going to make it very hard—if not impossible—to prove Tris's innocence.

Very hard—if not impossible—to make life better for Juliana and Corinna.

In her dejected state, the ride home seemed twice as long as the ride out. Peggy, at least, was quite solicitous. "I'm sorry it didn't work out, my lady."

"It's not your fault." Alexandra tried for a grateful smile. "I truly appreciate the way you managed to worm your way in there."

Peggy shrugged. "Miss Armstrong is a witch."

Although Alexandra agreed, she didn't think it would be seemly to say so aloud. But though she knew it was wicked of her, she couldn't help feeling pleased that Miss Armstrong was still *Miss* Armstrong…still unmarried since she'd abandoned Tris.

"I don't like to see your heart in your boots," Peggy said. "Is there anything I can do?"

She really was a dear. "I don't think so. Unless you can remember anyone else who might have worked at Hawkridge and since left."

Peggy frowned for a moment, then shook her head. "I cannot recollect anyone else."

"I think I will talk to everyone again, though, and see if anyone remembers any departed staff members. The possibility hadn't occurred to me before, so I never asked."

The maid was silent a moment. "If you don't mind my saying so, my lady…"

"Yes?" Alexandra knew Peggy had her best interests at heart. "Please, speak freely."

"Well, it's just that I overheard you and his lordship discussing this last night. Not that I was listening, you understand."

"We did raise our voices," Alexandra admitted, chagrined.

"Yes. Well, and don't you expect he might be upset if you talk to everyone again?"

"I'm sure he will be." She sighed. "But I must do this. There's too much at stake." She ran her fingers along the chain that held her cameo. "I shall have to face his wrath and try to make the best of things."

Peggy folded her competent hands in her lap. "I could do it for you."

"Pardon?"

"I could ask all the others and make a list of any departed servants and their current whereabouts, if known. That way you'll have the information without angering his lordship by asking more questions."

"Oh, Peggy, would you?" It was a perfect solution. "I'd be forever grateful."

"Consider it done." Peggy smiled. "It might take me a day or two, mind you, since I'll have to work around my other duties."

"I understand," Alexandra assured her. "I shall be very undemanding until you are finished!"

Once again, Peggy passed the time with a constant stream

of chatter. Although she'd regained a shred of hope, Alexandra felt exhausted by the time they returned home. Perhaps breathing the gas had affected her more than she'd thought, though she was inclined to think it was all the emotional ups and downs of the past few days. In either case, though she never slept in the daytime, she went straight upstairs, changed into Juliana's nightgown, and took a nap.

## FORTY-FOUR

*T*RISTAN ARRIVED home that evening eager to see Alexandra. It wasn't raining. The problem at the gasworks was finally solved. And he was starving.

After poking his head into the most likely ground-floor rooms and failing to find his wife, he took the stairs two at a time, anxious to see how she was faring after this morning's mishap.

If it *had* been a mishap.

But right this moment he didn't want to think about that. He wanted to kiss Alexandra and hear about her day and share the success of his. Preferably over a large and satisfying dinner.

Vincent appeared, as he often did, to meet him outside his bedroom door. "Your lady is sleeping," he said quietly.

Concern—and guilt—slammed into him. "Is she not doing well?"

"Peggy says she's well, my lord, only weary. Shall I arrange for a tray in your room? She may not wish to dress for dinner."

As usual, Vincent knew instinctively what was right.

"An excellent idea." Tristan paused with his hand on the doorknob. "Do you know if she went visiting today?"

"She did. She took the carriage."

That was a relief. If she'd been well enough to carry out her plans to meet the villagers, she couldn't be feeling too poorly. But he wondered how her visits had gone. While the villagers were dependent on him and therefore didn't snub him outright, his relationship with them was rather strained. They didn't like having their lord steeped in scandal

Then again, Alexandra had his servants eating out of her hand—literally—already. Perhaps she could bring the villagers around, too.

"Did Peggy go along with her?" he asked.

"And Ernest as well, my lord. And John Coachman, of course. I mean Charlie," Vincent corrected himself. They shared a smile. "Your lady is making a lot of changes around here, isn't she?"

"Positive ones, I believe." Tristan was gratified to hear Alexandra had followed his directions. He didn't know if he could handle any more excitement today. Now that her blasted investigation was over, he just wanted to see if they could settle into something resembling a marriage.

He turned and reached for the doorknob.

"She's not questioning anyone, either," Vincent added. "I know you were concerned about that, so you'll be pleased to hear that Peggy is doing it instead."

Tristan turned back. "Doing what?"

"Questioning the staff. Peggy came to me earlier, asking if I recalled anyone who might have worked here two years ago but has since left. She's compiling a list for your lady."

"Is she?"

"Yes. Isn't it clever of your wife to widen the search?"

"Quite." No one had ever accused Alexandra of being dull-witted. To the contrary, it seemed she was too bright for her own good. "She's not going to find anything, though. My uncle died in his sleep. Of a broken heart."

"Of course he did. But it's endearing that your lady wishes so much to prove otherwise."

*Endearing,* Tristan thought as he cracked open the door and slipped inside. That wasn't the word he would have chosen. *Exasperating* was more like it.

Why couldn't she stop poking around where she didn't belong?

She slumbered, huddled on her side beneath the covers, a small lump in his big bed. It occurred to him that now was his chance to dump her onto the floor. But he couldn't do it. Upset as he was to learn she was still pursuing her folly, after nearly losing her this morning he couldn't summon the anger he'd felt last night.

But dread of what she might find…*that* he could summon quite handily.

The room was dim but not yet dark. He walked over and stood by the bed. Her even features were outlined against the white sheets like the profile portrait she'd made of him so long ago.

"Alexandra," he called softly, half expecting her to sleep on like she had earlier. A hint of that panic came back, the terror he'd felt when he couldn't awaken her.

This time, though, she opened her eyes and yawned. "Tris?" she murmured sleepily.

She would never know how endearing he found it when she called him that. Yes, *endearing.* Stubborn fiend though she was.

"Are you hungry?" he asked.

"Not really." She struggled to sit up against the pillows. "How did everything go at the gasworks?"

"Very well. The construction is back on track." He sat

beside her on the mattress, his weight on the featherbed making her tilt toward him. "How was your day, then?"

"Disappointing." She sighed. "Mrs. Pawley recollected a scullery maid who'd left for Armstrong House to take a better position. I went—"

"You went to Armstrong House?" He blinked. "I thought you were going to the village."

"I *was* going to the village—I even made sugar cakes to take with me—until I learned about Beth." He thought he saw guilt darken her features, but it was immediately replaced by other emotions he couldn't read. "Then, when I got to Armstrong House, Miss Armstrong wouldn't let me in the door. Peggy had to talk to Beth instead." She swallowed hard. "I must confess, I didn't like your Miss Armstrong much."

"I don't care for her much, either," he said dryly, taking note of her furrowed brow and clouded eyes. She was more upset by the rejection than she was letting on. It was on the tip of his tongue to suggest that Leticia was merely acting out on old resentment, or say she had an exceptionally cruel nature—to assure his sweet, innocent, new Lady Hawkridge that she wouldn't have to face this sort of contempt every time she walked out her front door. He wanted to lie.

But she'd discover the truth before long.

She would get used to this treatment—and much worse—eventually. He knew she had strength and confidence and faith enough to survive it. He was less sure *he* could survive seeing her hurt over and over, and knowing all the time that he was the cause of her pain.

He could only hope—though it felt more like dread—that he wouldn't have to watch her suffering long. Whatever love she believed she felt for him would no doubt fade quickly under the strain. And when she returned to her senses, she'd return to her family.

It was only a matter of time.

"You shouldn't have gone there," he said with more regret than anger.

Guilt flashed again, this time followed by determination. "I had to find out if Beth had any information, Tris, don't you see?"

He didn't see. Or rather, he saw all too well that she wouldn't stop digging up his past, threatening his hard-won equilibrium, no matter what he did. He scooped a hand through his hair. "I thought you said it was over."

"You cannot expect me to ignore new information. I've asked Peggy to find out if there are any more servants who have left as well. If there's any chance—"

"I want you to stop."

"I cannot." She sighed. "I'm sorry. It's too important. This is our *life* and the lives of my sisters. We're married for better or worse, but I cannot help trying to make it better."

He sat silent for a moment, trying to accept that. It wasn't easy. If she continued asking questions, neither of them were going to be happy with the answers. But at least she was being honest. He hadn't known she'd been to Armstrong House, and she'd volunteered the information. She wasn't trying to hide anything, wasn't sneaking around behind his back.

Of course she wasn't. She was Alexandra.

"I don't want to fight," he said finally, determined to shake off his dejection. When he rode up to the house, he'd been so eager to see her. There was no sense ruining the entire evening. If their time together was limited—by her inevitable leaving—he wanted to enjoy her company while he could. "I'm very disappointed that you're not willing to let go of this. But I don't want another fight."

Her eyes grew misty, which cut him to the core, because he'd never seen Alexandra cry. "I don't want to fight, either."

A knock came at the door, and Vincent entered with their dinner tray. Or rather, two trays. And then he brought in a third. Mrs. Pawley had sent up a veritable feast. Alexandra composed herself and Tristan lit the gas lamps while Vincent put everything in the sitting room. The valet ducked back into the corridor to fetch a fourth tray holding a bottle of Hawkridge's wine, two glasses, plates, and cutlery. "Will there be anything else, my lord?"

"Thank you, Vincent." Tristan saw him back to the door. "This will do."

"This will do?" Alexandra asked when they were alone again. "There's enough food here to feed the entire household!"

"Well, come fix yourself a plate."

Shaking her head, she slid out of bed and made for the sitting room.

Following her, he stared, incredulous. "*What* are you wearing?"

"The nightgown I borrowed from Juliana." She stopped and twirled in the monstrosity, making yards and yards of white fabric and lace bell out and swirl about her. "Do you like it?" she asked, sounding a bit hesitant. "I know it's too short on me, but my own nightgowns are so plain, I thought you would prefer this."

His gaze traveled from the frilly ruffle beneath her chin to the four rows of tiered lace skimming her ankles. The wide sleeves were gathered at the wrist with a six-inch spill of froth that completely concealed her hands. But the worst of it was the body of the gown—there was so much material, he feared he could get smothered in it.

Speechless, he decided to offer her a plate instead of a response. Experience had taught him never to criticize a girl's clothes.

There was fish, roast duck, lamb cutlets, artichoke

bottoms, mushrooms, green peas, boiled cauliflower, plum pudding, apricot fritters, and bread. Alexandra took an artichoke bottom, three mushrooms, a small piece of bread, and some butter.

"That's all?" Tristan asked.

"I told you I'm not hungry."

Setting his plate aside, he laid a hand on her forehead. "Are you ill?"

"No. Just tired."

"Get in bed."

"With my food?"

"People eat breakfast in bed, don't they? Why not dinner?"

After she was settled against the pillows, he poured two glasses of wine and handed her one. She took a cautious sip.

"I'm going to stay home tomorrow," he said, divesting himself of his coat and cravat.

"Hmm," she said pleasantly, sipping again.

He unbuttoned his waistcoat and shrugged out of it. "I have a lot of paperwork to catch up on. And journal entries to record." He made short work of removing his braces, then loosened his cuffs and undid the buttons at the top of his shirt. "I'm weeks behind on that sort of business."

She licked her lips. "I suppose that's Griffin's fault."

"You said so, not me." He noticed her watching his activities with interest. Smiling to himself, he sat beside her on the bed to remove his boots. "It's just something I need to take care of."

"It will be nice to have you here," she said.

He felt her gaze still lingering on him as he peeled off his stockings. Looking up at her, he grinned. She gulped the rest of her wine and let him take the glass from her hand and set it on the bedside table.

"Eat," he said, pointing to the untouched plate on her lap. She nodded and reached blindly for her fork.

He walked through the sitting room to the dressing room, thinking—rather smugly—that a fellow appreciated a girl who could appreciate him. He could tell his wife was anticipating the evening ahead. But first things first. His stomach rumbled, while Mrs. Pawley's lovely dinner was going cold. Throwing on a dressing gown, he returned to the sitting room and filled a plate for himself. A generous helping of everything—after all, he would need his strength.

He took his plate back to the bedroom, planning to tell Alexandra as much and enjoy her shock.

She was sound asleep, her head lolling on the pillows.

"Alexandra?" He took the tray off her lap and set it aside. "Alexandra?" She slumbered on. He inhaled deeply to detect the telltale smell of a gas leak.

Not even a whiff.

He ate his dinner and tried again to wake her, shaking her shoulder this time. "Alexandra?" Still no luck.

He turned off all the gaslights. Then went back and double-checked them all. And triple-checked. "Alexandra?"

She was out cold.

He couldn't remember the last time he'd gone to sleep this early. But he climbed into bed beside her, pulled her against him...and held her all night.

## FORTY-FIVE

"WHAT IN heaven's name is that noise?" Alexandra asked the next morning at breakfast.

"Rex. I left him asleep in the study." Her husband gestured toward the connecting door. "I told you he snores."

"He's louder than your ram pumps," she marveled as a footman poured her tea. "I'm surprised he hasn't wakened us in the night."

"Nothing could have wakened *you* last night." She'd never seen Tris roll his eyes before. "I won't be giving you any more wine at bedtime," he declared.

"I cannot blame you for that." She didn't remember falling asleep, and she'd awakened to find herself alone. But the sheets had still held his scent, and she'd been aware all night of his arm encircling her, his body curled against her back. "I was sorry to see you gone when I woke."

"I woke to find myself in the kitchen," he admitted, disgruntled.

"On the floor?"

"No. Just standing there, eating one of your sugar cakes."

"Stealing sweets in the night again?" she teased over the continuing rumble of the mastiff's snores. "See, you sleep-walked, and nothing bad happened."

Tris gave her a look over his coffee. "We were talking about you dozing off on me," he retorted.

She felt her cheeks warm. "I can only drink half a glass of wine. Any more and I—"

"Fall asleep?" he provided with a raised brow.

"Or get very, very silly."

He speared a bite of ham, looking thoughtful as he chewed and swallowed. "I cannot imagine you silly; that would truly be a sight. However, I'm not sure I'm willing to risk you falling asleep in order to see it."

Two thunderous snorts came from the adjoining room, followed by blessed silence. Rex must have rolled over. Smiling, Alexandra reached for the jam pot. "Did you make a dent in your work this morning?"

"A rather large dent, as a matter of fact. I may even find time to get out and take care of some business later in Windsor." He sprinkled salt on his eggs, watching her spread jam on her toast. "It won't take long. I promise to be back in time for dinner."

"I'm not passing judgment on you. I know you have much to do, thanks in part to my brother."

She also knew she wasn't offering him much incentive to remain home, given the way she insisted on defying his wishes. She feared he might have begun pulling away, distancing himself from her emotionally.

She set down her knife. "I have much to do as well," she said, watching him frown at the jam pot. She wished he would look at her. She was trying her best to be cooperative. "I'm meeting this morning with Mrs. Oliver to go over—"

"No!" His hand darted out and snatched the toast from hers.

She blinked. "Tris?"

"It's strawberry." He swiped a finger across her toast and licked, turning ashen as he confirmed it. "Strawberry preserves, not cherry."

"Dear heavens." Her heart pumping wildly, she realized the skin on the side of her index finger felt prickly. Spotting a telltale streak of red preserves there, she quickly wiped it off. "I should have looked," she said, searching her hands for other traces of jam. Finding none, she released a tense breath.

When she glanced up, Tris had gone even whiter beneath his tan. "I must have switched the preserves in the jam pot." He scraped rigid fingers through his hair. "I've done it again —I'm trying to hurt you in my sleep."

"You are *not*." She didn't know which she found more disturbing: discovering strawberries on her toast, or his assumption that he was at fault. "It's a long way from eating a sugar cake to switching the contents of a jam pot. I'm certain this was an honest mistake. A kitchen maid who didn't know better must have refilled the pot."

"No. Mrs. Pawley assured me she would tell everyone you cannot eat strawberries. It was no mistake. I—"

"Do you even know where the jam pot is kept?" she interrupted. "Or the preserves?"

He paused a moment. "I must have hunted around."

"In your sleep? I think not. Mrs. Pawley must have neglected to inform someone—not deliberately, of course, but in error." Who knew how often the woman nipped from the sherry bottle? "Let's call in the kitchen staff and get to the bottom of this."

A few minutes later, the dining room was crowded with kitchen maids, scullery maids, and the small boys who did odd jobs belowstairs. Mrs. Pawley looked perfectly sober— and extremely concerned. Hastings stood solemnly in the back, watching the proceedings. Mrs. Oliver did the questioning.

"Did you know Lady Hawkridge cannot eat strawberries?"

"Yes, Mrs. Oliver."

"I did, Mrs. Oliver."

"Mrs. Pawley made that clear, Mrs. Oliver."

"And did you refill the jam pot or see anyone else do so?"

"No, Mrs. Oliver."

"I didn't, Mrs. Oliver."

"Absolutely not."

It went on and on, so long that Alexandra began to suffer from the headache, especially because all the denials were only strengthening Tris's delusional assumptions. At long last, everyone shuffled out.

"It was me," Tris said in a dull, resigned tone.

"Don't be ridiculous," she returned crossly, rubbing her temples. "One of them refilled the pot. I'm not surprised no one would own up to it and risk being dismissed."

Someone else *had* to have done it. She knew, deep in her bones, that an honorable, compassionate man like Tris couldn't do anything to harm her—or anyone else. Not even in his sleep.

She reached across the table to lay her hand over his. "You're only sleepwalking because you're anxious. You said that's when it happens, didn't you? It's a pattern. And as I've said before, I think there's another pattern at work here as well. You do things when you sleepwalk that you wish you could do while awake. Like kiss me or steal more sweets than you're entitled to."

It was a pretty theory, but Tristan wasn't convinced, let alone at all mollified. "You can argue that I went to the kitchen in the night for sweets. But your pattern theory doesn't explain why I would leave a gas line open."

"You didn't. Or at least, not on purpose. You got up—and perhaps dealt with the gaslight in some way since it had been left on—and took yourself downstairs to sleep in your study. I had angered you by questioning your staff against your wishes, so you were separating yourself from me in the night."

Had he really wanted to get away from her that night? He hadn't thought so. But even if her assessment was valid, there was another plausible explanation—another pattern in his sleep. One of mayhem. Violence.

Murder.

"It's the pressure," she said, squeezing his hand. "As soon as we clear your name, you'll be fine. I'd wager you'll never sleepwalk again."

He looked at her for a long moment, searching her eyes while a strained silence stretched between them. His gaze dropped to the cameo she wore on a chain around her neck.

His cameo. She'd take it off someday. Maybe someday soon.

"I'd feel a lot less pressure if you'd call off this blasted investigation," he said at last, pushing away from the table. "I'm going back to work."

## FORTY-SIX

*T*HERE WERE times in a woman's married life when she wished she could confer with her sisters. Even though she already knew exactly what they would say.

Juliana, the peacemaker, would tell her to abide by her husband's wishes. "Your marriage ought to come first," she would say, and advise Alexandra to be the dutiful wife and put Tris's happiness and their relationship before her own desire to right past wrongs.

Corinna, on the other hand—the rebel—would cheer on her efforts. "You're entitled to your convictions," she would say, and advise Alexandra to stand to her guns and let no one, not even her husband, sway her from doing what she thought best.

And Alexandra would be right back where she'd started. But at least she'd have some hugs and sympathy to bolster her. Here in this strange house, with Tris occupied most of the time, and no neighbors willing to welcome her—a point Leticia had driven home yesterday—she was beginning to feel lonely.

Still, the first part of her morning had proven quite

productive. She and Mrs. Oliver had gone over the household budget, reviewed the cleaning and repair schedules, and discussed all the lower female servants. Everything seemed well in hand. She'd left their meeting assured that Mrs. Oliver was a fine housekeeper indeed.

Afterward, she practiced on the harpsichord in the north drawing room for a while. It wasn't hard to play, but the double keyboard would take some getting used to. The sound was also different, thinner than a pianoforte's, and there seemed to be no way to play louder or softer. Although she was by no means a concert-quality pianist, she did enjoy putting some emotion into her pieces. But there were no pedals, and no matter how she hit the keys—tentatively or with great force—the resulting notes sounded the same. She wearied of it rather quickly.

Next she considered visiting in the village, but she wanted to take Peggy along to introduce her to everyone, and she'd prefer to have Peggy here, talking to the rest of the staff and compiling the list. The villagers would be there to meet another day. Pursuing the investigation was more important, and even more urgent given this morning's events. Quite apart from her sisters' future woes, her husband was miserable *now*, and apparently dead set on tormenting himself unless and until he was given irrefutable proof of his innocence—preferably hand-delivered on a silver platter and tied up with ribbons, she grumbled privately.

What the man really deserved was to have his ears boxed, but since she was trying to *save* her marriage, she would keep that opinion to herself.

And still more dire was the fact that the longer she continued her efforts—continued flouting her husband's wishes—the greater the threat to their relationship. She needed to fix this fast, and, in the meantime, somehow manage to stay on Tris's good side.

To that end, she decided to peek into the study and ask him to join her for luncheon.

But he wasn't there. Disappointed, she sat at his desk, idly straightening piles of papers and stacks of journals. He *had* told her he had business that might take him away for a while. It would have been nice, though, if he'd sought her out to let her know he was leaving.

She shrugged philosophically, turning the chair to gaze out the study's windows. Obviously, she still hadn't scaled that wall Tris had built, and she'd probably doubled the height with her own actions.

The study was in the back of the house, and through the windows the gardens beckoned—colorful formal gardens nearby, and then, behind them, an area of grass walks lined with hornbeam hedges and field maples that seemed to enclose smaller, private gardens. It was a glorious day, and she'd yet to explore them.

She decided she'd eat her luncheon out there. And take along some paper and her family's cookbook, so she could copy her favorite recipes while enjoying the sunshine.

A few minutes later, having grabbed a bonnet and arranged for luncheon, she made her way out the front door and down the steps, following the cobbled path that curved around the back of the mansion. A flash of motion by the river made her pause.

Tris.

She watched him toss a stick and Rex jump into the river to retrieve it. Mere moments later, the big, wet mastiff scrambled up the bank and shook violently, spraying Tris with water that left splotches on his buff pantaloons.

Thinking she'd be tempted to laugh if she wasn't so uncertain of his feelings, she hurried toward him. "What are you doing?" she called.

To her relief, Tris looked over and smiled. "Playing with

the poor beast. He's been dreadfully neglected of late." He eyed the book and paper in her hands. "What are *you* doing?"

"I was going to take luncheon in the gardens and copy some of my favorite recipes. Would you care to join me?"

"I'm sorry, but I cannot." Rex was panting at his feet. He bent to grab the stick and tossed it arcing out over the water, watching as the mastiff gleefully splashed in to fetch it. "I have business in Windsor."

She wondered vaguely what he needed to do. She knew Windsor was the nearest sizable town, but did he have his bank there? His solicitor? She'd expect those would be in London. She needed to learn these things if he wanted her to assist with the household finances as she had for Griffin, but they had yet to discuss anything like that.

And now was not the time. "When I couldn't find you," she said, "I thought you'd gone already."

"Without telling you? I'm hurt you'd presume me so thoughtless." Obviously reading her face, he reached to pull her close. "And you were hurt thinking I had. I'm sorry." He tilted her bonnet back and bent to place a soft kiss on her mouth.

Emerging from the water, Rex barked. "He hates me," she said.

"He doesn't." Tris took the stick from the dog's teeth and tossed it once more, farther out this time. "If he hated you, he'd have taken a bite out of you by now."

While Rex bounded back into the river, Tris took the book and papers from her and set them on the grass, then wrapped his arms around her and brought his lips to hers again. "I missed you last night," he murmured against her mouth. She slipped her hands under his coat, mindless of his damp, dog-splashed clothes. Her heart began to race, the blood rushing through her veins.

And she knew it was the same for him.

She was confused and unsure of his feelings from one moment to the next, but one thing she knew for certain: the spark between them would never go out.

Rex barked until they stopped kissing, then shook and sprayed them both. Alexandra laughed. Tris brushed ruefully at his damp coat. "I really must be going, and I fear Vincent won't let me off the property without a bath and a change of clothing. I promise to be home in time for dinner." He gave her another quick kiss, eliciting another bark, then started toward the house, the dog following at his heels. "Enjoy your afternoon," he called back.

Feeling warmed and reassured, Alexandra picked up her things and ambled around the house and through the formal gardens. Gravel crunched beneath her feet as she followed the paths bordering beds planted with brilliantly colored flowers. Finally she reached the area of grass walks that she'd seen, lined with hedges that enclosed many small, private compartments.

She smiled as she peeked into them, glimpsing not only a variety of rather wild-growing plants, but also a surprise in each area. Some hid copies of famous statuary, one a sundial, another a cozy bench for two. Choosing one with a tiny round white gazebo, she slid inside.

The structure's roof offered welcome shade, so she removed her bonnet and set it, along with her book, paper, and pencil, on the bench that curved against the back edge. No sooner had she taken a seat than a warm, motherly voice carried through the still summer air. "Lady Hawkridge?"

Alexandra rose and went to the opening. "Here, Mrs. Oliver!" she called, surprised that the housekeeper was bringing her luncheon personally. "In the gazebo!"

A moment later, Mrs. Oliver entered the tiny garden. But she didn't have any food. Instead she carried a small stack of letters. "I thought you might want these right away, my lady."

Alexandra took them and flipped through the pile. There were six, one from each of her siblings and female cousins. Thrilled, she smiled at Mrs. Oliver. "Thank you so very much."

"Enjoy them, dear," the housekeeper said and walked away.

With a happy sigh, Alexandra went back to the bench. She opened the two letters from her sisters first. Juliana and Corinna had both written cheerful notes, wishing her well and relating several amusing anecdotes as well as telling her all about a lovely picnic they'd shared with their cousins. Griffin's letter was shorter, mostly saying he missed her very much and threatening bodily harm to her husband should he fail to take good care of her. Rachael told her all about the goings-on at Greystone and her preparations for her brother Noah's return. Claire's letter mentioned the picnic again. And then Alexandra opened the letter from her youngest cousin, Elizabeth.

*We all miss you very much. It was Rachael's idea we should have the picnic, and also her idea that we should all write to you so you won't feel lonely in your new home. Wasn't that so very nice?*

Alexandra had been wondering how it was that six letters had arrived the same day. Grinning, she read on.

*I suppose you've heard that Juliana and Corinna were DISinvited to Lady Cunnington's country garden party. I vow and swear, that made me so livid I wrote to Lady C posthaste with my regrets—and a piece of my mind. Worry not, dear cousin, your sisters have much support. Rachael and Claire have said they will not attend, either.*

The letter fluttered from her fingers to the grass. Good heavens, it was happening already. And not only affecting her sisters, but her cousins, too.

Her throat tightened like it did when she ate strawberries, her breaths growing rapid and shallow.

A high-pitched voice snapped her to attention. "Lady Hawkridge?"

She quickly gathered the letters. "Here, Peggy! In the gazebo!"

Peggy hurried into the little garden, tray in hand. "Your luncheon, my lady." She squeezed into the tiny structure and set the tray on the bench, then pulled a folded paper out of her bodice. "And the list you asked for, completed."

"Oh!" Alexandra's breathing calmed as she took it. Once she cleared Tris's name, her sisters would be just fine. But she was disappointed to see only four entries. "Is this all?"

"Most prefer to remain at Hawkridge, my lady. Kinder employers are difficult to find."

"I know." And she knew she should be happy about that. She *was* happy. Just seeing the list was a huge relief. "Thank you. And for writing down everyone's direction as well. They all live close by."

Peggy shrugged. "Not many travel too far from the place of their birth."

People usually seemed more comfortable with the familiar. Which was a lucky thing, Alexandra thought, because she should be able to pay calls on these four in short order. Her spirits rose as she realized that, very soon, she might have the information she needed.

Her appetite had evaporated, but since Peggy went to the trouble of fetching luncheon, she thought she'd better eat something. "Let me just have a few bites, and then we'll be off. I want to ride today. It will be much faster than the carriage. Would you ask a groom to saddle three horses? And see if Ernest is free to accompany us again, if you will. Oh, and ask Mrs. Pawley to put some of my sugar cakes in a basket. Then meet me upstairs—I'll need to change into a riding habit, and so will you."

Peggy shuffled her feet. "I cannot ride, my lady."

"Pardon? I'll be pleased to give you a habit if you have none. I've one or two I'd like to retire. I plan to order some that aren't blue," she added with a soft laugh at herself.

But Peggy showed no signs of humor. "I cannot ride. I don't know how. As a housemaid I never had reason to learn, and the last Lady Hawkridge never rode anywhere. She was very proper and always took a carriage."

"Is that so?" Perhaps riding to pay calls wasn't strictly ladylike—A Lady of Distinction would probably cluck her tongue—but Alexandra had no time to waste. "Make it two horses, then. Ernest and I shall do fine on our own."

"Are you certain, my lady?" Peggy didn't look at all happy. "I believe his lordship would prefer you to take a carriage."

"Nonsense—he said that only because he was afraid breathing the gas had weakened me. I'm perfectly recovered by now." And the sooner she finished this investigation, the happier Tris would be—no matter what the outcome.

"I'd prefer to go with you," her maid said quite peevishly.

Alexandra couldn't figure why the woman would be so testy, but she decided to ignore it. "That's very thoughtful, Peggy, but there's no need. Two horses, please. I'll meet you upstairs in ten minutes."

# FORTY-SEVEN

*D*ELICATE NOTES from the harpsichord greeted
Tristan when he arrived home that evening.
Carrying the large, plain box he'd brought from Windsor, he
made his way upstairs and paused in the north drawing
room's doorway.

Alexandra sat with her back to him, focused on some
sheet music, her graceful fingers moving over the antique
instrument's keys. Watching her, he clutched the box tighter.
He hoped she would like what was in it.

Despite the promising intimacy of their wedding night,
lately everything between them seemed to be going so very
wrong. He wanted to give her a perfect night. Just one perfect
night.

And, all right, it wouldn't be so bad if the perfection
extended into tomorrow and the next day, too.

As he watched, she raised a hand from the lower
keyboard to the upper and hit a sour note. "Drat," she said
softly and resumed. More notes tinkled through the air,
sounding lovely for a few bars until she switched keyboards
again and made another mistake. "Drat!"

"Good evening, sweetheart."

She startled and snatched her fingers from the keys, turning on the stool to face him. "You're home," she said, sounding surprised.

"I said I would be."

Her cheeks turned a delicate pink. "I hope you didn't hear too much of that. I'm sure I'll get better with practice."

"There's no need to practice," he said cryptically, knowing she'd understand tomorrow. Already dressed for dinner, she looked beautiful in a pale green frock with a scooped neckline and his cameo on a matching green ribbon. She glanced curiously at the box in his hands, making him smile to himself. "Give me ten minutes to allow Vincent to fuss over me before dinner. Will you meet me in the dining room?"

"All right," she said, her gaze lingering on the box before she turned back to attack the keyboard with renewed vigor.

A quarter of an hour later, having instructed Vincent as to the box, he strolled into the dining room and bent to give Alexandra a thorough kiss. As he seated himself beside her, she blushed, her gaze going to the two footmen in the room.

"They didn't see or hear anything," he assured her in a whisper, and then louder, "How was your afternoon?"

"Peggy gave me the list of former servants," she said rather breathlessly. One of the footmen put a bowl of soup before her, and she lifted her spoon, the simple motion seeming to calm her. "Four names. I visited three of them and learned nothing."

He spooned some soup, wondering how he would get it into his mouth between his clenched teeth. But he wanted this to be a perfect night, so all he said was, "I wish you hadn't done that."

"I know." Somehow she managed to look both sorry and determined at the same time. "If it's any consolation, there's only one name left. A woman in Swangate. Unless she astounds me by being the only one to have seen suspicious dealings, I'll be finished after I talk to her."

Although she sounded mournful, he couldn't help celebrating privately. And he certainly didn't want to argue and ruin the night ahead. Instead, he made light conversation through the next two courses, his blood humming with anticipation.

At last the table was cleared. Hastings brought in and opened a bottle of port. A footman presented a platter of fruit and biscuits. No sooner had they departed when Mrs. Oliver walked in, placed the box—now gaily wrapped and ribboned—at the far end of the table, and promptly left.

Tristan poured Alexandra a very tiny glass of port—he didn't want her falling asleep tonight. He poured himself a larger one.

Alexandra glanced at the box, then lifted his empty dessert plate. "Grapes? Biscuits?"

"Surprise me," he said, impatient to surprise *her*. He sipped, savoring the heady flavor of the fine, sweet wine and enjoying the poorly concealed curiosity on his wife's face.

She filled his plate and took a single biscuit for herself. "How was your afternoon?" she asked, her gaze drifting again to the box.

"Extremely successful."

She took a small sip of the deep red port. "Your business in Windsor went well?"

"Exceedingly."

She hadn't touched her biscuit. "Would you mind if I asked what you did there?"

"Not at all." He popped a grape into his mouth, enjoying this exchange immensely. "I visited the shops." Seeing her startled gaze fly toward the box once more, he smiled to himself again. He seemed to be doing a lot of that tonight. "Would you like to open it?"

"Is it for me?" A tinge of excitement threaded her voice. "This was your business?"

He loved seeing her transparent joy. He hadn't given her enough since he'd brought her home. "Part of my business. Another parcel will arrive tomorrow." He moved the platter to make more room near her on the table, then rose, fetched the box, and placed it in the space he'd created. "Open it," he said, lifting his glass as he sat again.

The box was so large she couldn't see into it while seated. Slowly she pushed back her chair, stood, and untied the ribbon. The paper fell open, and she raised the lid, set it aside, and reached inside with both hands to part the tissue that protected the contents.

"Ooooh," she breathed.

"Take it out."

She did, lifting it by its handle. Polished silver gleamed in the gaslight. "A basket," she said reverently. "A...basket of silver?"

"Pure sterling," he confirmed. "For your sweets. The Marchioness of Hawkridge's specialties deserve much better than wicker." He sipped, watching her marvel at the gift. "It won't be too heavy to carry with you when you go visiting, will it?"

"No." She clutched it like she might never let it go. "It has a glass liner," she informed him as though he might not know.

"You wouldn't want to be trailing crumbs."

She still stood there, slowly turning it this way and that, watching the light bounce off. "It's the most beautiful thing I've ever seen."

"I'm glad you like it," he said, although *glad* seemed a very tame word. *Thrilled* would be more accurate. He'd wanted so much to find the perfect gift. He *hated* visiting shops—Vincent ordered all his clothes—but he'd walked round dozens of them all afternoon, being fussed over by every shopkeeper in Windsor. It had been his worst nightmare come true.

But her reaction made it worth it.

She was looking a bit overcome, so he rose and moved behind her to scoot her chair toward the back of her knees. "Sit!"

She lowered herself gingerly, holding the basket on her lap, her fingers tracing the chased and pierced embellishments, the floral swags and raised ribbons and bows all fashioned out of fine, delicate silver.

He moved the box from the table to the floor by her chair, where she could reach into it. "There are more gifts inside," he announced gleefully.

She was testing the basket's fancy handle, folding it down and back up. "There's more?" She looked up, dewy-eyed. "Why...when you have so much to do, why would you spend your day doing this for me?"

Because he wanted to give her a perfect night.

Perhaps that was an oversimplification.

Because he'd do whatever he could to make her happy, but he couldn't say the words she needed to hear. Because he'd do anything to make her stay, but his own deficiencies were the reason she should go. Because some foolish part of him was hoping against hope that a silly little trinket and one nice evening would be enough to make up for everything else.

But he couldn't say any of that. Not tonight.

"Because you deserve it," he said instead.

"I do not," she said, her voice thick. "I defy you at every turn."

"Every other turn," he disagreed agreeably. "At the alternate turns, you delight me."

She sighed and reached into the box, pulling out a book

bound in fine leather dyed robin's-egg blue. The cover was embossed with gold designs, the pages edged with gold leaf. "This is lovely," she said through an obviously tight throat.

"It's blank inside. For your recipes. After you copy the ones you like, I thought you could start your own tradition. Our family could add to it every year."

"Our family," she echoed softly, not quite meeting his gaze. She set the book aside and pulled the next item from the box, her eyes widening as the fabric unfolded. "Heavens above, what is this?"

"A nightgown," he said.

At that moment, two footmen returned to clear their dishes. Her cheeks burning, she stuffed the garment back into the box and plopped the book on top. "It's lovely, too," she said quickly, sounding uncertain.

It took everything he had not to laugh. "Shall we take it upstairs and have a closer look?"

He couldn't wait to see her in it.

## FORTY-EIGHT

*T*HE **NIGHTGOWN** was only the first of the garments in the box. There were *seven* nightgowns, in fact—one for each day of the week—of delicate silk, lovely georgette, and beautiful tiffany. As Alexandra pulled them out, she draped them on the bed. She'd never seen a nightgown that wasn't white, but these were almond and pale blush pink, powder blue and soft peach, with delicate edgings of lace and intricate, exquisite embroidery.

"They're stunning," she said. "Madame Rodale has nothing like them in her book of fashion plates."

Tris just grinned.

He seemed different tonight. More relaxed, less worried. She didn't know what had prompted his sudden good humor, but she didn't want to question it. She'd rather enjoy it instead.

After the afternoon she'd had—starting with Elizabeth's letter and ending with three fruitless interviews—she wasn't about to risk the one thing that seemed to be going right.

"Are you going to try one on for me?" he asked.

Her face heated.

He chose a nightgown off the bed, palest lavender with black lace and violet embroidery. "This one," he said, handing it to her. "Do you require assistance with your dress?"

"Just the buttons," she said, and turned to let him unfasten them. She shifted the nightgown in her hands. It felt so light.

"There," he said when the back of her green dress gaped open. He kissed her softly on the nape of her neck, then settled on one of the striped chairs, sipping from the glass of port he'd brought upstairs with him. "Use the dressing room. I'll be waiting."

In the dressing room, she shakily stripped out of her frock, chemise, shoes, and stockings, then dropped the nightgown over her head and smoothed it down over her hips. The fabric whispered against her legs. She turned to see herself in the looking glass.

Sweet heaven. She'd never imagined nightgowns like this existed.

Her nightgowns all had high collars that tied at the throat. This one had a wide, low neckline. Her nightgowns all had long, full sleeves. This one had tiny puffed sleeves that began halfway off her shoulders. Her nightgowns were made of yards and yards of thick, billowing fabric. This one was a slender column that left no curve to the imagination.

It was wicked.

"Are you ready yet?" Tris called.

Alexandra swallowed hard, reminding herself that he'd seen her in less clothing. And he *was* her husband. Still, wearing the nightgown for him somehow felt more intimate than wearing nothing at all.

She was as ready as she'd ever be.

Drawing a deep breath, she exited the dressing room, walked quickly through the sitting room, and paused in the bedroom's doorway. She dropped her gaze, then raised her lashes, giving him *the look*—the one Juliana had said would make men fall at her feet.

Judging from the expression on Tris's face, it was a good thing he was sitting.

The way he looked at her made her heartbeat accelerate. He rose and moved toward her. She met him halfway, licking suddenly dry lips. "Will you kiss me?" she asked softly, reaching up to sweep that always unruly lock off his forehead.

It worked this time. He kissed her but good.

~

*T*HIS—THE two of them completely alone, truly together, all obstacles cast aside—was the one part of Tristan's life that could never be tainted. He'd never felt closer to anyone, body and spirit, than he did now, in the bed he shared with his wife. He was suffused with Alexandra. He was drowning in her. She was everything.

But as soon as it was over, everything else came rushing back.

He lingered as long as he could, recovering his breath as he kissed her forehead, both cheeks, her nose. "I need to go now," he whispered before settling on her mouth.

"Hmm?" she murmured when he finally allowed them both to come up for air.

"I'm going to sleep in the Queen's Bedchamber. Vincent will lock me in."

She blinked hard, her soft mouth falling open. "You're going to *leave*?"

"Just until morning," he promised as he rose from the bed. "It's for your own protection. If I sleepwalk again, I don't want to be able to leave the room. I don't want to be able to get to you or to anything that might harm you."

"I don't want protection from you, Tris." He'd never heard such hurt and disbelief in her voice. It made his insides shrivel. "I want you here with me. Didn't tonight mean anything to you? Didn't it prove how much we mean to each other? And yet you still think yourself capable of wishing me harm?"

"I don't know—all I know is if there's any *shred* of a chance that I'm a danger to you, I cannot stay. How could I? What kind of man would that make me?"

She offered no answer, but her big, round eyes were silently pleading. They were going to destroy him, those eyes. Destroy his resolve, and snap the tenuous thread holding his life—and his marriage—together.

Before that could happen, he left.

## FORTY-NINE

*A*LEXANDRA LAY in her marriage bed, stunned. And alone.

She could scarcely believe Tris had left her. Not tonight. Her gaze went to the lovely lavender nightgown, to the silver basket and the beautiful book beside it. Presents, she knew, from his heart.

Perhaps he couldn't bring himself to say it out loud, but only love could drive him to spend a whole afternoon choosing such perfect gifts. Gifts that demonstrated careful thought. Gifts that showed he understood her. Gifts that fit *her*, specifically, not any other girl.

Well, with the possible exception of the wicked night-gowns. But she didn't want to think about other girls those might fit.

Of course, he'd left for Windsor before learning she'd gone off to interview three former servants. Perhaps he wouldn't have bought beautiful things for her if he'd known what she was up to. Had he really left her alone in bed as a protective measure? Or was he drawing away because he was angry? She didn't truly believe it was the latter, but how could she know for sure?

Oh, hang it. If he could jump to foolhardy conclusions, so could she.

And she wanted answers now. *And* she wasn't the type of person to sit and wait for those answers to come to her. Or lie in bed and wait for them, either. She was the type of person who went out and found answers for herself.

One would think her husband might have figured that out by now.

If he thought she'd just accept his decision and meekly go to sleep, he'd best think again.

She rose and washed up, then wiggled back into the lavender nightgown, in case she had to resort to seducing him to get him to talk. A few more kisses wouldn't be unwelcome, either, come to think of it. But business would have to come first.

After covering the nightgown with a very modest wrapper, she brushed her tangled hair and pinned the front off her face, then made her way from the room.

No sooner had she opened the door than Rex came trotting up and followed her down the corridor to the Queen's Bedchamber.

She knocked briskly on the queen's fancy gilded door. "Tris?"

Rex barked.

"I'm sleeping," Tris said.

Alexandra rolled her eyes. She knew he was lying— because if he were sleeping, he wouldn't have answered her, would he? Besides, he obviously wasn't in bed. She could hear him quite clearly, as though he were right on the other side of the door.

"I want to talk to you," she said.

"We'll talk in the morning."

She wondered whether he was sitting or standing. Whether he was upright or leaning against the door. "I want to talk now."

Rex barked again, adding his own demand.

But Tris was having none of it. His heavy sigh emanated from the room. "The door is locked, and only Vincent has the key."

"I'll get it from him, then. I want to talk. And I want you to come back to bed." She imagined him lying beneath the turquoise and gold canopy with the absurd ostrich-feather poufs at its four corners. "You hate this room."

"I'd hate hurting you even more. Vincent has gone to sleep—you're not to bother him. Go to bed, Alexandra."

"No," she said. She needed the door opened in order to entice him with the wicked nightgown. But she wouldn't bother Vincent. For one thing, she hadn't the slightest idea where the man slept. She needed to schedule another appointment with Mrs. Oliver to beg a tour of the servants' quarters.

In the meantime, she pulled a pin from her hair and stuck it into the lock, poking it around.

"What are you doing?" Tris asked after a moment.

"Picking the lock." She'd seen Griffin do this more than once, and she'd read of many a protagonist doing it in books. Surely it couldn't be that difficult. But despite the fact that she heard many clicks, nothing seemed to actually move.

Rex barked his encouragement, slapping the wall with his tail for good measure.

"Are you giving up yet?" Tris asked, sounding amused.

"No." She dropped to her knees in order to get a better angle.

"Now?"

"No." Clenching her teeth, she rooted around harder.

"Now?"

"Drat," she gritted out. This wasn't going to work. She plopped to sit on the floor and leaned sideways against the door. "This is ridiculous, Tris. You belong in our bed."

"It's only one night. A few hours. I'll see you in the morning. Good night, sweet wife."

"Good night, *dear* husband," she returned, but she didn't move. After a moment, she added, "And how many more nights will you abandon me in the name of 'protection?'"

Tris remained silent.

Rex gave her a pitying look and padded away, his huge paws thudding on the wood floor.

"The dog gave up," Tris said. "It's time you did, too."

She never gave up. Perhaps that was a character flaw rather than a trait to be admired, but regardless, there it was. If she couldn't tempt him back into their bed—or at least into more kisses—perhaps she could get some answers.

"Are you doing this because you're cross with me?" she asked.

"I'm doing it to protect you."

"Are you certain? Because I know you're unhappy that I won't give up the investigation."

"That's nothing to do with this," he insisted—rather patiently, she had to admit. "Except in a peripheral way. If you'd stop your investigation, perhaps I'd stop sleepwalking, in which case I might not fear doing you harm in the night. But it isn't anger driving me to do this. It's concern and sheer terror. Can't you understand that?"

She could, although she wouldn't admit it. That might encourage him.

She knew she shouldn't have allowed her hurt to get the better of her, but couldn't *he* understand the difficulty of *her* position? He'd convinced himself he was dangerous, and unless she proved otherwise, he would stay convinced. But he didn't *want* her to prove otherwise.

What an impossible mess.

But she did understand him. And she also understood that, in his own twisted way, he was doing this because he loved her, whether he knew it or not.

"I love you," she said.

He didn't answer.

She shifted to sit with her back against the door and drew her knees up toward her chest. She wrapped her arms around them. "You're acting like your father," she said.

That elicited a response. "What on earth do you mean by that?" A rather hostile response. "A single glass of port hardly makes me a drunk, and I rarely gamble."

"You said he was so convinced love would never happen for him again that he never bothered trying to find it."

"I also said I don't believe each one of us has a perfect person."

"You didn't mean that."

"I most certainly did. We're not all of us destined for bliss, Alexandra. The sooner you accept that, the happier you'll be."

"Like *you're* happy?" she countered softly.

He was silent so long, she wondered if he'd fallen asleep. But then he shifted against the door, and she knew he hadn't.

She'd have to give him more time. Three girls he'd loved had left him. No, make that five—his mother and his sister had left him, too.

The women he'd loved had been leaving him since he was seven years old.

She laid her head on her bent knees, hugging herself. "I'm not going to leave you, Tris. No matter what I do or don't learn tomorrow, I'm not going to leave you. Ever. Not next week or next month or next year. You married me, and you're stuck with me. If you open the door, I'll be right here. Always."

As it turned out, that wasn't true in the strictest sense. As the tall-case clock in the round gallery struck four in the morning, she woke, stiff and sore, and took herself back to bed.

## FIFTY

"**G**OOD MORNING, my lady." Peggy bustled into the bedroom and threw open the drapes. "It's nine o'clock, and I brought your breakfast." She placed a tray on the bed. "Shall I have the carriage brought round for your visit today?"

Nine o'clock? Alexandra blinked in the harsh light, wondering where the night had gone while at the same time happy those long, uncomfortable, restless hours were over. Sitting up against the pillows, she took a slow, bracing sip of hot tea. "I wish to ride again today. The sooner I complete this final interview, the happier my husband will be."

"I've been thinking, my lady. Perhaps, since you enjoy riding, it may be time for me to learn."

"That's a fine idea." Alexandra spread jam on her toast, checking first to make certain it was cherry. "We shall arrange for a groom to give you lessons."

"I meant today. I believe I should start riding with you today."

"Oh, I don't think so." Picturing middle-aged Peggy mounting a horse for the first time, Alexandra hid a smile behind her teacup. "I shall be in quite a hurry today, and you'll need a few lessons before you go galloping off. I believe I shall just take Ernest with me and get this done."

She'd quite enjoyed riding with Ernest yesterday. Unlike Peggy, who talked her ear off, Ernest was quiet. He never asked to come in during her interviews, nor did he ask what happened afterward. He allowed her time to think.

Peggy scowled, clearly unhappy that she would be left behind again. As she helped her mistress into a riding habit, Alexandra did her best to disregard the maid's bad mood. Peggy had been so pleasant and accommodating for the most part—even going to the trouble of making the list—and it *was* good of her to want to learn to ride.

When Alexandra was dressed and coiffed, she handed Peggy her gorgeous new silver basket, waiting for a reaction.

There was none. "Yes, my lady?"

"Please ask Mrs. Pawley to fill this with the rest of my sugar cakes. I shall meet you in the main parlor."

"As you wish," Peggy said coldly and took herself off.

Alexandra heaved a sigh as she started downstairs. If the woman was going to sulk whenever things failed to go her way, perhaps she'd be happier with a different lady's maid, after all.

When she entered the main parlor—or rather, tried to—her mouth dropped open. "What's this?"

Two muscular strangers were blocking the door as they maneuvered a large object through it.

An excessively large object.

"A pianoforte," one of them said in answer to her question.

"I can see that." She hurried around to the front and read the name above the keyboard. "Erard," she breathed in wonder, running her hand over the shining, dark mahogany. Sebastien Erard was known to build the very best pianofortes

—why, it was said that Beethoven himself owned one. "And it's *six* octaves."

"Begging your pardon, ma'am, but we need you to move."

"Right. Of course." She looked toward three footmen who were inside the room rearranging the furniture. "Might any of you know where Lord Hawkridge is at the moment?"

"The vineyard, I believe." One of the Johns hefted a small table onto his shoulder. "Or so I heard him tell his valet before he left this morning."

"Thank you," she said and turned away—then turned back. "Um…where is the vineyard?" Hopefully it wasn't as far from the house as Griffin's. "Will I need a horse?"

"Not at all." The man set down the table. "Just walk across the west courtyard, past the icehouse and through the hornbeam arch. You cannot miss it."

It was a pleasant walk. The icehouse was brick with a domed roof, and she found the long hornbeam arch to be delightfully shady. At the far end of the leafy tunnel, she exited to find sloping land covered with rows and rows of staked vines, the spaces between them only wide enough to walk single file. Spotting Tris in the middle, speaking with a man, she hurried toward him, her skirts brushing the vines on either side.

"Excuse me," she heard him say as she came up. "I'd like a moment with my wife." The man tipped his cap and walked a decent distance away, bending to tend to a vine.

"A pianoforte?" Alexandra said the moment he was out of earshot. "An *Erard* pianoforte?"

Tris's eyes looked silver in the sunshine. She thought perhaps she saw an apology in them, mixed with excitement at surprising her. "I did say another parcel would arrive today."

"That's quite a parcel," she said, determined to forget last night. Or the last part of last night, in any case. "Thank you. Thank you ever so much."

She threw her arms around him, relieved when he wrapped his arms around her, too.

"I hope you'll enjoy it," he said into her hair.

"Oh, I will. I was so keen to try it, the parcel delivery men were forced to eject me from the parlor."

The world seemed brighter this morning, as though the Queen's Bedchamber last night had been no more than a bad dream. She breathed deep of the fragrant air, reaching to touch a bunch of grapes. "How fat they look!"

"In a month, they'll be ready for harvest."

She began walking along the row, touching a plant here and there. "The vines seem so sturdy. Their trunks are so wide."

"Compared to Griffin's vines, you mean?" Sounding amused, he followed behind. "A hundred years from now, their trunks will be wide as well."

"If he can make his vineyard pay well enough to keep it."

"He can make it pay. With the duties raised during wartime to nearly twenty shillings a gallon, French wine is no longer affordable on a moderate income. People will be happy enough to stock their cellars with what Griffin produces."

"If it tastes as good as yours does, they will." She paused to pluck a grape and sniff it. "Is this a certain kind of grape?"

"Doubtless, although I confess I don't know the variety. In the old records they're noted only as English sweet-water grapes."

"Well, they make truly wonderful wine," she said, popping the fruit into her mouth.

"I'm glad you think so," he said and added teasingly, "as long as you drink only half a glass at a time." He shot a glance to the other man. "I'm afraid I'm not finished here."

Swallowing the sweet flesh, she nodded. "I must leave, anyway. Ernest will be waiting with our horses. We're going to visit with the final former servant. Lizzy, her name is."

"I wish you wouldn't." A hawk wheeled overhead, and a sudden breeze kicked up, making the vines rustle around them. She saw something twitch in Tris's jaw. "I sleepwalked again last night."

"I'm sorry," she said, meaning it. He looked haunted. "Have you suffered these incidents so closely together in the past?"

"Never. It's always been weeks—if not months or years—between episodes. But this morning, after locking myself in that room, I woke to find the window wide open." He sounded totally disgusted that his plan hadn't worked. "The lock kept me from sleepwalking around the house, so I sleep-walked outside instead."

"Did you wake up outside?"

"No, but that doesn't mean I didn't go out. In the past, I've often ambled around and ended up back in my bed."

"But the Queen's Bedchamber is upstairs. You would have injured yourself climbing out that window. I'm sure you simply opened it for fresh air." When she saw that he was going to argue, she put a hand on his arm. "Let me go see Lizzy. And then this might be over, and maybe you'll be able to sleep."

He just looked at her for a while. Just looked. And it made something tighten in her chest, because every time she thought they were making progress, stepping forward together, it seemed they took two steps back.

But she *had* to go see Lizzy. Her sisters were being ostracized already, and this was her last chance to discover information that might lead to a solution for them all. Her last chance to prove to Tris that he wasn't dangerous.

"You may not be happy with what you learn from Lizzy,"

he finally said, the warning sounding bitter on his tongue. "And it's not going to change anything." Then he turned and left her, his shoulders looking tense beneath his dark blue coat as he strode away.

The hornbeam arch didn't seem nearly as delightful when she traversed it in the opposite direction. And at the other end, Vincent, Hastings, and Mrs. Oliver all stood waiting for her.

"May I help you?" she asked, puzzled.

Hastings glanced at the other two and then spoke for all three. "May we have a word with you, Lady Hawkridge?"

"Of course."

"Lady Hawkridge," Hastings repeated, then stopped.

"Yes?"

"We're concerned," Mrs. Oliver continued. Her kindly chocolate eyes *did* look concerned. "These mishaps that keep occurring..."

"We fear that if someone did indeed murder the last Lord Hawkridge," Vincent hurriedly finished for her, "he may be trying to kill you now to stop you from finding him."

Alexandra blinked, taken aback by the mere idea. It hadn't, of course, occurred to them that Tris might be causing the mishaps while sleepwalking, since other than Vincent—and she was certain he'd keep Tris's secret—they probably had no knowledge of his night wanderings. But it had never occurred to *her* that it could be anyone else.

For a moment, her heart raced.

Then she told herself not to be ridiculous. "I appreciate your concern," she said carefully, "but I truly believe both incidents were accidents."

"But what if they weren't?" Hastings asked.

"Everyone has assured me the marquess's death was natural," she reminded him.

"But what if it wasn't?" Mrs. Oliver blurted. "What if

there's a murderer among us? Should you continue your investigation, even worse could happen."

It was obvious that recent events had them nervous and suspicious. Even of each other. Mrs. Oliver was looking at Hastings. Hastings was looking at Mrs. Oliver.

And they were both looking at Vincent.

"We brought this up for your own good," Vincent said now, his gaze steadfast. He had too much dignity to shrivel under their scrutiny. "We worry for you. If you would quit—"

"I cannot," she interrupted firmly. "You're all dears to worry for my safety, but I will not stop asking questions until *every* avenue has been exhausted."

The three of them exchanged glances and subtle sighs.

"Do please be careful, then," Hastings finally said.

"I will, I assure you. Thank you for coming to me with your concerns. I consider myself very lucky to be surrounded by such caring people."

She watched them walk off, praying that she was right and they were wrong. She felt a little shaky. The thought of Tris attacking her was one thing—it was too ludicrous to believe. But the thought of someone else...

She didn't believe that, either, she decided firmly.

And if it turned out to be true...well, that possibility had its advantages.

## FIFTY-ONE

*T*HE QUIET RIDE with Ernest had done little to calm Alexandra's nerves.

She was still shaking when she dismounted in front of Lizzy's small cottage. For the second day in a row, Hawkridge's villagers had stared at her as she rode through. Between that, defying Tris, and learning she might be the target of a murder plot, she felt like a wreck.

Walking up Lizzy's pretty flower-lined path, she half hoped this interview would lead nowhere, because that would mean this would all be over. No, she thought with an inward sigh…she didn't really hope that.

Though perhaps she felt she should.

The woman who answered the door had soft white hair, kind blue eyes, and a pronounced stoop. "Yes, dear?"

"Might you be Lizzy?" Alexandra knew that, unlike the others, Lizzy had retired rather than leaving for a new position. Still, she hadn't expected someone quite so old. Lizzy looked ninety if she were a day. "I'm Lady Hawkridge."

"A new Lady Hawkridge!" Lizzy's weathered face crinkled with delight. "Come in, my lady, come in."

Alexandra waved to Ernest where he was patiently waiting with their horses, then stepped inside. The cottage was a single room with a living area on one side and a bed on the other. "Would you care for a sugar cake?" she asked Lizzy, pulling one from her silver basket.

"Why, thank you." The woman pulled a chair out from the simple oak table and gestured for Alexandra to sit. "I will have one, if I may."

"I've been told you were employed at Hawkridge Hall when the last marquess died."

"And for sixty-two years before that." She munched on the cake, seating herself across from Alexandra.

"My husband, the current marquess—"

"I remember your husband, dear." Lizzy licked crumbs off her fingers. "Bless you. It's long past time that poor boy's innocence was proven."

For what must have been the dozenth time, Alexandra's hopes soared. "Did you see anything that night or morning? Anyone suspicious? Have you reason to believe anyone at Hawkridge Hall may have wanted the marquess dead?"

"Alas, no." Lizzy's hand inched toward the basket. "But someone must know something. Whom have you talked to so far?"

"Everyone," Alexandra said with a sigh, handing her another sugar cake.

"Names, my lady. I want names."

Lizzy devoured two more sugar cakes while Alexandra recited the list.

"How about Maude?" Lizzy asked when she was done.

"Maude?"

"The marquess's old nurse—after his wife and children passed on, she was the closest person to him. If anyone saw anything that night, it'd have been she. She left very soon after he passed…I wonder if she's still alive." She reached for yet another sugar cake, her face wrinkling so much in contemplation that her eyes all but disappeared. "Maude was old as dirt even then."

Alexandra felt an urge to laugh, from some mixture of elation at her lucky break and amusement at hearing this wrinkled old woman call someone *else* old as dirt. "Do you know where Maude went, by any chance?"

"When she left, she was headed for Nutgrove. Maude was born there, and she said that there she'd die."

Alexandra could only hope she hadn't already.

She gave the rest of the sugar cakes to Lizzy as a thank-you and hurried back outside, marveling at her good fortune. Not only was Maude her most promising lead yet, but she'd passed through Nutgrove on the way here. In mere minutes, she might be with Maude, learning the answers that would cure all her ills...

Giddy, she slanted Ernest a glance. "Are you up for a good gallop?"

"If my lady pleases," he said stoically.

She mounted, shoved the basket handle over her arm, and lifted the reins.

Tris had an excellent stable, and she had borrowed a fine mare. She flew over the countryside, the horse's hooves pounding the dirt road at a measured, rhythmic clip. Her hat tumbled back, held on only by its ribbons. She laughed, enjoying the fresh air, the light wind, the renewed hope.

She didn't hear a snap. There was nothing to warn her. Her saddle just slid sideways and off—and she screamed as she went with it.

## FIFTY-TWO

*C*LUCKING HER tongue, Peggy placed a glass of water by Alexandra's bedside. "Whatever did you learn from old Lizzy that made you ride off so recklessly?"

"I don't wish to speak of it now. My head hurts."

"Hmmph." Peggy leaned to plump her pillows, which Tristan suspected only made Alexandra's pain worse. "Serves you right for going off without me there to watch out for you. If you ask me, you should go home until all these dangerous happenings cease. I vow and swear, if you ask me—"

"No one asked you," Tristan interrupted, rising from one of the striped chairs. *He'd* be vowing and swearing if he had to listen to her a single moment longer. "Leave us. Lady Hawkridge needs her rest."

"Well!" Peggy said and took herself out the door, closing it more forcefully than necessary.

Alexandra winced at the resulting *bang*. "You could be a bit kinder to her."

"Why in blazes do you put up with her?"

"She has her moods, but she's nice and helpful most of the time." She threw off her covers. "I'll have a talk—"

"Stay in bed!"

"I'm fine, Tris." As though to prove it, she sat up and swung her legs off the side. "A little bumped and bruised, is all—"

"You're *not* fine." He walked closer and slid his hands into her hair, probing gently. His fingers met a hard, raised lump. "No wonder your head hurts."

His heart had nearly stopped when Ernest rode up with Alexandra, scraped and bleeding, the two of them sharing the same horse with her mare tied behind. Thankfully, most of her wounds were superficial and had cleaned up nicely, but he cringed to see the multitude of bruises just beginning to color.

And that was only on the parts of her he could see—the rest was concealed beneath Juliana's hideous nightgown.

He stepped back. "You took several years off my life. You're going to be the death of me, Alexandra, if you don't manage to kill yourself first. Or if *I* don't manage to kill you," he added in a tone of disgust.

"Don't start that again. You were miles away when this happened."

"Leather straps don't simply split all by themselves. Someone must have sabotaged the saddle sometime before you left." He paced over to the fireplace and leaned on the mantel, feeling drained. "Like me, last night, when I climbed out that window."

"Leather can weaken over time," she argued. "And you didn't climb out a window. The room felt overwarm in the night, so you got up, opened the window, and went back to bed." A thread of exasperation—or perhaps desperation—tinged her voice. "Must you make everything more complicated than it has to be?"

But it couldn't be as simple as she was claiming. This incident fit the pattern perfectly. The window had been wide open in the morning, and he had no memory of opening it. And, once again, his wife had been injured by an *accident* he'd had clear opportunity to arrange.

"Come sit by me," she said after a tense moment of silence. She patted the mattress beside her.

He crossed the room and sat, but not too close.

He felt too guilty to touch her.

"You would never do anything to hurt me, Tris," she said quietly. "If I believe that, why can't you?"

Because his nights were voids in his memory. Because too many coincidences were impossible to ignore. Because someone else had died on a night when he knew he'd wandered.

He sighed. "This has to stop."

"I can't stop. That would mean dooming my sisters to dreary spinsterhood and ourselves to a troubled marriage."

"You *must* stop. Hastings came to me after you left, along with Mrs. Oliver and Vincent. They said they speak for the entire staff and are concerned that someone may be after you."

"They're just being overcautious," she insisted stubbornly.

"What if they're right, Alexandra? Our own servants are worried for your safety. Have you any idea how panicked that made me while I waited for your return?" He was surprised he had any hair left, he'd run his hands through it so many times. "And then you rode up, all battered and bloody—"

He cut himself off and lurched to his feet, moving away from her. He needed to calm down. She was injured, and her heart was in the right place. He didn't want to yell at her, he just wanted to make her understand.

Leaning on the mantel, he took several deep breaths before continuing as calmly as he knew how. "Someone could be after you in order to stop this investigation, or it could be me during my stressful, sleepwalking nights. Either way, you must cease."

"I won't," she said stubbornly.

It seemed she said everything stubbornly. He'd never met anyone quite as stubborn as Alexandra. That made it very hard to maintain his hard-won calm.

"They're looking at Vincent," he said, turning around to watch her reaction. "He's the only one who was new at the time, and his skin is darker than theirs, and they're *looking* at him."

"I'm sorry for that." She truly did look sorry. "Is he overwrought?"

He shook his head. "*I'm* overwrought."

"I'm sorry for that, too. But can't you see, Tris? If these three incidents were accidents, there's no reason for me to discontinue my efforts. And if they weren't accidents, that's even *more* reason for me to persevere. Because if someone is after me, that would mean your uncle was, in fact, murdered —and if there's a killer, that means we can find him and clear your name."

Tristan stared at her, mute, unable to believe his own ears. He was stunned by her convoluted logic.

Was he supposed to be grateful she was putting her life on the line in order to prove his innocence?

Well, *he wasn't.*

He finally found his voice. "Am I to understand you actually think it's good news that someone might be trying to kill you?"

"Precisely."

He hadn't really been expecting a different answer, but he flinched just the same. He wasn't sure which would be worse: to have Alexandra's investigation prove he'd committed the murder himself, or to have some other murderer cut short her search by cutting short her life. Either possibility was too appalling to contemplate.

And that wasn't even taking Vincent into acccunt. If this continued, people would be looking for a scapegoat. The man could be prosecuted and convicted regardless of the truth—a Jamaican ex-slave was unlikely to find justice in this world.

But she was hurt, he reminded himself. And so he said very calmly, but firmly, "You must stop." And then it occurred to him: "Why are we even arguing about this? Wasn't Lizzy your final witness? You interviewed Lizzy, and now you're finished."

"I'm sorry," she said, and she really did look sorry again. "But Lizzy gave me another name. I'm not going to stop until I've talked to Maude."

"Maude." A vivid picture of a sweet old lady flooded his mind. How odd. He hadn't thought of the woman in years. Not at all. It was as though she'd evaporated from his memory.

"You knew her?" Alexandra asked.

"Uncle Harold's old nurse. His nanny, actually, when he was a child. She was kind." Talking about her was making him uneasy, though he couldn't think why. He'd liked Maude. "She was his children's nanny after that. And when he lost heart and fell ill, she nursed him all over again."

She shifted on the bed to face him. "Why didn't you tell me about her?"

"I didn't remember her." Strangely enough, it was true. Not that he'd have volunteered the information if he *had* remembered. All he wanted was for her to stop.

Maybe if he told her several hundred more times, she might start listening.

Probably not.

"Evidently nobody else remembered Maude, either," she said. "I find it very odd that she wasn't on Peggy's list."

"She was a little bird of a woman, quite elderly. I wonder if she's even still alive."

"Lizzy wondered that as well, but I'm hoping she is. As she was closest to your uncle, she's my best hope for information. Ernest and I were on our way to see her when I took my little tumble."

"Little tumble?" he scoffed. Leave it to Alexandra to trivialize such a thing. "For pity's sake, you could have broken your neck!" Remembering something, he dug a small bottle out of his pocket. "I fetched this for you."

"What is it?"

"Laudanum." He handed it over. "I thought it might help you. Dull the pain and help you to sleep."

"How old is this?" She popped the cork and sniffed.

He shrugged. "I have no idea."

"There's hardly any in here."

"You'll want to take only a little, anyway. You can overdose on laudanum."

"I don't hold with taking medicine. Not unless I have to, and I've told you, I'm fine." She replaced the cork and handed back the bottle.

"Lie down at least," he said with a sigh. "Your head will feel better if you rest."

For once, she listened, which made him suspect she felt worse than she'd admit. "It's dented," she said mournfully when she was once again settled on the pillow.

"Your head?"

"My beautiful basket." She gestured to where someone had set it on a table. "It took the tumble with me."

He rose and went to examine it in the light from the window. "It's not too bad. I don't expect anyone would ever notice, although I'm certain we can have it fixed."

"No." She gave him a shaky smile. "I believe I shall think of it as a battle scar."

"I only hope your own battle scars end up being so minimal." He set down the basket. "Maybe Peggy was right. Maybe you *should* go home until everything here settles down."

"This *is* my home," she said quietly.

The simple statement moved him. Despite all his worry, all his dread, all the anger beneath the surface of his calm, he felt a rush of warmth and gratitude. It lifted him.

"I'm not sleepy," she said. "I'm sore, but I'm not tired."

That was why he'd brought the laudanum, but he wouldn't force it on her. He should have guessed she'd be too stubborn to take it.

Her family's cookbook and the blank book he'd given her were stacked together on the bedside table. "Here," he said, handing them to her. "You can copy the recipes you wanted." He shifted on his feet, and then, unable to help himself, added, "And think about whether continuing this investigation is really wise."

Her eyes flashed, as he'd known they would. "If Maude knows nothing, there will be nothing left to investigate. But I'd be a fool not to question her."

He'd known she would say that, too. "It isn't foolish to protect yourself, nor to abide by your husband's wishes."

She kept quiet for a moment, but something in her expression hardened.

"This is beautiful," she finally said conversationally, turning the blue leather book over in her hands. After another moment, she looked up at him. "But I hope you haven't been trying to buy my cooperation with these gifts, because my convictions aren't for sale."

He *hadn't* known she would think him so calculating. The warmth inside him went cold as he left her in peace.

# FIFTY-THREE

## *LEMON PUFFS*

Beat the whites of four eggs till they rise to a high froth. Then add as much sugar as will make it thick; then rub it round for half an hour, put in a spoon of lemon peel gratings and two spoons of the juice. Take a sheet of paper and lay it on as broad as a sixpence and as high as you can. Put them into a moderately heated oven half a quarter of an hour, and they will look as white as snow.

*Give these sweet-and-sour biscuits to a sour person you wish to turn sweet. My husband has never proved immune.*

—Elizabeth, Countess of Greystone, 1747

*A*LL THAT LONG afternoon and evening, Alexandra had a lot of time to think.

After a short nap, her head felt better. The rest of her was achy, but not intolerably so. She copied some of her favorite recipes as Tris had suggested, then called for Peggy to help her dress for dinner. The maid was still in a snit, so for once she didn't babble, which suited Alexandra just fine. When she was ready, she waited for Tris to come escort her to the dining room.

A tray arrived for her instead.

She ate little, the food sticking in her throat. She knew she had hurt Tris terribly. *I hope you haven't been trying to buy my cooperation*...even as she'd said it, part of her had been shocked to hear the words come out of her mouth. She wondered what had happened to traditional, ladylike Alexandra. This crusade for truth and justice had turned her into a girl she scarcely recognized, and turned her fairytale romance into an ugly cycle of hurt, anger, and guilt.

She'd managed to destroy her marriage inside of a week. It had to be some sort of record.

At ten o'clock she changed from the dinner dress into one of her new nightgowns, a blush-colored confection that she hoped would help soften Tris's resentment. She belted a wrapper over it and waited. The clock struck midnight before she heard footsteps in the corridor.

She hurried to open the door, to welcome him, to do what whatever it took to mend things between them. But he wasn't coming toward her. At the far end of the corridor, he was opening the door to the Queen's Bedchamber.

Wearing only tight trousers and a white shirt, with the collar open and the sleeves rolled up to expose his forearms, he looked worn out and wonderful all at the same time.

"Tris," she called softly.

He turned. "Good night."

"You're not going to sleep in there again, are you?" She started down the corridor, forcing her lips to curve in a smile. "If you're going to go out a window anyway," she said lightly, "there hardly seems a point."

"I had bars put on the windows. I won't be going anywhere tonight."

"Bars?" Having reached the room, she looked past him and inside. It was dark outdoors, but she could just make out faint stripes that must be iron rods outside the glass. "That seems a little extreme, doesn't it?"

"Nothing is too extreme to protect you," he said, unblinking.

Indifferent. Uncaring.

She swallowed hard, any pretense of normalcy gone. "I'm sorry for what I said. Please don't pull away from me, Tris. I love you."

"Good night," he said again and turned to enter the room.

Although she certainly hadn't expected to hear those three words echoed back at her, neither had she expected them to be ignored entirely. "Wait," she said, grabbing his wrist.

She'd been fighting it all along, but she knew what she had to do. She'd thought of little else for the past few hours.

He glanced dispassionately down to her hand. "Yes?"

His skin felt warm, but his arm felt tense. She grasped him tighter. "I'm not going to do the last interview. I'm not going to talk to Maude."

He blinked at her. "Why?"

"It's the only way I can prove my love. Prove that I'll stay with you even if we remain in disgrace for the rest of our lives. I don't care about society, Tris—I don't need their parties or their approval. I never have. I've been doing this for you and for my sisters. But my sisters will cope. You're my husband, and you're more important. My loyalty to you comes first."

She couldn't think of anything else to say. So she waited. He looked down again to where her fingers gripped his arm, and she released him and waited some more.

"All right," he said at last. "Thank you. I'm sure I'll sleep quite soundly tonight." Then he stepped into the room and closed the door—without even so much as a kiss.

While she stood there, stunned, Vincent walked up, as if

on cue, and slid a key into the lock. "Are you all right, my lady?"

"I'm fine," she said woodenly. "I believe I shall go make some sweets."

"Now?" Vincent asked in surprise. His gaze went to her bare feet.

"Now," she said, belting her wrapper more tightly.

She refused to spend another night on the floor outside her husband's room.

"Well." He seemed at a loss. "The ovens will be cold. Let me accompany you downstairs and light them for you."

She fetched her new recipe book before following him down the gaslit staircase, flipping pages as they crossed the great hall to the back passage.

"Lemon puffs," she decided. According to some long-dead cousin or aunt, they were supposed to turn a sour person sweet. Heaven knew, given Tris's current attitude, she could use all the help she could get.

In the kitchen, she gathered eggs, sugar, and lemons while Vincent started the brick ovens. Just as she began separating the first yolk from the white, Mrs. Pawley walked in. "What's going on here?" she asked through a yawn.

The cook's round body was covered by a voluminous white nightgown and her feet were as bare as Alexandra's. Dressed as always like a perfect gentleman, Vincent answered with great dignity. "We're making lemon puffs."

"We?" Alexandra and Mrs. Pawley said together.

"We," he confirmed, reaching for a lemon.

Mrs. Pawley went to a cabinet and took out a bottle of sherry and three glasses. When she filled Alexandra's to the brim, Alexandra didn't protest. Instead she took a generous sip and felt the rich wine warm her all the way down her throat and into her stomach.

She hadn't realized she'd been so cold.

She pushed up her sleeves and cracked another egg.

Grating sugar, Mrs. Pawley eyed a bruise on her arm. "You had a rough day, from what I've heard. Are you up to this, my lady?"

"Oh, quite. I'm halfway healed already." She took another sip, deciding the sherry must be healing her even faster. "Tomorrow I'm sure to be good as new."

Two kitchen maids wandered in, also wearing plain night-gowns. "What's going on here?" one of them asked.

"Come in," Alexandra said brightly. "We're making lemon puffs." She took another sip. "However did you know we were in here?"

"They sleep right down the corridor," Mrs. Pawley said, fetching another bottle of sherry and two more glasses.

There was much beating to do of the egg whites, in order to make them nice and stiff. And after that, they were supposed to be rubbed together with sugar for half an hour. Alexandra appreciated all the help. She *was* a bit sore for such strenuous work, and while the others had their turns, she could relax and drink more sherry.

Before long, three housemaids and two footmen had joined them, and it was quite a while before her turn came to beat the eggs. In fact, she was so busy sipping sherry that she missed her turn twice. When they weren't occupied beating eggs, the servants took turns telling jokes. Alexandra thought they were quite the funniest jokes she'd ever heard, and when she told one or two herself, everyone laughed even when she stumbled over the words.

She rather suspected they laughed mostly because she was their mistress, but their support cheered her all the same.

By the time the lemon puffs came out of the oven, shiny and white as snow, five bottles had been emptied and the kitchen rang with laughter. "You must serve these to my husband first thing in the morning," Alexandra told Mrs.

Pawley as she peeled the finished puffs off the brown paper on which they had baked.

"Our fine master cannot abide sweets in the morning," the cook pronounced with formal reserve. Then she dissolved into laughter that brought tears rolling down her plump cheeks. Everyone else laughed, too. One of the footmen—Alexandra couldn't remember his name—even snorted once or twice.

"For luncheon, then," Alexandra instructed. Noticing no scullery maids had joined them, she waved a hand magnanimously—or rather, flung it somewhat flamboyantly. "You may leave this mess until morning," she trilled as Vincent grabbed her to stop the momentum from tipping her over.

She quite liked her new servants, she thought as she giggled her way up to bed, Vincent close behind in case she should fall. She'd never had so much fun in the kitchen at Cainewood Castle.

The lemon puffs had better turn Tris from sour to sweet, because she wasn't going to be leaving Hawkridge Hall anytime soon.

# FIFTY-FOUR

*T*HE NEXT DAY, Alexandra was *not* good as new. To the contrary, her head ached abominably, her stomach felt queasy, and her body was stiff and more sore than yesterday. She didn't know whether Tris was served the lemon puffs with luncheon, since she couldn't seem to force herself out of bed. Even the daylight seemed to make her hurt.

Peggy came in from time to time, clucking and leaving Alexandra cup after cup of strong, hot tea. Alexandra wasn't certain whether the clucking indicated sympathy or disapproval, and she didn't really care. As long as Peggy left the drapes closed tight and the gaslights off, she could ignore her. She ignored the tea as well for the first few hours, but after a while she started sipping it, and after a few cups, she started feeling slightly better.

By late afternoon, she finally felt well enough to dress and rejoin the world. Since her battered body didn't want to move, she allowed Peggy to help her, enduring still more clucking. At long last, she stiffly made her way downstairs, going straight to the main parlor and the new pianoforte.

It was magnificent. She walked around it reverently, trailing a hand along the fine, polished mahogany. Finally, she stopped in front and hit middle C. The single note sounded so rich it sent a tingle down her spine.

She sat down to play, choosing Beethoven's Piano Sonata No. 14, long one of her favorite pieces of music. "*Quasi una fantasia,*" he'd called it…"Like a fantasy."

Indeed, only a few notes into the first movement, she lost herself in the fantasy. Her beautiful new pianoforte sounded like a dream. The minuet and trio that made up the second movement flowed effortlessly from her fingertips, and when she reached the stormy final movement, exhilaration seemed to carry off her burdens. All the pain and heartache she'd been carrying poured out of her and into the performance, leaving her with a sense of peace as the last note faded away.

She heard applause. "Brava," Tris called from the doorway.

She turned to him with a tentative smile. "You're not scandalized? Most of the older people of my acquaintance find Beethoven's style too passionate and therefore unfit for young, impressionable ladies."

"Do you think me that old?" he wondered aloud.

"When we were younger, six years seemed like a vast age difference."

He nodded slowly, as though he were remembering, too. "You played the piece wonderfully," he said, "scandalous or not."

"It's a wonderful instrument." She wouldn't feign modesty, because she'd played better on it than she ever had. "I thank you for it."

"I didn't buy it to bribe you," he said quietly.

"I know."

The two words hung between them. "Shall we go in to dinner?" he finally asked.

It was her turn to nod. He placed a hand beneath her elbow to help her rise. It seemed the curative powers of Beethoven were temporary, for all her sore and tender spots had returned.

Including the emotional ones.

If Tris wasn't dismissive, he wasn't particularly friendly, either. Their dinner passed in relative—and relatively awkward—silence, the rattle of dishes and clang of cutlery more prominent than conversation. It seemed ages before Hastings placed the bottle of port on the table and left them alone, closing the dining room door behind him.

"None for me," Alexandra said.

"Hmm." Tris poured some for himself, a wry smile curving his lips. "Could it be you overdid it in the kitchen last night?"

He'd heard. Well, of course he'd heard. Not only was he the lord of the manor, his own valet had been there as witness.

"I made some lemon puffs," she said, ignoring his implication.

"Yes, and they're quite delicious. I had two after luncheon. While you were sleeping off the sherry."

"I was sleeping off the pain," she protested. "My body is complaining even more today than yesterday."

He nodded. "That's not unusual. You'll be on the mend by tomorrow, no doubt." He paused for a long sip, then met her eyes, his own a penetrating gray. "And I will take you to see Maude."

She couldn't have heard right. "Pardon?"

"We'll take the curricle, since I'm certain you won't feel up to riding."

Tristan watched the parade of reactions cross her face: disbelief first, followed by relief and then cautious joy. "Are you sure?" she asked.

"I'm sure."

"I told you I was giving up. I meant that, Tris. It's what you wanted."

He took her measure for a moment and decided she was sincere. But he'd already known that. "Are you trying to talk me out of it?"

She shook her head emphatically.

"I appreciate your willingness," he told her. He appreciated it more than she'd ever know. "But I cannot allow you to give up. Not this way."

Glad to see hope returning to her eyes, Tristan kept his expression carefully neutral. He didn't want Alexandra to see the dread that had settled over him as he granted her wish. He'd realized he couldn't let her wonder all her life if her investigation might have succeeded—it would eat at her, the not knowing—but though he'd made the inevitable decision, he couldn't say if it was the *right* one.

In fact, he had a horrible feeling that it wasn't. That this could only result in one or both of them being put in harm's way. That's why he would accompany Alexandra on her last interview, much as he hated the idea. He couldn't let her venture out with only a footman for protection, not when a murderer might be after her.

Of course, he shouldn't be letting her venture out at all, but it seemed that somehow she'd managed to wrap him around her little finger.

"Thank you," she whispered, her eyes shining.

He nodded shortly. "Whoever is trying to stop you—if not myself—is obviously part of this household."

"They were *accidents*, Tris."

"Let's not go over this again, shall we?" He raised a brow to emphasize his point. "In case someone should try to follow us, I don't want anyone to know where we're going or what we're doing."

"All right," she agreed slowly.

"We shall say you require fresh air to aid your recovery, so we're going on a picnic. A honeymoon picnic."

"I suppose it won't hurt to be cautious."

"Have you told anyone about Maude?"

"No. I've been languishing in the bedroom since the accident." When he cocked his head at her, she added, "Maude's name never came up in the kitchen."

"How about Ernest?"

"Not with him, either. He doesn't care to talk much. Besides, we'd only just got underway when the strap on the saddle snapped. I didn't have time to say anything before, and after...well, on the ride home I didn't feel much like conversation."

He supposed she wouldn't have—she'd have been occupied gritting her teeth against the jarring pain of that ride. "Good. Then no one has any reason to suspect we'll be doing anything besides enjoying a honeymoon picnic." He rose, yawning. He hadn't slept much last night. Having one's wife offer up the sacrifice of her future happiness tended to disturb one's equilibrium. "We should both get a good night's sleep."

A hesitant smile curved Alexandra's lips. "Shall I go up and change into another of my new nightgowns? Or do you wish to come along and help me?"

"Neither. I'll be sleeping in the Queen's Bedchamber again. For your safety." He leaned and pressed a kiss to the top of her head. Hearing her disappointed sigh, he raised her chin and met her eyes. "Besides, you're still entirely too bruised and hurting. When we've finished this thing you've started, perhaps we'll both feel better."

For a long while after he left, Alexandra just sat in the dining room. She'd thought since Tris was being so kind, he'd want to be with her tonight. And she wanted so much to be with him…or even just in the same room with him. She'd take what she could get.

He was right: She was bruised, both inside and out.

On her way from the dining room to the stairs, she nearly collided with Mrs. Pawley.

"My lady! Will we be seeing you in the kitchen tonight?" The cook's blue eyes danced. "I expect we shall have a great crowd to assist in the sweet making. There are many who are sad to have missed our little impromptu party."

Alexandra hated to disappoint the staff, but a party was the last thing she felt like tonight.

"I'm afraid not, Mrs. Pawley," she said, watching the light fade from the older woman's eyes. "Perhaps another time."

# FIFTY-FIVE

"*I*'M SO PLEASED to see you're feeling more the thing today," Peggy said in Alexandra's dressing room the next day.

"Oh, I truly am." Alexandra wondered at her maid's sudden good mood, but she wouldn't risk ruining it with any questions. "I'm going on a picnic today!" she said brightly instead. "What do you expect I should wear to picnic with my husband?"

"With your husband?" Peggy flipped through a few dresses, then held up a pretty blue frock for Alexandra's approval. At her nod, the maid started toward the bedroom, slanting a sly glance over her shoulder. "Aren't the two of you rather estranged?"

Following her, Alexandra sighed, supposing their separate sleeping arrangements had prompted much speculation belowstairs. It was so tempting to tell Peggy the truth about everything, but she'd promised Tris she would stick to their story. "I'm hoping a picnic will help us reconcile," she said carefully as she dabbed on a little perfume. "And—"

A knock at the door interrupted her.

"Yes?" she called, hurrying into the dress.

Tris poked his head in. "Mrs. Pawley has requested your silver basket to fill with our picnic luncheon."

A clever ruse to support their story. She fetched the basket and brought it to him. "Please ask Mrs. Pawley to include some lemon puffs," she said, thinking she needed some sweets to take to Maude. "I haven't found a chance to even try them yet."

"Will do." He planted a light kiss on her lips, a kiss that unexpectedly turned into more. He pulled away with a foolish grin. "Are you about ready?"

He hadn't kissed her for days. Her lips tingling, she wondered whether the kiss had been for show or for real. "Almost."

He smiled. "I shall wait for you in the curricle," he said, then walked away.

She slowly closed the door.

"It looks like you're reconciled already," Peggy commented as she did up her buttons.

Alexandra blushed. "We're both trying." She took a seat at her dressing table so the maid could work on her hair.

"I wish to apologize for being such a crab the past few days," Peggy said from behind her. "I admired you so for your investigation, and I was disappointed to find myself no longer part of it." She deftly twisted and pinned. "Do you expect you could ever forgive me?"

"Of course," Alexandra said. Peggy had been her strongest ally until that first time she went off without her, and she'd missed having a woman here at Hawkridge to confide in. "I collect I haven't been a very pleasant person myself the last day or two."

"But you're the mistress," Peggy pointed out. "You're allowed to be a crab." They both laughed; then Peggy sobered. "I fear for you, though. All the buzz in the servants' quarters is that someone is after you—perhaps you should be leaving Hawkridge to save your life, not to go on a picnic."

The woman's concern was kindly meant, Alexandra knew, if misplaced. "I know tales of danger have been bandied about belowstairs, but I assure you there's nothing to fear. A few unfortunate accidents do not a plot make. Besides, my investigation is all but over. I have only one person left to interview."

In the mirror, Peggy looked surprised. "Did you fall from your horse before visiting Lizzy, then?"

"No, I spoke with Lizzy. She told me of another departed servant called Maude." Too late Alexandra remembered Tris's wish to keep their final interview secret—and Peggy's propensity to gossip. She watched the maid's face in the mirror. "I wonder why she wasn't on your list?"

"We all thought the old woman was dead," Peggy said, looking shocked. "Are you certain she isn't?"

"Lizzy wasn't sure, but I hope not. I collect I will find out tomorrow when I try to pay Maude a visit."

"You'll take me along this time, won't you?"

"If I'm still not up to riding, most assuredly." Alexandra turned to her maid, putting a finger to her lips. "Tell no one else, I beg you. You know his lordship doesn't want me continuing this investigation. I cannot risk any word reaching him concerning my plans for tomorrow."

"Mum's the word," Peggy promised. "But I do believe the old woman is dead. Why make the journey at all when you'll most likely put your reconciliation in jeopardy for nothing?"

"Perhaps you're right." Hoping to keep her maid in such good humor permanently, Alexandra made a big show of sighing. "I shall think on it," she told her and rose to collect her bonnet.

## FIFTY-SIX

"**P**EGGY THINKS Maude is dead," Alexandra told Tristan as he helped her into the curricle. "But I want to try to visit her anyway. You won't mind, will you? Even if the journey proves to be fruitless?"

"I said I'd take you, and I don't intend to go back on my word. But whyever would Peggy say she's dead?" He climbed up beside her and pulled the hood over their heads to shield them from the bright sun. "I thought no one knew about Maude."

She winced. "I mentioned her without thinking. But I made her promise not to tell," she added quickly as he lifted the reins. "And she also believes that I plan to visit Maude tomorrow, not today. I made the timing very clear."

Annoyance tightened his jaw, but he didn't want to start this outing with a disagreement. As he drove away, he told himself firmly that what was done was done. Nothing untoward was likely to come of it, since it was plain no one was following them. By all appearances, everyone had bought their story that they were off for nothing more interesting than a honeymoon picnic.

Alexandra took up the silver basket and wrapped their luncheon in one of the large napkins, leaving only the lemon puffs in the bottom. "For Maude," she explained. "Thank you so much for doing this. It means a lot to me."

He slanted her a glance. "It means a lot to me that you were willing to forgo it."

"I'm glad," she said softly and left it at that. They rode silently for a few minutes before she turned to him again. "Would you care for something to eat?"

He shook his head. "I'm not hungry."

"Neither am I. I'm too nervous to eat. This is our last chance…"

She trailed off, and little was said for the rest of the ride.

But he hadn't missed the "our." *Our* last chance.

Like most servants, Maude hadn't gone far from the place of her birth to find employment. Nutgrove was less than an hour away, an hour Alexandra spent leaning against Tristan, smelling faintly of lemon puffs and the same perfume he'd noticed earlier that morning when he'd kissed her.

The kiss had been intended for show—he hadn't meant to get carried away. No, he thought ruefully, that had been his sweet, innocent wife's doing. She was either a natural born seductress or a very quick study, and gradually…so gradually he was only just beginning to recognize his doom…she'd been spinning a web around his heart.

*Blast it!* He wasn't ready for this.

Even if he *was*—hypothetically—prepared to love again, he couldn't allow himself to fall for her now. She was about to reach the end of her search, see her hopes for their future fade once and for all. She was about to finally accept that her life with him would never improve. After that, it wouldn't be a question of *if* she would leave, but *when*.

As she'd said herself, this was their last chance.

And then he'd be left to go on without her. The thought

was almost too much to bear. He imagined never getting to touch her or kiss her again. Never knowing where she was or what she was doing. Never knowing if she was happy or if she missed him.

Alexandra had changed the very essence of his existence, the very substance of his home. Even the servants walked with more spring in their steps and smiles upon their faces. He imagined the music, the light, the life she'd brought with her to Hawkridge Hall—things he hadn't even realized were missing until her arrival—fading back into a dull, gray hush.

He didn't want to go back to the way it had been without her. He could hardly imagine living there without her. In fact, he *couldn't* imagine living there without her.

He couldn't imagine living *anywhere* without her.

*Blast it.*

And this, of course, was assuming one of the best possible outcomes, that their interview was merely fruitless. If instead Maude confirmed Tristan's guilt or, heaven forbid, the true murderer somehow got to Alexandra...

Well, scenarios could only get darker.

So he sat beside her in the curricle, upright and tense, alternately praying and cursing the impossible muddle he found himself in, until they passed the signpost that read NUTGROVE.

Alexandra immediately straightened and called excitedly to an elderly gentleman walking a tiny dog. "Good sir! If I may bother you...might you know the direction of a woman who goes by Maude?"

And it was the oddest thing...but just hearing Alexandra say "Maude" again, that vague, niggling sense of unease Tristan had felt two days ago came back.

The old man cupped a hand to his ear. "Eh?"

"Maude!" she shouted as they rolled along beside him. She turned to Tristan. "What is Maude's surname?"

He shrugged. "I never thought to ask." He'd forgotten her. How was it that he'd forgotten her?

"Maude!" Alexandra yelled again. "Might you know anyone named Maude?"

"Ah, Maude." The man smiled, revealing gaps where he'd lost several teeth. "Down the corner," he said, gesturing and pulling his dog's leash in the process, nearly choking the poor little beast. "Turn left. Honeysuckle Cottage."

"She's alive," Alexandra breathed, her brandywine eyes brimming with excitement. "Goodness, I hope she knows something that will help us."

"It could be someone else named Maude," Tristan cautioned, that sense of unease growing stronger.

"It isn't. I just know it."

Somehow he also knew it wasn't someone else. And in any case, there was no sense arguing the matter, when they'd know for sure soon enough. "Honeysuckle Cottage," he muttered. "That isn't much of a direction."

"The man seemed to think it would do," she said as they turned the corner. "Look! There it is!"

Sure enough, about halfway down the lane stood an old stone cottage wreathed in pale-flowered honeysuckle vines.

No sooner had the curricle rolled to a stop than Alexandra hopped down, basket in hand, and started for the door. Tristan just sat there for a moment, feeling the unease tangle into a knot in his gut.

Finally, he climbed down and followed her. "You're supposed to wait to be handed down," he said peevishly.

"Oh, bosh!" She knocked on the weathered wood. "This is hardly the time for propriety."

How much she had changed since he first met her. She'd always shown remarkable poise, but now she'd gained the shrewd self-assurance of someone much older than seventeen.

She shifted on her feet. "What's taking her so long? Dear heavens, I hope she's home. Lizzy said if anyone saw anything that night, it'd have been she."

And suddenly he knew why he'd forgotten Maude. He *hadn't* forgotten her. He'd deliberately pushed her clear out of his mind.

She'd been the person closest to his uncle. The person most likely to have seen him if he'd sleepwalked into his uncle's rooms that night.

The door swung open, and Maude stood on the other side, leaning on a cane and looking much like Tristan remembered her. A faded cotton dress hung on her slight frame. She'd always seemed so frail she might break.

"Good afternoon, Maude," he said.

Her pale green eyes widened, looking apprehensive. "Lord Hawkridge?"

She knew something. She wouldn't look like that unless she knew something. The knot tightened in Tristan's gut.

He wrapped an arm around Alexandra's shoulders and forced a smile. "This is my wife, Lady Hawkridge."

Alexandra reached into her basket. "Would you care for a lemon puff?"

"No, my lady. Thank you." Maude's blue-veined hand went up to pat her gray curls nervously. "Why are you here?"

The knot twisted. "We wish to talk to you," he said. "May we come in for a moment?"

She looked like she wanted to say no, but then turned abruptly, her cane tapping across the wood floor as she led them inside and to a small table. "These are all the chairs I have," she said, her voice wavering.

There were two. And they were rickety. "I'm perfectly content to stand," Tristan said, helping the elderly woman to sit while Alexandra took the second chair. He made a mental note to send the old nurse some decent furniture next week—

that was, assuming he wasn't locked up in some prison. He'd been the marquess for less than a day before she'd departed, but that was no excuse for not seeing that a long-term employee was comfortable in her retirement.

Perhaps he'd have done that if he hadn't forgotten her.

Maude held on to her cane, still leaning on it even while she was seated. Alexandra reached across the little table to touch her other hand. "I've been told you were very close to the last marquess," she began gently.

"Y-yes." The old woman's eyes looked everywhere but at her.

"Do you remember anything that happened the night he died?"

"Y-yes."

Tristan stopped breathing.

"Did you see anyone go into his room?" Alexandra continued. "Anyone who might have done him harm?"

"Y-yes."

Alexandra sent Tristan a startled glance—a hopeful glance —before she looked back to Maude expectantly.

No further information seemed to be forthcoming. Tristan feared he'd expire if he didn't breathe. He wished Maude would accuse him already, so he could breathe.

Alexandra's gaze darted to his again before her smooth hand tightened over the wrinkled one. "Who was it, Maude?" she whispered, her eyes flooded with not just hope, but also a measure of self-protective doubt.

The cane crashed to the floor as Maude covered her face with her hands. Beneath her cotton dress, her bony shoulders shook with silent, racking sobs.

Petrified and resigned, Tristan crouched beside her chair. "Maude? What is it?"

"I'm sorry. I'm so sorry," came a muffled wail through her fingers. "It was a mistake, I swear it."

"Of course it was a mistake, but that doesn't make me any less guilty." Ignoring Alexandra's gasp, he eased Maude's hands away from her face. "Whether intentional or not, I'm still responsible for his death."

His life was over. Or at least it was meaningless, which was the same thing.

"I'm s-sorry," Maude repeated. She stared into space, tears rolling down her parchment cheeks. "It was a mistake."

Except for the painful knot, he felt only numbness. But she looked downright distraught. "Maude, what was a mistake?"

Her tears flowed faster. "The l-laudanum."

Tristan dug a handkerchief from his pocket. "The laudanum?" His memory flashed on the nearly empty bottle he'd taken from his uncle's rooms and tried to give to Alexandra. *You'll want to take only a little,* he'd told her. *You can overdose on laudanum.*

He hadn't thought the knot could tighten more, but it did. He must have poisoned his uncle with that very same bottle.

"I just wanted him to stop hurting." Maude took the proffered white square and dabbed her eyes with it, then balled it in her fist, staring at her hands in her lap. More tears splashed down on them. "H-he was coughing. He couldn't sleep. I gave him too much. Too much. I used all of it." She was babbling so fast Tristan couldn't seem to keep up. "Perhaps I gave it to him twice that night. I didn't intend to. I couldn't remember. My m-memory isn't what it used to be..."

"Could you mean..." A mist had obscured Tristan's brain. He'd stopped breathing again. He took both of Maude's hands. "Do you think you may have accidentally caused my uncle's death?"

She nodded and met his gaze, her eyes reddened. "I should have died instead of him."

"No." He couldn't catch his breath. His vision clouded. His pulse felt thready and weak.

"I told you," Alexandra murmured.

He was innocent. He was innocent.

Relief flowed through him, blessed relief after more than two years. He felt weak and lightheaded and giddy, like Alexandra when she drank too much wine.

*Alexandra.* She'd had faith in him all along.

"Maude." He swallowed past a lump in his throat. "Will you tell this to the authorities?"

A sob escaped her. "Th-they're going to hang me."

"I won't let them." His knees hurt, but he remained crouched there, holding both her hands, when all he wanted was to collapse in relief. "You did your best, didn't you? Always. You cared for my uncle when he was a child, then his children, then him again. I won't let them hang you for doing the best you could. Everyone makes mistakes."

He heard a little noise from Alexandra and turned to see her. A fat tear rolled down her cheek, cracking his heart.

"They're going to hang me," Maude repeated.

"No." He looked back to the older woman. "I will protect you. I promise your safety, Maude, if you'll only explain what happened to the authorities."

She stared at her lap. "You promise?"

"I do. No one will hurt you. You can come back to live at Hawkridge, if you'd like. We'll take care of you."

A long moment passed when all Tristan heard was the beat of his own heart pounding in his ears. At last Maude lifted her red-rimmed gaze to meet his, her eyes filled with gratitude and relief of her own.

"I'll talk," she said. "I lied to the sheriff before, but this time I'll tell the truth."

## FIFTY-SEVEN

*W*HEN MAUDE'S door closed behind them, Alexandra and Tris paused on the garden path and turned to each other. And just stood there, looking at each other, for a very long time.

"Alexandra," Tris finally murmured. He took the basket from her hand and set it on the gravel, then gripped both her shoulders, searching her eyes. "I've never seen you cry before," he said.

"I'm not crying," she said as her eyes glazed, making a liar of her. "It was just that when you said everyone makes mistakes...well, I'm sorry for mine, Tris. I'm sorry I was so obstinate that I drove you away."

He held her face in unsteady hands. "I'm not sorry you were obstinate. Look where it led. I was too obstinate to see you might be right." He shook his head. "I even thought Maude was confessing *my* guilt instead of her own."

"Everyone makes mistakes," she reminded him with a watery chuckle. She blew out a shaky breath. "Goodness, Tris, we did it."

"*You* did it," he said. "Sweet heaven, you did it." Grinning foolishly, he swept her up to twirl her in a wide circle right there in the cottage's little garden.

She laughed, lifting her face to the sky. "I told you," she crowed as he set her on her feet. "I told you that you weren't capable of causing harm to your uncle." She poked a finger into his chest. "And you aren't capable of hurting me, either."

He raised both hands in surrender. "You were right about that, too. They were just accidents." Then his hands darted out to seize her, yanking her to him.

"Oof!" she said, feeling the tenderness of her bruises. "Maybe now you *have* hurt me."

"I'm sorry." He kissed her and set her carefully away before he bent to retrieve her basket. "But I've never been so happy to hear *I told you so* in my entire life."

He led her back to the curricle and handed her in, then clambered up beside her. Seizing her once more, he kissed her so thoroughly she forgot her bruises altogether.

"Let's go home," he said, lifting the reins.

The curricle jerked as they pulled away. She unwrapped their luncheon, spreading the napkin over her lap with all of Mrs. Pawley's offerings. She was famished. She couldn't remember ever being so hungry.

"Everything is going to be so marvelous," she said, taking a big bite out of a chicken leg. "All of society will have to apologize to you, and my sisters are both going to marry dukes."

"Marquesses aren't good enough?" he asked with a raised brow.

She slapped a chicken leg into his open hand. "I suppose marquesses will do."

They ate and laughed all the way home, talking about their future. Tris still hadn't said he loved her, but she really didn't care. She was certain he did, and if it took him ten years to admit it, she could wait.

Was it her imagination, or had she never seen the sky a more brilliant blue? The sun sparkled on the Thames. Birds trilled in the trees. Everything seemed unnaturally bright, including her joyful husband.

"I've never seen you so jolly," she teased as they headed up Hawkridge Hall's drive. "Now that I know you're capable, I shall expect you to remain so."

"Constantly?"

"Indeed. We'll be the jolliest couple in England."

His laughter trailed off as the house loomed into view. The sight seemed to sober him slightly. "It *is* jolly to know I'm in the clear, but let's not celebrate until the authorities have taken Maude's statement. At the rate the law moves, she could die before they get out to Nutgrove."

"Oh, no—"

"I was jesting," he said with a lopsided grin. He pulled up before the steps. "That old bird will probably outlive us both. Besides, I'm going to find the sheriff right now and drag him there directly. Let me take care of tying up the details, and we can celebrate tonight."

*Tonight.* His tone sent a shiver of anticipation down her spine. Which nightgown would she wear?

Passing the reins to a groom, Tris lightly jumped to the gravel and came around to hand her down.

The powder blue one, she decided, offering her hand. He grinned up at her. "You waited this time."

"I would wait forever for you, Tris."

"I shan't be gone that long," he murmured, forgoing her hand to grasp her under her arms and swing her down. "Don't tell anyone the news—I want to announce it together tonight, after everything is settled."

He kissed her forehead, her cheek, and finally her mouth. Drawing back, he smoothed a stray curl from her face. "You must be exhausted, considering your injuries. I hope you'll rest while I'm gone."

Her senses still spinning, she nodded her assent.

He reached back into the curricle for the silver basket and pushed it into her hands before dropping one last kiss on her lips. "Go, will you? Before I'm tempted to accompany you upstairs."

She went straight up to their bedroom. She *was* exhausted.

Peggy seemed to be nowhere about, so she kicked off her shoes and burrowed, fully dressed, under the covers, where she dreamed of her marvelous new life while her husband secured their future.

## FIFTY-EIGHT

*A*LEXANDRA WAS still snug in bed when she heard the door quietly close, followed by the *clack* of an engaging lock.

She opened her eyes and yawned. Light streamed through the windows, and she hadn't expected her husband home until dark. Everything must have gone well.

"Tris?" she queried, rolling languidly to face the door. She couldn't wait to see him.

But instead she saw Peggy.

Holding a gun.

For a moment, that was all that registered: Peggy holding a gun. It was surreal, really. Why would Peggy be holding a gun?

Then Alexandra's sleep-fogged brain cleared a little, and she bolted upright in the bed.

"I'm sorry," Peggy said, walking closer. She hadn't aimed the gun; she just held it in her right hand. But the hand shook. She was nervous. Which made Alexandra more nervous than she already was, which was very nervous indeed. Her heart was hammering against her ribs and threatening to climb out her throat.

Her maid was walking toward her, holding a gun.

And then Peggy raised it, and Alexandra was staring down the barrel of a gun. A gun pointed at *her*.

It was, quite undoubtedly, the most frightening moment of her life.

She stared down that barrel, thinking it the longest, darkest, most menacing thing she'd ever seen.

But she couldn't just sit there staring at it. She had to get her mouth to work. She had to say something to stop this. "Y-you cannot shoot that," she stammered, still wondering why Peggy had a gun. "It'll be heard. You'll be caught."

"But my mother won't," Peggy responded through clenched teeth. "And that's all that matters."

"Your mother?" Alexandra squeaked, inching toward the edge of the bed. Peggy was too old to still have a mother. Or at least she'd never mentioned a mother. What in heaven's name was she talking about, and why did she have a gun, and would that hand ever stop shaking?

And then something clicked in her head, just as her feet hit the floor. "Maude is your *mother*?"

"Yes," Peggy gritted out, and she brought her second hand up to steady the first, and her shaking finger moved toward the trigger.

Alexandra didn't think anymore. She just sprang, one palm hitting the maid's chest while her other hand grasped her wrists and forced them up toward the ceiling. A sharp *bang* rang out, the recoil making them both fall as plaster rained down on top of them.

Peggy dropped the gun. Or rather, it skittered from her hands and went clear under the big bed.

Relief sang through Alexandra's veins. The bullet was spent. Peggy couldn't shoot her anymore, at least not without reloading. And first she'd have to get the gun, which was under the bed. All Alexandra had to do was get out of the room. She'd run for help.

She scrambled up and dashed for the door, reaching for the key.

"Oh, no, you don't," she heard just before hands clenched painfully on her still-bruised shoulders, wrenched her back, then bodily tossed her on the bed.

Whoever would have guessed Peggy was so strong? Alexandra twisted on the mattress to see her, then blinked, her heart racing even faster than before. This wasn't Peggy, not the Peggy she knew. Or thought she knew. Peggy the maid didn't have such a deranged look in her eyes.

And this deranged woman was coming after her.

There was no way to get to the door without going through Peggy. Alexandra slid off the far side of the bed and went under it.

It was dark, and she didn't fit very well, but she squirmed and squirmed some more, forcing her way under the bed, straining to reach the gun. She didn't think Peggy had supplies to reload, but she wasn't going to take any chances. Her heart beat so loudly it seemed to be thundering in her ears, ricocheting around the cramped space. If she couldn't get the gun, maybe at least under here she'd be safe from Peggy, and Peggy's crazy eyes, and Peggy's strong, vicious hands.

A fist began pounding on the door. And then another, and another, all accompanied by wild, angry barking.

"Lady Hawkridge!" Mrs. Oliver called. "Was that a *shot*?"

"Are you all right?" one of the footmen asked.

"Open up!" That was Vincent, followed by a vicious kick at the door.

Alexandra had warned Peggy people would hear. But being right brought no satisfaction. The doors at Hawkridge were thick, and the hinges were heavy, and there was nothing Vincent or anyone else could do.

"Oh, no, you don't," Alexandra heard again, then felt Peggy tugging on her foot, dragging her backward. She yanked her ankle from the maid's grasp and wiggled farther under the bed, trying to regain lost ground.

The pounding on the door grew louder as more servants arrived, adding voices and fists to the commotion. Alexandra stretched toward the gun, almost touching it. Almost.

Then a cackle echoed under the bed, and a hand reached out and snatched the gun from her grasp.

Peggy. She'd scooted in from the other side.

And now she was pointing the gun at Alexandra under the bed.

*It isn't loaded*, Alexandra told herself, forcing herself to breathe. There was nothing to do but back out, wiggling in reverse as fast as she possibly could, which wasn't nearly fast enough.

"You won't get away," Peggy said. "I am *not* going to let you take my mother."

Alexandra kept wiggling. Her heart was pounding, and her blood was pumping, and she was gulping spastically and trembling all over. But Peggy wasn't trying to reload the gun. What did she want with the dratted thing anyway, then?

Rex's barking seemed to be getting even louder. "Lady Hawkridge!" the servants shouted. "Let us in!"

If only she could. She and Peggy rose from beneath the bed at the same time, on opposite sides, and as Peggy rounded the bed, coming toward Alexandra with her arm raised, it became clear what she was planning to do with the gun.

Hit Alexandra with it. Very hard, if Alexandra could judge by the maniacal look in the woman's eyes.

Panic rising in her throat, Alexandra scrambled backward, her eyes darting all around. A glint of silver caught her eye. As Peggy bore down on her, she snatched her sterling basket off the table and bashed it down on the woman's blasted, curly head.

The maid collapsed like a sack of flour.

Alexandra rushed across the room to unlock the door, her trembling fingers slipping off the key, then knocking it to the floor. As she bent and snatched it back up, she heard a moan behind her and whirled.

Peggy was rising up from the floor.

The maid's eyes—unreasoning eyes—were a sick, poisonous green. One over-strong hand flexed, as though she itched to clench it around Alexandra's throat. Amazingly—petrifyingly—her other hand still held the gun.

With a cry of rage, she sprang to her feet and rushed headlong. With no time to think, Alexandra pivoted and jammed the key into the lock, turning it just as Peggy seized her by the hair and began dragging her backward.

The door burst open, and there stood the most beautiful sight Alexandra had ever laid eyes on: a drooling Rex, barking his enormous head off and bounding straight at them. Taking advantage of Peggy's astonishment, Alexandra wrenched herself free.

She managed to dive out of the way just as Rex's huge paws came up and knocked the maid on her back. Before Peggy could so much as scream, he'd draped his body full on top of her.

Pinned by two hundred pounds of dog, she couldn't budge. In fact, from the looks of it, she couldn't even draw breath. From his perch, Rex appeared quite pleased with himself, which Alexandra thought entirely appropriate.

As the servants poured in, she sat quietly on the floor, catching her breath. A quick probe confirmed that all of her hair was still attached to her head, for which she was thankful.

Eventually, Peggy regained the use of her lungs enough to howl, but her protests were lost among the staff's excited chatter and Rex's thundering barks. Amidst it all, Alexandra remained on the floor, content to just sit quietly and breathe and let the maids and housekeeper fuss over her.

Until she heard a shocked *"What...?"* and glanced over, through many livery-clad legs, to see her husband standing in the doorway.

He looked whiter than Juliana's nightgown.

The noise subsided as Tris pushed into the room. "For heaven's sake, what happened here?" he husked out. "Where is Alexandra?"

"Peggy happened." The liveried legs parted to reveal Alexandra where she sat. "Maude is Peggy's mother. She thought I wasn't going to see Maude until tomorrow, and she was trying to stop me."

"With a *gun?*" Tris stared horrified at the pistol he'd nearly tripped over, left unattended where it had fallen.

"The bullet is already spent." Peggy's hands had seemed as much a weapon as the gun, anyway, Alexandra thought as she let Tris pull her to her feet.

He wrapped her tight in his arms. "Maude is Peggy's *mother?"*

"I am," Maude said from the doorway.

Every pair of eyes followed as she walked slowly toward her daughter, her cane clicking as she went. Rex's ears perked up at the old woman's approach, as if he, too, were waiting to hear her explanation.

"I was but eighteen when I arrived here at Hawkridge," Maude began. The rhythmic clicks accompanied her words. "I thought I'd landed in heaven when I was offered a position as nanny to the marquess's son. But at twenty the head groom raped me, and I landed in hell instead."

The clicking stopped, and she gazed down at her daughter pinned beneath the massive dog.

"Had the master known I was with child," she continued, "I would have been turned out without a reference. I was a mite plumper in those days, but at seven months I was forced to feign illness and return home. After birthing the child, I left her to my mam to raise. When she reached the age of fourteen, I found a position for her here, but we never told anyone we were related." She heaved a great, shuddering sigh. "My dear Peggy, what have you done?"

Maude's eyes rolled back in her head as she collapsed in a rather graceful heap.

A collective gasp drowned out Peggy's scream. Ernest knelt to feel Maude's blue-veined wrist for a pulse.

"Mother!" Peggy was shouting repeatedly, with impressive volume for someone who currently had a mastiff compressing her chest. "Mother! I didn't want to hurt anyone! I just wanted to scare her away. But she wouldn't leave, the stubborn chit—"

"Maude's only fainted," Ernest announced.

Peggy sagged in relief, while everyone released their held breaths.

"Excellent," Tris said. "Please move her to the bed and then go fetch the sheriff. The man is earning his keep this day."

He was still holding Alexandra. While they waited for the authorities, he finally released her and took her hand instead, clutching tight as they told their rapt audience all about Maude and his uncle's accidental poisoning.

Maude woke from her faint, rolled over, and went to sleep. Rex remained sitting on Peggy until the sheriff arrived and hauled her away. It seemed hours before the servants finally drifted back to their duties, leaving Alexandra and Tris alone in their room.

Well, except for a slumbering Maude and a slobbering mastiff.

Tris was still holding Alexandra's hand. "Good dog," he told Rex, then turned to her. "See, I told you he doesn't hate you."

"He saved my life," she marveled.

"There's no need to give him quite that much credit. There were twenty-odd servants waiting to rescue you if he hadn't. They all love you, Alexandra. And so do I."

"You...what?" Was he really saying what she thought he was saying?

He glanced again at Rex, then at Maude still in their bed. With a long-suffering sigh, he drew Alexandra from the room and down the corridor. "I love you," he stated quite clearly.

And with that, he pulled her into the Queen's Bedchamber, used one booted foot to slam the door shut in Rex's face, and crushed her to him.

The kiss was fiercely possessive, and she responded with equal intensity. The warmth between them built into a heat that seared her senses and overwhelmed her awareness, making her forget everything except the three words that wouldn't stop repeating themselves over and over in her head.

*I love you, I love you, I love you.*

She'd known he did, but she hadn't known how much it would mean to hear it. Tears sprang to her eyes.

"You cannot cry now," he admonished. "I cannot kiss a sobbing woman." He kissed her nose and her cheeks. "I love you. Have I told you I love you? You may not have saved my life, but you rescued it from oblivion, you stubborn chit."

She laughed. "I did it for myself as much as for you. I'm a selfish chit as well."

"You're an irredeemable chit," he said, pulling back a little. He brushed at her dress. "How on earth did you get so dusty?"

"I scooted under the bed to hide from Peggy."

"I love you," he said and laughed, either finding it funny she'd been under the bed, or perhaps from nervous relief—she wasn't sure which. And she didn't really care. She felt free and easy with him for the first time ever, and that mattered so much more.

"I shall have to have a talk with Mrs. Oliver," she said, looking down at herself in disgust. "There is no excuse for such muck to be under the beds."

He laughed even harder. "I love you," he said.

"Where did Peggy get a gun?" she suddenly wondered.

Tris shook his head. "She nearly killed you," he murmured, suddenly looking rather pale.

"I guess she did." Alexandra slanted a glance at him. "Are you going to tell me you told me so?"

He shook his head again, his forehead creased in concern.

"How can someone named *Peggy* have done such terrible things?" she asked. "It's such an innocuous name, don't you think?"

That seemed to bring him back. He laughed, the tension flowing out of him, and wrapped his arms around her, so tight she groaned in protest. "Sorry," he said. "I seem to keep forgetting you're still bruised. But that's because I love you. I think I will tell you I love you every five minutes for the rest of our lives."

"That won't be necessary," she told him with an amused smile. "But I love you, too. And I'm glad you finally figured it out."

He nodded, skimming his knuckles over her cheek. "I couldn't admit it before. Not even to myself. I was too afraid of losing you. I thought I would lose you when you chose to leave, but instead I almost lost you when Peg—"

"Hush," she said. "I know."

He nodded again, lifting her chin with his thumb and forefinger to fix her with a serious silver-gray gaze. "All right, just once more for good measure. I love—"

She silenced him with a kiss.

# EPILOGUE

## *CHOCOLATE PUFFS*

Beat the white part of a good-sized egg till very stiff and then add a handful of sugar. To this add finely grated chocolate and then put small spoonfuls on a flat buttered pan with an area between them. Bake in an oven not overly warm for an hour or until the puffs are very dry.

*Everyone loves chocolate, so these are perfect to take on a family picnic!*
—Anne, Marchioness of Cainewood, 1773

**TWO WEEKS LATER,** on the peaceful rise overlooking Griffin's vineyard, in the last sweet days of summer, Tristan and Alexandra picnicked with her family once again on the red blanket. Her siblings and cousins gasped as she told the adventurous story of her quest for truth and justice.

At least, she made it sound adventurous. Griffin suspected it had been rather more dangerous than she was letting on—and he wasn't happy about that.

Brooding, he watched Claire lift the silver basket and turn it in her hands. "This is gorgeous. But it's dented."

"In two places," Alexandra agreed. "Peggy's hard head left quite a mark."

"I can fix it," Claire offered, having taken up an old family pastime of making jewelry.

Alexandra smiled. "I think not. I like it just the way it is."

Apparently still mulling over the tale, Corinna reached for another of the chocolate puffs Alexandra had brought. "So Peggy offered to make that list in order to control who was on it?"

"Exactly," Alexandra said. "There were others who knew Maude was alive, even if they didn't know Peggy was her daughter."

"And Tristan hadn't done *any* of those things while sleep-walking," Elizabeth said, her green eyes wide.

"Of course he hadn't." Alexandra scooted closer to her husband and leaned dreamily back against him. "I knew he hadn't all along."

"Have you sleepwalked since then?" Juliana asked him.

"Not once," Tristan said.

"And I'm sure he won't ever again," Alexandra declared.

"I wouldn't wager on that," her husband disagreed wryly, tilting her face up and back for a quick upside-down kiss. "Something tells me this irredeemable chit is likely to cause more trouble sometime in the future."

Everyone laughed. Except for Griffin. He was glad to see his sister happy, but that didn't alleviate his misgivings.

Alexandra frowned at his clenched jaw. "What's wrong with you?"

"You should have come home," he gritted out. "When all that was happening, you should have come home."

"That's what Peggy wanted, but Hawkridge is my home now." She exchanged a glance with Tristan, apparently realizing Griffin was as disappointed with his friend for not making her come home as he was with her for not doing so on her own. Extricating herself from Tristan's embrace, she rose to her feet. "Let's walk," she said to Griffin, taking his arm to pull him up before he could protest.

"I could have lost you," he said as they headed down the rise to the vineyard.

"Have you not figured out yet that you're not going to lose any of us, Griffin? Not even after we're all married and gone from Cainewood. You're stuck worrying about us forever," she said all too truthfully and cheerfully.

They walked for a few minutes, sharing a companionable silence that relieved his temper. When they reached the vineyard, they headed into the middle of it, toward where Rachael wandered in the distance.

"What's wrong with *her*?" Alexandra asked.

"I don't know. Would you care to ask her?"

"I'll let you ask her."

"Hmmph."

She bent to touch a minuscule grape. "Your vines are bearing fruit!"

A ridiculous sense of pride washed over him. "Nothing worthy of wine yet, but it's something to celebrate."

"We'll toast your success with Hawkridge's wine in a few minutes." She wandered the row, still heading toward Rachael. "Are they English sweet-water grapes?"

"They're Rhenish." A few months ago he wouldn't have known the variety, but the vineyard truly felt like his now. "Since when do *you* know anything about grapes?"

"I have a vineyard now, too, you know. It's my responsibility to learn everything about Hawkridge."

His eldest sister always *had* been rather responsible. But she was different, Griffin thought. He couldn't put his finger on how, but he knew the change was for the better.

"You should have come home," he repeated doggedly,

"but I must thank you for persevering. Because of you, Juliana and Corinna have fine prospects."

"Thank you for allowing me to marry Tris," she returned, then shot him a grin that was much more impish than the old Alexandra. "And for the excellent advice you gave me the night before my wedding."

He felt his face heat and suspected he was as red as the blanket on the hill. "I think I shall talk to Rachael now," he said and walked off.

Rachael turned as he approached, her cerulean eyes laced with distress. "Leave me alone," she said miserably. "I came out here to be alone."

"My sister sent me to talk to you."

"Do you always listen to your sisters?"

"Only when I agree with what they say." He stepped closer. "Tell me, Rachael. What's wrong?"

"Oh, thunderation," she said, then pressed herself into his shirtfront and sobbed.

He patted her awkwardly, feeling her warm tears soak through his shirt. Even miserable, she was stunning, and embracing her made him uncomfortably aware of that fact. He sent a murderous glance back toward Alexandra before patting Rachael some more. "Whatever it is," he said sooth-ingly—at least, he hoped he sounded soothing—"it cannot be that bad."

"I'm not a Chase," she whispered through a sob.

"What?" His hands froze on her slim back. "How can that be?"

"I found a letter." She pulled away, swiping at her swollen, reddened eyes. She didn't look quite as stunning now, Griffin told himself. "This morning, when I was clearing out the master suite for Noah's homecoming. It was from my mother to my father. From before I was born."

He dug a handkerchief out of his pocket, and she took it and blew her nose. Noisily and not prettily.

Much better, he thought. Aloud he said, "What was in the letter?"

"It said…it said she would always be grateful to him for wedding her even though she was a widow already with child. She prayed I would be a girl so he wouldn't be stuck with another man's son as his heir. She—"

"Did she say she loved him?" he interrupted pointedly.

She nodded. "But—"

"They were in love, Rachael. Anyone could see it just looking at the two of them. Don't you ever doubt it."

She shrugged, following that with a long, sorrowful sniff. "But he wasn't my father. Whoever my real father was, he wasn't a Chase."

"Did the man who raised you ever, for one minute, treat you as anything but his daughter?"

"No." The tears continued to flow as she shook her head. "But I'm not a Chase. I don't know what I am if I'm not a Chase."

"You're Rachael," he said. "Noah and Claire and Elizabeth are still your brother and sisters. You still live at Greystone. Nothing has changed. What does your surname matter? It will change when you marry, anyway."

But her family name wouldn't change if she married *him*, another Chase. And he was aware, quite suddenly and uncomfortably, that the cousin standing before him wasn't actually his cousin.

Thankfully, she hadn't seemed to make that connection. "You're right," she said, straightening her shoulders and taking a big breath.

She didn't look like she really believed him, but she looked like she *wanted* to believe him. And the shaky little smile she aimed at him had nothing to do with seduction and everything to do with family consoling each other.

"Thank you," she added. "I don't know when you became so reasonable, but I do appreciate your calm, considered approach."

He could have had a hearty laugh at that one. He'd been anything but calm and considered since inheriting the marquessate. To tell the truth, he'd felt calmer on campaign with bullets whizzing around him.

*Panicked* would describe his current state better.

He had two more sisters to marry off, an estate that came with entirely too much responsibility, and now a cousin who wasn't his cousin.

And since she'd stopped crying, she was suddenly looking quite—what was the word Tristan had used?

Oh, yes. *Sultry.*

"I am glad I could help," he said stiffly.

"I think…" she said, licking her lips, "I think I'm ready to go back to the others."

"Thank goodness," he said under his breath.

"Hmm?"

"I'm thankful to God that you feel much better."

She cocked her head at him, as though she might not believe him. But she followed him back down the row, and for that he was thankful, too. Mostly because she was behind him, which meant he didn't have to watch her hips swaying down the aisle.

*She's your cousin,* he reminded himself forcefully. *Your cousin.*

*Except she wasn't.*

It was a good thing she'd said she'd never marry him, because the last thing he wanted was a wife.

# AUTHOR'S NOTE

~

**DEAR READER,**

Do you know any sleepwalkers? Two of my children occasionally sleepwalk, so I know firsthand that it doesn't look as scary in real life as it's usually portrayed in movies. Sleepwalkers look and act quite awake—if a little bit addled—but they never remember anything of their escapades in the morning.

Much mystery has been attached to sleepwalking, yet it's really no more mysterious than dreaming. The main difference between the two is that a sleepwalker's brainwave patterns are a combination of the type produced during deep sleep mixed with awake patterns. This second type of brainwave reflects waking behaviors like walking and talking while the person is still asleep enough so that he's not aware of what's happening and isn't forming memories of his actions. In adults, sleepwalking is most likely to occur during times of emotional stress and usually stops when the source of anxiety disappears.

As to whether sleepwalkers can be dangerous, although violence while sleepwalking isn't common, sleepwalkers aren't allowed in the armed services of the United States, in part because of the threat they pose to themselves and others when they have access to weapons and are unaware of what they're doing while asleep. There are at least twenty documented cases where defense against a murder charge was "I was sleepwalking and therefore, ladies and gentlemen of the jury, I was not myself at the time I killed him and so deserve acquittal." The argument has proved successful more than once.

If you're musically inclined, you may know Alexandra's favorite piece of music, Beethoven's Piano Sonata No. 14, as the "Moonlight Sonata." It wasn't given that name until after Alexandra's story, though. Beethoven wrote the sonata in 1801 and dedicated it to the seventeen-year-old Countess Giulietta Guicciardi, with whom he was said to be in love. In 1832, several years after Beethoven's death, the poet Ludwig Rellstab compared the music to moonlight shining on Lake Lucerne. Since then, it's been known as the "Moonlight Sonata."

Tristan's hydraulic ram pump was invented by a Frenchman, Joseph-Michel Montgolfier, in 1796. In 1821, *Ackermann's Repository*, a very popular magazine, published an article with instructions on how to build a ram pump, calling it "A simple Hydraulic Engine, which will raise Water to a very considerable elevation, without manual force or assistance." The article included engravings very similar to the drawings Tristan sketched in this book, which you can see on our website. Ram pumps are still built and used today.

Unfortunately, Tristan was too optimistic when he predicted that slavery would soon end in Jamaica. Slavery wasn't abolished until nineteen years after this story, in August 1834, and, as he feared, the transition from a slave economy to one based on wage labor proved difficult.

Although gas lighting is often thought of as a Victorian invention, it actually came into use during Regency times. It was developed by a Scot named William Murdock. The story is told that, as a child, Murdock heated coal in his mother's kettle and lit the gas that came out of the spout. In 1794, he heated coal in a closed iron vessel in his garden and piped the resulting gas into the house. That was the first practical system of gas lighting to be used anywhere in the world. In 1805, gas lighting gained public awareness when the Prince of Wales (later the Prince Regent) had it installed in Carlton House, his London home. Two years later, gas lamps were installed in Pall Mall, the first street to be lit by gas. The UK's first gasworks was built in 1812 to light the City of Westminster, and 288 miles of pipes had been laid in London by 1819, supplying more than 51,000 gaslights.

Most of the homes in my books are inspired by real places you can visit. Cainewood Castle is loosely modeled on Arundel Castle in West Sussex. It's been home to the Dukes of Norfolk and their families, the Fitzalan Howards, since 1243, save for a short period during the Civil War. Although the family still resides there, portions of their magnificent home are open to visitors Sundays through Fridays from April to October.

Hawkridge Hall was modeled on Ham House, a National Trust property located just outside of London. Known as the most well-preserved Stuart home in England, Ham House was built in 1610 and remodeled in the 1670s. The building has survived virtually unchanged since then, and it still retains most of the furniture from that period. The house and gardens are open Saturdays through Wednesdays from April to October.

I hope you enjoyed *Alexandra!* Next up is Juliana's story in *Juliana*. Please read on for an excerpt as well as more bonus material!


Always,

Lauren Royal

Read on for an excerpt from

# *Juliana*

Book 2 of
*Sweet Chase Brides: The Regency* series
by Lauren & Devon Royal

Lady Juliana Chase loves playing matchmaker—and she's good at it, too. So why does the eligible James Trevor, Earl of Stafford, insist on ignoring her sound advice and shaking up her sensible plans?

### SPICE CAKES

Take three scoops of Flower and put into it a Spoon of ale-barm, crushed cloves, mace, and a goode deal of cinnamon. To a halfe Pound of sweet Butter add a goode deal of Sugar and mixe together. Stir in three Eggs and work until good and stiff, then add a little cold Rosewater and knead well. Knead again, pull it all in Pieces and bake your Cakes in a warm oven.

*I 've heard tell that should you eat one of these before a gathering where you are likely to meet available men, their spiciness will clear your head and allow you to choose wisely. This did not, however, work when I baked them for my daughter. In any case, they are delicious.*

—Amethyst, Countess of Greystone, 1690

*London, 1816*

**JAMES TREVOR,** the young Earl of Stafford, hadn't been to a ball in ages. And he hadn't particularly wanted to attend this one, either.

However, being a good-natured sort of fellow, he'd chosen to regard tonight as an opportunity for renewing a number of neglected acquaintances. Among these was Griffin Chase, now the Marquess of Cainewood.

But his old schoolmate was looking rather sullen. James approached with caution.

"At whom are you glaring, Cainewood?"

"My sister." Cainewood's frown deepened. "She's not dancing."

James's gaze followed his across the ballroom. He lifted his quizzing glass and squinted through it. "The little blond one?"

"The girl in yellow, yes. That would be Juliana, wasting precious time."

"She appears to be agreeably engaged."

"With our sister. But Juliana is *supposed* to be meeting gentlemen. I despair of ever finding her a husband."

James chuckled at that. Lowering the quizzing glass to dangle on its long silver chain, he refocused on Cainewood. He hadn't seen his old friend since their time at Oxford, and he'd never met his family, but still he sensed an easy familiarity between them. He felt well within his rights to laugh at the fellow's consternation.

"Juliana is seventeen," Cainewood added as though that explained everything.

"That doesn't sound particularly old."

"No, but I'll still have Corinna to settle after her." He gestured toward his other sister, a pretty brown-haired girl. "I'd hoped to get them both married off this season, but Juliana is overparticular. And unfortunately, I believe she's already met everyone here..." His green gaze narrowed on James. "Except, perhaps, you."

"Me?"

"You. Won't you at least suffer an introduction? You're an earl now, are you not?" He flashed a crooked grin. "An earl in need of a wife."

An earl in need of a wife—the exact same words James's mother had used to describe him earlier this evening as she'd all but dragged him from the carriage into this house.

But although James had inherited the title more than two

years ago, he still had a hard time thinking of himself as an earl, let alone *an earl in need of a wife*.

His older brother was supposed to have been the Earl of Stafford.

Straight out of Oxford, James had been perfectly content with his parents' plan for him to be a captain in the cavalry. Good-natured as he was, contentment was his natural state, and, in fact, he'd been pleased when his father bought him the commission. Unfortunately, less than a week into active duty, a wound ended his laughably short stint in the army.

He shifted and flexed his left knee, which always ached in this type of cold, wet weather. On days of this sort he still walked with a slight limp, which made him feel conspicuous and much older than twenty-five. But he was profoundly grateful the army surgeons had managed to save his leg rather than amputating it. So grateful that, needing a new occupation after his recovery, he'd decided to become a physician.

He hadn't been long in medical school before he'd realized he'd found his calling. For the first time in his memory, James had been more than just content with his life—he'd been truly happy. Especially after he fell in love.

Then everything fell apart.

His brother had died first, leaving James shaken by grief and the realization that he'd someday inherit. He didn't *want* to be an earl—he *liked* being a physician. He liked helping people, and he liked feeling that he made a difference. Every day was surprising and challenging, and there were always successes to balance the disappointments. Managing an earldom seemed tedious and superficial in comparison.

Then, while he was still reeling from the loss of his brother, his father's heart had stopped, and suddenly James *was* the earl.

After that came a dark, miserable blur. It was some time—he knew not how long—before the cloud began to dissipate. He simply found himself awakened one morning, not by the paralysis of grief or the weight of obligation, but by the sun. Gradually he began to feel that his despair was subsiding—by, say, a thimbleful per day—and he was growing used to his new role. His work *could* make a difference in the lives of his tenants and in the stodgy House of Lords. And his lovely new bride, whose resilience had kept him afloat, showed him that he didn't have to do as society expected—he could be an earl *and* a physician.

Harnessing the vast Stafford fortune, James had opened a facility in London where those who were too poor to afford doctors could get smallpox vaccinations, an endeavor dear to his heart. At last, he saw true happiness peeking over the horizon. Life was looking good again.

Then Anne died in childbirth, and their baby, born too early, died along with her.

No physician, himself included, had been able to make a shred of difference. And James was certain he'd never be truly happy again.

A year later, he'd regained some measure of his old contentment. But his mother was pressuring him to take a new wife, and, while the idea pained him, he knew it was an earl's duty to sire heirs. Though he couldn't love another girl, he might as well at least consider making his mother happy. So he'd allowed her to drag him to this ball, and, by the same token, he would allow Cainewood to introduce him to his sister.

"Yes, I'd be delighted to meet Lady Juliana."

Cainewood wasted no time marching him across the ballroom and introducing him to both of his sisters. It had been so long since any girl made an impression on James that he was surprised to find his gaze locked on Lady Juliana's as he bowed over her hand. Her eyes were so full of life. He felt drawn to her energy.

And that felt incredibly wrong.

But Cainewood's sister was a pretty thing, and he couldn't seem to wrench his gaze from those eyes. Green eyes. No, blue. He couldn't decide. They seemed to change as he watched.

"Will you honor me with a dance?"

He wasn't sure whether he'd asked out of impulse or obligation, but he was glad when she responded with, "It would be my pleasure."

She let him lead her out onto the floor. He hadn't danced since Anne died. He felt a wave of panic—what if he didn't remember how? But there was a waltz playing, and Lady Juliana fairly melted into his arms.

He remembered.

"What color are your eyes?" he asked.

She gave a merry, tinkling laugh, a laugh that matched her eyes. "Hazel. Why?"

"I couldn't tell. They looked green at first, but now they look blue."

"Well, they're hazel," Juliana repeated, wishing he would stop staring into them. It seemed almost as though he saw right through them into her head, as though he could guess exactly what she was thinking and feeling. And that was unnerving, no matter that she had nothing to hide.

She glanced away, her gaze landing on her older sister. Alexandra had come to town for the season while her new husband claimed his seat in the House of Lords. How happy they looked dancing together, Alexandra's dark eyes locked on Tristan's steady gray ones. Their road to wedded bliss had been a rocky one, but they'd been fated to be together from the first—as Juliana had known, of course.

Where was *her* great love? Was fate taking a protracted holiday?

Still feeling Lord Stafford's gaze on her, she met his stare dead on, daring him to look away. He didn't. His eyes were a warm brown, reminding her of chocolate. She loved chocolate. But she had to look up to see those eyes. Way up.

She could get a crick in her neck dancing with such a gentleman.

"I haven't seen you at any other balls," she observed. "You must take your duty to Parliament seriously."

The corners of those warm eyes crinkled when he smiled. "That and my profession."

"Your profession?"

"I'm a physician."

"I thought you were an earl," she said.

One of his dark brows went up. "Can I not be both?"

"Of course you can," she said quickly, although she'd never heard of an earl-physician. "What do you do, exactly? Have you many patients?"

"Some, although I'm not taking on any new ones. Most of my time is spent at my facility, the New Hope Institute."

"New Hope," she mused. "I've heard of that. Something to do with smallpox?"

"I provide vaccinations, yes. Mostly to London's poor."

"That sounds like very important work," she allowed. He was a most unusual young man. And an excellent dancer. Having noticed a slight limp as he'd initially approached her, she wouldn't have thought he'd move so nimbly.

Still, much as she loved dancing, finding a gentleman who excelled at it wasn't her priority. After all, it wasn't as though she had a shortage of dance partners—she danced her feet off at every ball, with or without Griffin flinging every eligible bachelor her way. She had no problem meeting young men; the problem was finding one she considered husband material. And Lord Stafford was definitely not what she had in mind.

When the music came to an end, he led her by the hand off the dance floor. "It was a pleasure, Lady Juliana."

His voice was warm like his eyes, low and smooth, reminding her again of rich chocolate. "Thank you," she said.

The musicians struck up a country dance, and as he was still holding her hand, she half expected him to lead her straight back to the dance floor. Instead, he raised her fingers and, rather than kiss the air above her hand, he actually pressed his lips to her glove.

Scandalous! Equal parts appalled and amused, she hardly knew how to arrange her face. *What* an unusual young man.

She could have sworn she felt the kiss—a tingly sensation —through the white silk.

"Thank you," she repeated more faintly.

"Thank *you*," he echoed with a vague smile.

She couldn't help wondering if he was dazed or just bored.

No sooner had he turned to leave than Griffin descended. "Well?"

She watched Lord Stafford walk away. The cut of his tail-coat emphasized broad shoulders. Dark, tousled waves grazed his velvet collar. Many fashionable men achieved a similar look with pomade and curl papers, but his coiffure looked *genuinely* tousled. Like he was too busy to bother with it.

"His hair is too dark," she said.

"Pardon?"

"You know I prefer golden-haired gentlemen. And he's entirely too tall—I felt like a child dancing with him."

Griffin looked down on her, both literally and figuratively. "Face it, Juliana—you're short."

As though she hadn't noticed. "He works," she said. "He has a *profession*."

"And you find this unacceptable?"

"He wouldn't have any time for me." She wanted a grand love, like Alexandra and Tristan's; she wanted a husband who loved her to distraction. She wanted special outings and thoughtful surprises and long, lingering, endless hours together. And faith, *this* fellow couldn't even find a few minutes to comb his hair. "I'm sorry, but he just won't do."

The fact that Lord Stafford's work was important made him admirable, but no more suitable—and the fact that she *may* have enjoyed his chocolate eyes and his impertinent kiss had no bearing whatsoever. Even if she could fall for a too-tall, too-dark earl-physician, their attachment could only end in tears.

Griffin released a long-suffering sigh. "I shall keep looking."

"You do that," she said, patting his arm and silently wishing him luck. The spice cakes had clearly been a waste. Poor Griffin. "In the meantime, I must speak with Alexandra."

She scanned the ballroom and finally found her married sister talking to Aunt Frances.

"Who was that you were dancing with?" Alexandra asked as she approached.

"Lord Stafford."

"He's very handsome."

"His hair is too dark. Can you come to the Berkeley Square house this Wednesday afternoon?"

"I expect so. Why?"

"I need help making clothes for the Foundling Hospital babies."

"Your newest project, I take it?" Alexandra's brown eyes

gleamed with mischief. "What have you got yourself into this time?"

If only she knew. "Corinna wanted to see the Hospital's art gallery, but oh, the poor foundlings were heartbreaking. And their mothers." Thinking back on the anguished yet hopeful faces of those young women, Juliana wanted to cry. "I *must* do something to help them."

"Of course you must," Aunt Frances said. "With you, it's always something."

That much was true; Juliana wouldn't deny it. "And what does that make me?" she wondered. "Impulsive? Interfering? Overwrought, overdramatic, overbearing?" She stopped there, knowing she was all of those and more.

Which was why she wanted to hug Alexandra when she said, "No, that makes you compassionate, giving, hopeful. Good-hearted and unselfish and sensitive. And lovable— that's what it makes you most."

Juliana *did* hug her sister. Her perfect, responsible, *married* sister, who always managed to summon the right words to fix everything.

But a small part of her couldn't help wondering...if she was so lovable, why couldn't she find someone to love?

∾

**AVAILABLE NOW!**
**Learn more about *Juliana* at**
**www.DevonAndLaurenRoyal.com**

# ENTER FOR A CHANCE TO WIN
## a sterling silver replica of the cameo Tris gave Alexandra in this book!*

Visit the Contest page on Lauren & Devon's website
at www.LaurenandDevonRoyal.com
and answer a question to be
entered in the monthly drawing.

No purchase necessary. See complete rules on the site.

*Please note: Depending on when you enter, the prize may be another p ece of jewelry
associated with one of Lauren & Devon's books. The authors reserve the right to
discontinue this promotion at any time.

# ABOUT LAUREN & DEVON ROYAL

~

**LAUREN ROYAL** decided to become a writer in the third grade, after winning a "Why My Mother is the Greatest" essay contest. Now she's a *New York Times* and *USA Today* bestselling author of humorous historical romance novels. Lauren lives in Southern California with her family and their constantly shedding cat. She still thinks her mother is the greatest.

**DEVON ROYAL** is the daughter of romance novelist Lauren Royal. After attending film school, she wrote an award-winning TV comedy pilot and worked in digital video production before turning her focus to fiction writing. Devon lives in Southern California with her husband and son. She also thinks her mother is the greatest.

# ACKNOWLEDGMENTS

∾

**OUR HEARTFELT THANKS:**

To Lauren's BFF and fellow historical author Glynnis Campbell, for calling around Napa Valley to find the elusive grape-growing information we needed (thank goodness Lauren has such a good friend, since both of us would rather text than call anyone).

To Sara Rodger, librarian at Arundel Castle, for tracking down and sending nineteenth-century floor plans (twice... thanks to a less-than-reliable postal system).

To all the honorary Chase cousins in our Chase Family Readers Group, for their enthusiastic support.

And to all of our readers, whose wonderful letters, kind words, Facebook posts, and tweets make us want to sit down every day and write.

Thank you, one and all!

# CONTACT INFORMATION

≈

## Newsletter

littl.ink / News

## Facebook Readers Group

facebook.com / groups / ChaseFamilyReaders

## Website

www.DevonAndLaurenRoyal.com

## Email

royall.ink / Email